The Survivors

Book I: Summer

V. L Dreyer

Copyright © 2013 V. L. Dreyer
All rights reserved.
ISBN: 978-0-473-25627-2

Dedication

Dedicated to Alyssa, for being the sister of my heart that genetics failed to give me.

V. L. Dreyer

THE SURVIVORS
The Survivors Book I: Summer
The Survivors Book II: Autumn
The Survivors Book III: Winter
The Survivors Book IV: Spring

Table Of Contents

Chapter One	1
Chapter Two	11
Chapter Three	23
Chapter Four	31
Chapter Five	39
Chapter Six	51
Chapter Seven	67
Chapter Eight	85
Chapter Nine	97
Chapter Ten	111
Chapter Eleven	127
Chapter Twelve	155
Chapter Thirteen	169
Chapter Fourteen	191
Chapter Fifteen	209
Chapter Sixteen	223
Chapter Seventeen	241
Chapter Eighteen	255
Chapter Nineteen	277
Chapter Twenty	303

Chapter Twenty-One	329
Chapter Twenty-Two	359
Chapter Twenty-Three	383
Chapter Twenty-Four	395
Kiwiana Language Guide	407
Credits	409
About The Author	411

Acknowledgements

This book would never have been finished without the loyalty and dedication of my family. Without your eternal faith in me, Sandy's adventure would have forever remained untold.

To all of my fans from my early days as a graphic novelist, thank you as well. Your love and endless stream of inquisitive questions gave me the strength to carry on in the darkest hours, and opened my mind to all kinds of new possibilities.

To Holly, my editor, for her incredible patience and high degree of tolerance to my idiosyncrasies.

And most of all, to Alyssa, for being my Skylar. Where would I be without you? You pick me up when I'm feeling down, smack me down when my ego gets too big, and call me out on my grammar at every turn. Thank you.

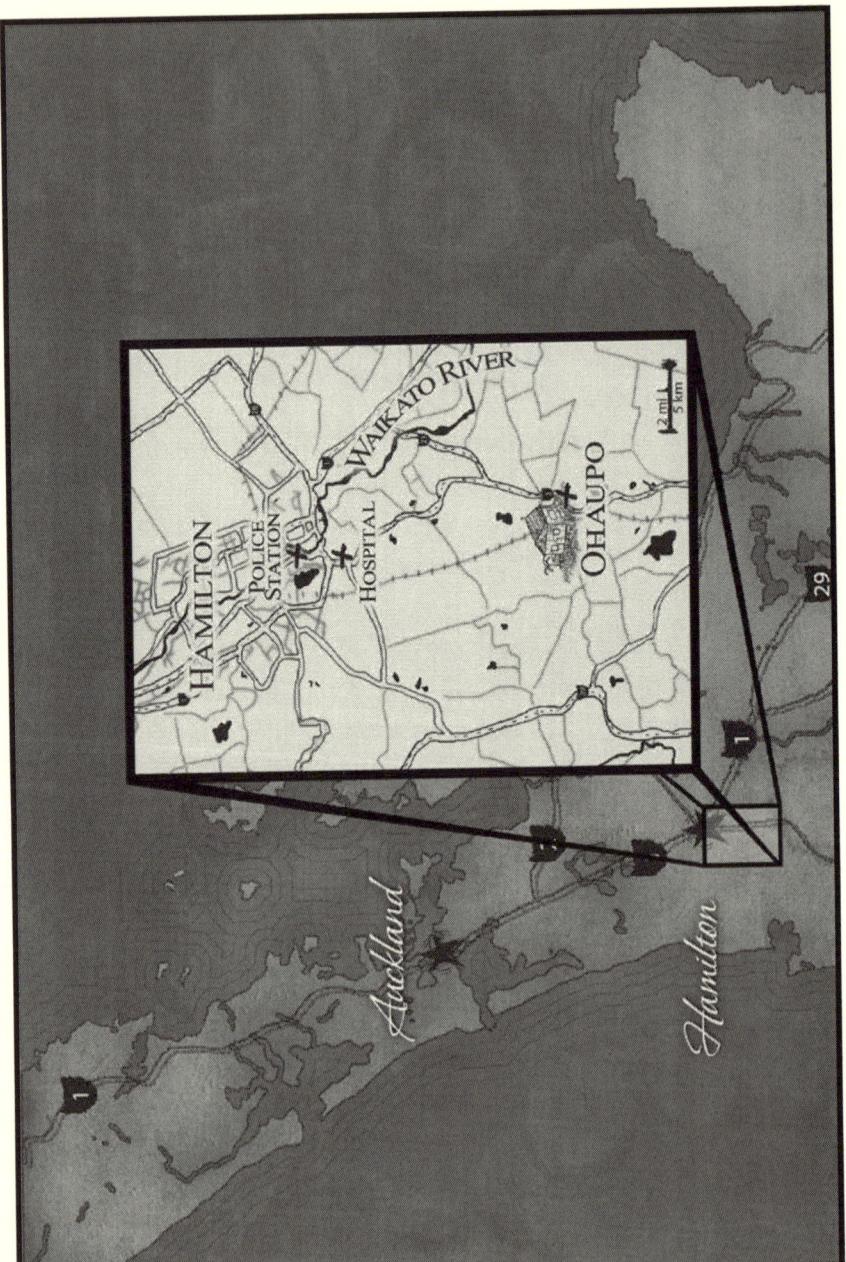

Foreword

The Survivors series is set in New Zealand. In order to preserve the authenticity of the setting and the heroine's voice, this novel has been written in New Zealand English.

New Zealand English (NZE) is an off-shoot of British English, but the geographical isolation of the country has given rise to a quirky sub-dialect that is neither entirely British, nor Australian.

I have attempted to make this novel as easily accessible as possible for readers around the world by providing contextual explanations for most words. However, as the language variations are subtle and frequent, it is not always possible to do this.

A more in-depth article on the language used in this book is available on my website, where you also have the facility to ask me questions.

http://www.vldreyer.com

Chapter One

It seemed like a cruel irony.

I had survived the brutal end of civilization and watched our world fall from grace; I had stood by helplessly while all of my friends and family died, or were reduced to the walking dead, one by one. I lived on and yet now, a decade later, my salvation lay behind a worn, old movie poster for a film named *Zombieland*.

Crouched between a dumpster and a stack of decaying boxes, I stared at the faded, ruined poster, wondering at life's morbid sense of humour. I remembered that movie. It had been a few years old at the point when the world ended, so it seemed strange to have it hanging in the window, but places like this backwater little town tended to be behind the times. I used to enjoy that kind of thing, back when I was a teenager and the world was still whole. The zombie fad had been so popular – there were copies of *The Walking Dead* in the window, too.

If only we had known what was to come.

The virus that struck us down was nothing like any of those movies. There was to be no *Dawn of the Dead* for us, no *28 Days Later*. I was eternally grateful for that fact, actually. My reality was very different to the fantasies dreamed up by Hollywood.

There was one of them in the DVD store across the road from me: An old man. I could just see him past the tatty photograph of Jesse Eisenberg, shuffling back and forth between the shelves. He wandered tirelessly, trying to organise his stock with hands no longer capable of gripping.

Some of the undead were still dangerous, but most of them were slow and heart-wrenchingly pathetic, like the little old man in the store. I'd take him over a fast-moving, angry movie zombie any day, even if it did break my heart to look at him. The difference came down to which one was more likely to eat my brain. Frankly, I liked my brain right where it was. The real undead weren't interested in brains – or anything else, really.

There was nothing left on the shelves now; the old man had knocked all the videos to the ground long ago with his limp-fingered efforts, and then crushed them beneath his wandering feet. He was far gone after all these years. His flesh was half-rotted, and his eyes were unseeing. Only instinct kept him moving in his relentless, unattainable quest for perfection.

A lot of the infected seemed to retain the basic memories of their lives, but only the things that they had repeated so often that the action ended up deeply ingrained within their subconscious. The core of their personalities seemed to linger as well, but it was just an echo of the person they used to be.

That made them unpredictable.

I had seen a great many different kinds of infected over the years, and their behaviour seemed to vary depending on the person they were before death. Mothers still rocked the withered husks of their dead babies. Soldiers gunned down non-existent foes until the chamber of their weapons ran dry. Most of the infected just went on about their un-lives, oblivious, like that old man in the store. Even though his conscious mind was completely gone, he stayed in the place that he knew best, going through the same motions now as when he was still alive.

The old man must have really loved that little store. Ten years was a very long time.

The virus came from somewhere deep in Central Africa; a mutation of the deadly Ebola virus. They named this new strain the Goma ebolavirus, after the city where the first cases were found. By the time they'd decided on a name, it had killed a hundred thousand people and infected millions more.

The media nicknamed it Ebola-X, and that version stuck. It had more of a ring to it.

In the beginning, diagnosis and research was slow. The doctors, nurses and scientists studying the pathogen kept getting infected, no matter what they did to prevent it. Level four biohazard containment was not enough. Nothing was ever enough.

It was funny how much a kid like me learned about biohazard containment in those first few years. Not so much "funny-ha-ha" as "funny-horrifying", though.

The thing that made Ebola-X so terrifying was its virulence. It spread so fast that no one could hope to contain it. It had infected half of the African continent before the rest of the world even realised that it was a threat.

It was vicious and untreatable. What it did to the human body was horrific and irreversible; like other strains of the Ebola virus, it liquefied healthy cells.

Unlike its ancestors though, the thing it destroyed first was the delicate tissue of the brain. Within hours of infection, the temporal lobe began to disintegrate, taking with it speech, memory and perception. The rest of the cerebrum followed soon after, leaving only basic motor function behind.

Eventually, the motor function went as well, but by that stage the body was usually starting to fall apart. Given enough time it destroyed the entire infected body, but it took years to get that far. Even a decade after the infection first hit us, there were still plenty of undead wandering aimlessly around the landscape.

Some of the victims died within hours, but others survived for many years after the infection erased their conscious minds. It had been almost ten years since the first reported case arrived on New Zealand's shores, and nine and a half since they stopped telling us what the body count was. It was safe to say that most of the people that used to live here were dead.

I had seen a few other survivors over the years, but experience left me wary of strangers and I always gave them a wide berth. Resources were limited, and a lone female in a world without rules was easy prey. My sense of self-preservation told me to keep to myself, so I did.

For me, the worst part was that I didn't know if the infected were conscious or aware up until the end, or if they felt any pain. I had no way to ask them. It still made me feel terrible to put them out of their misery, even after so many years. They were human beings, or at least they had been, and no one deserved to suffer like that. Somehow, killing them felt like an act of mercy.

Before the roar of the media shrank to a whisper, they told us that there was a small percentage of the population who had been born with a natural genetic abnormality which made us immune to the effects of the virus. The only thing separating me from that poor old man was one tiny twist of fate. I was still infected, but my immune system had the rare and precious ability to fight it off. I had no idea how long my immunity would last, though. The virus could mutate at any time, leaving me defenceless.

Einstein was wrong. God did play dice, and I was lucky enough to roll high this time.

The virus was aggressive and indiscriminate; it was in the water, the air and was even carried by some of the animals. For the people who weren't as lucky as me, transmission was unavoidable. If you were near an infected, and you were not immune, then you were going to die. It was just a matter of time.

Within a year of the first reported case, a billion people were gone.

There was no cure.

There was no antivirus.

There was no hope.

After so many deaths, there was no one left alive to study the virus and look for a cure, at least not as far as I was aware. Perhaps there was a bunker somewhere full of scientists working diligently to try and find a solution that would preserve humanity from extinction, but if there was, they didn't invite me. I wasn't surprised. I was eighteen years old when the plague devastated my world. Just a useless kid, I hadn't even decided what I was going to do with my life. Now, I no longer had the choice. I was a survivor, and that was all I'd ever be.

The infected man in the store, he had been a person once, too. A good man, probably. An innocent man. In my imagination, it was his life's dream to retire to this little town and spend his twilight years running that tiny store.

I wondered if his wife was dead, too. His children. His grandchildren. Thinking about it made what I had to do so much harder.

I couldn't just leave him like this, though. It wouldn't be right. There was no way for me to know if he was in pain, but it sure as hell looked like he was suffering. No one would want to spend the rest of their existence shuffling around mindlessly until their legs finally fell off. As one of the lucky few that won the genetic lottery, I had an obligation to free him from his torment and let him move on to whatever came next.

With silent care, I slipped my backpack from my shoulders and set it on the ground at my feet, then paused to check if anyone had seen the motion. Nothing else moved except me. Me, and my decomposing friend across the street.

I rose to my feet and crossed the cracked roadway in a dozen quick steps, drawing from my pocket the single most effective weapon in my arsenal: A small hand taser. In most cases, it was enough to put down one of the infected once and for all. Why a non-lethal weapon was lethal to the pseudo-dead, I really didn't know, but what I did know is that it was quick, bloodless and hopefully painless – that was what was important to me.

I thumbed the switch to the *on* position as I entered the store; the taser crackled to life in my hand, ready to discharge its high-voltage payload. The clerk did nothing. He just stood there, helpless, shuffling the one lone DVD case left on the shelf back and forth with a limp hand.

"Hey," I called softly, hoping to draw his attention. "You okay, buddy?"

Of course he wasn't, but I had to be sure in case the old man wasn't really undead. Sometimes a survivor just went completely off his nut. It happened occasionally in our short and brutal existence. The old man just stood there, staring off into space, oblivious. I let out a soft whistle, trying a different frequency to get his attention.

That time, it worked.

His head rose and turned to look at me with blind eyes, worn over by cataracts long before the virus compounded his problems. His brow knitted into a frown, and he opened his mouth as though to speak but no sound came out.

I cringed. He looked so much like my grandfather, who died when I was a little girl. Even after all these years, I still remembered holding my Poppa's wrinkled old hand as he lay on his deathbed, gazing up at me with those sad, blind eyes. In retrospect, I could take comfort from the fact that Poppa didn't have to watch the world crumble into ruin, but that didn't ease the pain.

Slowly, cautiously, I circled around the old man. His head jerked side to side, seeking the sound that had drawn his attention.

Most of the infected weren't really dangerous. I'd yet to see a strain of the disease turn them into violent monsters, like the ones in the movies. They were stripped of their awareness but they still resembled the people they'd been in life. A gentle person was still gentle; a violent one was still violent. The virus stripped away the laws of civility that once helped them to fit into a neat and well-ordered society; it erased from their minds the rules that kept them from giving in to their natural impulses.

"It's okay, buddy. I'm just going to put you to sleep." I kept my voice low and calm; like animals, the pseudo-dead responded more to tone of voice than the words themselves. "I'll make the pain go away."

He didn't turn to face me or even move from the spot, but just stood there shuffling his limbs listlessly. One of his hands moved absently in mid-air, shifting a non-existent video case towards a better imaginary location, while I stepped carefully over the real cases that were scattered all over the floor. Crushed plastic and cracked discs crunched ominously under my feet, like dry old bones picked clean and left brittle in the sun. There was nothing left of them to salvage, they were damaged beyond repair by the old man's shuffling feet.

The taser made a soft crackling sound when I pressed it to the nape of the old man's neck; he collapsed like a sack of potatoes at my feet. I knelt beside him to check, but the old man was already gone. To Heaven, I hoped, or whatever came next. Anything was better than lingering in purgatory while your body rotted away around you.

I hung my head to reflect and to offer a silent prayer for the old man's soul. Although I was raised as an atheist, spending so much time surrounded by violence and death made me wonder if there was something more. I hoped so. It hurt too much to think about so many good, innocent people just ceasing to be.

I'd been alone for a very long time. Even so, killing someone who looked like a person that I loved still affected me more deeply than I could express. I sometimes wondered if it would be easier to feel nothing at all, but the pain kept me grounded in reality. They weren't monsters, they were people. Just like me, just like my family, just like everyone else. The day I stopped feeling something towards them was the day that I became the monster.

Years ago, I made myself a promise: if the day ever came when I stopped feeling grief and remorse for what I had to do to survive, then I would put my gun against my head and join my family in the hereafter.

Chapter Two

Ten Years Earlier

Fresh from school and full of energy, I pulled open the front door, trotted inside and flung my school bag into its usual corner by the door. It landed with a heavy 'thunk', full of books and all the other junk I had to bring home at the end of the school year.

"Mum, I'm home!"

My voice echoed down the hall as I headed for the kitchen in search of something cool to alleviate the summer heat. Although it was only mid-December, it was hotter than Hades and muggy to boot. The cheap polyester of my school uniform clung in all the wrong places, and it did not breathe at all.

I yanked open the fridge, and relished the wave of cool air that smacked me in the face like a glorious arctic ice floe. When my mother didn't respond, I glanced over my shoulder and called her again. "Mum?"

After grabbing a can of lemonade from the top shelf, I shouldered the fridge closed and went off in search of my missing parental unit. I wasn't worried, but I wanted to talk to her and she was always home at this time of day to greet me. It was a family tradition for us to hang out for a couple of minutes after school and work, just to talk and catch up on the day. I was always bursting with gossip, and she was happy to listen. That's just how my mum was – she was a listener, and she was always there for me no matter what.

I stuck my head into the stairwell and called out to her again.

"Mu-um?" I paused, waiting impatiently for a response.

"She's not he-ere." The reply came in my father's voice. My curiosity was doubly-piqued now – Mum was out and Dad wasn't at work? My home environment was usually very organised and well-ordered; it was unusual for things to be out of place. Following the sound of his voice up the stairs, I made my way into his office.

"Why aren't you at work?" I asked, curious.

"Why aren't you at school?"

"Dad, it's after four." I laughed and shook my head. "School let out an hour ago."

His brow furrowed into a look of confusion. I glanced over his shoulder at the computer screen behind him, and caught a glimpse of some gruesome photographs on what looked to be a current affairs website.

As soon as he realised where I was looking, my

father spun and switched off the monitor, then turned back to give me an awkward smile.

"I guess I lost track of the time."

"Uh-huh. You know they talked about that thing in school, right? You don't have to hide the photos." I layered on the sarcasm, the way I always did.

Dad bolted from his chair and grabbed me by the shoulders, a movement so sudden that it startled me right out of my cavalier mood. "They did what?"

"T-they talked about the thing happening in Africa." I stared up at my father wide-eyed, shocked by his vehemence. "We got a big lecture about hygiene and stuff in the final assembly today. I don't get it. It's just another SARS, it'll blow over soon enough."

My confusion must have been written on my face, because his expression softened as he looked down at me. Finally, he released me and turned away, rubbing the bridge of his nose between finger and thumb; a familiar anxious habit of his.

"I don't think so, sweetheart. This is different." He glanced at me again; the look on his face was one I'd never seen before, and that scared me.

My heart skipped a beat.

"Daddy?"

"Go get out of your uniform, Sandy. I'll make us some smoothies and then we'll talk. Okay?"

Dad always knew how to get my attention, and he knew I loved a good smoothie.

"Okay," I agreed, happy to put the morbid conversation aside. I left the office and crossed the hallway to my bedroom door, which stood ajar to reveal the mess within. The sight struck me as strange, because my mother usually picked up after me while I was at school. Perhaps the impending 'talk' I was about to get from my father was the one about how I was old enough to clean my own damn room.

Blast, I'd been trying to delay that one as long as possible.

The door closed with a soft click as I pushed it shut behind me. I sat myself down in front of my vanity and unlaced my shoes. When the laces came free, I kicked them off and leaned down to yank off my sticky socks as well. My clothing was sweaty and repulsive, so I stripped off my skirt and polo shirt and tossed them into the laundry basket by the door. Silently cursing the humidity, I stood flapping my arms like a demented duck for a few seconds to cool off. My mother often joked that you needed gills to survive an Auckland summer, and as far as I was concerned she was very, very right.

My household was just an ordinary, average Kiwi family. Mum, dad, two kids and a fat old cat, living in a fairly nice house in an upper-middle class area of Auckland's North Shore. The house was big enough that my little sister and I each got our own rooms, but it wasn't huge. We went to good schools and our parents were always happy to help with our homework. It was true that we never went on amazing, globe-trotting family holidays, but our grandparents were well-off and owned a holiday house at the beach. My little sister and I were happy to spend our summers playing in the sun, swimming and building sandcastles on the beach.

Dad was an accountant, and Mum had been an office manager until she got pregnant with me. After I was born, she decided to become a stay-at-home mum instead. We were financially stable but not rich, and we survived comfortably on Dad's income alone. I both loved and respected my parents beyond words.

When I cooled down enough to feel human again, I pulled on a pair of shorts and that baby doll tee Dad hated because it showed a little sliver of my belly. I enjoyed teasing him about it, and saying that he was just jealous because he couldn't pull off the look. He always laughed, but I doubted he'd see the humour today.

My hairbrush sat waiting for me, so I grabbed it and turned to face the mirror. A pretty little pixie-face looked back at me, with large blue eyes framed by long lashes, but all I saw were flaws: my breasts weren't big enough, my thighs were too fat, and there was a zit on the side of my nose that looked like Mount Vesuvius.

Of course, I knew full well that the flaws weren't half as bad as they seemed — Harry chided me all the time for being self-conscious. It was a girl thing, though. I figured I'd grow out of it when it was time.

I sighed heavily and grabbed my hairbrush, and then pulled out the elastic band that held my tresses back in a practical schoolgirl ponytail. With a shake of my head, golden curls bounced down around my shoulders. Whatever else I thought of myself, I did love my hair. Dad always said that it was a gift from my mother. He was olive-skinned with black hair, while my sister and I looked like Mum: fair skinned and prone to freckles, with blue eyes and naturally curly blonde hair.

The down side was that fair skin meant I burned like a lobster if I spent too long in the sun. In the summertime, I turned into a mass of freckles instead of getting a tan. It was only mid-December, and I already had a plague of them dusting my nose.

Today had been my last day of high school, so I had the entire summer ahead of me. My next step was deciding what I wanted to do with my life. Maybe I should get a job? Or should I go to university next year? My grades were usually pretty decent, though I wouldn't have my final results until early next year, so it was really just a matter of figuring out what I actually wanted. I already knew that I didn't want to be either an accountant or a homemaker, like my parents.

As usual, I relegated the decision to the 'too hard' basket, and moved on without really answering the question.

With my hair freshly brushed and hanging loose around my shoulders, I stood and padded barefoot down the stairs to join my father. He was in the kitchen as he promised, with the blender out on the bench, fruit everywhere, and glasses waiting for the impending delicious smoothie goodness. His back was to me as I entered, his attention intensely focused on slicing a banana into little, mushy pieces.

"Mum will kill you if you make a mess," I said as I

slipped onto a stool at the end of the breakfast bar. My warning made him jump. He shot a glare at me, but I grinned impishly and planted my elbows on the counter, resting my chin against my knuckles to watch him work. When he didn't say anything for a couple of minutes, I decided to break the silence.

"Hey Daddy, can I borrow twenty bucks?"

"Eh?" He paused in his banana-murdering and shot me a confused look.

"My friends are going to the movies tonight to celebrate graduation. I wanna go with them." I paused for a breath, and then lathered it on a bit thicker. "Please, Daddy? I'll wash your car tomorrow. Mum's, too."

"I—" Dad hesitated, then looked back down at his fruit. "I don't think that's a good idea, sweetheart."

His answer surprised me. It was true that I could be a bit cheeky on occasion, but I was generally a good kid. I never stayed out late, never went boozing and hardly ever got myself into trouble. Dad knew that he could trust me, because I respected his trust in return.

They knew that Harry and I were intimately involved, but they also knew that they had raised me smart enough and worldly enough that I would never come home on drugs or pregnant. As far as my parents were concerned, teenagers would be teenagers regardless of what their parents wanted them to do, and smothering a teenager never worked out well. They wanted me to be comfortable enough to come to them with questions or if I ever needed help — and I was. They weren't just my parents, they were my friends.

That was what made his response so strange. That, and the fact that Dad had never turned down a chance to have someone wash his car before. The thing drew bird poop like a magnet, so offering to wash Dad's car was generally a guaranteed way to get whatever I wanted.

"Why not?" Confused, I tilted my head and sought clarity. "It's just Harry and Katie and a couple of others, you know all of them; you know their parents, too."

"Oh— that's not it, honey." He looked at me and smiled weakly. "I trust you, and I know your friends. It's just—" He finally paused and put down his knife, then turned to look at me fully with that same strange expression. "Sandy, I'm home today because they've quarantined the central business district."

"*What?*"

I was just a kid, but even I knew what a big deal it was if they closed down the centre of Auckland City. It was the biggest financial hub in the entire country, where more than 80,000 people lived and worked on any given day. I could not believe my ears.

"Well, a quarantine is when they—"

"I know what a quarantine is, Dad." I rolled my eyes. I swear, sometimes Dad still thought I was five. "I mean, why?"

"Oh." There was a pregnant pause, and then he sighed deeply. "The infection is here, sweetie. They said on the news last night that there is someone being held at Auckland Hospital that tested positive for the disease."

"Oh, shit."

"Hey, language. But— yes. This morning my supervisor called me, and told me no one was to come into work today. The next thing I knew, it was all over the news that the council had declared an emergency, and set up a quarantine zone around the hospital. The authorities just extended the zone to cover the entire central city and the surrounding suburbs. No one goes in – and no one leaves."

My brow furrowed. "No one leaves? But doesn't that mean that the people stuck inside the zone are at risk of infection?"

"Yes." He grimaced and looked at me, and there was a flicker of something in his eyes that I barely recognised – fear. "The authorities have been talking about it all day on the news. They say the risk of exposure to anyone inside the zone is pretty much guaranteed, but if they let anyone out there's a risk to everyone else in Auckland – maybe even the entire country. Anyone that's inside that zone, stays in that zone."

"But what about my friends?" I stared at my father wide-eyed. "They all live in the city. I haven't heard from them since we left school. When did they extend the quarantine? Do you think they might be inside the zone?"

Before Dad could answer, the front door opened; we both nearly jumped out of our skins. Mum shuffled in, struggling to juggle a couple of very full grocery bags, with my eight-year-old sister, Skylar, whining for attention behind her.

"Mum!" I squeaked in alarm and jumped up to go help her with the bags. I snatched a couple from her hands before she could drop them, then almost did so myself. "Whoa, these are heavy. What have you been buying? Rocks?"

Mum looked up, and shot me an uncomfortable smile. "Canned food and bottled water. A lot of it."

"Geez, is the apocalypse coming or something?" I asked. My parents exchanged a glance.

"I was just about to tell her," Dad said, and then looked back at me. "Sandy, they're going to lock down the whole city soon. They haven't told the public yet, but you remember how your uncle Rick works for the council? He saw the plans on someone's desk to extend the quarantine zone. So you, me, Mum and Skylar, we're going to go for a bit of a road trip. We're going to get out of Auckland tonight, and try and get as far away as we possibly can. We'll go to Palmerston North and visit Grandma, and see where it goes from there."

I looked at him for a long time, and then I switched over to stare at Mum instead. I could see in both their eyes that they were deadly serious, and that they were scared. Really, really scared. As much as I wanted to ask about my friends, the look in their eyes made me think better about pushing for an answer.

Then I looked down at little Skylar, and saw that she wasn't oblivious to the mood in the room either. She sensed the fear Mum and Dad were trying to hide, and clung anxiously to our mother's hand. With no other safe recourse but a healthy dose of sarcasm to try and lift everyone's spirits, I looked over at Mum and quirked an eyebrow.

"Uh, Mum? If we're leaving again in a few hours, then why did you bother lugging all that stuff inside?"

My mother blinked owlishly at me, then looked down at the bags scattered around her feet as though seeing them for the first time. As I turned towards the stairs, I heard her muttering a muffled curse, and the sound of my father's laughter. At the foot of the stairs, I turned back and shot an impish grin at my father.

"So, can I swear *now*?"

V. L. Dreyer

Chapter Three

    I'd never imagined that ten years later I would be dragging around the corpse of a rotten old man. I thought I'd be something special by now: A doctor or a lawyer, maybe a scientist or an astronaut. Maybe someone's wife. Maybe someone's mother.

    I had never thought that I would be a survivor.

    The things that you learned as a survivor were hard and brutal life lessons, like how to ignore the smell of decay. How to push aside your every instinct and kill when you have to. How to ignore the feelings of guilt, and the incessant gnawing of depression around the edges of your psyche. I was not very good at any of those things, but I had no choice.

    "I'm sorry," I whispered to the old man as I dragged him out of his beloved store as quietly as I could. He had a nametag on. His name was Benny. Knowing that made it so much harder to ignore the pain; it made him even more human in my eyes. He wasn't just meat, he was a person, just like I was, just like my family was. A good, loving person who sure as hell didn't deserve the bum fate that life had given him.

And he didn't deserve to spend the rest of eternity rotting between a dumpster and a stack of mouldy cardboard boxes.

I stood and looked down at the worn old face, etched with age and diseased torment. He wasn't there anymore, I reminded myself. Maybe he hadn't been there for a long time. He wasn't a nice old man named Benny anymore, just meat, rotting meat that was going to attract rats if I left him too close to where I was sleeping.

If there was one thing our new civilization did have in droves, it was rats. At least they seemed to be immune.

There was one good thing about Ebola-X, though. Once the infected organism was dead, the virus went into overdrive and consumed the rest of the remains fast. Usually, within a few weeks, not even the bones were left behind. Not always, though. Sometimes the virus burned itself out before the remains were entirely gone. There were skeletons everywhere; five million people didn't just vanish into thin air without a trace.

I often wondered what would happen once the last of the infected finally fell, and their remains dissolved into eternity. What would happen to the disease? Would it just die out, or would it mutate to survive? Would it find a way around my immunity so that it could consume me, too? Or would it go the way of the dinosaurs and become nothing but a terrible memory, leaving a bleached bare world for me and my descendants to reconstruct over the next hundred generations?

More hard questions. I was just too tired to think about it today.

With one last look at the old man, Benny, I grabbed my backpack from where I left it and turned my back to him. But a twinge of guilt plucked at my heart and made me hesitate. I looked again; his blind, old eyes stared blankly up at the clear blue sky, focused on nothing. Could I live with myself if I just left him there, in the open, to be eaten by the birds and rats? I tried to tell myself that I had to, or I'd end up digging a grave for every corpse I saw. Being the world's most prolific gravedigger wasn't quite the legacy I planned on leaving for my children.

Still...

It was a haphazard grave at best, but I grabbed a few of the grimy cardboard boxes and gently piled them atop the old man's corpse to cover him up with as much respect as I could manage in the circumstances. Although it wouldn't really keep the rats at bay, at least it would keep the birds from taking his eyes. That bothered me a lot. I guess it was a phobia.

With my civic duty done, I tried to put poor old Benny out of my mind and turned my attention back to setting myself up a nice little base of operations. At least, that was what I hoped to achieve. The store looked promising from afar: A stand-alone building at the end of town separated from the nearest other buildings by a decent sized car park on the right, a road on the left, and a narrow walkway behind that separated it from the old motel in the rear. From what I could see, it looked like there was a loft above it, probably where the owner used to live. If I was lucky, there might even still be power.

The power grid had been spotty for a number of years, though the fact that it was still on at all was amazing. I had heard rumours of a selfless group of survivors working in one of the big power stations, trying to keep the electricity flowing for as long as possible. Whether that was true or not, I didn't know.

When had I arrived in town early this morning, there was a single street lamp glowing brightly in the semi-darkness, like a beacon of hope drawing me in with its wordless promises. Perhaps this place would offer a respite from the trauma I had suffered in the south. Maybe I could stay a while, and be safe and comfortable. I hadn't felt either of those things in a very long time. So far, I had not seen any signs that indicated anyone else lived in this area; after the abuse I'd suffered over the years, I had become very good at detecting the signs of danger. A tui had sung on the power lines overhead as I'd tiptoed past the sign that welcomed me to the township of Ohaupo, and its song was a familiar memory from my childhood.

The township was a tiny, quiet place, a blip on the map somewhere between Hamilton and Te Awamutu. At first glance, there wasn't much here – a small group of shops clustered around the main street, a handful of homes and a motel, and a few farmsteads further out.

It was the kind of place that a snobby Aucklander should turn her nose up at and drive right on through.

But I was no snobby Aucklander anymore. To me, this little hamlet set in the flat green pastureland of the Waikato was a relief to both the eyes and the soul. Most of the survivors congregated in the shells of the old cities, picking out a living from amongst the shattered ruins torn apart by ten years of storms and earthquakes and flooding. I learned a long time ago that tiny townships like this one often provided a bounty of supplies, if I was lucky enough to be the first one to land there.

Once again, it looked like I had rolled high. The only sign of life was Benny, the tui, and a couple of cheeky magpies that chided me as I crept down the barren streets near their nests. As far as I could tell, there didn't even seem to be all that many rats. Like the survivors, the pests tended to be more attracted to city life.

I left Benny to his eternal sleep and returned to the shattered remains of his livelihood to see what I could salvage from the wreck. If the place proved to be liveable, then I would go back and move his corpse further away, but there was just no point in wasting my energy unless I knew this place was worth the effort.

I passed through the front door and crept back inside in a low, stealthy crouch-walk, my body as conditioned as a soldier's by years of having to survive on my own against all the odds. The main room of the store was a mess. Shattered discs formed a hazardous carpet that crunched underfoot as I checked between the shelves for any signs of danger. I found nothing, only dust and discarded merchandise. Content that I wasn't going to be jumped from the shadows, I picked my way to the front counter to investigate what lay behind it.

I ducked behind the counter and paused to take stock of the contents of the refrigerators, then glanced towards a narrow doorway to my right. My heart sank when I noticed the lock, still intact and shiny even after all these years. Refusing to give in to disappointment, I looked down and around, and used my booted foot to shove aside piles of cracked plastic until finally the glint of steel caught my eye. Correction, several different glints of steel.

Jackpot.

Careful not to cut myself on the mutilated shards, I pried the key ring out from beneath the rubble and held it up to the light. To my eternal relief, all the keys looked more or less intact. I crossed to the door and tried a couple in the lock until one of them turned. The door popped open to reveal a small office, decorated simply with a couple of desks, some computer equipment, a filing cabinet and large framed painting of brightly-coloured lilies hanging on the wall.

Then the stench hit me and sent me reeling back, gagging. Afraid that I was about to find another corpse, I dropped my backpack outside the door and yanked a small cloth mask out of one of the cavernous pockets of my cargo pants. This wasn't the first time I'd had to deal with stench. In a world where almost everyone was dead, you had to find ways to keep the odour at bay. My method was a strip of cloth soaked in the strongest perfume that I could find.

I dove into the stinking gloom and looked around. Thankfully, I didn't find another body, just one little glass jar sitting open beside an old computer. It was a very, very rancid jar, that presumably had once contained some kind of pickle. Now, after a decade's worth of decomposition, the olfactory nightmare had sprouted fungus almost ten centimetres high.

Suddenly feeling amused, I briefly considered keeping it to try and harvest penicillin.

I didn't, of course. The smell was just too horrifying. Instead, I yanked open a window and dropped the doom-pickle into the long grass below, careful not to break the glass or make a sound.

Beyond the office, I spotted a second doorway. I went over to open it and found a set of stairs leading up into semi-darkness. From within one of my many pockets, I drew out a torch and clicked it on, then scampered up the stairs as quietly as I could. One of them creaked ominously underfoot, making me flinch. As unlikely as it was that anyone was alive up there, you never knew. I hadn't survived this long by being careless.

At the top of the stairs, another door opened onto a small, dusty landing, decorated by ancient furniture and lit from above by a little rectangular skylight. Another piece of art hung on the wall; this time, it was a painting of a beautiful landscape, a quaint little village bustling with life. I stopped, and stared. It took me a minute to recognise that it was a painting of Ohaupo township, the way it had been before the plague came and turned this lovely place into a ghost town.

God, how that brought back memories.

Chapter Four

Ten Years Earlier

The drive south felt like it was taking forever, with a nervous eight year old constantly begging for attention. Where were we going? How much longer would it be? Why weren't we going home? It seemed like Skylar had a million questions.

She was driving me crazy, but I was worried about her. She was my baby sister, after all. I was ten when Skylar was born, an unexpected burden on a family that had been perfect just the way it was. My parents had only planned on having one child, and I remembered listening to them argue when they found out that Mum was pregnant again. A second child interfered with all their plans for the future, their financial stability and their hopes for my education.

I had been too young to understand the problem; I was intrigued by the idea of having a baby to play with. The arguments continued right up until the day that Skylar was born, but once they saw her little face, they couldn't help but fall in love with her. The burden of a new baby became a blessing.

Just not right now.

"Skye, please shush." Mum was eternally patient when it comes to her kids, but even she was getting frustrated. The stench of fear in the car was so thick that you could cut it with a knife. The three of us were jammed into Mum's tiny hatchback, while Dad followed behind in his bigger sedan. Her logic didn't make any sense to me, but for some reason Mum insisted that we travel with her, while Dad carried the supplies and the cat in his car. I realised that she was feeling extra protective, and that her maternal instinct had gone into overdrive the moment that her babies were threatened.

I was upset, and Mum knew it. My parents had insisted that I not contact anyone, not even my best friend Katie, or Harry, my boyfriend. I wasn't even allowed to check if they were okay, and it was driving me crazy. Normally I was willing to accept that Mum and Dad knew best, but in this case I thought it was completely unreasonable. They'd even had the nerve to take away my cell phone.

"But Mum, I need to pee!" Skye whined from the back seat, dramatically clutching at herself as though that would make her plea look more genuine and urgent.

"Just hold on a couple of minutes longer, there's a petrol station right up the road." Mum's voice carried an element of frustration, but she struggled to stay calm and reasonable. "You don't want to pee in the bushes like Mushkin, do you?"

Mushkin was our elderly tabby, who had a bit of a bladder problem.

"Mum, Mushkin doesn't pee in the bushes; he pees on the little rug by the door," Skye said matter-of-factly, with admirable wit for one so young.

"He does what now?" Mum exclaimed and glanced back over her shoulder at Skylar. "Damn, I was wondering where that smell was coming from, but I could never find the source."

"Language, Mother," I said dryly.

My mother shot me a dark look, but it didn't last for long.

"Honey, I need you to help me. Please?" This time, her tone was one of earnest appeal.

She sounded exhausted, but concern for my friends made me tense and angry. Although I knew it was petty, I decided that the silent treatment was in order and said nothing.

"Sandy, please? I can't do this by myself. I know you're angry at me, but we'll talk about everything later, I promise. We'll work everything out, but we shouldn't discuss it in front of Skye."

Mum was pleading pathetically, and trying to appeal to my good-natured side. It worked. I was not made of stone, even when I was annoyed at her. I sighed and looked at her.

"Fine, but I'm holding you to that promise. What do you need?" I asked gruffly, doing my best to maintain my show of being the injured party.

"Send a text to your father. Tell him we need to

stop at the next town for a rest," she answered. With one hand on the steering wheel, she fumbled in her purse for my phone and then offered it back to me.

I hesitated, staring at it as if it might explode in my hand. "But I thought you didn't trust me?"

The wounded look that she gave me made me immediately regret saying it.

"I do trust you, honey. There are just some things that we need to keep to ourselves. Promise me you won't text, call, email or Facebook anyone without my permission, okay?"

"What about Twitter?"

"No, no twitting either."

"Tweeting, Mum. The verb is tweeting."

"Well, whatever it is, none of that. Promise me." She suddenly reached over to grab my hand; her palm was sweaty and tense. That broke the last of my resistance. I couldn't stay mad when she was trying so hard to be brave for our sake. I had been trying to gloss over the seriousness of the situation to make it seem less scary, but I was not oblivious to it. There was only so long that I could deny reality before I would have to accept it and deal with it, even if I didn't want to.

"Okay. Okay, okay, I promise. I won't contact anyone." I summoned a weak smile to reassure her, then switched on my phone and thumbed through a text to my father to pass on the message.

Once it was sent, I resumed staring out the window. A green government-issue road sign rolled past, announcing that the township we were about to enter was some little town called Ohaupo, a tiny place that was nothing more than a blip on the map.

***

Present Day

I stared at the painting, thinking back over the way I felt when I first came here at the age of eighteen. I had been passing through on my way to somewhere else, but my first impression of the place was that it looked dull, like one of those little country towns where old people go to die. Back then, it had been alive and full of people.

Well, not full in the Auckland sense of the word, but there were people nevertheless.

It looked like they were all gone now. They were either dead, lingering in the purgatory of undeath, or had left for other places. There was a thick layer of dust on the little decorative table directly beneath the painting, and the tiny china figures were faded and dirty.

Faded and dirty, kind of like Mum and Dad and little Skylar, I thought. The idea brought tears to my eyes. I hadn't seen any of them in so long. It hurt just to think about them.

I shoved that thought back into the little corner of my mind that kept me awake at night, and tried to focus on the task at hand. There were only a couple of hours of daylight left, and it was best for me to use them wisely.

At the end of the hallway stood yet another door,

this one hanging slightly ajar. An angular beam of afternoon sunlight shone through the crack, making the dust stirred up by my footsteps sparkle like fairy dust. I pressed the door open with one hand, the other resting on the pocket where I kept my taser, just in case.

I needn't have bothered. Nothing stirred within.

The place had stood undisturbed for years, a time capsule dating back to a whole other era. The landing opened into a small living room, with an antique couch and a plump armchair sitting in front of a box television that was probably older than me.

Dust coated everything, shimmering in the rays of afternoon sunshine that filtered through net curtains. Behind the television, large windows overlooked the street below, framed by thick curtains in an old damask print that gave the room a special kind of rustic charm. Shelves covered in knick-knacks decorated the walls, and an old, framed black and white photograph of a happy couple on their wedding day took centre stage directly above the television.

Beside the photograph was a small urn, just big enough to hold a person's ashes. I stepped closer and stared at it, then reached out to brush away the dust that blurred the inscription. It bore a woman's name and a short verse.

Margaret.
Beloved wife, beloved mother.
Rest forever in Heaven.

I stood back to consider it, feeling an unexpected rush of relief course through me. It hurt to think of an innocent little old lady going through what Benny had to suffer – or worse, having to watch him go through it. But she had been dead long before he became infected. She was already at peace, and never knew what would happen to her home and her world. That thought gave me some sense of peace, as well.

Perhaps later on, I would bury them together. It seemed like the right thing to do.

V. L. Dreyer

Chapter Five

I sneezed violently.

Mum would be so proud, I thought dryly as I rubbed my nose. God knows that I never did this much dusting at home. Still, if I wanted to make this little loft into my new home then it would have to be clean. It was hard enough to find food and water without a crusty layer of dust getting all over everything.

An hour earlier, I had finished my inspection of the little apartment, and found that there really wasn't much to it. A tiny kitchen opened up off the living room, with a stove, a fridge and a decent-sized pantry. At the far end of the living room, a door led into a small bedroom with an attached en suite. It was just right for one person, maybe two if they didn't mind getting a bit cosy.

For me all on my lonesome, it was perfect.

The bad news was that the dust was just as thick everywhere else as it was in the living room, and the kitchen was a disaster area of a whole other stripe. The good news was that when I tried a light switch, I discovered the place was still attached to the power grid, and the grid was miraculously still going.

Thank you mysterious heroes, whoever you may be.

I was going to have to invest a substantial amount of time in getting the place clean, but it was water-tight, wired, and very secure. There was no sign of rats or roach infestations, which was a blessing. I hated rats. While I was immune to Ebola-X, that immunity did not extend to all the other diseases that could be brought by pests – and if something were to happen to me, where would I go for treatment?

Being a survivor meant being self-sufficient, but it also meant being a bit of a neat freak. It was just better to stay healthy to begin with than to have to try and pull myself back together after a nasty bout of the flu – or worse.

As soon as I had finished my inspection and judged the place fit to be my new domicile, I went back down to retrieve my backpack so that I could leave it somewhere safe while I cleaned. No time like the present; the sooner I got started, the sooner I'd be finished.

I discovered a small vacuum cleaner hidden in the back of the linen cupboard, but my inner survivalist was loathe to give away my position over something as minor as a little dust. Our world was a silent place now, without the drone of traffic and human voices; the noise of a vacuum cleaner would carry over half the township. As far as I was concerned, there was no reason to assume that I was safe and alone just because

I hadn't seen anyone yet. After the pain that I'd been through, I chose to err on the side of caution.

Luckily for me, it seemed that Benny had been a rather fastidious fellow in his former life, and kept the place well stocked with cleaning supplies before his untimely infection. In no time at all, I had the windows open to let the apartment air out and I'd tossed the worst of the dust right back outside where it belonged. In some places, the dust was so thick I didn't even need to use a dustpan; I just picked it up with my fingers and it all came up in one big wad of filth.

The spiders were another story. They were a little territorial. Thankfully, any arachnophobia that I might have once suffered from was a distant memory.

"Sorry, mate, but this is my house now," I told one particularly large daddy longlegs as I swept him off the ceiling with my broom, and shook him out the window.

Good thing that spiders were also immune. Could you imagine a zombie tarantula?

That thought made me chuckle, even in the face of so much horror. I figured that you had to keep up your sense of humour, or you'd go crazy.

I suppose when you had spent the better part of the last ten years alone, it didn't really matter if other people thought you were crazy, did it? All kinds of things stopped mattering when you no longer had society watching and judging you, and from what I'd seen it seemed to be different for every person.

For some survivors, personal hygiene seemed to be one of the first things that they abandoned, but I still considered it vitally important. Perhaps it was because I'm female, and we were just more sensitive to that kind of thing. I hated that unspecified itchy feeling when your skin was all filthy and sweaty, and I loathed being able to smell myself. Most of the male survivors that I'd met didn't seem to care. I could only guess that they couldn't smell their own stench the way I could.

Yet another reason to avoid them, as if I needed any more after what had happened the last time I saw another living human being.

I let the broom head drop to the floor, and stood back to admire my handiwork. Not perfect, but it was a start. There was still the matter of the bed, though. The last person who had slept in that bed was Benny, and that was years ago. I hated to think what kind of foulness lingered in those stale, old sheets. They'd have to go.

With a determined stride, I crossed to the bedroom and set about stripping off all of the bedding. Sheets, duvet, and pillows alike, I flung them into a pile on the floor. When I reached the mattress, I was relieved to discover that it was still in excellent condition, with no signs of fungus or pests aside from a tiny bit of mildew on the underside. A wee bit of mould wasn't enough to deter me from sleeping in it though, not after I'd spent the last couple of years living in the back of an old shipping container.

It gave me the shivers just thinking about sleeping in a real bed again.

I gathered up the old linens and dumped them in a

pile in the living room so that I could deal with them another day. As filthy as they were, a survivor threw nothing away if there was any chance it could be saved. Waste not, want not. After the end of the world, you became the ultimate recycler.

From the linen cupboard, I fetched the spare set of bedding. Despite the years, the sheets were relatively clean and mould-free. I unfolded them and flapped them out the window, giving them a damn good shake to get rid of any excess dust.

There would be time to wash all the bedding out another day, but not tonight. I was working against the clock, with not much time before the sun set. Knowing that the power was still on did relieve the tension of impending darkness, but I preferred not to rely too heavily on something that could abandon me at any moment. It was not terribly surprising that we suffered a lot of blackouts in this day and age.

When the new bedding finally passed my critical inspection, I returned to the bedroom. There, I flicked the bottom sheet over the mattress and quickly mitred and knotted the corners the way my mother had taught me when I was a little girl. A pang of longing and loneliness twisted my heart when I thought of her, but I fought it off. If I gave in to despair, I might as well have killed myself right then and gotten it over with. Mum wouldn't have wanted that.

Besides, I still had to deal with the kitchen, and I wasn't looking forward to that at all.

***

By the time I finished sanitising the kitchen, I decided it was appropriate to coin a whole new word to describe the state it was originally in. 'Epigross' seemed appropriate, or perhaps 'grodetacular' was better.

I wonder if Oxford is still taking submissions?

The kitchen held all kinds of smells in unexpected places, and none of them were good. Most of them came from the fridge, which I was sad to discover had burned out years ago. Given enough time I could probably have fixed it but there was no real need to do so. What would I refrigerate? Everything I ate came in cans or packets, or was fresh out of the ground. I settled for scraping out the contents and giving the fridge a quick wash, then I left it alone.

The pantry was in no better state, and everything that was in there soon went into a rubbish sack as well. Sadly, my good friend Benny was not the kind of fellow that kept a stash of canned food in case of emergency. Rather selfish of him, if you ask me. I did come away with a couple of tins of baked beans and minted peas. Not an amazing haul, but decent enough. Combined with what I'd brought with me, it would be enough to keep me going another couple of days – long enough to explore this pretty little town and map out the available resources.

What was important was that it meant I wouldn't have to eat cat food or bugs for dinner tonight. Been there, done that. Not fun.

When the pantry was clean, I put my tins back in and lined them up in an obsessively neat little row with their faded labels facing forward. Tidy little soldiers, all standing at attention, ready to be devoured at my leisure. Om nom nom.

By that stage, I was starting to lose the daylight.

"Time to batten down the hatches," I murmured to myself as I glanced out the window at the setting sun. While I had artificial light if I wanted it, I did not want to go advertising my position to every Tom, Dick and Harry in the local area. Don't poke the bear.

Bear? What bear? I crinkled my nose; I was really starting to go a bit peculiar, and apparently my head was full of delightfully inappropriate clichés.

I shook my head and decided to let that one go. I'd worry about my mental health later, along with my many, many other problems. Such as figuring out if the plumbing in my new home still worked. Oh, how I longed for a hot shower. That would have been just lovely.

Taser in one hand and keys in another, I trotted back downstairs and peered cautiously out at the office through a crack in the door. Nothing stirred.

Then I crept into the main room of the store, and inspected that just as thoroughly before proceeding. Still nothing.

I stuck my head outside, and looked up and down the street. Once again, I found no signs of life except a pair of magpies chatting about how silly I was for being so paranoid.

You think that's paranoid, maggies? Just watch me.

Still not satisfied, I slipped outside and circled the

store in a low crouch, peering into bushes and over obstructions to make sure beyond a shadow of a doubt that I really was entirely alone. One full circuit completed, I turned right back around and went the other way, checking that my footprints were the only ones visible.

Satisfied at last, I returned to the front door of the shop and paused to examine the debris in the doorway, making sure everything was exactly as I'd left it. It was.

I was safe and alone.

Part of me wondered if that was a good thing or a bad thing, but the part of me that remembered the pain of violence most vividly reassured me that it was definitely a good thing. In this messed-up world, there was no one that I could trust, no one that I could love – no one that would put my safety above their own. I was alone in every sense of the word.

With a sweep of my foot, I cleared away as much of the debris from the doorway as I could, then shoved the outer door closed and turned the lock. I didn't have much faith in the door's strength, given that the glass was badly cracked, but it would do. At least if someone – or something – tried to come through it, I'd have plenty of warning.

And the taser wasn't the only weapon in my possession.

Retracing my steps, I retreated back behind the counter and paused to examine the old refrigerator that had once housed drinks for sale to the public. I didn't trust the various kinds of soft drinks and juices, but there were a number of bottles of water inside that were still sealed.

Gathering up an armful, I took them with me as I retreated back into my new home, closing windows and locking doors behind me. First, the office was locked up, then the door to the stairs, and then the door at the top of the stairs as well. Apparently, Benny was as paranoid as I was, or at least liked the security of having several locked doors between him and the rest of the world.

I wasn't sure what Benny's excuse was, but who could really blame me? I had barely survived my last encounter with other people, and the experience had left me scarred both mentally and physically.

Once I was finally safely confined to my new home, I lined up my water bottles on the kitchen bench – more neat little soldiers destined to sacrifice themselves to fill my belly. I broke the seal on one and sniffed at the contents, then tasted it cautiously. Nothing but fresh, clean water. A little tainted by the plastic over the years, but it wouldn't kill me – at least, not anytime soon.

'Have a drink!' the bottle encouraged, with its happy little cartoon mascot dancing for my amusement.

"Don't mind if I do", I said to myself, and swigged from the bottle as I meandered through my little flat, to close up the windows that I'd opened earlier to let in the afternoon breeze. It was getting cooler, I realised as I studied the setting sun. Clouds were rolling in from the west, obscuring the sunset. It had been fine all day, but it looked like this evening there would be rain.

Not that I minded. I was safe and sound, inside an elevated building well away from the risks of city life. It could rain all it liked. I didn't mind at all.

***

I discovered that the bathroom fixtures still worked, but hot water was a lost cause until I had time to look at the tank. A cold shower was better than no shower though, so I stripped down hastily and stepped beneath the icy flow, determined to get clean before the sun slipped away completely. With the aid of a bar of soap I found under the sink, I sloughed away the day's grime from my skin, and enjoyed the feeling of relief that cleanliness brought.

A few minutes later, I stepped out and dried myself on a towel liberated from the faithful linen cupboard, feeling like a whole new woman. Right up until I caught a glimpse of myself in the mirror, and realised that new woman looked like a crazy woman.

My hair was a mess, unbrushed for days and yanked back into a messy braid. I still wore it long in memory of my mother, but apparently I didn't groom it nearly as much as I should. I usually didn't have time for that kind of thing, but for some reason, today I felt the need.

I dug around in one of the medicine cabinets until I found a comb and set about taming my bird's nest as I wandered out of the room with the towel wrapped around my naked body.

Boy did it hurt to get all those knots out, but it felt

good regardless. Who did I think I was going to impress, anyway? Just me and the magpies, I guess. But it didn't matter – this was for me, not anyone else.

Just as the sun dipped below the horizon, I paused my grooming to close the curtains, making sure that the thick fabric joined perfectly in the middle to block the light. There were no windows in my bedroom or in my bathroom, but the light might still shine through to the living room if I wasn't careful.

I decided to err on the side of caution once more, so I closed myself into my new bedroom with only a single small lamp above the bed to give me light. That was enough for me to finish combing my hair, then have a basic meal of cold baked beans straight from the tin. I wasn't going to need the light for very long.

As soon as I finished eating, I set the tin aside and snuggled down beneath the relatively clean sheets, enjoying the softness of the mattress beneath me. It felt so good after months of sleeping on cold concrete padded with dirty, scavenged rags in a pathetic attempt at bedding.

I was exhausted, and fell fast asleep a moment after my head hit the pillow.

Chapter Six

I awoke to the sound of heavy rain on the tin roof above my head, a familiar and pleasant sound. I blinked, then squeezed my eyes closed again, focusing on that sweet noise. It brought back images of summers spent on the beach and winters with family close by. It rained all year round in New Zealand, and the end of human civilization did not change our climate at all.

I often wondered if it had in other countries. We were lucky, down here in little Aotearoa. We possessed no nuclear reactors, no major military installations. Nothing that could break down and poison what was left of our tiny little island nation beyond all repair. Our power stations were either fossil fuel, hydroelectric or thermal, all relatively clean energy sources compared to nuclear.

I wondered what it was like in Europe and America. Had their nuclear reactors failed and spewed toxic poisons into their skies, now that the people who kept them running were all dead? Did their few survivors live under the perpetual cloud of nuclear winter?

Was there even anyone left alive over there? I had no way to know. Communications were basically gone. There were only a few limited ways for survivors to communicate with one another and they were spotty at best. The mobile phone networks still functioned in some places, but they were useless without knowing the number of the person you were trying to reach. Radio was the only way left to bridge the oceans that separated us from our nearest neighbours, and I had never gained access to one of those. In some ways, that kind of isolation kept us safe.

If only it had been enough to keep us safe from the plague itself.

***

Ten Years Earlier

Skylar leaned against me as we sat in the kitchen, drinking milk and eating the cookies Grandma baked for us that morning. We had been banished to the kitchen while the adults huddled around the television in the next room, watching the news. Mum made me promise to keep Skylar away so she wouldn't see what was happening in the world outside. She was just a little girl, but she was bright for her age and knew that something was going on.

"What're you drawing, Skye?" I asked, trying to keep her attention focused on happy thoughts. She glanced up from her colouring with a mouth full of cookies, and gave me a bright smile.

"Zombies," she answered cheerfully, spraying me with crumbs.

"Zombies?" I blinked like an owl caught in sudden light. That was the last thing I had expected her to say.

"Yup." She nodded and went back to her colouring like it was the most normal thing in the world.

"Why are you drawing zombies? Zombies are yucky," I asked her, curiosity overwhelming my caution.

"Cause they're coming," she answered simply. With delicate little fingers, she selected a bright red crayon from the box. I watched as she applied the red crayon to her artwork, scribbling over the figures that looked like members of our family. The sheer volume of crimson that she used bothered me immensely; I was suddenly overwhelmed by the need to talk to my mother.

I stood carefully, so as not to disrupt my sister's artistic endeavours, but she barely noticed. She was thoroughly engrossed in destroying her own creation.

Now I was *really* bothered.

With barefoot stealth, I crept down the hallway that separated Grandma's kitchen from her lounge, and quietly pushed open the door to sneak a peek. A noise that sounded like a muffled sob jolted me; I shoved the door open the rest of the way to see what was going on. I found my mother with her face buried against my father's chest, while Grandma clung to their hands. None of them seemed to notice me.

On the television, people screamed and surged against police cordons, the low volume of the TV muffling their cries. It was a riot. A full blown riot. In the background, I could see the shopping centre where Katie and I had spent so many afternoons hanging out together and doing nothing, as teenagers are wont to do.

Then suddenly, there she was: My best friend in the whole wide world. Her tear-stained face was split in a scream as she strained against the cordon with the others. Begging to be let out of the quarantine zone. Begging for a chance to live.

My breath caught in my throat, and it was my turn to muffle a cry when I saw that familiar face in distress. Dad heard me, of course. It was too late to protect me now, so he just beckoned me closer and invited me to join the huddle on the couch.

"Is that why you wouldn't let me call them?" I whispered as I sandwiched myself in between my parents, afraid to hear the answer. Mum clung to me, unable to reply. It was Dad who answered, his voice trembling as he tried to stay strong for our sake.

"Yes. They were already in the zone, Sandy. It was too late for them." He hugged us both tightly. "Your mother and I knew you wouldn't let them go without a fight, so we had no choice but to protect you from the truth. I'm so sorry." He looked at me, his eyes full of so much pain and fear that I couldn't be angry at him. "Now, the entire city is quarantined. All of Auckland. No one can leave. The infection is spreading too fast, they can't stop it. Thank God we got out in time."

"I don't think we've gone far enough, Dad." In my

doe-eyed teenaged wisdom, I had no idea how right I was. "It's only been a week. We need to... go further away. Get away from people. Get away from the towns."

"No, we'll be fine right here. We're five hundred kilometres away; we'll be safe for sure," Dad insisted stubbornly. My grandmother knew better though, and interrupted him with her own wisdom.

"Don't be stupid, Roger. She's right. This isn't the flu we're talking about here. It's come all the way from Africa. It will reach Palmerston North." Her wrinkled face furrowed. "We'll go to the beach house. I'm not sure anywhere is safe, but at least it's isolated. Maybe that will give us a chance."

Dad started to protest, but he was voted down by all the women in his life. We knew in our hearts that nowhere would be far enough to save us, but still we had to try.

Then from behind us came a soft little voice, a voice that filled me with dread.

"I told you." Skylar stood in the doorway hugging her favourite doll, her red crayon still clutched between tiny fingers. "They're coming."

***

Present Day

By the time the sun rose, the clouds were clearing and the rain had come to a halt. The day dawned with a flawless blue sky, adorned with the lightest dusting of high puffy clouds around the ring of the horizon.

Another beautiful day in my dead world.

As I often did, I found myself wondering what the date was, but I had given up trying to keep track a long, long time ago. It was at least December, maybe January; perhaps it was Christmas Day? I had no way of knowing. The date is one of the many things that stopped mattering when society vanished from the earth.

I mean, what difference did it make if it was December or January? The only difference to me was how far away winter was, and I would figure that one out when the birds started flying north. In this part of the country, we suffered from no real weather extremes. There was no snow in winter, and the temperature rarely climbed above 30 degrees Celsius in the summertime.

Without the climate to dictate my actions, the days blended together into an endless cycle of day and night. Time only mattered in the abstract and in the most literal sense. When it was dark, I slept, in the mornings and afternoons I worked, and at midday I rested until the heat of the day passed. I had a vague sense of the weeks, months and years drifting by and my body gradually getting older, but no real sense of scale.

I wasn't even sure when my birthday was any more. I just counted myself a year older with each summer that passed, but sometimes I had trouble remembering what I was up to. I thought I was about twenty-eight.

I stretched languidly in bed, enjoying a moment of peace while I could, then I rolled myself out of bed and padded into my little en suite to indulge in another cold shower. Ten minutes later, feeling pleasantly clean, I dressed and devoured a quick breakfast of minted peas and bottled water before I set off about my day.

I'm going to need to find some kind of protein soon, I thought to myself as I disposed of my trash; I could feel my muscle-mass waning by the day. I put the thought aside for now, and just kept my hopes high that I would find some canned meat during my day's exploration. If I didn't, then I would have to consider hunting and killing something – and that was something that I despised. I had killed before and I probably would kill again, but I was not *a* killer.

Feeling safe with the security the loft provided me, I left my backpack behind and took only the necessities I needed for salvage. I could move faster without the burden of my pack, and with the keys to the store safely deposited in one of my cavernous pockets I felt confident that no one would be able to steal my few precious belongings.

In some ways I was like a skinny blonde turtle. Everything I owned had to fit in my backpack and be light enough for me to carry when I travelled on foot. Even though I was young, fit and strong, I was bound by my natural limitations; there was only so much I could carry and still be able to walk and fight effectively. Whenever I decided to add something to my pack, I had to justify its weight. If it wasn't worth it, then I had to leave it behind.

My necessities were few, but practical. Like every

teenager, I had owned a slick-looking smartphone, but now there was no one for me to call, and it could be days or even weeks between opportunities to charge it. When I figured that out, I discarded the thing in favour of an old GPS unit with a long battery life. The software was ten years out of date, but without city councils changing street names and building new subdivisions, things weren't exactly changing very fast. I did wonder how much longer the satellites would continue to function, but for now they still seemed to be working just fine.

Like everything else I owned, the GPS had proved its worth many times over the years, but today it would stay at home. I didn't need a map to show me around this tiny little township. I'd already seen most of the town on my way in, so now I was just going to go back and investigate it in more detail.

Like most other survivors, I lived by scrounging supplies from the ruins of old towns like this one. While I had water aplenty in my new home, my food supplies were running low. Still, water was more important than food and I had lots of it, both safely bottled drinking water and running water from the tap. I didn't really trust the tap water for drinking unless I boiled it thoroughly, but at least I could use it to wash in or to flush the toilet.

In this day and age, that kind of extravagance was a luxury that a lot of us didn't have.

Food was a problem, though. For the past several years, I had lived in the ruins of the town of Te

Awamutu, about 20 kilometres to the south. I was the only person there, because the place was a total disaster zone. Years before my arrival, a terrible earthquake had reduced the entire town to rubble. There was enough there for a clever survivor to live off for a while, but not indefinitely. Eventually, I had exhausted the supplies I could get at without seeking help from others, so I was forced to come north in search of food.

Compared to Te Awamutu, Ohaupo was in nearly perfect condition. Although there were signs of storm damage everywhere, the buildings all appeared to still be more or less structurally sound. There were a lot of shattered windows and few fences were still standing, but most of the buildings still had their roofs and their doors and porches were intact.

I hoped that meant that I would be able to find plenty of food stashed around the town. At the moment, I was down to a half-dozen tins of unknown quality, one of which was cat food. I was saving that for last. Eating cat food was one step above eating bugs, and I had no intention of doing either of those things any time soon.

Of course, if I wanted to keep avoiding it, I would have to find other options fast.

The tiny shopping centre was the logical place to start, and also the closest; it was only about half a kilometre down the road. The buildings stood sad and vacant, adorned by faded Old West-style signs that marked what they had once been used for in the simplest of terms. 'Cafe', one proclaimed vibrantly; 'Bar', said the one next door; 'Function', advised the third.

That's a little vague, I thought, peering suspiciously at the ambiguously-named function building.

Of course, 'Fish N Chips' stood out, in its bright blue and white TipTop colours, now so faded that it looked far less appetizing than it had long ago. I decided to skip that one; abandoned takeaway joints were a haven for rats and cockroaches. There was rarely anything worth salvaging in them anymore.

Across the road, another small storefront attracted my eye, one that was simply labelled 'Ohaupo Store'. The front window was smashed, the faded Lotto logo barely visible through the spider-webbed glass, and the old magazine racks that framed the doorway were tattered beyond all recognition. Old spray paint proclaimed a mixture of biblical end-of-days prophecy and faded swear words.

Still, despite the damage, I drew my taser and approached the doorway with silent-footed caution.

The door swung in the wind, squeaking rhythmically with each gust. I paused and drew a deep breath of the clean, cool air, made pleasant by last night's rain, then ducked through the doorway into the waiting stench. Crouching just inside the entrance, I waited until my eyes adjusted to the dark, breathing shallowly through my mouth to keep the inevitable stink at bay.

The place appeared to have been ransacked.

Not surprising. In the riots during the final days of

civilization, many places had been devastated by the panicked populace as they tried to flee the cities, or by the undead who simply didn't know any better. Most of those people were dead now, or they were like me – picking a living from the ruins of the old world.

Regardless of the destruction, I snuck deeper inside with my taser at the ready. Most of the time there was still something left in these old, trashed general stores. You just had to know where to look.

Glass crunched underfoot as I crept along the end of the aisles to check for unwelcome guests of any stripe. The only sign of life was a nest of mice behind the counter, full of angry babies that hissed at me when I passed, but to them I was big and scary, so they fled when I got too close.

Behind the counter, I spotted a closed door. I moved closer to examine it, and found that it was made of solid steel with a modern lock. It was still intact despite dents that spoke of repeated attempts to burst it open. I tried the handle and found it firmly locked. A quick hunt turned up no keys nearby, so I would have to return later to try and figure out a way inside. It would take some creativity for me to get through that.

I was always up for a challenge – particularly since there was probably a storeroom back there with stock that didn't fit on the shelves, which could well be a gold mine for someone like me. As it was still sealed, the chances were extremely good that no one else had gotten in there yet. I added the location to my mental map and moved on.

Picking over what was left on the store's shelves did not yield quite the bounty that I hoped for. Most of the tinned goods were long gone, and the dried goods were well past the point of being remotely edible. Piles of decay sat in what had once been displays of fresh vegetables, and rancid-smelling slivers of glass was all that was left of the preserves.

Even the cash register was cracked open, and hung sad and empty inside. A tiny mouse stuck its head out of one and squeaked in horror, then fled back into its sanctuary.

That's not to say the store was useless, though. In the back of the store, I found a small stash of hardware that no one had thought to steal during the riots. I came away with half a dozen knives, two metal can openers, and a few small hand tools. To a scavenger like me, those kinds of things were a treasure trove almost as exciting as an entire crate of tinned spaghetti.

I stuffed my treasures into a plastic bag liberated from behind the counter, and left the store behind.

***

By midday, I had picked over most of the other stores in the district as well, and come away with enough food and bottled water to last me for a few weeks, with some careful rationing.

Even more exciting, I found a small automotive workshop fully equipped with machinery, and a few cars that I thought I could salvage with enough time and determination. Not that I planned to go anywhere, but if I needed to get out of town in a hurry, then having a functioning vehicle made it so much easier. Plus, with a vehicle I would be able to visit the outlying farms more easily, and see what treasures waited for me there.

I was feeling rather buoyant and pleased with my morning's work. The pantry was filling up nicely and I even found a few treats along the way. I was practically salivating at the thought of the large tin of peaches I found in the back room of the cafe. They were long past their 'best before' date, but a girl could still hope.

As a reward, I decided to stop for lunch and crack open the peaches. To my delight, I found that they were still good. They tasted a little metallic, but I couldn't complain; it was rare to find fruit that was still edible in the towns these days. I did hope to find a local orchard that might have some fruit growing wild, but it would be a few days before I was prepared to go that far out of town.

In the meantime... ah, I could practically taste the vitamin C. De-lish!

Peaches in one hand and fork in the other, I wandered back down the stairs. In front of the store was a battered bench, left for people passing by to sit and rest their feet; now it was my turn. Like everything else, the bench had seen better days, but in my imagination I could picture this as Benny's favourite place to sit and watch the evenings go by. It was mine now, and I gave silent thanks to the poor old fellow for his foresight.

All in all, I was feeling pretty relaxed by that stage. I

had almost finished securing the town and seen none of the tell-tale signs of danger, so I felt more or less at ease. I let my guard down for a moment, to enjoy the warmth of the sun and the simple human pleasure of eating.

Needless to say, the ambush took me completely by surprise.

I was so startled that I almost dropped my food when the tiny kitten suddenly leapt from the bushes onto the seat beside me.

"Mew?" The kitten queried, its little face canted at a curious angle as it watched me eat.

Some ambush. Beware the fuzzy terror.

Still, the kitten's arrival was completely unexpected, and its fearlessness struck me as peculiar. I immediately worried that it might be diseased, but it showed no signs of any illness that I was familiar with. Rabies had been eliminated from my country decades before Ebola-X decimated us, and this tiny cat showed none of the telltale symptoms of carrying either of those diseases. Its eyes were alert, and... well, it was quite vocal. The walking dead are not.

"Mew?" It cried again, inching closer to me on cautious paws, not quite confident enough to touch me but too inquisitive to back away. Likewise, I was too curious to shoo it off, but too wary to try to touch it.

I put another slice of delicious peach in my mouth and chewed thoughtfully, which drew yet another demanding cry from the kitten. I blinked and held the tin down low enough for it to smell the contents, and it immediately lost interest.

"Yeah. You don't eat peaches, kitty," I told it dryly, and resumed eating them myself. Mmm, tasty.

Rebuked, the kitten sat down and started grooming its little paws with intense concentration, pretending that it didn't see me at all. My heart softened. It seemed hungry, with the way it was crying at me, and it was so young – no more than six weeks old. Maybe its mother was dead, like mine?

Damn it. What am I, made of stone?

"Stay here, kitty." I sighed and rose carefully so as not to disturb the fluffball, then headed upstairs to find that dreaded cat food. Well, at least if I fed it to the kitten then I wouldn't have to stomach it myself. My morning's exploration had turned up plenty of supplies, so I could spare one can for a hungry kitten.

Even after all these years alone, I still had my human compassion. The day I lost that, is the day I wouldn't be a human being any more.

I returned upstairs to find the can right where I had left it – hidden right at the back of the pantry behind my new-found bounty, where I wouldn't have to think about it unless things got desperate. I cracked open the pop-top lid, scooped a couple of spoonfuls of the foul-smelling pseudo-meat into a bowl liberated from Benny's cupboards, then carried it back downstairs.

In the doorway, I stopped and looked around.

The kitten was gone.

V. L. Dreyer

Chapter Seven

    I found myself surprisingly disappointed by the kitten's disappearance. As much as I tried to ignore it, I longed for some kind of companionship, anything to help keep the loneliness at bay. I was tempted to call for the little cat, but I didn't want to risk giving away my position in case there were larger creatures around. With few other options, I set the bowl down on the ground beneath the bench and left it there. There was still much of the town left to explore, and perhaps while I was gone the kitten would return.

    There were only two stores left on the main drag for me to investigate – a little antique store, and the simply named 'Function' building. I wasn't expecting much from either, but instinct said to check anyway. At least then I'd sleep easier at night, because I would know the buildings were safe. Lacking any particular inspiration, I flipped a mental coin and headed for the antique store.

    As it turned out, 'antique' was a fancy name for 'second hand'. The store had survived the riots surprisingly well, mostly due to the fact it stocked very little of conventional value. The lock on the door had been forced, and the contents of a few shelves strewn across the floor, but mostly it was just dusty and quiet. I took in the entire room at a glance, soon realising that there was nothing of great value to me either, but I still felt drawn inside.

The shelves that were still standing contained things that fascinated my inner child. Along one high shelf was a row of tiny porcelain tea sets in miniature, with little teapots, sugar bowls, teacups and saucers all to perfect scale, and resplendent with beautiful, hand-painted patterns. Unlike just about everything else, porcelain survived the years without fading; the painted flowers were still just as bright and vibrant as the day they felt the artist's brush.

I found that fascinating. Even after all this time, there were still some things made by human hands that stood the test of time. But it wasn't the cheap, mass produced things from my generation; it was the old, beautifully hand-crafted items that survived the best.

Some morbid part of me hoped that if the human race survived long enough to flourish again, in a thousand years archaeologists would come to dig through these ruins and find these beautiful little things. Maybe that way, our distant descendants could look back on our civilization with some sense of pride, instead of with shame.

I picked up one tiny teapot and turned it over between my fingers, half-expecting it to crumble to powder at my touch. It didn't. It just sparkled prettily, its glossy paint as flawless as the day it was made. I wanted desperately to put it in my pocket and take it with me, but I knew it would not survive the rigors of my journey and it felt like a sin to destroy something so beautiful. With reverence, I set it back down with its little teacups and moved on.

There were a great many things in this store that served no real purpose, or whose function I could simply not name. They were things that had once been so important to society, but their purpose was forgotten long before I was born. Now that the generation who remembered them was gone, there was no one left to understand them.

But there were some things I understood, like the beautiful doll house beside the counter. Oh, I remembered longing for something just like it when I was a little girl, a doll house so perfect in every detail. I bent down to peer inside, and in the living room I found a family of little figurines, humanised bunny rabbits – a mother, a father, and two little girls. They were dressed in human clothes, old fashioned but perfect in their own way.

In my memory, I heard Skylar's sweet little voice cry out with delight. Suddenly, I remembered that once, long ago, we had stood in this very store together admiring that doll house.

A pang of grief socked me in the gut, and I stood sharply to leave. I was halfway to the door before a sense of longing overwhelmed me, and forced me to turn back and look at that little family again. They were so perfect, happy and sweet.

I felt such a sense of abandonment at the thought of leaving them behind that I just couldn't bear it. Those little dolls reminded me of my own lost family. I could justify it if I thought about it. There was no harm in one tangible keepsake to remember them by. They weighed next to nothing.

So I took them, my little family, and I put them in my pocket.

Tears blurred my eyes as I left the antique store behind, putting as much distance between it and myself as I could. There was one last port of call for today, that vaguely-named 'Function' building. I assumed it was used by the community for events, possibly even as a multi-purpose church or chapel, but beyond that I really didn't know what to expect.

Following my usual protocol, I kept my weapon in hand while I slipped open the door and moved into the building. I hovered in a half-crouch while my eyes adjusted; when they did, I found myself in a short hallway with a double-door in the centre and a single door on each wall flanking it.

I tried the left and right doors first and found them both unlocked, revealing small, basic offices beyond. The religious paraphernalia told me that they were probably used by the preachers who gathered their flocks here, and that there was little of use to me.

I was just about to close the door to the second office, when something out of the ordinary caught my eye. In a clear plastic bag on the desk was a quantity of tiny prescription bottles. A very large quantity.

Overcome by morbid curiosity, I crossed the room to the bag and pulled out a couple of the little bottles, and then turned them over to read the faded labels. Trilam, Riopnol, Hypnovel and Laroxyl? I was no pharmacist, but I have had a lot of time to read. I knew what those tablets were: Sleeping pills and antidepressants. Strong ones. Every single one of those little prescription bottles was empty.

I had a bad feeling about this.

The claws of dread tangled in my gut as I returned the bottles to their bag and retraced my steps to the hallway. There, I hesitated in front of that last set of double-doors. I wasn't entirely sure I wanted to open that door, but I needed to know for sure.

I'd seen a lot of death in the last ten years. What were a couple more bodies? On the other hand, curiosity killed the cat.

My hand shook on the door handle as I turned it, but I swallowed hard and pushed it open anyway.

A moment later, I slammed it closed again and burst into tears.

✤✤✤

Ten Years Earlier

This was not how I pictured spending my first New Years as a legal adult. I wasn't the kind of girl who would go out drinking and dancing on tables and flinging my knickers at anything with a penis, but anything would have been better than spending the night crammed in a car with a panicked mother and stressed-out grandmother. Not my idea of fun.

Mum was in a panic because Skylar, ever the adoring Daddy's Girl, insisted on travelling in Dad's car. When Mum had tried to force the issue, my sister threw such a tantrum that I was afraid she would wake the dead.

Now the problem had grown. We'd lost sight of Dad's car an hour ago, and none of us were able to get a cell phone signal to try and call him.

We pulled into the driveway of Grandma's holiday home on the coast, but the sedan was nowhere to be seen. The holiday house was miles from anywhere, totally isolated from the rest of civilization. It had taken most of the night to get there; by the time we arrived, the sun was rising over the ocean to the east.

As soon as we stopped, I leaped out and climbed up onto the roof of the car to look for Dad. I stretched up on tiptoes and shaded my eyes with one hand, staring long and hard into the gloom behind us, but there was no sign of him.

"Do you see anything?" Mum asked, her voice shaking. The fact that she let me stand on her car without kicking up a fuss told me just how upset she really was. I shook my head, and looked away so that I wouldn't have to see the tears well up in her eyes. Instead, I hopped down as fast as I could without breaking an ankle and I wrapped my arms around her, holding her tight as she cried helplessly.

"Oh God, Roger," she sobbed, shaking convulsively in my arms. "I have to go back for him. I-I have to—"

"No, you can't." I tried to keep my voice even, but I could hear it shaking despite my best efforts. "They're going to come here looking for us soon, and if you're not here then Dad will panic. They'll make it, I promise they will."

Grandma's cool hand landed upon my shoulder, and I looked at her over my mother's head, staring deep into her concerned eyes. I gently released my distressed mother into her care, and she led her off towards the house.

"Come along, sweetheart. You're very tired, let's get you to bed. I'm sure they'll be here by the time you wake up," she cooed, leaving me to tend to Mushkin and the supplies we carried in Mum's tiny hatchback. Silently, I prayed that Dad and little Skylar would arrive soon, so that my beloved family could be whole again.

But they never did.

***

Present Day

I sat in the sun on my little bench with my head between my knees, gasping for breath as I struggled to get my racing heart back under control. Tears rolled freely down my cheeks, but I didn't have the willpower to wipe them away. You would think that after this long, my heart would be hardened to this kind of thing, but it wasn't. I was still a person, still a human being.

Just like they had been. There were at least a

hundred of them, all crammed into that hall together. A decade later, their skeletons lay in the positions in which they'd died. Clinging to one another, curled up in as though in sleep.

So many bodies... so very many bodies – and the smell... oh God, the smell. I couldn't get it out of my head.

I muffled a sob and wiped my nose on my sleeve. Not the most elegant thing to do, but as I was having a bit of a breakdown and there was no one else around to see me so it didn't really matter. There was only so much one can person could handle before it became *too* much.

There were so many of them: Men, women and children alike all crammed into that dusty hall. They weren't even infected. Maybe a couple were, but not many. The skeletons were still there, bleached by the humid air over the years, their clothing preserved from the elements by the shelter of the hall. If they had carried the infection, then there would be no bones left, or at least not nearly as many.

They might have lived!

My mind rebelled at the idea. Some of them could have been immune, but they didn't dare to take the risk. So they chose to die together, huddled in a dark building for all of eternity. Husbands and wives, friends and neighbours, and even parents and children alike.

The parents – how could they do that? How could they murder their own babies?

But it was to spare them the horror of becoming

like poor, poor Benny. I could understand that. I couldn't bear knowing my children might end up like that.

But they might have lived!

If I don't find some way to calm myself down, I am going to lose my peaches. That thought made me laugh, but it was a hysterical kind of laugh that did nothing to stop the sobs from wracking my body. It had been awhile since I'd had a full blown break down, so I suppose I was entitled to one.

I'd seen suicides before, but never so many all at once. A lot of people had chosen to take their own lives rather than let the disease run its course. My own mother did, as did my grandmother. But I'd never seen so many in one place before. I was completely overwhelmed.

"Mew?" A soft head bonked against my hand; I looked up and found myself staring down into a pair of huge golden eyes, set into a fluffy little tabby face. The kitten had returned.

How did the animals always know?

***

Ten Years Earlier

Mushkin purred contentedly in my lap, oblivious to the shaking of my hands as tears rolled silently down my cheeks. No, oblivious wasn't the right word. He wasn't oblivious. As soon as I started crying, he climbed up into my lap and started purring, rubbing his soft head against my hands until I patted him. He knew something was wrong. He always did.

Mum was the first of us to get sick. It had started a week ago, with a fever. When Dad and Skylar failed to arrive, it was like all the strength had drained right out of her and with it had gone her will to live. She hadn't let me out of her sight, she was so terrified that she might lose me as well.

It had ended up being just the three of us huddled around the television while the latest updates were read out by an exhausted and frightened news anchorman.

"That man needs a shave," Grandma had commented dryly as we sat together, with her usual irreverent sense of humour. My parents had always joked that I inherited my sense of humour from her, and they were probably right. At that moment though, even I hadn't felt like jokes. I was watching my mother more than the television. Once I became aware of how pale she'd become, I became more and more anxious.

"Mum, are you all right?" I'd asked, reaching over to take her hand. She had turned and looked at me with dark, sunken eyes, and then shrugged.

"I don't feel very well." Her voice was husky, and her skin felt hot and clammy to the touch.

"Well, off to bed with you, then." Grandma had hidden her emotions behind a mask of strength like she always did, and bundled Mum off to rest.

That was a week ago. The fever didn't break, and Mum was starting to have trouble speaking. Grandma had banished me from the room while she tended to my poor mother, so I was curled up on the couch watching yet another news report. This one was about the immune. They'd discovered that some people were resistant to the disease, and they hoped that immunity would give the scientists enough information to protect the rest of us.

The anchorman still hadn't shaved.

It was then that I realised that I hadn't seen any other people on the news in days. I wondered if they were all sick. Was this anchorman the only one left? That thought scared me, so I hugged Mushkin tight and buried my face in his rumbling warmth. Maybe if I wished hard enough, Mum would be okay, and Dad would arrive with Skylar in tow. We'd be safe and happy forever.

Grandma's cool hand landed on my shoulder and interrupted my wistful delusion. When I looked up and saw her expression, dread clamped its ice-cold talons around my heart.

"You need to go say goodbye to her," Grandma told me softly. All the humour was gone from her voice, but somehow she stayed strong. Her daughter lay dying and yet she managed to keep her wits together. It didn't occur to me until much later that Grandma felt like she had to stay strong for my sake.

I picked Mushkin up, and headed for the bedroom where my mother spent the final week of her life. I made no attempt to wipe the tears from my cheeks. There was no point; I knew I'd be crying again soon enough.

I also knew that I was about to lose my mother forever, and that there was nothing in the world I could do to stop it.

Mum lay limp in her bed, propped up on as many pillows as we were able to scavenge from around the house. Her skin was so pale she looked like a porcelain doll. There was a clammy sheen of sweat on her brow that never seemed to go away.

I wondered briefly why Grandma would let me near her when she was so sick, then I realised that it was already too late for us both. If my mother had the disease, then we'd both been fatally exposed already.

It was only a matter of time.

I sat down beside her and reached out, taking her clammy hand in mine. I gave it a gentle squeeze; she opened her eyes and looked up at me helplessly. Although she tried to speak, when she opened her mouth nothing came out.

"She can't talk anymore," Grandma explained softly, her expression unreadable. I was about to lose my mother, but she was about to lose her only daughter. I could not imagine how she felt.

I made no attempt to stop the tears rolling down my cheeks as I leaned over to stroke my dying mother's forehead. I couldn't think of what to say. Everything seemed inadequate. How do you say goodbye to the one person you love more than anyone else in the world?

Lacking any other option, I just told her the simple truth.

"I love you, Mum."

The only response she gave me was a tiny smile and a gentle squeeze of my hand. She was too far gone to reply, but she still understood. Then suddenly, Grandma was bundling me out of the room, though I fought to stay longer.

"Please," I implored her, feeling completely helpless, "at least let me stay with her until the end."

Grandma caught my shoulders as I tried to get by her and held me firmly. "You can't, sweetheart. I made her a promise when she could still speak; now I have to keep it. Take Mushkin outside, I'll join you soon." She turned me around and ushered me out the door. With no other option, I took my fat old cat out and sat down on the doorstep to wait.

A few minutes later, a single gunshot shattered the silence. My head jerked up in surprise. Not long afterwards, Grandma stepped up beside me, her face a mask of grief. There was a small handgun clutched between her frail fingers. I looked up at her in horror, and she looked at me with more emotion than I'd ever seen on her face before.

"She made me promise." Grandma's voice was choked up, grief and guilt warring on her face. She sat down beside me on the stoop, staring down at the gun in her hand.

Then she looked at me. I realised with a jolt that her skin was clammy, and now that same sheen of sweat shone upon her brow as well.

"Sandy, I need you to make me a promise."

***

The promise had been the same one that my mother swore her to. When the disease took them to the point where they became helpless, they chose a quick and painless death over waiting for the inevitable.

My grandmother and I buried the body of my mother in the back yard. A week later, I buried my grandmother alone. Then it was waiting, waiting for weeks, waiting for the fever to claim me as well. All alone, just me and my cat, living on the supplies we brought with us from Auckland and what was already in the house.

Eventually, they ran out and I started to get hungry.

After a month passed, I realised that if I wasn't sick now then I wasn't going to get sick. I was one of the immune – alive but all alone. I needed to leave, to find food somewhere, but without my parents to guide me I couldn't even think of where to begin. I was absolutely terrified, but I was so hungry I could think of no other option. My choice was either to lay down and die with my family, or find to some way to survive.

I chose to live.

I took Mum's car and drove away, with Mushkin curled up on the seat beside me. For the first year or so, he was my loyal companion and followed me everywhere. But he was already old by the time the plague hit. One night, we curled up to sleep together, and he just never woke up.

After he died, I really was all alone.

***

The kitten was aggressive with its affection and demanding but it helped me to centre myself, to bring me back to the present and to focus on what needed to be done. I patted it gently, letting its soft fur bring back pleasant memories from childhood, happy memories of nights spent curled up with my beloved Mushkin, safe and warm in bed.

I tried not to think about the fleas.

Eventually, I calmed down enough to function. It took a while, but the kitten's sweet-faced inquisitiveness helped. Whenever I started to slip away, she nudged me with her little head and brought me back to the present. Finally, after I cried my way through utter despair and out the other side, I felt strong enough to get up. I would have to do something about that damn 'Function' building, or else I would not be able to sleep tonight.

There was an unspoken code amongst survivors. A way to both respect the dead, and warn others away from something they really didn't want to see. I had come across a few marked sites during my years on my own, and I knew without anyone ever having to tell me what the black mark meant. With that in mind, I set off in search of tools.

I found what I needed stashed away in the workshop I discovered earlier. While I was gathering things, an idea began to grow in the back of my mind. I initially planned to bury Benny and his beloved wife together, but it seemed more appropriate for them to spend their eternity with the community that they loved.

A coil of rope slung over my shoulder and a can of spray paint in my pocket, I returned home to fetch Benny and Margaret. It was not a pleasant trip, dragging a decaying corpse a few hundred metres along the street in the bright summer sun. He was already starting to fall apart, but I managed to keep him intact long enough to get him into the function centre.

I left Benny in the lobby. I couldn't bring myself to open the inner doors and take him all the way inside. I reassured myself that Benny would be happy just being close to his friends. It felt right. I straightened up his rotting limbs with as much respect as I could and set the jar of his wife's ashes into his wrinkled old hands and his wedding photo on his chest, then I stood back and looked down at him.

"Rest in peace, Benny," I whispered.

Leaving them to their eternal sleep, I backed out of the function centre one last time, pulling the outer doors closed behind me. I slipped the coil of rope from my shoulder, and then I wound it around the door bars and pulled it tight, knotting it a few times until I was satisfied.

A few knots wouldn't be enough to stop a determined survivor, but it would keep anything inside from getting out, which was really the point. I rattled the doors to check that my knots were tight, and then fished my can of spray paint out of my pocket.

It took a bit of shaking to get the thing going, but

when I did, I painted a large, black X across the doors, the universal sign that meant 'you really don't want to see what's in here, buddy'. I went over it a few more times, making it as bold as possible, then below it I added three simple letters: R I P.

I didn't think I could be any clearer than that.

Chapter Eight

The kitten padded after me as I spent the rest of the day keeping myself busy. Occasionally, would she vanish, only to appear again a few minutes later in the most unexpected of places. After a quick cold scrub to get the stink of death off my hands, I hunted down the hot water cylinder of my new home to see if I could figure out what was wrong with it.

I was no electrician, but I had learned enough over the years to be self-sufficient. My father had taught me the basics of automotive engineering when I was a teenager, and I'd picked up a bit at school as well. The rest was really just logic, combined with large amounts of trial and error.

It didn't take me long to figure out that the heating coil was blown. I could replace it, but I would have to find another one in order to do so. There were quite a few homes scattered around the outlying reaches of town. With any luck, one of them might have a spare.

Another problem for another day.

On the plus side, at least now that I knew where all

the bodies were, I was less worried about stumbling over a corpse in an unexpected place. You never quite got over the horror of tripping over a dead person when you didn't expect it, particularly if the corpse belonged to a child.

I eased myself out of the cupboard where the hot water cylinder lived and stood up, and then I moved to the window to check on the weather. There were clouds rolling in from the west again, thicker and darker than the ones the night before, warning me of foul weather yet to come. I opened the window and stuck my head outside, drawing in a deep breath through my mouth and nose. Sure enough, the tell-tale taste of a storm was on the air.

Probably best to stay indoors then, rather than out in the open.

There were still a few hours left before dark, and at least a couple before the storm arrived, so I decided to use them wisely. I returned to the automotive workshop, to see if I could salvage one of the cars.

They were a pack of rust-buckets after so many years without maintenance, but not entirely without hope. There were even a couple of different choices. There was a sedan up on the hoist, and another out in the yard, a hatchback parked by the gate, and a four wheel drive under shelter. I chose the four wheel drive, for practicality and comfort.

After the end of the world, you couldn't really trust the roads to be well-maintained.

I found the keys in the office, discarded amongst

piles of records that probably once meant something to someone, but not to me. I didn't care who the owner of the vehicle was. If they were still alive, they would probably have taken it already. No one had claimed it, so that made it mine.

It was a good machine, a double-cab Hilux with a canopy over the back; solid and well-built. One thing I'd learned is that Japanese cars really were made to last, and the parts were common and easy to find.

After a quick peek through the windows to check for corpses and rats, I unlocked the driver's door and climbed behind the wheel. The interior was still in good condition, less dusty than most due to being safely sealed for almost a decade. The smell was a little off, but that could be fixed with a bit of airing out. Resting one hand upon the wheel, I put my foot on the brake, slipped the keys into the ignition and turned.

Nothing.

Ah well, you didn't get something for nothing in the scavenger's life. I tried the key again, listening closely for telltale sounds that would let me know what was wrong. Again, there was nothing.

I concluded that the battery was flat, and hauled myself back out of the driver's seat. Not all that surprising; most of them died after a while. I popped the bonnet and propped it up with its little metal arm, then leaned in to get a closer look. A few cobwebs, but not much in the way of rust. That was a good sign. The battery terminals could use a good clean, but I knew how to take care of that with no trouble at all.

I didn't bother trying to find another vehicle to jump start the battery. After ten years, there was just no point. It was safe to say that the other cars were just as dead. However, I did strike it lucky and find a mobile charger not two metres away, in good enough condition that it looked like it would still work. It took me a couple of minutes to disconnect the battery and move it to the charger, but when I did the lights glowed steadily, reassuringly.

It would take all night to charge up, so I filled in the time with general maintenance. I checked the fluids, and found that there was still a full tank of gas that looked fine, but the oil was congealed and dirty. That was probably one of the reasons that its old owner had brought it in for maintenance all those years ago.

Ah, well. No time like the present, right?

***

By the time I was finished draining the old oil and cleaning the components that needed it, the storm was getting close. As I hauled myself out from beneath the Hilux and wiped the grease from my hands, I spotted the kitten watching me from a workbench nearby. Her little head was canted curiously as she regarded me, as if she were trying in vain to figure out what I was about. I offered her a hand, but she turned her nose up and danced away from me, playing hard to get.

"Have it your way, then," I told her, and walked over to a sink nearby instead. With some difficulty, I cranked open the rusted tap to wash my hands. There was some old, harsh soap nearby, crusted up over the years, but still useful enough for scrubbing the grease from my skin.

Craaaacka-boom, the sky agreed.

Startled, the kitten inflated like an angry puffer-fish and vanished down behind the workbench.

"Pussy." I chuckled to myself, amused.

Then the rain started, an explosive downpour that set off a deafening cacophony on the roof above my head.

Hm. Perhaps the kitten was right.

Even though there was still more than an hour until sunset, the clouds obscured the sun and left me in near-darkness — a situation that I'd never really much cared for. I always preferred to be somewhere safe, secure and easily defensible when darkness fell; danger often lingered in the shadows.

The workshop was more or less waterproof, so I left the battery charging and decided to return home for the evening. There was an old oilskin coat hanging by the doorway, which I liberated and shook free of spiders, then draped over my head. I was going to get drenched one way or another, but the token gesture made me feel a little better.

Out into the weather I went, huddled beneath my oilskin as I darted from shelter to shelter, keeping close against the edge of the buildings so that I could avoid the rain as much as possible. Despite my best efforts, I was soaked by the time I finally burst through the door of the old video store. I dropped the coat somewhere in the dark interior and shoved the door closed behind me, muttering soft profanities under my breath.

Mum would've been so furious if she'd heard, but I was a grown up now and could swear as much as I damn well liked. Still, I cringed and apologised to her memory inside my head, like I always did.

Sorry, Mum.

I shuffled through the sea of plastic shards and retreated upstairs, locking each door behind me. I'd left an upstairs window open that morning to let in some fresh air, so now one of the curtains was sopping wet, and there was a puddle on the floor.

I hurried over to close the window before it became a flood, and then retreated to the bathroom, shedding clothing along the way.

My boots will be wet for days, I thought morosely, wishing I that I owned a spare pair. I didn't even have a change of clothes. I did have a few spare pairs of underwear, but that was really about it.

Clothing was yet another thing to add to the weight I had to carry around on my back from place to place. Unfortunately, you couldn't eat clothing so when it came to a choice between clothes and food, it was the clothes that got left behind.

I removed my taser and the other contents of my cargo pants from their pockets and dried them carefully on a towel, then set them in a neat, organised row on the dresser. Each one of them could mean the difference between life and death one day, so each of them was assigned a specific place.

Off went my underwear and bra, flung over my shoulder into the bathroom and replaced a moment later by a spare set of knickers and an undershirt from my backpack. It wasn't really cold despite the weather, so I just stayed that way. There was no real need for modesty beyond a little personal grace, since there was no one around to see me.

Left with little to do to pass the time, I returned to the living room and stared out the window at the raging storm — and found myself face to face with a bedraggled, miserable-looking tabby.

"Mew?" she mouthed, the sound muted by the glass, as she perched haphazardly on the windowsill waiting to be let in.

"Well, aren't you a determined little thing?" I smiled to myself and cracked open the window just enough for the kitten to squeeze through. In a blaze of fur she was inside, just as soaked to the bone as I was. By the time I closed the window again, she had claimed the couch as her own and settled in to groom determinedly.

"How the hell did you even get up here?" I watched the kitten with amusement, but of course, she didn't answer. The logical conclusion was that she climbed up, but no one ever said my imagination was a logical place. In my head, she bounced up like a cartoon character, and that was how she got her new name: Tigger.

***

The storm raged outside as I tinkered with the

television, curious to see if I could get any life out of it. Not that there were any shows worth watching anymore, but there was still the news.

As I had discovered in the months and years following the outbreak, that poor, unshaven man my grandmother had criticised was one of the immune as well. Every evening at 6 o'clock sharp, he came on and spoke for an hour about whatever he felt anyone wanted to hear about. The 6 o'clock news was an old tradition, and he seemed determined to keep it going for as long as he was alive. I appreciated his stoicism, and I respected it. It was nice to have one thing left in life that I could rely on.

Plus, he was kind of cute.

Over the years, he had been the only form of male companionship I felt I could trust in any way, so I had developed a bit of a crush on him. Of course, I mocked myself mercilessly for it since I knew full well the anchorman didn't even know I existed.

I wondered what would happen when he died.

I had no idea where he broadcasted from. Would someone find his old studio and take over? Or would yesterday's traditions die right along with him? It was something that I didn't like to think about, but death was inevitable.

I often wondered how he got his news. In the past, he'd mentioned that people could call his studio and gave a cell phone number and a radio frequency, so I guessed it just came from other survivors. I had no news to give, so I'd never tried it. In my little world, keeping away from other people was the only way to stay safe.

There was a soft click as I reconnected a loose wire, then the telltale hiss of snow. I wriggled out from behind the television and sat down in front of it, fiddling with the tuning and scanning channels until finally I found the one I wanted.

The anchorman's solemn face filled the screen, a week's worth of whiskers fuzzing his jaw as he spoke into the camera. He was a handsome fellow, in his early forties with dark hair and bright blue eyes that somehow always looked so sad. His shirts were always crumpled, his hair looked like he'd probably cut it himself in a mirror, and his chin was perpetually overgrown. In some strange way, he always seemed to embody the way I felt at the end of the day – rumpled and worn, and far older than my years.

Something about that was comforting.

"...Repeating our top story, survivors in the Greymouth region are encouraged to relocate at the earliest possible time to another location, as supplies have run out. A bus departs tomorrow morning at dawn from the town hall for Nelson, and all survivors are encouraged to take it..." His voice was a morose drone, repetitive yet strangely restful. I relocated from the floor to the armchair, and curled up to watch.

It was morbidly fascinating, watching the news after the end of the world. There was never any good news. Everyone was dead except for a handful of us. The anchorman was our only form of communication aside from actual word of mouth or the occasional two-way radio.

Still, the sound of another human voice was pleasant and welcome, even if it was from someone as obviously depressed as our anchorman. I leaned my head on my hands and closed my eyes, letting the sound of his voice soothe me.

Eventually, it lulled me into sleep.

***

I awoke to the sound of static and birdsong the next morning, still curled up in the armchair like a sleepy child. Unlike all the times that I'd fallen asleep on the couch as a child, this time there was no Mum or Dad to carry me off to bed, so I had spent the night where I was.

I sat up and uncurled, my joints protesting at the discomfort of having slept in such a peculiar position, yet I felt physically replenished. Outside my window, a tui sang a love song to its mate, a pleasant and familiar sound. The kitten sat on the window sill, observing the songbird outside with intense interest, oblivious to my awkward stretching. Once my limbs were awake enough to cooperate, I moved over to the window to look out as well.

The sky looked grumpy and overcast, but it was not raining at the moment. That seemed appropriate, since I felt a little grumpy myself. The thought of spending the day in wet boots did nothing to help my mood.

My clothing was still damp, and clung unpleasantly

as I pulled it on, but what other choice did I have? I cheered myself with the thought that perhaps, if I got the car going, I could visit some of those outer homesteads; maybe find some clean, dry clothing and spare shoes. That would be nice. I wouldn't be able to take them with me when I eventually left this town, but having them for now would be a treat.

At least breakfast was readily available, which always cheered me up. Tigger joined me, and ate some more of the cat food from a bowl on the kitchen floor, while I indulged in another can of baked beans. Oh, what I wouldn't have given for some real beans. I'd just about forgotten what they tasted like. Maybe one of the homesteads would have some of those, too.

Maybe they'd have chickens. Chickens, even wild ones, meant eggs that could be stolen. My new home came with a working stove and cooking equipment. Perhaps tomorrow morning I would have a real omelette for breakfast. Now, that idea really cheered me up.

All of a sudden, my capricious mood was gone and I was raring to go.

I packed my essentials back into their pockets and laced on my wet boots, then padded off to check on my Hilux. The air smelt fresh and clean, and it was pleasantly cool after the heat of the last few days. Although the sky was still low and threatening overhead, it was nice enough outside and the thought of fresh food spurred me on.

When I arrived at the garage, I ducked in through

the side door and checked the room for uninvited occupants; again, I found nothing out of the ordinary. The battery was showing fully charged now, so I reinstalled it in the engine and closed the bonnet. Fighting down a wave of excitement, I climbed back into the driver's seat and tried the ignition again.

The utility roared to life. It didn't sound terribly happy, but it was functional. Functional was what I needed. Keeping it going long term would probably be impossible, but it worked for now and that was enough. I disengaged the engine and tried it again, and got the same response. Content that it was going to work for one more day at least, I hopped back out and scampered over to the big roller doors that blocked my exit.

They screeched in protest as I hauled them up, and then screeched again when I closed them behind me. I didn't mind. I was suddenly in possession of the freedom of wheels, and that pleased me immensely.

Just let the other survivors find me now; I'll run them over and they can be damned!

Chapter Nine

My first week in Ohaupo passed peacefully, with my days spent exploring the outlying countryside, and my nights spent tinkering and sleeping. It wasn't a good life or even a satisfying life, but at least it was a life. I was, more or less, content.

Several of the farms did have chickens, and a number of them had vegetable gardens as well. Like the chickens, the gardens had gone wild but that didn't bother me one bit. Wild or tame, fresh food was delicious and it made me feel a good deal happier than I had for a long time. After a few days on fresh vegetables and protein-rich eggs I felt strong and fit and ready to take on the world – or at least, my tiny corner of it.

The Hilux thrummed contentedly beneath me as I drove out to one of the few homesteads left to explore, hoping this one would yield more treasures to add to my growing stash. I had yet to find a functioning element for my hot water cylinder, and I still longed for a nice, hot shower.

I pulled the Hilux up the winding driveway to the homestead, carefully negotiating the rugged potholes and overgrown limbs hanging from the trees that framed the path. The house was a large one, someone's retirement mansion after many years of hard work, but just like all the others it was run-down and abandoned. Nature had reclaimed much of what was hers over the years.

Rose vines crept across the entire front of the house, covering it in a complicated lattice of foliage. Even at a distance, I could see fat, happy bumble bees darting from bloom to bloom, glutting themselves on sweet nectar.

I parked my truck and slipped out with my taser at the ready, and approached the old home to see what I could find. The smell was unexpected; an overwhelming mix of sweet, cloying scents from a dozen different kinds of flowers that warred for sunlight. I swept my gaze around, alert for danger, but detected nothing more hostile than the bees.

The gardens were a beautiful sight. Like the bees, I took a moment to enjoy the loveliness that spread out around me, then I turned and picked my way up what remained of the front walkway. Along the way, I bent to pluck a particularly perfect bloom from its stem and lifted it to my nose to savour the scent. After so much death and decay, the flower smelt like heaven on a stem.

With cautious fingers, I stripped away the thorns from said stem and then tucked the flower behind my ear. It was a silly little thing, but the woman in me longed to keep that beautiful scent close to me for a while longer. It reminded me of my grandmother. I thought of her wistfully, remembering the beautiful flowers she had once grown around her home in Palmerston North.

Maybe one day I'll go back and plant roses upon her grave. She'd like that.

With the softest of sighs, I ducked beneath an overhanging vine and slipped up the front stairs to the porch. I tried the front door and found it unlocked, so let myself in. I doubted there was anyone home to complain. A quick glance around the dusty interior told me that I was correct – no one had been home for a very long time.

The front door opened into a large and spacious dining room, resplendent in hard woods and rose-print fabrics. The floor and fittings were all varnished oak, which had survived the years almost untouched. All it would take was a touch of polish to bring out their shine and have it looking like new again.

A dinner set waited in a wooden hutch to my left, the kind of good porcelain crockery that stood up well to the years. Much like the miniature set I found in the antique store, these were resplendent in rose prints with a hint of gold around the edge of each plate. The good china, waiting for the family to come home to celebrate Christmas lunch.

They'll be waiting a while, I thought with a dreamy kind of sadness.

To the right of that was a set of wide glass doors that led out to an overgrown veranda. Wall hangings and paintings that spoke of better times decorated the walls, mounted with good, solid wooden frames rather than the cheap, plastic junk that had become more common in the later years.

A table with enough chairs for six people sat in the centre of the room, and off to one side an archway led towards a kitchen. To my right, a long flight of stairs led upwards into shadow.

Foliage blocked most of the sunlight coming through the windows, but it was only dim inside rather than truly dark. I could see what I needed to see. I paused to ponder, thinking how beautiful the place must have been in its prime, when it was clean and cared for and the garden was groomed.

I could imagine a Christmas tree in the far corner, ready to welcome the grandchildren that came to visit on Christmas morning. They were probably all dead now, along with their parents and their grandparents.

That thought was sobering and brought me back to the present. There was nothing I could do for those people now, except kill them if I saw them shuffling about vacant-eyed at the end of their half-life. For their sake as much as mine I needed to survive, so that one day my descendants could live like this again.

I went for the kitchen first, as I always did. Ignoring the smell from the long-dead fridge, I made a beeline for the spacious double-door pantry. It was well stocked with all the necessities of life, though most of them well past their best-before date. On the lowest shelf was a veritable treasure trove of canned goods, just waiting to be plundered by a little pirate like me. Arrrrrrr.

I grabbed an old rubbish bag from a higher shelf, and knelt down to gather up my bounty, pausing to examine each can before I put it into the bag. There was no point lugging something back that was guaranteed to be rotten on the inside, after all. I learned long ago what survived the years and what didn't, and which things were iffy.

Then, suddenly, I spotted something at the back of the pantry that made my heart skip a beat.

You knew you were a survivor when the most excitement you'd had in months revolved around finding a single, unopened can of Campbell's Creamy Mushroom Soup in the back of a dead person's larder, wedged behind a huge bag of rotten potatoes. I pulled it free and held it up, drawing a deep breath to try and contain my excitement.

This flavour had been my favourite in my old life. It brought back memories of snacks shared with my mother in winter, sitting around the table at the end of the school day. Talking, sharing funny stories, and enjoying soup together.

It was so corny that we could have written scripts for commercials. Back in the days when commercials still mattered, and Mum was alive, that is.

I knew as well as anyone that canned soups were hit or miss after this long. Chances were good that the contents of this can were a mass of congealed black goo by now, completely unrecognisable as any form of food product. But, for the sake of my memories, I would try anyway.

I reverently added the soup to my sack of booty and finished clearing out the rest of the cans. To my distaste, I discovered that amongst them was a large amount of cat food. Great, just what I needed. More cat food. Tigger would be happy. Me, not so much. At least I could reassure myself that I had a decent firewall of other food between me and the dreaded cat food.

Once I was done with the cans, I looked around. A neat row of decorative storage tins painted in pretty colours drew my attention next. Carefully prying them open one by one, I found milk powder, rolled oats and several kinds of pasta, most of which still looked edible courtesy of careful storage a decade ago. I added them – tins and all – to my sack, along with a couple of bags of white rice that I found tucked away in the back.

White rice lasted forever if the pests didn't get at it. I practically lived on the stuff when I had access to cooking facilities. Needless to say, I was sick of it but at least it was food. Not terribly nutritious, but it kept the hunger pangs at bay.

Sweeping my gaze upwards, I examined the top shelves and found little of interest.

Wait... no, what's that? That tin up there, the one painted with the Christmas decorations? I reached up on tiptoes and pulled the tin down, to stare at it suspiciously.

Fruitcake. It had to be.

I remember the old urban legend that fruitcake was so full of preservatives that it would never go stale, so I couldn't help but be curious.

I cracked the tin open and peered inside, then promptly closed it again and returned it to the top shelf. Myth successfully debunked; fruitcake did *not* last forever. Frankly, I was a little relieved. If it had still been good, then I'd have been morally obligated to eat it at some point. The thought of eating decade-old fruitcake was less than appetizing.

The memory of my grandmother's Christmas fruitcake twisted my gut; no other fruitcake compared. Hers was actually edible – and quite tasty, in fact. The last time I ate it was the Christmas just a few weeks before she died.

Shaking off the wave of sadness, I bundled my loot up on my shoulder and carried it out to where my Hilux waited faithfully. It was a heavy burden, but one of the perks of being a survivor was that you were never in need of a gym membership. If you sat around doing nothing, you died. Simple. Staying alive kept you fit and strong.

I grumbled a few choice words under my breath as I unfastened the back canopy of my utility and hauled the heavy bag up onto the deck. I left the truck unlocked in a rare moment of carelessness and headed back inside.

My reasoning was simple; who on earth was going to steal my supplies all the way out here? The nearest human being was many kilometres away.

I mounted the stairs to search the first floor, where I found myself in a dusty land of yesteryear. Old photographs faded with age decorated the walls, and there were a number of empty rooms that seemed to exist for decoration rather than any real purpose. Through one doorway, I saw a sitting room. Through another, a sewing room. A third was a hobby room, where a huge model train set took centre stage, rusting away amidst its carefully detailed landscapes.

Things were in good condition aside from the usual layer of dust, but I left most of it where it was. I took only some spare linens and a couple of pieces of clothing that looked to be around my size, and the rest of it I confined to the inventory map in my head.

In the world beyond the decline of man, you never quite knew what might come in handy one day. Whenever I saw something that I might need someday, I made a mental note of it in case I needed to find it in future. It was the survivalist's mental encyclopaedia: useful only after the expiration of human civilization.

It was also handy to know where things were if you ever needed to find something to trade with other survivors. Be it physical items or just information, it all had value. You could never have too much knowledge.

That thought froze me in my tracks as I was passing back by the sitting room door, and the bookshelves that I had ignored on the way through. Books were heavy and you couldn't eat them, so I generally left them behind when I was out on salvage missions. This time though, I had a safe berth to return to, a good supply of food, and time on my hands. It would be foolish not to use the time wisely, so I stepped through the doorway and went over to look at the shelves.

Nothing struck me as particularly interesting. The shelves were mostly filled with cookbooks intended for use with ingredients I could no longer get, old magazines advertising businesses long since dead, and books on trains. Oh so very many books on trains.

I was about to leave when something finally caught my eye. Tucked in between the magazines was a small, worn paperback, a tatty copy of some silly romance novel I'd never heard of. All things considered, it seemed like an appropriate way to waste my time, indulging in fantasies that would never be.

I tucked the book into my pocket and went on my way.

***

Further exploration of the property revealed more chickens, an old dairy cow grazing in a huge paddock behind the house, and to my delight, a small orchard. I armed myself with plastic bags, and spent much of the afternoon out amongst the trees, gathering up as much windfall as I could.

There were peaches, plums, apples and pears, a veritable feast for someone in my position. Needless to say, it was the peaches that drew me like a magnet drew iron. I plucked a soft, golden peach from a low-hanging bough and held it to my nose, drawing in a deep breath of the ripe scent.

It was too much for me to bear.

I took a huge bite and closed my eyes to savour the sweet, sweet taste on my tongue. Oh, how long it had been since I'd eaten a *fresh* peach! I devoured it in moments, juice running stickily down my chin, then snatched up another, and another. Finally, my sense of self-preservation kicked in. It took a hell of a lot of willpower to hold myself back from feasting until I exploded, but the last thing I needed was a tummy ache to go with all my other problems.

I drew a deep breath to steady myself, and knelt to gather up as many peaches as I could fit into my bags. There were so many on the ground I didn't need to pick any more from the tree itself. So many that finding ones not yet eaten by the birds and bugs was no trouble at all. It was unlikely that I would be able to eat them before they went bad, but there was no point letting them go to waste, right?

I was in the process of lugging the heavy bags back to my Hilux when I was distracted by something even more tempting than a fresh peach. Who knew that was even possible? I stopped for a moment to rest my aching biceps when I caught a whiff of a scent on the breeze. It was a familiar scent, a wonderful scent; a scent that took me back to childhood all over again.

The scent of strawberry bushes.

It was kind of a miracle that my nose was still so sensitive after all these years of abuse, but apparently it was. I could smell them, quite clearly from however far away, even over the overwhelming scent of the flowers.

So many lovely strawberries, and so close.

I passed the Hilux en route to the patch, and deposited my bags of precious fruit on the front passenger seat. Then I scampered off in search of strawberries, as excited as a child. Every so often, I paused to sniff the cool breeze, following my nose to what turned out to be a very pretty little vegetable garden tucked away behind the house.

It was full of weeds and half of the plants had gone to seed, but I didn't care. I smelled strawberries and I must have them. Careless in my footing, I scampered through the overgrowth until I found the strawberry patch.

That would be a moment that I would come to regret, very, very soon. Busy as I was stuffing my face with sweet, overripe strawberries, I paid no attention to where I put my feet. I didn't notice the old board hidden amongst the bushes until it was too late.

More importantly, I didn't notice the nail.

At first, I didn't feel the wound; just was a strange sensation, like a prick, followed by a weird, invasive cold. I tried to step backwards to see what had bitten me, but my right foot wouldn't move. It was trapped, impaled through the arch on a six inch housing nail that was hidden amongst the weeds.

A flash of panic struck me right about the same time the pain did; I threw back my head and screamed. Even in agony, I possessed enough presence of mind not to give in to the urge to fall on my backside to try to take the pressure off the wound. God knew what else was hidden in the undergrowth, and it would be very hard for me to get back up again with my foot trapped the way it was.

Trapped on a nail. A dirty, filthy nail. A sharp and probably rusty nail, I thought with gritted teeth. I fought the urge to scream again as I shifted my weight carefully into a better position to lever my foot free. There was no one I could call, no one to come and help me. I was alone. I had to do this myself.

The nail ground against the bones in my foot as I jerked it free. I couldn't hold back the scream any longer. The pain was overwhelming. I half-limped, half-crawled out of the vegetable garden and got as far as the garden path before I collapsed, panting, in too much agony to go any further. I sat heavily on the paving stones and dragged myself further into the clear so that I could see my foot.

Or see through my foot, I thought.

Okay, I was being dramatic. I couldn't see *through* my foot. The tension of my muscles held the wound closed, but... man, it really, really hurt. Through tear-filled eyes, I struggled to focus on the wound as I wrestled to get my boot off. The pain was so intense I bit my lip to try and keep myself from screaming myself hoarse.

My boots had done me well for a number of years, but the soles were worn thin from all the walking I'd done; they had offered little protection against the sharp spike. It had gone straight through the sole, through my foot, and penetrated the top of the boot as well.

There's not as much blood as I expected, I considered absently as I wrestled with the bootlaces. *Why isn't it bleeding more? And when did it get so hard to undo a double-bow?*

My fingers were trembling, slick with sweat and what little blood there was. It took twice as long as it should to get the laces undone and it felt like an eternity. I could feel the hot surge of my pulse in the wound, though the blood only oozed sluggishly.

"Oh, Christ!" I gasped as I finally pulled off my boot, and then stripped off the sock to lay the wound bare. It didn't look so bad, but the pain was nearly unbearable. Any number of terrible images flashed through my head.

Infection. Blood poisoning. Tetanus.

Oh God, when was my last tetanus shot? Before the plague, I thought. Panic rose in my chest. *Oh my God. Oh my God. What do I do?*

I didn't really know. I'd learned a little about first aid over the years, which was a necessity for surviving on your own, but I'd never been seriously injured before.

"Stop the blood flow," I hissed between clenched teeth, giving orders to my shaking hands. With one, I bundled up the sock and pressed it against the entry wound, while my other hand fumbled with one of the pockets of my cargo pants in search of the small emergency kit I carried out of habit. Awkwardly, using one hand and my teeth, I got the kit open and peered at the contents.

There was antiseptic, which I was quick to pour on the wound, but beyond that I felt lost. I had nothing to prevent a worse infection. People died from blood poisoning, from tetanus, from any number of ailments.

I had to find antibiotics.

I owned nothing more powerful than an over-the-counter dose of painkillers, and I knew there was nothing better to be found in this little township. I needed a pharmacy – or better yet a hospital. Although there would be no one there to help me, at least I could find the medication and administer it myself.

I hated needles, but I hated dying more. I refused to die. It was not my time and I was not ready.

I would have to go. Leave my little safe haven and go someplace else. I'd seen some hospitals in my travels to the south, but they were many, many miles away. Te Awamutu was picked clean, and I couldn't go further south without running the risk of encountering the very men I'd fled north to escape. So my only option was to go further north, to the city of Hamilton. There were bound to be survivors there, too, but what choice did I have?

I wasn't just afraid. I was fucking terrified.

Chapter Ten

I thought that I'd known pain and what it felt like to be totally helpless, but none of my past experiences compared to what I felt as I dragged myself to my feet and hobbled back to my Hilux, nearly crippled with agony.

Tears ran freely down my cheeks, but at least the bleeding was stemmed for now. It was a pretty knock-up job, to be frank, but it functioned adequately. I used my sock for gauze and bound it up tight with the one pathetic bandage in my first aid kit. It wasn't enough, but I had to keep going.

Unfortunately, I wasn't one of those badass soldiers that can stitch up their own wounds and be fit for battle ten minutes later. I was just an ordinary human being stuck in extraordinary circumstances, and right now all I wanted to do was curl up in a ball and cry until the pain went away.

It felt like a kilometre, though it was really only a couple of hundred metres. It felt like it took an hour, though it was really only about ten minutes. Eventually, though, I made it back to my truck. Leaning heavily against the Hilux's flank, I fumbled open the driver's door with a hand that trembled uncontrollably, and suddenly I was glad that I'd left the vehicle unlocked.

Keys in the ignition, too. Good thing no one was about or I'd really be in a pickle.

Even in my damaged state, I took a second to check the rear of the cab, to make sure no one was hiding back there waiting to take me by surprise. I was in no position to do anything about them if there was, but paranoia was a hard habit to break.

Getting into the car proved easier said than done, even with two good hands and one good foot. Everything I did seemed to knock the injury around and send white-hot stabs of pain all the way up my leg. I swore inelegantly every single time, then apologised to my mother's memory right after.

Under the circumstances, I was sure that Mum would have understood, but that wasn't the point. I apologised for my sake, not hers. Trying to keep my mother's memory alive helped to keep me grounded and civilized. Sort of.

I braced myself on the handhold on the roof and literally hauled myself the last few centimetres into the cab. Shoving my butt as far back in the seat as was possible, I grabbed a hold of the fabric of my cargo pants for leverage. My leg didn't seem to want to bend right now, so I hauled it in with my hands.

Then I realised suddenly that there was another problem. It was my right foot that was injured. My driving foot.

"Aw, Christ." I gritted my teeth, trying the pedals with my bad foot. Nope, not going to happen. I could barely move it, not until the swelling went down anyway. I was going to have to learn to drive with my left foot.

"Just what I need," I groaned to myself. "Bleeding, in pain, and a menace on the roads. I better put a seatbelt on."

Would that even make a difference?

I thought about it for a second, then buckled the belt anyway. Safety first. Didn't want to go getting myself killed, after all; I was fairly certain the other survivors would do it for me if I gave them half a chance. Still, I had no other choice but to expose myself, or suffer a terrible death by infection.

Thinking about that sent a cold shudder down my spine, so I focused on figuring out how to drive with the wrong foot. It was hard, like learning to drive all over again, but better that than thinking about what happened the last few times I'd encountered other survivors. I knew from experience just how bad desperate people could be.

At least I'd learned as a result that I never wanted to be like them. Ever.

***

By some miracle, I made it back to Ohaupo without hitting a tree or rolling into a ditch. There, I met with a dilemma. Did I return to my haven and get my things before I left, knowing that if I took them there was a chance I would have them all stolen by the survivors in Hamilton and be left with nothing? Or did I go on without them, and risk being stuck in a situation where I needed them but would have to make do without?

One thing was for sure – I needed my GPS, and I needed my gun. That meant figuring out how to tackle stairs on one good foot.

I managed to make it out of the truck and into the store without falling on my face, which I considered a small victory in and of itself. The store was another story; I was forced to shuffle awkwardly amidst the plastic shards in a valiant attempt to avoid injuring myself any further.

Of course, like a diligent survivor I had covered my tracks each time I came through here, so now there was no clear path for me to follow. I ended up with a collection of nasty scratches by the time I made it to the office, but none significant enough to worry me any more than the bloody great hole I already had. I didn't have the strength to close the door behind me, but that didn't seem to matter. Everything was as I'd left it. There was no one about but me.

And Tigger, apparently. She appeared behind me as I was crawling up the stairs on hands and knees, watching me with a curiously-tilted head. I could practically hear her thoughts. What on earth is that silly human doing? Oh, she's bleeding? Goodness gracious, I better go beg for food, post- haste. You know, in case she forgets that I'm a stomach with legs.

Sure enough, as soon as I made it to the top and struggled to my feet, she came bounding up after me and almost tripped me over.

"You know, you're supposed to be a wild cat. You're not meant to be this friendly," I told her dryly, to which she replied with a heart-felt mew. I guessed she was born and bred in the area so she'd never learned the wild cat lessons to fear big, scary humans. I was a big, scary human that administered food, which made me perfectly okay in her book.

Even in my injured state, the need to nurture rose in me. I dragged myself into the kitchen to fill the kitten's food dish, giving her the last of a tin I opened that morning just for her. I'd been feeding the kitten regularly over the last week and she'd gradually become tamer, but she was still playing hard to get and wouldn't let me touch her again.

Now I felt like that was a good thing; I didn't know if I was going to survive this trip, so I didn't want her to be too dependent on me. My reasoning for feeding her to begin with was that she was too young to be hunting on her own, but she was bigger now and I felt a little more confident she would be fine without me.

Truth was, she'd probably have been fine without me from the beginning, but a part of me wanted something, anything, to care about in this dead world. No, not wanted. Needed. Even without physical contact, little Tigger helped to alleviate the loneliness. My eyes blurred, and I brushed the tears away impatiently. No time for that now.

"I'll be back if I survive, I promise," I told the little kitten, who ignored me with great vigour. She was far too busy to notice me; her face was crammed into her food dish as she gobbled down her dinner. I left her to it and I hobbled out of the kitchen to the bedroom, looking for my pack. There was a better first aid kit in there, and I needed to clean that wound before I went anywhere.

Needless to say, that was a painful experience. By the time I was done, Tigger had fled from the sound of my gasps and cries. Personally, I was just amazed that I managed to stay conscious. It was a close call at times, when the pain got so bad that that I started to see stars and got light-headed, but somehow I made it.

Hell, if that's how much it hurt to clean the wound and wrap it in proper gauze and a bandage, I didn't know how all those fictional soldiers were supposed to have been able to do their own stitches.

I probably did need stitches, come to think of it, but I'd pass out for sure if I tried to do it myself. I didn't have time for that. The wound bled sluggishly, but the tension of the muscles in my foot staunched the worst of it.

"God, this hurts like a giant flying inflatable bejebus," I groaned and closed my eyes for a second. "Drugs. I need drugs. I think I have some in here somewhere."

I dug into my pack, and down in the bottom I found a box of painkillers so old that the brand name had faded away over time. As I popped back a couple and washed the bitter tablets down with water, I hoped that they'd still have the desired effect. They were just the cheap non-prescription kind, that I had found in a ransacked store years ago, back when the brand was still visible.

"I really hope this stuff doesn't go off – or go toxic," I muttered to myself. "Well, I guess I'm about to find out."

I didn't have any time to waste on thinking about it, so I put the thought aside and focused on what I needed to do.

My boot was gone. I had left it back at the farmstead, and there was no time to go back and fetch it. Luckily, a few days earlier I'd found a pair of athletic shoes in my size. With my injury, they would probably do a better job, anyway; they were old and worn by time, but the soles were soft and thick and they'd help me keep moving for a while.

I stripped off my other boot and tossed it aside, since it was useless without its mate. The only thing worse than wet boots was mismatched boots. I was having enough trouble walking without my balance being off due to uneven weight distribution from ill-matched shoes.

Scooting along the bed on my behind with my bad foot awkwardly elevated, I stuck my nose over the edge to search for my new shoes and a clean pair of socks, the old set were kind of a mess now. I found both fairly swiftly, by throwing aside mounds of miscellaneous scavengings until I got my hands on them.

The wound hurt terribly as I carefully pulled on the new footwear, a hot, rhythmic throb in time with my pulse, but once there was pressure on it I was surprised to find that the pain diminished a bit.

Maybe I've done the bandages up too tight, I pondered with a brief flash of morbid amusement. *Ah, well. Not complaining unless my toes drop off.*

Mission accomplished, I flopped backwards onto my bed and allowed myself a couple of minutes to rest and recover. I closed my eyes and drew long, deep breaths, trying to visualise the pain flowing away. Whether it was the meditation or the medication, the pain did seem to lessen a little.

In all honesty, it was probably just the fact that I wasn't trying to hobble around that eased the pain.

What's the incubation period for tetanus, anyway?

I tried to think back to high school health class, but I couldn't remember. I did remember that time when Katie cut herself at camp, though. They rushed her off for a series of injections straight away.

How much time do I have?

That thought stirred me out of a doze. It was getting dark. Could I stand to wait until morning? Normally, I refused to go anywhere after sunset – it just wasn't safe. Unfortunately, right now my choices were kind of limited.

"Just go now. Get it over with," I told myself, and eased my aching body back up into a sitting position. There was plenty of food in the car, and if I locked this place up nice and tight it would be fine without me. I estimated that Hamilton was about an hour away by car, less if I drove like a maniac, so in theory I could be back before dawn. I would sleep when I got home.

Filled with sudden determination, I grabbed my backpack and began sorting out the items I would take with me. The first aid kit, of course, in case I needed to change my bandages. My GPS, since I'd never been to Hamilton before. A couple of emergency pairs of socks and underwear – you know, just in case. My sewing kit, for the same reason. My taser.

And last but not least, the box containing the one thing I hated looking at most in the world, and the one I couldn't discard. The thing that brought back so many terrible memories.

The last gift from my grandmother.

The very thing that had taken her life, at my hand.

I opened the box and looked at it, checking that the 9mm Smith & Wesson handgun was still in its place. It was, nestled alongside a couple of boxes of spare bullets that I had collected over the years.

With a shaking hand, I removed the gun from its place, and checked over all the moving parts, making sure nothing was rusted or stuck. It seemed to be fine. Trying hard not to think about how it felt when I put the barrel against my beloved grandmother's head and pulled the trigger, I slipped it back into its box and closed the lid

I'd only fired it a few times since then. Each time, it'd been at another survivor rather than at the walking dead. Well, no. That was a lie. I did try to shoot one of the infected once, but all that did was cripple the poor thing.

They no longer felt pain, and the only part of the brain left that was vulnerable was their brain stem, which was a small target and difficult to reach. The taser worked better on infected, and since it was rechargeable it just made more sense. The gun was a weapon of last resort.

I added the box that contained the gun and its ammunition to the small pile of items I would take with me. The food in the car was more than I'd need; enough to feed me for a couple of weeks at least. Still, I was in no condition to remove it so it would have to come with me. Even if I didn't eat it all, I could potentially use it to trade.

I paused for a moment and thought. I should take money as well. To most survivors, cash was about as useless as monopoly money – our currency was essentials, like food, water and personal effects. Still, there were a few people out there that clung to the old ways. To most, the bags of fruit I carried were far more valuable than money, but knowing my luck I'd find the medicine I needed in the hands of the one person left who still wanted hard currency.

Most of the time, I didn't bother to carry cash since it was basically just dead weight, but I did carry a few hundred dollar bills in case of emergencies. I fetched them out and stared at them, not entirely convinced that they would be enough for what I needed. Life-saving supplies did not come cheap.

I closed my eyes, and thought back over the layout of the town. Suddenly, I realised that in my exploration of this very building, I hadn't seen a safe. There must have been one. Someone paranoid enough to put four locked doors between himself and the outside world would not have left his cash sitting around in an unsecured lock box.

"If I were a paranoid old man, where would I put the safe?" I asked myself. My head was spinning and it was getting hard to think, but verbalising my ideas seemed to help. "The office would be the logical place, wouldn't it?"

The reasoning made sense to me, so I decided that I would check on my way out. I wasn't sure I would be able to make it back up the stairs again, so it was better to plan my movements carefully. I repacked my bag, dumping out everything non-essential, and then triple-checked that each of my tools was in its proper place.

In my head, I went through a mental checklist like I'd done a thousand times before. I removed each item in order and examined it, then returned it to its pocket. It was a ritual more than anything, and helped me ensure I always had everything I needed and never wasted weight on anything I didn't.

Something small and soft poked my hand midway through my checks. I blinked and reached further into the pocket, then pulled out that little family of toy bunnies I had found the week before. One by one I set them on my palm and stared at them. In my head, they weren't just bunnies; they were a representation of the family I'd lost so long ago.

The smallest one, in her tiny pink dress – oh how she reminded me of my baby sister. The bunnies had been there ten years ago, when we first passed through this little town. Sitting together in their little dollhouse, waiting for the right person to come along and buy them. Mum had left me in charge of Skylar while she stopped into the local grocery store for some more supplies, and Skye dragged me over to stare at the precious things on display in the antique store's front window.

How clear her young voice was in my memory, full of wonder and delight. She begged me to buy her those bunnies, along with just about everything else in that store. When I told her I couldn't, she cried and cried as though her little heart would break – right up until Mum found us and gave her an ice cream treat instead.

I'd been here before. So, why couldn't I remember the face of the cashier behind the counter? That bothered me; the cashier was a human being, just like me, just like everyone else. Did she die in that horrible hall along with all the others? Or did she wander the earth restlessly, waiting for the end to come?

I closed my hand around the tiny, velvet-soft forms, and set them on the old wooden dresser as I rose. My tiny family, always perfect, always happy and never lost and all alone. I would leave them here, where they were safe. I took one last long look before I walked away, and shuffled awkwardly into the kitchen.

There, I added a couple of water bottles to my pack

and slung it over my shoulders. That would have to do. I couldn't carry much more in my current condition, and it would be a stupid idea to try.

It took me a while to get back down the stairs again, mostly because I ended up having to scoot down on my butt. Ah, how that brought back memories of playing silly games with my little sister, though our games were never in life-or-death situations.

Thinking of little Skylar made me so sad. Again, I wondered what had happened to her. She'd been such a sweet little girl, so innocent, all fairies and princesses and unicorns at the tender age of eight. I hoped her death had been quick and painless. She didn't deserve to suffer. I couldn't bear to think of her suffering.

I sighed, and resigned myself to never knowing for sure.

At the bottom of the stairs I hauled myself back to my feet with the aid of the door frame, and looked around the little office. I saw no sign of a safe or anything that resembled one. The room was so small that I should have seen it straight away, unless it was hidden somewhere.

Hidden somewhere?

With a sudden flash of cognition, I remembered the painting on the wall, the one that I instinctively felt was out of place in the room. I hobbled over to examine it more closely. Sure enough, behind the painting was a recess in the wall. Within it was a small safe.

To my relief, there was no combination or numerical pad, just a keyhole. That made life easy, since Benny's keys were in my pocket. I tried them, one after another, until one of them clicked. The safe swung open.

"Easiest burglary ever," I mumbled as I peered inside. Hey, at least my sarcasm-bone was still intact.

There wasn't a lot of cash in the safe, but there was some. The plastic notes were sticky but showed no sign of fading or decay. The Reserve Bank made things to last, too. I took the small stack of bills, probably about $500.00 in tens and twenties, and stowed it in my pack. Some was better than none.

It struck me as kind of funny how my dad used to gripe at us kids about how money didn't grow on trees. It sure did now. Everywhere you turned was free cash, and it was all worth a grand total of nothing. You couldn't even burn the stuff for warmth, since it was all made of plastic.

There was a box of coins in the safe as well, probably the float Benny used for his cash register, but the weight outweighed the value. You could find coins everywhere and they were only really useful if you had a vending machine and you were too lazy to pop the lock with a crowbar.

"Well, that's it," I told myself. "No more excuses, time to go."

Man, I was not looking forward to this little adventure, but I had no choice. Go and maybe die horribly, or stay and definitely die horribly? I had to go, for Mum's sake, for Dad and little Skylar. They wouldn't want me dying of any kind of infection, not after I had been lucky enough to survive Ebola-X. I was the only one left to carry on their memory and keep their bloodline alive. I was the only one left to remember how much they had been loved.

I shouldered my pack and hauled myself up straight, doing my best to ignore the renewed pain in my foot. I locked the door to the stairs, and then backed out of the office and locked that door as well.

Where's Tigger? I wondered, peering about. The last time I saw her was at dinner, so I hoped that I hadn't locked her inside. Then I spotted her, curled up fast asleep on the still-warm bonnet of my Hilux.

Cheeky little bugger.

I Indulged myself in a weak smile as I locked the front door to the store, then hobbled over to shoo the kitten off. She ignored me. Losing patience, I went to pick her up and shift her myself, but she hissed and swatted at my hand.

"Have it your way, kid." I snatched back my hand before she could draw blood. "But you're not going to like what happens next."

I checked the cab again, then opened the door, threw my backpack into the rear and hauled myself in. The keys slipped into the ignition and the engine roared to life.

Hey, look at that. I'm a prophet.

The kitten inflated like a hedgehog and practically levitated off the bonnet in a mad dash for the safety of the overgrowth. I immediately felt guilty for giving her a scare, but reassured myself that I didn't really have a choice. I needed to go now and she was being stubborn.

I was also glad she was nowhere nearby when I awkwardly pulled the truck away from the curb and hit the road. It would have just about killed me if I ran the poor little fuzzy over.

I was such a sucker for cats.

Chapter Eleven

The trip to Hamilton was unpleasantly long, but uneventful.

I'd never been much of a fan of travelling, but at least when I was driving I didn't get car-sick. Still, given a choice I would probably have just settled down in one place and stayed there forever, or at least until the supplies ran out.

I planned to do that in Ohaupo, but now I didn't know what I was going to do. It was my hope that I would be able to return, but my gut was all twisted up with a sense of foreboding. I chided myself with the fact that I was probably just worrying over nothing, like I usually did. I'd always been that person who was over-prepared for every situation, the one who churned themselves into a tight little knot of anxiety thinking about everything that could possibly go wrong, even the ones that were completely unlikely. Hopefully, this would be just another time when I got myself all worked up over nothing.

The road cut a swath across the broad, flat green

land, dotted with cows and sheep that grazed on, oblivious to the loss of their farmers. Most domesticated animals flourished in the wake of the outbreak, their numbers unchecked. New Zealand had no predators to speak of, or at least nothing that could have taken down a full grown cow.

I had heard on the news that a few lions were spotted near Wellington Zoo a few years back, but I doubted they would get this far north. And if they had, I imagined those cows out there would have been looking a hell of a lot more worried.

Right now, they seemed to be more bothered by the growl of my engine as I tore past their busted fences and wild paddocks than any risk of predation. Bovine heads came up as I passed, watching me with suspicion in their long-lashed eyes. To them, I was a noisy, alien menace that disrupted their contented, cud-chewing world, and they were glad to see me gone.

As the sun slipped below the horizon and plunged the world into darkness, I flipped on my headlights. This far from any kind of significant township, there was really no light aside from the stars. Once, there had been street lamps lighting the way at regular intervals, but at some point in the past the wind had claimed their lives; they lay scattered along the roadsides like fallen supermodels after someone greased the runway.

I made a mental note. There would be a lot of good metal and wire that could be gathered from them, with the right tools and enough determination. Maybe even light bulbs. Light bulbs were more precious than gold.

Living in the world after the fall of humanity meant being creative with the resources at hand.

I found myself absently wondering how strong the wind must have been to rip those street lamps out. There were still some standing in Ohaupo, so it seemed like a localised kind of destruction; perhaps a tornado had ripped through here. With no one around to fix things, once stuff fell over it just stayed where it landed.

It also occurred to me that with darkness falling, I should probably slow down. Goodness knows what would happen if one of those street lamps had fallen across the road and I hit it at high speed – or if a cow decided to sleep on the road. It had probably been years since they last saw a car; they would have no idea they were supposed to stay off the road. That could potentially get very messy, very fast.

I decided to err on the side of caution again, and eased the Hilux down to a more sedate pace. I flicked the headlights on to high beam and leaned forward over the wheel, focusing intently on the road ahead. The asphalt was in terrible condition, with long cracks running in all directions; grass grew through the cracks, making it hard to tell where the tar seal ended and the verge began. Debris of all kinds littered the way, and often I was forced to slow or swerve to avoid something that might damage the car.

A green-and white sign flashed by: Cambridge exit, two kilometres. Right lane only.

There were lanes? I saw nothing. The years had stripped away the road-markings, leaving it a simple ribbon of dark grey. What were the old rules again? Keep left? Keep right? It didn't even matter anymore. The chance of meeting someone else on this dark, deserted highway in the back end of nowhere was one in a million. Maybe more.

Cambridge exit, one kilometre.

The signs were made of a reflective material that glowed like a neon sign in the beam of my headlights, even after ten years of wear. Did I want that turn-off? I didn't think so, but I grabbed my GPS off the dashboard and consulted it anyway. No, I needed to keep on going. There was nothing in Cambridge I wanted right now. The supplies I needed might have been there, but I didn't have time to risk it.

I was headed straight for the biggest hospital in the area, the one located on the southern fringe of Hamilton city. I wanted to spend as little time as possible within the city itself, and since I was coming from the south that hospital was the one that made the most sense.

The dread in my gut turned my stomach like I'd eaten rotten eggs.

***

I had no idea what time it was when I hit the outskirts of the city, but I guessed it was almost midnight. The sun set later in the summertime and it had taken me far longer than I estimated to negotiate the overgrown roads. Fatigue was starting to catch up to me, and I found myself struggling to keep my eyes open.

As I eased the Hilux into the city proper, I noticed that there were signs of devastation everywhere; the riots had hit this place hard. Road signs had been torn down or defaced, and the cracked white paint flashed by like old bones when my headlights caught them.

Real bones lit up as I passed by as well, some full skeletons still dressed in the clothes they died in, some just random limbs or skulls bleached bare by the scorching heat of the long summer days. Many people had died here, and not all of them from the sickness or there wouldn't be so many bones left behind. I wondered how many were suicides and how many were murders; how many innocent people died in the riots that the police were unable to contain?

I slowed to a crawl as I negotiated the city streets, scanning the shadows for any signs of life, death, or anything in between. I saw nothing, but I didn't trust my own limited vision in the darkness. The street lights in this part of the city appeared to be out, or the power grid was having a fit. Aside from the occasional flash of a crumpled street sign when my lights grazed it and the distant glow from other parts of the city, it was too dark to make much sense of anything I saw.

It made me feel so exposed. If anyone was looking, they would see me long before I saw them unless they were stupid enough to walk right in front of the truck.

I checked my GPS, and found myself close to one of the old entrances to the hospital grounds, so I pulled over and stared into the darkness. I couldn't see anything, so I fished my torch from its pocket and clicked it on, then shone it out the window at the roadside. A high metal fence topped with spikes barred the gap between the footpath and the car park beyond. There was no way I was getting past that in my current condition – at least, not without a blow torch.

I drove forward slowly, searching for a break in the fence or some kind of entrance that I stood a chance of negotiating. A few metres further on, I caught sight of something that looked a little like a guardhouse coming up on the right, so I inched the truck closer to get a better look.

Suddenly, light flared up, blinding me momentarily. I shielded my eyes with my hands, cursing softly beneath my breath. When the initial glare faded and my vision adjusted, I found the area lit up nicely. The street lamps were back on, along with spotlights around the car park and hospital grounds; I just happened to be unfortunate enough to have one of those spotlights pointed straight at me.

Just a blackout, I concluded with relief. Maybe things weren't as bad as I thought. With the lights on, the place seemed less scary all of a sudden. I could even see light shining through a couple of the windows of the hospital itself. Maybe things would be all right after all.

Yes, there were skeletons all over the place, but there were skeletons everywhere in this day and age. I could handle skeletons... in small doses. I'd gotten used to them over the years. Many people had chosen to die by their own hand rather than let nature take its course, and just as many died of the infection before it reached the point it would devour them whole. Human remains were impossible to avoid.

They were still gross, though.

I took the time to look around my newly-lit world in more detail. The grounds surrounding the hospital were a mess, littered with all manner of refuse – everything from old newspapers to the decomposed remains of human beings. A banner flapped in the breeze amid a forest of road cones flung about like skittles; the plastic hazard tape that stretched between them was limp and faded with age.

Hey, road cones – they might be useful someday. My mental inventory updated, but aside from sarcastic jokes and witch hunting, I was unable to imagine any real use for the things. But, who knew? Maybe something would come up.

A strong gust of wind caught the banner and pulled it straight for a moment, long enough for me to read the biohazard quarantine warning. The words were marred by brown-black stains that were most likely blood, or perhaps paint. I suspected as much – the hospitals were the first places the infection broke out, for the obvious reasons. Where else would you go when you were sick and terrified? You went to hospital, hoping for salvation and a miracle, like you saw on all those TV medical dramas.

Unfortunately, there was no miracle for the infected. Most of those poor people had gone to hospital to die.

Of course, that fact also meant that the hospitals usually had the highest concentrations of undead loitering within. Although most of them used to be hospital staff and tried to be helpful, a zombie with a syringe was still a zombie with a syringe. I would keep my taser close at hand.

As I turned into the car park, the fallen barrier arm crunched beneath my tyres; I wondered briefly what happened to it, but there was no way to be sure. Perhaps it had been smashed in the riots, or torn down in the storms, but for whatever reason the arm that once held back unauthorised traffic now lay shattered on the ground. The car park was edged with small, powerful spotlights that lit the area well enough for me to see, so I switched off my headlights and nudged the Hilux forward carefully.

A doorway loomed before me, its doors hanging open like a gaping, toothless maw. The hallway beyond was pitch black aside the distant flickering of a fluorescent light bulb well past its prime. Deeper within, I could see a steadier glow, but this entrance was dark and foreboding. I pulled the Hilux to a halt directly in front of the door and stared as far down the hallway as I could see.

Nothing moved as far as I could tell, but the flickering light bulb made it hard to be sure. I considered my options, pondering whether it was worth driving around looking for another entrance or whether I should go with what I had.

I decided to just roll with it and move as fast as possible.

I put the truck in park, and fetched my pack from the back seat. From within, I drew out the box that contained my gun, feeling its unhappy weight in my hand. I hated this thing, but it was a necessary evil. With careful fingers, I slid out the magazine and checked the contents, then slid it back into place with a solid click. I was ready.

Setting the gun on the dashboard, I checked the shadows one more time before I struggled my way out of the cab, my foot stiff and swollen. As I put my backpack on and slipped the gun into the pocket closest to my hand, I hoped that it wasn't the first stage of infection setting in.

Another reason to move my ass, just in case.

I locked the truck and took the keys with me when I left it this time. The truck was my best means of a quick escape, so there was no way I was risking its security. Even though I couldn't see anyone, there might be any number of people watching from one of the dozens of dark windows all around me and I would never know. Biding their time. Watching, waiting.

Creepy.

Feeling horribly exposed, I moved as swiftly and carefully as I could to the entrance of the hospital, tolerating terrible pain in an effort to hide my limp. Show no weakness, lest the wolves decide you're dinner. I turned and stared behind me, searching the deepest dark recesses all around, before finally turning to confront the terrible shadows within.

I drew my torch from one pocket and clicked it on, my other hand fumbling to fetch my gun as I stepped forward into the darkness.

And promptly tripped, almost falling on my face before I could even get inside. That was a promising start.

Nice one, Sandy.

I swung the torch down and dropped a mental curse or two as I spotted an old black pushchair blocking the doorway at a level just below the line of my torch. It was rusted and dirty but small, so I gave it a gentle nudge with my shin to push it out of the way. Its rusted wheels gave way and it tumbled sideways, scattering the tiny bones of its former occupant across the floor.

A baby. There had been a baby in there.

Bile rose in my throat and I fought down the urge to cry. Poor little baby. I didn't know. I didn't mean to do that, to send its little corpse flying. Silently whispering apologies and prayers, I stepped around the scattered bones and forced myself to look away. I must keep moving, find the medicine, get somewhere safe again. If I let myself break down every time I saw a dead child, I would never achieve any of that.

The hospital was deathly silent. Not even the drone of the wind reached this far inside. It was creepy, like an old horror movie. A weird, chemical smell overlaid the ever-present stench of decay.

I never did much care for hospitals. Too many

movies as a kid, I guess. They both gave me nightmares, and now I had to live the nightmare. Great fun.

I shone my torch side to side, and finally spotted a sign that hadn't been completely defaced during the riots: Maternity Ward.

I'm in Maternity? Oh Christ, that's just what I need.

I swore beneath my breath. If I found a zombie baby, I was going to turn myself right back around and go die of tetanus in my truck. On the scale of horrification, zombie baby beat death by tetanus any day.

As I snuck further inside, I spotted doorways flanking the hall, each of them just as dark and ominous as the hallway itself.

I wondered if the power was still out to this part of the building, or if a surge a some point in the past burst all the bulbs. There seemed to be light further up, so it was reasonable to assume that it must just be this part. Ten years was a long time to leave the lights on.

Sweeping my torch from side to side, I checked the first room for hostiles, then the second, and moved methodically down the hall. No bad guys. No zombie babies either. I chalked one up for the 'Thank Christ For That' brigade.

Sorry, Mum.

I was wound up tighter than a starlet's Spanx as I approached the T-intersection ahead, my brain set to a hair-trigger. I moved under the flickering light, half-expecting to be attacked the moment I stepped into the light, but nothing happened.

The closer I got to the corner, the brighter the light grew, though 'bright' was a relative term. The hallway was lit only by old, dull emergency lights that bathed the corridor in a dirty, artificial glow.

I raised my gun as I slowly approached the junction, keeping close to the left wall. Although I moved with the natural stealth of a survivalist, my uneven footsteps sounded loud enough to wake the dead, and my breath was deafening to my own ears. I was almost afraid to breathe at all. In truth, they were barely audible, but in the silence with my ears tuned in for the slightest sound, I felt like a rampaging elephant.

Keeping near the left wall meant I could scan down the right arm of the junction before exposing myself on the left. I saw nothing. As smoothly as I could, I slid around the corner to stare along the left arm, again seeing nothing.

Instinct made me stop to assess the distances between myself and the next junction in either direction, to take stock of the rooms I needed to risk passing in order to continue. The hallways were short in both directions, branching after a half-dozen metres into more corners, more risk, more places for enemies to hide.

I made a snap decision. I didn't want to stay exposed for too long, so I chose the left hallway and hobbled around the corner with my gun tucked in close in front of me. There was a room just down the passageway, and I limped towards it to see what was inside. The lights were on, so I clicked off my torch and held the gun carefully with both hands.

My foot was starting to really hurt as the painkillers wore off, and my heart was hammering in my chest at a mile a minute. The sense of urgency I felt was growing more and more overpowering, leaving me feeling increasingly panicked and vulnerable.

This is a terrible idea. Why didn't I wait until morning? I mentally cursed myself for being such an idiot.

Of course, it didn't occur to me until much later that with my shuffling gait, my gaunt frame, my tatty clothes and my tangled hair, I probably looked more undead than alive from behind.

I limped into the side room, looking for supplies, any kind of supplies that might help with my injury. There was a locked cabinet on the far side that contained a promising array of little bottles, jars and prescription boxes. I shuffled towards it and stared at the contents, trying to make out what was inside before I decided whether it was worth the risk of breaking the glass.

Something shattered beneath a heavy boot right behind me, and I froze. Reflected in the glass cabinet, a dark shadow loomed in the doorway. A second later, my self-defence instincts kicked in and I spun to face the incoming threat. Or at least I tried to, but my damn foot gave out in the process and I ended up in a heap on the floor.

That fall saved my life.

The shotgun blast shattered the window right

above my head as I fell, showering me in shards of glass and hot shrapnel. I screamed and covered my eyes with my forearm to protect myself, fully expecting a second shot to tear me apart at any second. I would say that my life flashed before my eyes, but it didn't; I just found myself wondering if it would hurt to die.

Would I see Mum again? Dad? Skylar? Were they waiting for me? Or would I just... cease to exist?

The second shot never came

"My god, you're alive!" A deep voice gasped, a voice that was male and strangely hoarse, then a strong hand latched around my forearm and hauled me to my feet before I could react. "Are you crazy? What are you doing here at this time of night? I almost shot you – you could have been killed!"

The survivor was tall, dressed in worn, dark blue combat armour, the upper half of his face concealed by a helmet and night vision goggles that gave him a terrifying, alien look.

I didn't even stop to think. I just reacted.

Now, I was a scrawny thing. While I was pretty tall for a girl, malnutrition had robbed my frame of any body fat that I once possessed; I was maybe 50 kilograms soaking wet, so I didn't look like much. However, every gram that I had left on me was muscle, driven by a mind that long ago learned the only good defence was a swift and brutal offense.

Long story short, I did not hit like a girl.

I clocked him square in the jaw with every bit of my physical strength, and the man's head snapped back.

He stumbled away from me, tripping over an old chair and almost falling. Weighed down by his armour and the combat shotgun, it took him a second to right himself.

That was enough for me.

I snatched my gun and my torch from where they'd fallen, and then I was off like a... slow-moving, half-gimped shot. It wasn't very fast, but it was as fast as I could go.

I was terrified, my heart pounding in my chest and adrenaline tingling through my extremities. Every time I tried to pick up to a run, my foot sent a stab of pain all the way up my leg that was so bad the limb almost gave out on me, so I was forced to be satisfied with a shambling trot.

I was out the door before the man could recover, and headed deeper into the hospital, frantically searching for someplace to hide. I needed to get away from him – him and his terrible shotgun. Every moment of my past experience told me the only thing that could come from an armed man was pain, humiliation and death.

Sweat beaded on my brow. It felt like I was moving in slow motion, swimming through treacle, except that instead of treacle it was pain and a gammy bloody foot. I was never going to make it in time, I realised with painful clarity. I had hit him hard, but not hard enough. I could hear him stumble out into the hall just as I was about to round the nearest corner, and heard him scream at me.

"No, don't go that way, they'll kill you – get back! Get back!"

I shot a look behind me and found that he wasn't even aiming at me, just frantically running after me with a panic-stricken look on what little I could see of his face. My fear turned to confusion.

Then, I heard the growl.

It was a deep, low rumble from a dark doorway not far from where I was. The fear surged back up again. I wasn't his target, I realised with dreadful certainty. There was something else here, something terrible.

And now it was after me.

The thing emerged from the shadows with a disturbingly sinuous grace, moving on all fours with its head held low, its bloodshot eyes fixed on me. Its frame looked human, like any other one of the infected – but the infected did not move like *that*.

I was frozen, like a deer in the headlights. This thing, it was outside any of my experiences, something I'd never seen before. Every ounce of my being screamed at me to flee, and yet I couldn't get my muscles to obey.

The creature squatted, regarding me. It seemed to be considering me, its horrible eyes roaming up and down my body – the stare was almost sexual in its intensity. I felt nauseated, but too terrified to move. There was blood all over it, from head to toe, and its clothing was shredded and almost unidentifiable. Then suddenly, it straightened up, and I recognised the deep blue scrubs of a nurse.

Christ, I was going to get killed and eaten by an undead nurse. Not quite how I pictured my death.

At the same moment the armed man caught up with me, the creature sprang. The stranger's bulk struck me hard and shoved me clear. A fraction of a second later, he swung his shotgun around to bear. The muzzle flash blinded me as I fell, my torch and gun once more clattering away. When my vision cleared, I saw the creature lying in a crumpled heap not two feet away from me.

It was still moving.

Even with its face caved in and the liquefied remains of its cerebellum leaking out of the terrible cavity that had once been the front of its skull, it was still struggling to get up. Still trying to get me.

Human fingers bent into ragged-nailed talons clawed in my direction, and I muffled a shriek as I scooted out of its reach. The scattershot had done a real number on the creature; half its head was gone and shrapnel burns covered the entire upper half of its body. I was fairly certain that I could see the bloody remains of its brain stem, shattered by the shell.

That should have done it. That should have killed it. It should *not* still be moving.

"How the hell is it still moving?" I whispered, as much to myself as to the other survivor, but he still heard me and gave me the answer.

"It's a mutation. We don't know how it's happening, but this is the fifth one we've seen this month — the second in a week. We think the virus is evolving." His voice was harsh, like he'd been running for a few hours without stopping to catch his breath.

As I scooted away from the horrible thing, the stranger put himself between me and the creature again, in a protective move that surprised me. With a glance over his shoulder, he spoke softly to me.

"Stay back. There's only one thing that we know for sure kills them."

There was a bottle in his hand, a red metal flask about the size of a drink bottle. With gloved hands, he unwound the cap and emptied the contents of the flask over the crawling undead. From the smell, I realised immediately it was either kerosene or lighter fluid.

He returned the empty flask to one of his pockets and pulled a box of matches from another – like mine, his clothing bore a lot of pockets. I noticed his hands shook when he struck the match and dropped it onto the bloody creature, but he didn't hesitate. As the flames spread, he hopped back away just in time to avoid being burned, then turned to look at me.

By the time he finished setting the creature aflame, I was a few metres away, trying in vain to put distance between myself and danger. To my frustration, my body still didn't want to respond. He moved closer, cautiously offering me a hand to help me up. I shoved it away, afraid to let him touch me.

A surge of adrenaline hit suddenly, and gave me the strength to get up on my own, and as soon as I was up I started backing away. I needed to use the wall to support my weight, which made my retreat inelegant, but it also made my fear quite obvious.

In my mind, I was remembering all the terrible, painful, violent things that men had done to me, and forced me to do to them. Even though he had helped me and seemed to want to help me again, my instincts were reluctant to forget those terrible things that human beings were capable of doing to one another – and to me.

He hesitated as he watched me scoot away, uncertainty etched on what little I could see of his face. Finally, he reached up and slid his night vision goggles up onto his head, letting me see the rest of him. He was handsome in an angular sort of way, and his eyes made me hesitate. They were gentle and full of concern for me despite my resistance.

"Hey, it's all right." His gruff voice was soft, as though he were trying to make himself as nonthreatening as possible – as if I was a wild animal that he could tame with gentle tones. "I just want to help you. Survivors have to help each other, right?"

"Not in my experience," I snapped back, my voice almost as harsh as his. It had been a long time since I'd held a conversation with anything that actually understood what I was saying.

His expression changed, from concern to sadness, and he closed his eyes for a moment. When they opened, he reached up to his chest, and pointed out a faded logo.

"Miss, I'm a police officer." He drew my eye to the faded word printed above his left pectoral. "I didn't mean to shoot at you, I swear on my life. I'm sorry. I thought you were one of them. I came here to hunt the mutants."

Then he looked down, suddenly noticing my gun at his feet. With a quizzical glance at me, he stooped and picked it up. I tensed, expecting to be shot with my own gun, but he didn't. He just turned the weapon around, and offered it back to me hilt first without a word. A peace offering. A gesture of trust.

I snatched the gun away and turned it on him, pointing the weapon straight at his handsome face – but I didn't pull the trigger. He held up his hands, trying to show me that his intentions were good. Although one of those hands did hold a shotgun, the gun was pointed about as far from my direction as it possibly could be.

Behind him, the fire cracked. The undead thing was still writhing. Oh god, it was still alive. My panic was fading, leaving me shaking from tension and sick to my stomach. The smell of burning flesh and hair in an enclosed space was nauseating. The survivor followed my eye to the writhing corpse, then swiftly stepped to his left to block my view.

"Don't look, please. You look like you've seen enough terrible things to last a lifetime," he said softly, his gruff voice barely audible over the crackle of flames. With slow, measured movements, he extended a hand towards me.

This time, it was in the form of a handshake.

"I'm Michael. Constable Michael Chan. I'm part of

a group of survivors that live around here." He glanced at my foot, obviously aware of my injury, then looked back up and offered me a wry half-smile. "One of my friends is a doctor."

I stared at his hand like it was a serpent that was going to bite me. The sound of hands striking flesh, my flesh, echoed in my memory, bringing with it the remembrance of pain. Then I looked up at his face, and saw only concern in his kind eyes. My gut did a flip-flop. There was a certain honesty about that face that my instinct said wasn't faked.

I lowered my gun, feeling uncertain and confused, unsure of what to do. He waited, his hand extended, an open invitation of— what? Friendship? I didn't understand friendship anymore. But, he was a police officer, sworn to protect and serve. He knew a doctor. I needed a doctor, so badly. And the way he was looking at me, that sweet, earnest concern.

Finally, my intuition as a human being overcame my learned paranoia as a survivor. I reached out to take his hand. A moment before our fingers would have touched, a blood-curdling shriek echoed through the empty corridors, cutting short our greeting. It was swiftly joined by a second, then a third.

All of a sudden, Michael wasn't so scary after all. Not compared to whatever was making those terrible sounds.

He spun and stared down the corridor beyond the burning corpse, his face suddenly intense. Careful steps brought him back towards me, and this time I didn't flee. I had to admit, after hearing those sounds, I really wanted a nice, big meat shield between me and whatever was making them. I didn't care if I was being self-interested.

But then I damn near jumped out of my skin when he turned unexpectedly and shoved his shotgun into my hands.

"I'm going to pick you up." His voice was calm and soft. "And then we're going to run for our lives. Please refrain from hitting me or shooting me until we're out of here."

Despite the warning, I still squeaked in surprise when he scooped me up into his arms, and fumbled to keep hold of the pair of guns. My torch was gone now, rolled away when he'd bowled me over to save me from the undead.

Another one screeched, this one closer.

Forget the torch. Forget the scary man. Fucking run! My instincts screamed at me. Apparently his did as well, because Michael took off with me in his arms, heading back the way we both came. I clung to him, surprised to find myself considering him the lesser of two evils at this particular moment.

The screeches were drawing closer and closer, like the baying of wolves. They were closing in on us, following our scent. Hunting us.

Just as we arrived back at the T-junction, another shriek joined the fray – this one was directly in front of us, from the direction Michael must have come, the opposite leg of the junction from the direction I had chosen.

"Wait." Self-preservation overrode my fear of him. Right now, my only hope for survival rested in the arms of a strange man who claimed to have once been an officer of the law. I was not ready to die. I shot out an arm, pointing to the right, through the Maternity Ward. "Go that way! There's an exit, I have a car waiting."

I didn't have to tell him twice. He turned and was off like a shot down the dark corridor. I found myself praying that nothing snuck in behind me after I cleared this corridor a few minutes ago. The shrieks were coming more and more frequently, drawing closer and closer, making my ears ring with their volume and ferocity.

Chancing a glance over Michael's shoulder, I saw nothing yet, but I was sure that at any moment I would see those horrible creatures scrambling to devour us.

Suddenly we were outside, the bright spotlights that bathed the car park startling after the dark corridor. My truck was where I left it, like a beacon of hope that we might yet survive this night.

"The keys?" Michael was gasping, out of breath from his frantic run while bearing my weight, but he made no effort to put me down even as I fumbled to get the car keys from my pocket. He held me close, protectively, bracing me against the door until I found the right key and shoved it in the lock. Central locking did the rest.

Unexpectedly, he yanked me away from the driver's door, and somehow managed to juggle my weight long enough to open the rear cab. I felt a flash of panic at the strength of his hands, but all he did was lift me in gently and sit me in the back seat. With a moment of understanding, I realised that he intended to drive and that he'd seen all the supplies piled on my passenger seat; the back seat was just the quickest and safest option for us both.

Despite my inner paranoia screaming in protest, I thrust the keys into his waiting hand. He slammed the door as soon as I was safely inside, and then dove behind the wheel. The engine roared to life, and he threw the car into reverse.

As the car swung around, the headlights flashed up the corridor, briefly lighting the figures that were loping towards us. They were horrible, hunched, their strides uneven. There were four or five, and they were coming fast.

"Michael!" I cried, their demeanour shooting pure, animal terror into my heart. I'd never seen undead move like that. It was like something out of one of those goddamn zombie movies I watched as a kid.

"I see them. Put your seatbelt on." His voice was still calm somehow, and I fumbled to obey. As soon as he heard the click of my belt sliding into place, he put his foot down.

The Hilux leapt forward, careening out the gate I had snuck through so carefully before; the combination of speed and weight crushed that fallen barrier arm into splinters beneath us. He swung the car to the right and deeper into the city, gaining speed at a dangerous rate.

I clung to the hand hold on the roof above me, suddenly more afraid of his driving than of the zombies.

Luckily, he seemed to know the streets and their obstacles well, and we miraculously survived our high-speed dash. As we drove I saw the flash of murky water to our right. I stared at it, trying to piece together what I saw with what I remembered from looking at my map, but my brain was too tired to co-operate.

"I'm taking a circuitous route to lose them." Michael spoke up suddenly, as though reading my mind; I was just getting myself all worried wondering where on earth he was taking me. "Our base is only a few kilometres from the hospital grounds. I'd hate to lead those things back home."

"They can track?" I was surprised. Being able to hunt was a sign of intelligence, and that seemed unlikely from what I'd seen of the creatures in the past.

"We're not really sure, but I'm not taking any risks with the lives of my friends. I hope you understand."

I did understand. I took the moment to catch my breath instead and fell into silence, staring out the window as I considered his possible motives. He seemed so genuine, so honest. Those were things you couldn't really fake.

Could you?

I'd been alone for so long that I had lost my knack for reading people. Feeling overheated despite the cool evening air, I rubbed a hand across my forehead and slumped back in my seat.

Then a thought struck me, and I turned to peer at

the back of Michael's head in the dark.

"You knew they were there. You came here all alone, at night, to a place where you knew those things were living. Why?" I asked softly, watching what I could see of his body to gauge his reaction.

Even I understood what it meant when I saw the way his hands tightened on the steering wheel; I could imagine his knuckles going white inside his gloves. I knew what that kind of tension meant.

"They killed one of my... friends. Two days ago." His voice was so low I could barely make it out over the sound of the engine. My sympathy bloomed into understanding. "We've only seen them attack during the day, so I hoped to catch them unaware at night. I won't let them take anyone else. I can't. For her sake. I'll kill them all, if I have to."

"You were close," I surmised, curiosity getting the better of me. It surprised me that I was interested in this stranger's motives at all, but what better way to understand someone than to learn about what drove them to kill?

"Yes." He paused, his husky voice almost a whisper. I wondered if there were tears in his eyes, but I couldn't see from where I sat. "She was my niece. My brother's little girl. She was only twelve." I heard him swallow and could imagine him trying to centre himself, just like I would do in his place.

My heart softened when I heard the pain in his voice. I knew that pain so well; I felt it every day. Every time I saw a child's toy or a little pair of shoes, I thought of my baby sister.

For him, the pain was still so raw, so recent. I understood that, too.

In spite of myself, I found myself reaching out to touch his shoulder. I don't know if he could feel it through the body armour, but it didn't matter. He was motivated by revenge and a powerful need to protect what little was left. I could understand that. More importantly, I could respect that.

I sat back in my seat after a brief moment of contact, pondering what had happened over the last few hours. With the back of one hand, I wiped my forehead and found that I was sweating despite the cool night air. Strange. A minute ago I'd felt like I was boiling alive, and now I was freezing. A wave of sparkles danced in front of my eyes, which left me feeling a little light-headed. I'd put the strange feeling down to adrenaline at first, but now that I was calm I wasn't so sure.

I laid my cheek against the glass of the window beside me, letting its coolness draw some of the heat from my cheeks. My mind wandered, and I found myself bouncing from one thought to the other without connection as I stared off out the window.

Today had not been a good day for me.

***

By the time we reached our final destination, I was feeling dizzy and disoriented, and was having trouble focusing both my thoughts and my eyes. I felt the engine stop, and then Michael was saying something, but I couldn't quite understand what he said.

If he was talking to me, then why was he so far away?

My eyes were closed but I wasn't asleep, just too dizzy to focus on the road anymore. I cracked my lids open and saw his concerned face peering back at me in the half-light. I managed a weak smile, then laid my head back down against the window again. It felt so nice and cool.

I heard a door slam.

A moment later, the window I was leaning against moved and I felt myself slipping towards the ground. Strong arms caught me, and a cool hand pressed against my forehead and cheeks. I wondered at it, but it didn't seem to matter so much anymore.

I was so tired. All I wanted to do was sleep.

I felt myself being disentangled from my seatbelt, then gathered up and held close to someone, but I wasn't sure who it was anymore and it didn't seem to matter. I heard worried voices, but when I tried to open my eyes it felt like the lids were weighted down with bricks.

No, lead.

No, bricks made of lead.

Bricks of lead tied to my feet.

So tired...

Chapter Twelve

Eventually, the fever broke.

One minute I was lost in the land of nonsense dreams of times long gone, happy times spent with family and friends. The next, my eyes were opening and I felt lucid and alert for the first time in what seemed like forever. I blinked slowly as my vision cleared, then reached up to rub the crust from the corners of my eyes and lips.

Every part of me ached. How long had I slept? I rolled myself up into a sitting position, shaking my head to clear away the cobwebs. As I sat up, the thin blanket slipped down to my waist, and I realised with a flash of shock that I had been stripped to my knickers and undershirt.

My cheeks coloured, first in fear and embarrassment, and then in anger as my memory came crashing back.

How dare he? After all his talk about trust, after the way he went on about wanting to help me, he'd betrayed me just the same? A sense of overwhelming outrage shot through my breast, sending spasms of energy to the furthest reaches of my limbs. I darted a glance around the room, intent on escape, looking for anything I could use as a weapon to defend myself.

There, on the table by the door: a gun!

...and a taser. A familiar-looking taser. My taser. Actually, that gun was pretty familiar too, come to think of it. Next to the weapons, my other belongings sat stacked with care. My clothing was washed and folded, with my shoes placed neatly atop the stack. They'd even gone so far as to clean my shoes for me while I slept.

My anger evaporated.

A cocktail of confusion and guilt replaced my anger as I came to understand. There was a bucket of water on the floor beside my bed, with a pile of wet rags near it. I vaguely remembered the strange feelings as I drifted away in the car, and now realised that I had been sick. A fever. They only removed my clothing to keep me cool, to try and keep the fever at bay.

They'd left my things untouched, aside from washing my clothing, and left me untouched as well. I knew the feeling of violation very well, and I did not feel it now. I shifted my foot and found the pain was muted, and the wound was dressed in clean bandages.

There was even a tiny purple flower sitting on the table beside my bed, in a makeshift vase made out of a shot-glass.

A flower? That's strange, I thought as I stared at it. I was so focused on the bloom that at first I didn't notice the door crack open, nor the little face peer through. My attention snapped to the doorway when the child peeking at me giggled, but she shut the door before I could get a good look at her.

Someone was out there and they knew I was awake. Animal instinct kicked in.

I swung my legs out of bed and examined my foot, finding it stiff but relatively functional. I resisted the urge to tear the bandages off and douse the wound in bleach; the bandages were far neater than anything I could have done myself, so I could only hope the wound had been thoroughly disinfected.

Feeling woozy from fever and possibly painkillers, I managed to get out of bed and limp the three steps to my clothing before the door burst open again. Michael hurried in, followed closely by a stocky older gentleman and a small girl of six or seven years of age.

I was still so weak and disoriented from my recent illness that when Michael swept me off my feet and tucked me right back into bed again, I didn't have a chance to protest. Probably a good thing, for his sake; there was a huge green-black bruise along his jaw from where I'd hit him and it was only just starting to fade.

Something else for me to feel guilty about, when he had been so nice to me. I'd add that one to the list.

Everyone was suddenly talking all at once and I was having trouble keeping up. I didn't know how to respond to so many questions, coming from all angles. It was like a verbal barrage and I didn't know how to counter-attack. After so long alone, it was hard enough to follow one line of conversation, let alone two or more.

Amazingly, it was the little girl who saved me.

"Shh." She silenced the adults with a sharp gesture, then fixed them with a pointed stare until they fell quiet. She pointed at me with one little finger, and with wisdom beyond her years got right to the heart of the matter. "She has been alone outside, probably for a very long time. Talk one at a time so she can understand you."

I couldn't help but smile at the precocious child, and she smiled back at me. She leaned in close and whispered to me. "I picked you a flower. I hope you like it."

Aww. Well, that explained that.

"Sorry," I apologised automatically. "But she's right. It's been a few years. Longer, I think." My voice was dry and croaky from thirst, but it gave validity to my claim. Michael smiled, looking a little embarrassed, and the older gentleman frowned deeply.

"How are you feelin—" Michael started to ask, but the older man cut him off with a gesture.

"You hush, young man. Who is the doctor here? I am. I go first, and you may talk to her afterwards." He scowled at Michael, who held his hands up in self-defence. The doctor then turned penetrating hazel eyes back to me, and eyed me over the scratched lenses of his spectacles. "As for you – I am going to touch you, as I must examine you. Please refrain from hitting me. The boy says you pack quite a punch."

The gentleman had a strange accent that I couldn't quite place. His demeanour, though less than friendly, spoke of a professional candour that put me relatively at ease. I nodded my consent, and braced myself for the unfamiliar sensation of human touch.

Must not freak out. Must not freak out. Must not freak out.

To my own amazement, I managed to refrain from panicking, as the examination was blessedly short. He leaned over me to check my temperature with the back of his hand, and then felt behind my ears with calloused old fingers. He checked my pulse, peered into my eyes, ears and the back of my throat then finally ended up asking me the exact same thing Michael had tried. "How are you feeling?"

"Sore," I admitted, absently rubbing one of my shoulders. It felt like I'd slept on it for a long time, long enough for my arm to go to sleep. "A bit stiff. Really thirsty, too. How long was I out?"

"Three days. It was touch and go for a while there; you were very ill," the old man answered, and his expression softened just the tiniest bit. He opened one of the drawers beside the bed to show me the contents. Inside, a couple of bottles of water were flanked by several precious items of personal hygiene – toothpaste, a toothbrush, a bar of soap and a few other things.

Things that were once life's necessities, but were now rare and valuable. I was surprised to see them; putting them in the drawer beside my bed was obviously an offer for me to use them. It was generous beyond belief.

I was suspicious.

I looked at him uncertainly then looked at the water, afraid to reach for it in case it was a trap. With a disapproving click of his tongue, the man snatched a bottle out and put it right in my hand. He even opened the lid for me, then made impatient hurrying gestures until I drank deeply and quenched my intense thirst. I immediately felt better as the cool water poured down my dry and scratchy throat. I supposed running a fever did that to a body.

"Where did you come from?" he demanded while I was still swallowing the last sip of my water.

I peered at him questioningly. "Originally or most recently?"

"Most recently, of course." He frowned at me, as if I were silly just for asking. The older fellow was a bit grumpy, I decided, but he was a doctor and that counted for a lot in this day and age. Behind him, I saw Michael hide a chuckle behind a cough, and pretend to be fascinated by something on the floor. He looked amused, but I was so isolated that I couldn't figure out what he found so funny.

"South. I've been travelling around the south for the last few years. Most recently in a rural area about twenty kilometres south of here," I answered, although I was wary of the question. My distrust ran deep, though I didn't have the courage to ask why he wanted to know.

"Rural?" he repeated my answer, and I nodded. "Mm. Did you see any horses? Or pigs?"

"No, just sheep, some chickens, and a few cows." The pieces were coming together; his line of questioning suddenly made sense. He was trying to work out my chances of exposure to tetanus and other infections. "A lot of the fences were down, though. There could have been horses in the past, I can't be sure." I paused to consider. "I wasn't attacked though, so I doubt there are any pigs left in the area."

"Attacked?" The doctor's brow furrowed, and behind him Michael looked equally confused.

"Attacked by the pigs?" I peered back at them. Were we speaking different languages here?

"Why would pigs attack you?" The doctor asked, bewildered.

"Because of the infection?" I was incredulous, but the looks on their faces said they didn't have a clue what I was talking about. "Do you guys live under a rock or something? Pigs can catch the infection. It makes them crazy and violent. Kind of like..." I trailed off when something clicked. Michael stared at me, wide-eyed with understanding, and I stared back.

"Great." When the news had sunk in, Michael squeezed his eyes closed and rubbed his forehead with his fingertips. "Psychotic zombie-pigs. They're really a thing now. Please tell me you're kidding?"

I shook my head, and he groaned.

The doctor sat down heavily in an old wooden chair beside my bed, and pinched the bridge of his nose with his fingers. "Ah, just what we need. At least that explains how the mutation happened."

"I think I remember reading that humans and pigs are genetically similar." I suddenly felt sick in the pit of my stomach. I'd only encountered a pig once in my travels, and it was so riddled with infection that it screamed a horrible sound and charged right for me. Like any sane person, I had panicked and fled. The only reason I'd survived was because both of the animal's back legs were so badly mutilated that it couldn't keep up.

The men looked horrified when I shared the story with them, and I shot a worried glance at the little girl, but she seemed totally disinterested in the grown-up talk. I wondered briefly how traumatic her short life must have been, but given her age it was the only life she had ever known.

"What about survivors?" The doctor decided to change the conversation, seeking information from me. "Did you see any other survivors? Why did you come north?" The questions came quick and fast, forcing me to take a second to process them before I replied.

"No, no other survivors where I was most recently. I-I usually stay away from other survivors." I looked down at my hands, twisting the edge of the sheet nervously between my fingers. "I came north because I lacked the medical supplies or expertise to treat the infection I was bound to get from that." I gestured at my foot. "I stood on a nail in an orchard. I knew there was a hospital here, so I hoped to find antibiotics."

"An orchard? That explains the fruit." Michael smiled at me. Despite the smile, I felt my stomach lurch. He must have read the concern in my expression, because his smile faded quickly. A look of uncertainty flitted across his face, as though he wasn't sure how I would react. "I didn't want to leave it in your truck to rot. I put it in our cold storage for you."

"You didn't eat it?" This time I was genuinely surprised, and pleasantly so. I had expected from the moment I awoke in a strange place that I would have been robbed of all my supplies and left with nothing.

"Of course not!" Both the constable and the doctor looked mortified at the very thought. "We are *not* thieves. What kind of people do you think we are?"

I looked at my hands, feeling a sudden rush of heat in my face and neck as embarrassment and guilt curdled once more in my belly. Again I'd misunderstood, applying the template of past cruelties against good people who didn't deserve it, and now I had upset my benefactors. I felt like crying, but that wouldn't really help anything. Everything was just so confusing.

"I-I'm sorry," I apologised softly, not sure what else to say.

A small body alighted on the bed beside me, and a pair of skinny little arms wrapped around me. I glanced sideways and discovered the little girl looking up at me with huge, doe brown eyes. She translated my unspoken thoughts to her elders, then gave me a tiny smile. "She thought that we were going to hurt her and take her food."

Tears blurred my vision and I hurried to brush them away, afraid to show weakness before others. How could this child have known me so well, and yet the grown men did not understand me at all? I felt so confused, so out of place. The child wasn't the traumatised one, I realised suddenly. I was.

I was so broken that I needed a seven-year-old to translate my reactions to rational adults.

I finally looked up, and found the old doctor looking worried and Michael standing nearby looking confused and upset. He was the first to speak, his gruff voice a little grainier than usual. "We would never do that to you, or to anyone else. We're good people. I would rather die than steal from you."

He sounded like he really meant it, too. I lowered my head, feeling ashamed of myself for judging them before I knew anything about them. Seeing the hurt on his face stung like a snake bite, even though I didn't quite understand why I cared at all.

I guessed it was because I'm still human, and human beings are innately social creatures. Even me. *Especially* me.

"We must do your next injection, and then you should rest." Looking embarrassed, the doctor hurried to change the subject again. He leaned over to grab a small leather satchel that was beside my bed and fussed around inside it.

If it was a tetanus shot then I agreed wholeheartedly, but I was feeling shy and reclusive now, too ashamed to say a word. The little girl was still hugging me, watching my face intently. I understood that she was trying to comfort me, and I felt no urge to push her away. She was so small, unthreatening and sweet. Even my somewhat overzealous self-defence mechanism didn't kick in over her touch. While the doctor was preparing his medication, she tried to distract me with her childish cheer.

Leaning up against me, she whispered in my ear. "My name is Madeline. What's yours?" Then she gave me such a sweet little smile that even I couldn't resist.

"Sandy." Out of instinct alone, I put an arm around the girl's gaunt frame and gave her a little sideways hug. "Thank you for the flower."

"You're welcome." She beamed brightly, and then pointed at the old man. "That's my granddaddy." Her finger shifted to Michael, who had finally relaxed enough to look amused by the exchange. "That's Mister Officer Chan. He looks after me and Granddaddy; and Mummy too, before she died."

"Maddy-monkey, come down from there and leave the young lady be," the doctor scolded gently, busy filling a syringe from a small, official-looking medicine vial

"It's okay." I suddenly felt protective. "She's fine. She reminds me of my sister." I looked at the girl and added softly, "My sister was about your age when I last saw her."

"Is your sister dead, like Mummy?"

I flinched. Oh, from the mouth of babes. There was no point denying it, this child clearly understood death better than most.

"Probably." I nodded, sadly. "I didn't see her die, but the last time I saw her she was driving away with my daddy and I never saw either of them again."

"Aw. I would have liked to play with her." Madeline looked crestfallen.

"All right, enough of that. Injection time," the doctor advised, shuffling closer to me with a syringe in one hand and a cotton swab soaked in cleaning alcohol in the other. I tensed up immediately, since I'd never liked needles, and drew a disapproving sound from him. "Hold still now. This will only take a moment. Unless you *want* to get tetanus, of course?"

He did have a point. I nodded curtly, and looked away.

I felt the fluff of the swab on my arm as the site was being cleaned, then the prick of the needle followed by that creepy sensation of something being injected into my body. As much as I hated that feeling, I held still like a good girl. One little prick was a hell of a lot better than getting lockjaw. Like he promised, it only took a second and then he was pressing a clean rag over the tiny wound to staunch any bleeding.

"There, all done." Despite his stern face, his voice was soothing. I took the rag from him as soon as he would let me, and kept pressure on the wound.

"You were a real doctor, weren't you?" It sounded like a stupid question after I'd asked it, but he seemed to understand.

"Yes, I was a general practitioner. I'm sure there's

an office around here somewhere that still has my name on the door. I also studied pharmacology, which has come in rather handy these days. I make most of our medication, when I can find the resources." He paused when he noticed me staring at him expectantly. "My name is Dr Cross, but you may call me Stewart. We are rather informal around here."

"Thanks," I answered with a sudden surge of sarcastic humour. "I wasn't looking forward to having to call you 'Granddaddy'."

Madeline giggled, Michael laughed, and even Dr Cross cracked a smile, the first one since we'd met. I felt a little better after that, a little more accepted. Maybe they would forgive me for assuming they were thieves and murderers.

At least, I hoped so.

Chapter Thirteen

The other survivors interrogated me a few minutes longer, and then left me in peace with instructions to rest. I couldn't fall back to sleep so I just lay there staring at the bare concrete walls for about an hour, trying to figure out where I was. The place looked like a bunker, designed to withstand a bomb blast or an assault by armed forces, but I couldn't think of a reason for Hamilton to have a bunker. Hamilton was small by city standards, with only a couple of hundred thousand residents in its prime. It was mostly a farming hub for the lush Waikato region, and all the businesses required to support that industry. Why on earth would it have a bunker?

The more I lay there and thought about it, the more I realised that I wasn't going to get an answer without asking — and the more I started to realise that I was going to need a lavatory soon. That was an uncomfortable feeling. Someone must have been dealing with my biological needs while I was unconscious, but I was in no way ready to trust anyone with that while I was awake.

Stuff doctor's orders, it was time to get up.

I shoved back the blanket and swung my feet to the floor, then stretched my arms up over my head to get the blood-flow going again. Despite the fact that I hadn't really slept, I felt pretty good, or at least better than when I first woke up. Who knew daydreaming was good for the body *and* the soul?

With great care, I rose to my feet, keeping my weight on the heel of my injured foot. Although that made walking awkward, Dr Cross had warned me repeatedly not to go tearing my stitches. Still, I was restless and it was time to move. They had implied that there were other people here, which meant more potential risks that I needed to assess.

I also kind of felt the need to apologise to Michael for bruising his jaw.

While I was dressing, I decided in a rare moment of trust to leave my other belongings where they were. If these people had wanted to rob me, then they would have done it while I was unconscious. They'd chosen not to, so I could not imagine that they would suddenly change their minds. It would just make no sense at all.

Once I was properly clothed, I opened the door and stuck my head out into the hall. I found myself in a long concrete corridor, lit by fluorescent bulbs that cast the passages in a dull artificial glow. Occasionally one flickered, reminding me of the hospital – I shivered at the thought. Still, people lived here, so there must be a lavatory somewhere. One problem at a time.

I picked a direction at random, and headed off along the corridor, limping slowly to avoid putting undue strain on my foot. There was a doorway up ahead on my left, which turned out to be another small room with a cot much like mine. Judging by the scattered toys and the mountain of pink clothing, I assumed that it must be Madeline's room. A second cot, neater than the first, lay against the opposite wall. Although I couldn't be as sure, I guessed that was likely to be the doctor's bed. Neither of them were there, so I moved on.

The next doorway along was on the right. When I looked inside I found a small kitchen area, with a table, chairs and a couple of tatty couches. It probably used to be a break room for the people who worked in this building forever ago, but right now it was empty as well.

There were a few more rooms on the left which appeared to be storage rooms. They were packed with goods appropriated from around the city, everything from food and clothing to old computers and cell phones. There were a couple of large refrigerators which I imagined must be the 'cold storage' that Michael mentioned, and a few big metal drums that I assumed contained fuel, water or possibly rice.

For survivors, they were quite well stocked. No wonder they didn't feel the need to steal from others; they would not have to go hungry any time soon.

Beyond the storage rooms was a dead end, so I headed back the way I came to try another direction. The place was quite extensive and solidly built. I could understand why they had chosen this as their base of operations; it wasn't pretty, but it sure felt safe.

I passed more rooms, a couple of which had been converted into bedrooms, a few were obviously storage, and some seemed to serve no purpose at all. A noise from one of the rooms further down the hall drew my attention, so I slipped up to the doorway to see who was inside.

I found Michael Chan sitting on a narrow, metal-framed cot, whittling away at a wooden plank with a chisel. There were a few other pieces of wood scattered around him, along with a hammer, screwdriver, nails and other tools. As someone who had always been interested in handcrafts, I noticed he wasn't very good at woodworking, but at least he was trying. Effort always counted for something.

His head was down so he didn't notice me at first, which finally gave me the opportunity to really study him. He was tall, probably a good three inches taller than me, which would put him at a little over 6', and he was built quite large, with broad shoulders and muscular arms that told me he spent a lot of time engaged in physical activity.

Unusually large for someone with a Chinese last name. I pondered that thought, and although I was curious, I didn't know him at all and couldn't really guess at his origins. Right now, he was dressed in civilian clothes. Jeans, boots and a t-shirt that was a little too small for his powerful frame.

I found that I didn't mind. After all these years and

so much abuse, it was strange to admit that I found him rather handsome. Well, he was handsome. Almost beautiful, in that sculpted way Chinese men could sometimes be. He possessed a strong jaw, angular cheekbones and a fine, straight nose, with short black hair combed straight back from his forehead.

It was still his eyes that fascinated me, though. They were dark brown, fathomlessly deep and yet so kind and gentle.

I was off in my own little world, getting myself all addled with conflicting thoughts and emotions, when he suddenly sensed my presence. His head shot up, startled. For a moment I thought he was going to leap to his feet and defend himself, but then he seemed to recognise me, and relaxed.

"You're supposed to be resting." His gruff voice was somehow both scolding and caring simultaneously. It finally occurred to me that the gruffness wasn't from hostility, but rather the result of an old accent that my ear just wasn't used to hearing.

"I did rest." I lifted a brow pointedly. "But nature's calling, and no one told me where the loo is."

"Oh." His laughter was a friendly sound; I decided that I liked it. He set aside his woodworking and rose, to move over to where I peeked around his doorframe. I retreated, my instincts making me naturally skittish, but he made no attempt to touch me. "I'll show you the way. This place is pretty big."

He headed off and I fell in behind him, resting one hand on the wall as I walked to help keep my weight off my foot.

"I would offer to carry you again, but I'm afraid you'll hurt me." He shot me a teasing look over his shoulder, but kept his pace slow enough for me to keep up.

"I can walk." I snorted in mock indignation. "Just not very well."

He chuckled and turned a corner, and I hurried to keep up with him. For some reason that I didn't want to think about too closely, I found watching him walk quite fascinating. The ill-fitting outfit was flattering on his lean physique. As I watched him, I found myself experiencing an unexpected rush of emotion, the kind of feelings that I hadn't dealt with in a very, very long time.

I was so distracted by trying to decipher what those feelings actually meant that I didn't notice straight away when we reached our destination. The lavatory turned out to be a large, military-style bathroom, with a row of toilet stalls along the back, a wall of lockers and benches down the middle, and a half-dozen shower stalls to our right.

The shower stalls had originally been open-faced, but the survivors had hung colourful shower curtains in front of each to provide some degree of privacy – a fact for which I was grateful. I inspected the room thoughtfully, before making my way towards the toilets. Halfway there, I noticed something that made me gasp.

"You have toilet paper? Real toilet paper?"

"And hot water, too."

His dark eyes twinkled with mirth when I spun around to stare at him in surprise.

"Really? Hot water?" I could hardly believe it, after how hard I'd worked trying to get the tank working back at Ohaupo. "Can I—?"

"Knock yourself out." He moved over and opened one of the lockers with a dramatic flourish, revealing that it was being used as a makeshift linen cupboard. Neat stacks of towels in an assortment of cheerful colours filled it, along with various personal hygiene items.

"How do you guys have so much *stuff*?" I blurted. Given how hard I had struggled just to survive, seeing such a stockpile was mind-boggling.

"Well, I've been using this as a base since the outbreak happened." He shrugged sheepishly. "This is the underground portion of the police precinct. Since I was serving here, it just made sense. There were hardly any other survivors in this area to begin with, so I've had time to collect stuff. There isn't a lot of competition."

"The others weren't here with you from the start?" I tilted my head inquisitively and looked up at him.

"No. It was just me and Sophie – my niece – for three or four years before I found Stewart and his family. He's from around here, but his son's family were down in Otago. He went all the way down there looking for them, only to find out his son was already dead. He found his daughter-in-law was still alive, though, and that she had a little baby with her.

"They managed to get back to Hamilton, and I found them one day while they were scavenging in the ruins." He smiled shyly and shot me a sideways glance. "I couldn't very well leave them out there, so I brought them back here where it's safe and warm. We've acquired a few other stragglers since then, and, well, here we are."

"Huh." I looked down at my feet thoughtfully. I guess I was the latest straggler. That was food for thought.

After a moment of silence, Michael waved and made to leave. "You do your thing. Just call if you need me. Sound travels down here, so chances are good that I'll hear you – or someone will."

Then he was gone, leaving me alone in that big bathroom. I stood there, pondering, for a couple of moments before I realised that I was wasting precious shower time.

I quickly ducked into a stall to relieve myself, before turning my attention to enjoying the longest, hottest shower of my adult life.

***

They had soap. They had shampoo and conditioner. They even had razor blades. Shaving wasn't exactly something you had time to do when you were surviving in the ruins of a shattered civilization, but I did it every chance I got. I hated the feeling of hairy legs almost as much as I hated being sweaty. It might have been a bit pedantic, but I liked to feel clean.

The hot water was amazing. I practically roasted myself washing and shaving every part of my body that I could reach. It was a difficult prospect with doctor's orders to keep the bandages dry, and in the end I just gave up. A hot shower trumped clean bandages any day of the year.

After three shampoos and a conditioning, my hair felt cleaner than it had in a very long time. Oh, the sweet, glorious smell of shampoo, I'd almost forgotten how wonderful it was.

I must have spent at least half an hour in there, getting nice and clean, but when I finally convinced myself it was time to get out I felt absolutely wonderful. The world seemed like a brighter place. I was so clean, so very clean. Pruney, but clean.

Of course, feeling good never seemed to last long for me, in my fucked-up little life. Something always went wrong.

I dried myself and dressed back in the clothing I was wearing previously, and then braided my hair to keep it out of my face while it dried. Sodden towel in hand, I looked around for an appropriate depository for soiled articles but couldn't find one, so I took it with me as I left the bathing hall.

I made my way back in the direction I suspected the kitchen was, and heard voices speaking softly in a room nearby. Curious, I inched closer until I could hear what they were saying.

"She's emotionally scarred, son. I'm not sure it's good for the others to have someone like her around here. Look what she did to your face."

The voice sounded like Dr Cross, and 'son' turned out to be Michael.

"Of course she's emotionally scarred. Put yourself in her shoes and think about what she's been through. You and I have always had someone with us to keep us real, but she's a pretty, young girl all on her own. I'm not at all surprised that she hit me; I must have scared the hell out of her. The poor thing."

Michael thought I was pretty? I felt my cheeks burn, and leaned in closer to listen.

"What if she's dangerous, or crazed? You don't know anything about her. She's clearly a loner, and that says things about her mental state. What if *she's* a thief? What if she's a serial killer and playing on our pity?"

Michael's deep voice was firm and commanding, and rose to my defence. "The only thing it says about her mental state is that she's been through a lot of pain, doc. You saw her face when we were talking. Even Maddy could see it. She honestly thought we were going to rob her or kill her – or worse. Just think about what it must have been like to live like that for so long."

I heard footsteps, but they weren't coming closer; it sounded like he was pacing.

"We can't just abandon her." It was Michael's voice again, low and solemn. "If she wants to go, that's one thing. But forcing her out would be wrong – it's both immoral and unethical. Frankly, doc, I'm a little disappointed that you would even suggest it. She's a human being, just like all the rest of us, and she's traumatised. She needs us."

My heart leapt into my throat, and the flush faded almost as soon as it began. Dr Cross wanted to throw me out? It felt like someone dumped a bucket of ice water over my head. I wasn't surprised though, really. I probably wouldn't want me around either.

There was silence in the room, apparently as the men were thinking over their decisions, while out in the hall I slumped against the wall. Tears ran down my cheeks, and I wiped them away with a corner of my towel.

"Ah, what is it with you and picking up strays?" There was a heavy sigh. "I suppose you're right. She does deserve a chance. But I must insist that if she becomes any kind of threat to Madeline, you evict her immediately or we will leave. You understand, of course."

The sound of footsteps came again as the men parted ways, heading in opposite directions. I didn't know where the doctor went, but it was Michael who emerged from the doorway where I was eavesdropping. He turned to head in the direction of the bathroom, then froze when he saw me right there, in tears.

"If your friend doesn't want me here, then I'll go," I said softly and sniffled, not wanting to blow my nose on their nice towel. With as much dignity as I could muster, I shoved myself away from the wall and drew myself up to my full height. Then I gave the handsome young man a long, hard look, trying my best to pretend I hadn't been crying like a baby a second before. "It's okay, I understand. This is your home, not mine. I wouldn't feel right staying here if it made you and your friends fight."

I gave him the faintest of smiles, then turned and limped my blubbery mess off in the direction I was at least slightly certain my room was. The truth of the matter is that I wasn't comfortable with the situation at all and I wasn't sure how to react. The whole thing was overwhelming, and my automatic response to the unknown was to retreat.

Behind me, Michael swore under his breath. The sound of his footfalls behind me sped up, so I picked up the pace to try and outdistance him. Injured and vulnerable as I was, he caught up with me easily; his big hands captured my shoulders from behind.

I tensed, automatically expecting to be beaten or violated. Even though I had already come to understand that Michael was a gentle man by nature, my instincts were so warped that I was ready to defend myself in a heartbeat. But one thing held me back: No matter how hard I fought, violence wouldn't fix the terrible emptiness that I felt at the thought of being alone all over again. I had tasted the simple joy of human acceptance, and I longed for it – but the last thing I wanted was to tear apart other people's relationships in the process.

Michael didn't hurt me, of course. He just held me gently, close enough to him that I could feel his body warmth on my back, but not quite close enough to touch.

"The doc's just a cranky old man, and he's always picking a fight over something." Michael's voice was hard at first, but it softened as he spoke. The last words were almost a whisper, and I sensed something in them that I didn't quite understand. "Don't pay any attention to him. *I* want you to stay."

I couldn't think of an answer.

He turned me around to face him, as gently as if I were a porcelain doll. I stared up at him silently, and saw the look of concern on his face.

"Nobody should have to be alone unless they want to be," he said, his voice calm and reassuring. "You don't want to be alone, do you?"

The tears sprang back unbidden. Although I tried to blink them away, the lump in my throat made it impossible. The pressure of spending all those years alone was just too much for me to bear. My head ached and I felt like I might burst at any second. I looked away and tried to think of an appropriately sassy response, but all I could think of was little Tigger, the kitten who had been my only companion in many years.

Did I really want to be that alone again? It hurt just to think about it. These people were so nice that it brought me back to another place and time. A time when I was young, before I needed to be afraid of everyone. Back to being with my family, safe and loved.

Did I really want to go back to the endless silence, where the only kind of conversation I could have was with myself?

No, I really, really didn't.

I shook my head and closed my eyes against the onslaught of pain. Michael seemed to understand my turmoil. He put his arms around me and drew me up against his broad chest, holding me so tenderly it was like he was afraid he might break me if he squeezed too hard. I tensed right up, before I realised that he was just hugging me in an attempt to comfort me. I hadn't been hugged since Grandma died. I barely even recognised what it was.

It felt... nice.

Lacking the experience to know what to do, I just stood there pathetically, my face pressed up against his chest. The tears flowed freely, and he held me as I cried. The longer he held me, the weaker my defences grew and the more the wordless emotion poured out of me. But even when my shoulders shook and I struggled to muffle the convulsive sobs that fought their way out, he was there for me, like a pillar of strength to hold me up while I was weak.

Something in me had burst. Over the years, I'd built up an emotional dam to survive. That dam had been full to bursting for a very long time, and every day it was a battle to keep it under control. Something about the warmth of human contact made it impossible to keep forgetting and keep suppressing, and so I wept.

I wept for all the things I'd lost, for all the things I'd never have, and for all the lives that had been snuffed out in futility all around me. For the unbearable pain I'd suffered in silence all these years, with no kind of vent or release to keep me sane.

I had no idea how long it was before I regained control of my emotions, but when I did I felt exhausted, drained and sore all over again. I leaned against him for almost a minute longer while I caught my breath, before I finally broke the embrace. He let me go, but kept his hands resting on my shoulders, his face full of kindly concern. Not a word of judgement, no questions, he just waited, giving me as much time as I needed until I was ready to talk to him.

"Bleh." My first word was not an elegant one. "I think I'm dehydrated now." I buried my face in the towel and scrubbed away salty tears with the dampest corner I could find. Michael blinked owlishly at my comment, and then cracked a smile.

"We better get you something to drink, then." His voice was soft and husky in a way that sent shivers down my spine. Without asking permission this time, he slid his arm around my shoulders and led me off toward the kitchen — and I let him. I was not in the mood to fight.

I let him seat me at the table and watched listlessly as he poured two glasses of cool water from the fridge. He set one down in front of me and seated himself across the table, sipping deliberately from his glass. I mostly just played with mine, more interested in figuring out the weird feelings that careened through my gut than drinking water.

It was a good five minutes before he finally broke the silence. When he reached out to me, it was with the dry, sarcastic brand of humour that I always resorted to; apparently he had noticed already, and turned my own verbal weapon back against me. He was trying to get a rise out of me, any kind of rise, so that he could assess the extent of my psychological damage – and I knew it.

"Are you moping?"

"Yeah," I answered without missing a beat, then heaved a dramatic sigh. "Apparently my brain is broken. I feel stupid and rude and– and–" I looked up at him, finally seeking out his kind eyes. "And I'm sorry I hit you."

"You do pack a mean right hook." He smiled and rubbed his jaw sheepishly. "Don't even worry about it. I understand. Big, scary guy sneaks up behind you in a dark, terrifying hospital, and almost shoots you in the butt? I'd have punched me, too."

"I didn't break your jaw, did I?" I felt a flash of unexpected concern.

"No, I don't think so. Doc says it might be a little cracked, but it'll heal just fine."

I stared at the bruise, noticing the fine stubble on his chin for the first time. It was nice, just a half day's growth but it made him a little less perfect, a little more human. Just the right touch of scruffiness. I wondered if the bruise made it hurt to shave, but I decided not to ask. Instead, I looked down again with another soft sigh.

"You've been so patient with me. I'm really sorry, for everything." I felt ashamed of myself and didn't quite know how to express it. "I'm just, you know..."

He reached across the table, and rested his hand over mine. "I know. You're broken." He smiled softly, and gave my hand a comforting squeeze. "It's okay. You've been through a lot. We'll talk about it, gradually, when you're ready. I'll help you get better."

"You mean that?" I asked softly, feeling hope for the first time in what felt like forever.

"Damn right, I do. We're friends now, okay? You and me. And Doc and Maddy, too. And the others once you get a chance to meet them. We're all friends, and we're here to support one another. Right?"

"Yeah," I agreed readily, although I barely remembered what it was like to have a friend. There had been a lot of friends in my early life, before the outbreak, but now I was in uncertain territory.

"Besides," he reached over to lightly chuck me under the chin in a friendly fashion, "if we ditched one another just because we were a little broken, this place would be completely empty."

I couldn't help but laugh. It was the first laugh I'd had in a while, too. The sound of it made him smile.

***

We just talked for a while about nothing in particular, about cartoons we watched as children and the places where we grew up. The conversation stuck to cheerful things. Skillful manipulation on his part, but I wasn't complaining. I needed it, to just talk about good times and forget all the bad ones.

He even broke out the food to keep me distracted, and we ate reheated spaghetti-from-a-can together while we chatted.

"Call me crazy, but I think the little sausages are the best part." He stabbed one of the tinned sausages with his fork.

"Yeah, I agree. I always begged my mum to get the kind with the sausages in it when I was little. She always said no, no, it's not good for you, they're more expensive, blah blah; but then she'd end up buying it anyway."

He was really good. Usually, whenever I thought about my mother, I suffered a terrible pang of grief; this time, all I felt was the wistfulness of remembering a happy memory. With an impish grin, he waved the little sausage at me teasingly, and then popped it in his mouth. I stuck my tongue out childishly in return, and found my own sausage to eat.

"Mich-ael?" A female voice called from some distance away, drawing our attention away from our lunches. A few seconds later, the voice called again. "Mi-ike?"

Michael grunted in annoyance. "She knows I hate being called that."

"I understand. I don't much care for my full name." I nodded understandingly, twirling spaghetti on my fork.

"What, Sandra?" He peered at me, curious.

"That's actually not it."

"Then what is it?"

"I'm not telling." I waved my fork at him in mock

threat. "If I tell you, then you'll be tempted to use it, and if you use it then I'll have to give you a shiner to match your jaw."

"Oh no, anything but that." He feigned terror briefly, then stood up and stretched. "I better go see what they want. They were out scavenging, so they probably found something big and want me to help them move it. You want to come meet them?"

"In a minute. I want to finish my food while it's hot; I'm pretty hungry." I gestured for him to go ahead without me. "Don't worry, I'll find you. You're kind of loud."

"I am not loud!" This time he was the one faking indignation, but it didn't last for long. His scowl melted into a grin, and he gave me a wink before he left the room.

I took my time finishing off my lunch, not entirely sure how I felt about meeting yet more potentially dangerous survivors. In spite of everything, I really felt like I could trust the three I'd met so far, but adding more strangers to the mix felt like I was pushing my luck somehow.

Still, Michael would probably bring them to me if I didn't go to them. I popped the last bite of spaghetti in my mouth and stood up to take my bowl and utensils to the sink. I rinsed them and left them to dry, then headed off in the direction my new friend had gone.

It didn't take me long to find them. He wasn't really all that loud, but voices did carry in these cold, concrete halls. I found him deep in conversation with a pair of young people, a man and a woman, over some item of salvage they wanted to bring back to base.

The male was a fairly short fellow in his early twenties, skinny as a rake with a shock of red hair and a plague of freckles across every inch of visible skin. By contrast, the woman was blonde and pretty, no older than eighteen or nineteen, with pale skin that showed just a touch of sunburn across the nose. Her hair was clipped at a practical shoulder length, and fell in tight natural curls that reminded me of my mother. I also noticed that she was heavily pregnant.

Some inexplicably jealous part of me hoped it wasn't Michael's baby.

"Hey," I called softly to announce myself, and the trio looked up from the map they were studying.

"Oh, hey, you must be Sandy. Michael was telling us about you. I'm Ryan." The redhead approached with a hand extended, and I managed to shake it without freaking out. I thought that was a pretty major achievement for Project: Tame Sandy – I didn't even hit anyone that time.

"Hi." My reply was a bit awkward but was functional, then I looked over at the young woman and froze when I realised that she was staring at me intently, looking puzzled.

"Sandy..." She repeated my name, as though trying it on for size, her brow furrowed. "Sandy McDermott?"

"Yes?" Something was going on here. How did she know my last name? I hadn't told anyone that. My brain shifted into overdrive. Then, something clicked and all the pieces fell into place.

The age, the hair, the complexion. This young woman was the spitting image of my mother from her old wedding photos. But, it couldn't be. It just couldn't be. Could it?

"...Skylar?"

Chapter Fourteen

There was a lot of squealing and bouncing and hugging as Skylar and I reunited. The men watched with bewildered expressions, clueless as to why we'd both suddenly gone mad – but we didn't care. We clung together making inarticulate noises, but too impossibly happy to form a rational thought.

After a whole decade, hundreds of kilometres of wandering, and against all odds, I had found my little sister alive and well. I could hardly believe it. Ten years I'd spent mourning for her, and all that time she was still alive. It seemed like a wonderful dream and I was afraid to think about it too much in case I woke up.

We were so noisy that we even attracted the doctor and his granddaughter from wherever they had been. With everyone gathered around, I finally managed to gasp down enough breath to explain the reason for our joy.

"This is my sister. My little, baby sister. Though not a baby anymore, by the looks of it." I eyeballed her pregnant belly and gave her a playful nudge, which made her giggle. Then the reality of the situation finally struck home and dampened my levity. "I thought you were dead, Skye. Where the hell did you go? Why didn't you meet us at the beach house?"

"I couldn't." Skylar clung to me like a limpet. I didn't mind – I was just as determined to cling back. "We got a flat tyre halfway there, so we tried to walk but we got lost. Dad found an empty farmhouse for us to sleep in, but I think he was already infected. He put me to bed one night, and when I woke up he was gone.

"Ryan's family owned the house. He was away at a school camp when the infection hit and had to walk home. When he got there, he found me hiding in his house and his family was all gone. He's been looking after me ever since."

"I can't believe it." Overcome by a surge of emotion, I squeezed my little sister so hard that she squealed in protest. "All these years, I thought you were dead. If I'd known, I would have come looking for you."

"I know. If I'd known you were alive, I would have done the same." Suddenly, she shoved me back and stared at me with huge, hope-filled eyes. "Is Mum alive, then? Grandma?"

My heart sank, knowing that I was going to have to break her heart all over again. I just shook my head.

"We made it to the beach house, but they got the infection anyway. I'm so sorry."

I hugged her tight and gave her a minute to absorb the information. She looked pretty crushed, but took the news well. I understood how she felt. I'd already mourned for Dad so much over the years that finally hearing for sure that he was dead didn't hurt nearly as much as I thought it would. That wound had scabbed over and turned into an old scar years ago.

"Well, at least I've got you again." Skye squinted up at me with tear-filled eyes, as though trying to figure out if I was the real thing. "Though, I do remember you being taller."

I shook my head and gave her a smile. "Nah, you were just shorter."

Suddenly, little Madeline decided that she'd heard enough of our nonsense. She stomped over and poked me unceremoniously in the bottom. I squeaked in surprise and looked down at her; her big brown eyes were narrowed suspiciously.

"Miss Skylar can't be your sister. Your sister is my age. You told me so." The little girl stomped petulantly, drawing a chuckle from the adults in the room. I stood awkwardly for a moment, not entirely sure how to respond to that. The childlike answer seemed like the best response, so I went with that.

"Well, she was your age when I last saw her, but she grew up. But, look." I poked Skylar's pregnant belly. "She's making a new baby for you to play with. That counts."

"But the baby won't be my age either," Madeline complained, pouting.

"She will be when she's your age." I selected a cryptic answer as though it made perfect sense.

"Ohhh." Maddy's eyes lit up as if she suddenly understood. "Well, I guess that's okay then. She can be your sister."

"Thanks for the permission." I smirked and shot an amused glance at the other adults in the room. Oblivious, Maddy skipped off and vanished down the corridor in search of something fun to do.

Awesome. Apparently I spoke fluent seven-year-old now. I should add that to my resume.

"That kid is so cute." Skye giggled and leaned up against me. Even as an adult, she was still a little shorter than me, but in some strange way that pleased me. At least she was still my little sister.

All grown up. Still alive. I marvelled at the fact. I could hardly believe it. After a decade, a whole decade, somehow we had both survived and found each other.

It was a miracle.

***

We didn't have much time to get reacquainted. As it turned out, Ryan and Skye had been off scouting for resources and had found a cache that had been opened up by the storm a few nights ago. An old tree had come down in the wind, taking out the wall of a building as it fell.

Once it had been a big general goods store, but the front of the building collapsed years ago, so whatever was inside had been sealed in ever since. When the tree fell, it exposed the stock room and all the merchandise that was hidden safely within. It was like a time capsule of retail greed and it was ours for the taking.

The good news, Skye told us, was that a lot of the stuff still looked viable – clothing, shoes, home wares and much more. The bad news was that we would have to be quick. The tree took out half the roof when it collapsed, so the stock was exposed to the elements.

"It's going to take us a lot of trips to get all that stuff back here. We could probably scavenge some shopping trolleys, but it's about two kilometres each way." Ryan peered down at the map spread out on the table as he explained the situation to us.

"We're going to need every able body." Skye shot me a pointed look. "You're on babysitting detail."

"Hey, I can help," I protested, feeling stung.

"With that?" Michael cut in, and pointed at my foot. "Oh no, you stay here." With one big hand, he reached out and gave my shoulder a gentle squeeze to soften the blow of what he had to say next. "With that injury, you're more of a liability than an asset in the field. You know that. Plus, someone has to stay here to protect Maddy if anything goes wrong."

My shoulders slumped. I didn't like it, but I knew they were right. Until it healed, my foot made me a liability. Still, I wanted to help in some way. This was my *sister*, for crying out loud. Her presence in this group changed everything.

"At least take my truck." I gave them a plaintive look. "It still has half a tank of gas, it should get you back and forth a few times."

"You have a truck?" Skye stared at me, wide-eyed. I squinted at Michael, who shrugged sheepishly.

"I forgot to mention it." He looked a little embarrassed. "I parked it in the garage with all the others, but none of them work and we don't know how to fix them, so we never really go in there."

"Huh." There were other vehicles? And these survivors didn't know how to repair them? I stored that piece of information away for later use. "Anyway, yeah, I resurrected an old ute. The back is pretty spacious."

"Thank you, Sandy. We appreciate the offer." Michael smiled that kind smile of his. "That'll help things go much more quickly."

I felt an unexpected flush of pride at his praise, but I just smiled back and nodded.

"All right, so we've got a plan." Michael turned to the others and took command with an ease that just seemed natural. "Sandy stays with Maddy, everyone else is with me. Has anyone seen Dog?" He looked around at the others, but they all shook their heads.

"He was off scouting this morning, like us." Skye shrugged. "I imagine he'll be back before dark."

"Hm, okay." Michael glanced over at me again. "If you see a skinny kid come waltzing in with a big black Labrador, don't panic. He's one of us. He's also deaf, so don't be offended if he doesn't hear you yelling at him. I'll leave a note for him on the fridge in case he gets back before we do."

I nodded my understanding.

"Right." Michael clapped his hands once, falling

into the leadership role by default. "Everyone, go get your gear. Ryan, come and help me get Sandy's stuff out of the car before we go." He looked at me. "You don't mind if we put it in your room, do you?"

I hesitated. They seemed perfectly happy to let me be selfish with my supplies, but for the first time in a very long time I felt like being generous.

"No, just add it to your stores." I smiled shyly. "You've all been so kind to me – I don't mind sharing."

Michael looked both surprised and pleased at my decision. He nodded his understanding, then clapped Ryan on the shoulder and vanished off down a corridor. The doctor left to gather his things, leaving me alone with Skylar. She beckoned for me to follow her, so I did. Together we made our way through the cold, concrete passages towards her room.

We walked in companionable silence, each of us hampered in our own way by our medical conditions – me by my foot, her by her swollen belly. Judging by the size of it, she must be at least seven months along, maybe even eight. She looked about ready to burst and yet she was still going, game to help with the search. I was impressed with her stubbornness and determination. That was a survivor's attitude.

Curiosity got the better of me at last; I just had to ask. "So, who's the dad?"

"Ryan, of course." Skylar grinned broadly and glanced over at me, her big blue eyes sparkling. "He's such a sweet guy, the way he's been taking care of me all these years. He was twelve when he found me, and I was eight of course, so we grew up together. A couple of years ago, we both kind of realised we were adults, things got a bit more serious, and, well—" She trailed off and rubbed a hand over her belly, smiling contentedly. "He's asked me to marry him, but we haven't found a living priest yet."

"I'm sure there's one around somewhere, we'll just have to find him." I gave her another mischievous little nudge – and tried to ignore the way relief flooded through me when she named her young companion as the father.

It concerned me a little bit that I felt that way, but it was a basic, animal kind of jealousy, even though I knew full well I had no right to feel jealous over Michael at all. He wasn't mine. I did find him attractive though, so perhaps some part of me wanted to claim him somehow. I wasn't sure. It'd just been such a long since I'd felt any kind of attraction to another human being. I didn't really know what to do about it anymore. I didn't even know if I wanted a relationship with any man, ever.

But when he gave me that quirky little half-smile of his, it made my gut do a backflip. I couldn't help but feel *something*.

"Hopefully." Skylar's voice interrupted my thoughts, and suddenly I felt the warmth of a small hand slipping into mine, just like when we were kids. "It doesn't really matter anymore. All that matters is the way we feel about each other, right?"

"Right," I agreed and gave her hand a squeeze.

"Aren't you worried, though? About the immunity, I mean?"

"What do you mean?" Her smile faded and she looked at me in concern.

"Well, I mean, about the immunity to the disease." I chewed my lip and stared down at my feet as we walked. "I guess you were too young. Before the internet went down, I found articles online from scientists that were studying the immunity. They said that they discovered the gene that makes us immune is a recessive gene—"

"What does that mean? Is my baby in danger?" Suddenly defensive, Skye stopped walking and grabbed me by the arms, her eyes wide.

"I-I don't know." I grabbed her in return and hugged her close, hating to be the bearer of bad news. "I just remember reading that they said there's no guarantee our immunity will be passed on to our children."

Skylar's lean frame shook in my arms. For a moment I was scared that she was crying, but when she pulled back and looked up at me I saw that her eyes were dry and her face set in a mask of determination.

"But there's a chance, right?" It wasn't a question – it was a demand. "There's still a chance my baby will be immune? I mean, Maddy was born after the outbreak, so there must be a chance."

"There's always a chance." She looked so resolute, and I had no evidence one way or another. It was the only answer I could think of.

I braced myself, expecting an explosion of some kind. Tears, shouting, blaming, something – but none of that came. She merely accepted my word with a curt nod and resumed walking. The only sign of whatever she might be feeling was that one small hand rose to protectively rub her belly.

I had no idea what to say after that, so I just stayed silent, feeling uncomfortable and confused. If it was me in her position, I would have been freaking the hell out and crawling up the walls.

Then it occurred to me that perhaps she was just tougher all around than I was. This was the only life she'd ever known, a life of death and struggle. Even if she lost her baby, she would still have Ryan to help her through it. That kind of emotional support was something that I'd never had.

I guess that was what made her so strong, while I was so fragile. I felt a little bit of envy creep into my thoughts, but it was suddenly dashed by a cold flash of realisation.

Crap. That means I'm the high-strung sister, doesn't it?

***

Skye and the others got their stuff together and left within ten minutes, leaving me alone in their bunker. As I limped along the corridors looking for little Madeline, I pondered over all the changes that had happened in my life in a few short days.

It'd only been a few hours since I first awoke from

my fever, and yet they trusted me enough to leave me alone with their possessions, including the most precious one of all – Maddy.

In return, I felt a sense of trust towards each of them that I hadn't felt since I lost my family. Skye's presence helped with that, of course, but that wasn't all. I felt a sense of trust towards Michael and the doctor that almost bordered on affection, despite the conversation I had eavesdropped on.

It had all happened so fast.

Michael's talk had reassured me and set my mind at ease. He helped me to understand that this group worked together, like an extended family. They weren't just a group of random castaways that had come together for mutual survival. I was surprised by how much they cared about one another. Each member was trusted just as much as any other. That was a rare thing in the world that we lived in since the plague.

Most of the gangs I had seen were just that – gangs, with one charismatic leader surrounded by a group of minions. They were not family. In most cases, they were hardly even friends. The gangs were held together by one thing: fear.

Despite the doctor's initial misgivings, they accepted me as one of their own. I felt both honoured and bewildered by their acceptance, but in such a short period of time I'd come to value it more than words could express. I had no desire to lose that trust, or do anything to violate it.

The behavioural conditions the doctor put on me

just made sense, and after everything I'd seen and suffered, I agreed with them. They were the very same conditions I would have put on him, if I were in his position. As upset as I was after hearing it, once I thought it through I realised that I understood his reasoning. I could respect that.

I was a little surprised that he had agreed to let me babysit Madeline, considering how worried he was at first. I could only guess that the revelation of my relationship with Skylar changed his opinion of the threat that I presented, since it kind of made me family too. It bound me to their group dynamic, and to their communal moral code. If I wanted to stay with my sister then I had to follow their rules.

I found Maddy in her room, playing with a couple of rag dolls. She didn't even look up when I entered the room, nor when I sat myself down on her bed with my back against the wall and crossed my legs comfortably. Whatever little game she had invented for herself was far more interesting than me.

Watching the little girl play, I thought back to when Skye and I were growing up together. I'd been ten when she was born, old enough to be fascinated by the new baby but young enough to not really understand her limitations. Mum had given me a thorough scolding when she caught me filling the newborn's crib up with every Barbie doll I owned.

I had been the only child up to that point, and the only grandchild as well, so I had a *lot* of Barbies. The memory made me smile. I was only trying to share.

Madeline looked up at me at last, her head tilted curiously to one side. "What are you grinning for?"

"Nothing. Just thinking." I covered my tracks hastily to avoid having to explain my thoughts to the little girl. "I like your dollies."

"Thanks." Maddy beamed and held up her dolls one by one as she named them for me. "This one is Granddaddy, this one is Mummy, and this one is Mister Michael."

The Michael doll had a piece of old Velcro for hair, and was so overstuffed in the chest that it took all of my willpower to keep myself from laughing out loud.

"What about that one?" I asked to distract myself, and pointed to a fourth doll that sat lonely in a corner, excluded from her games.

Maddy reached over and picked it up, frowning down at the doll. "It was Sophie. But Sophie died. Playing with her makes me feel sad."

Is that the sound of my heart breaking? Why yes, I believe it is.

I watched her set the doll back down, propped against the leg of the bed.

"I'm sorry to hear that. Was Sophie your friend?" I asked the question gently, hoping to gain a little insight into the group so that I could be careful of the subject in future.

"Yes. We used to play together lots and lots." Maddy looked even more upset now, and I suddenly realised I'd crossed a line. Michael had lost his niece, but Maddy had lost her only friend. I hurried to change the subject.

"Hey, I have an idea. Do you want to help me make something?" I asked swiftly, praying she'd take the bait.

She did.

"What kind of something?" The little girl asked, looking up at me curiously from where she sat on the floor.

"I was going to make everyone a big bowl of fruit salad to share for dessert. I could use a hand."

Generosity wasn't an emotion that I felt often, but when I did, it hit me like a sledgehammer to the face. Besides, there was no reason to let all of that fruit go to waste, when there were plenty of hungry mouths that could use the vitamins.

"Fruit salad, like from the cans?" She looked up at me with big brown eyes, curious. "Granddad lets me have those sometimes."

"No." I shook my head, then stood and offered the little girl my hand. "I mean a real fruit salad, made from fresh fruit."

"Fruit from a tree?" Madeline's eyes went huge, but she bounced up to her feet and took my hand anyway, following obediently as I led her from the room.

"That's right, real fruit from a real tree." I smiled down at her incredulous expression. "Not from a can. It even has skin on it."

"Fruit doesn't have skin." She gave me an owl-eyed look, like I was crazy.

"Yes it does, but they take the skin off before they

put it in the can."

"But, why does a fruit have skin?"

Okay, she had me there.

"Uh... I don't know." I shrugged. "To protect the soft, squishy inside bits, I guess. That's why *you* have skin. I'll show you and prove it, though. I brought some fruit with me, but Mister Michael put it into cold storage so we'll have to go find it."

"Okay." She agreed happily, and together we went off in search of fruit.

Our first stop was the storage room I found earlier, and the big commercial refrigerators within. I opened them one by one, until at last I found my bags of fruit. They were untouched and unopened, just the way I left them when I put them in the truck three days before.

I hoisted them awkwardly and hobbled off towards the kitchen with Madeline hot on my heels. When I set the bags down on the table in the kitchen, she was quick to hop up on a chair and look inside them.

"What's this?" she asked, holding up a glossy red fruit and staring at it in confusion.

"That is an apple." I felt so useful for having knowledge that someone else didn't have, even if she was a child. "It's delicious. You can eat it if you like, but make sure you wash it first."

She sniffed it and examined it thoroughly, then hopped off the chair and scampered over to the sink to do as I instructed. While she was busy, I opened each of the bags and began sorting out the fruit that was the ripest and needed to be eaten swiftly, from that which would last a while longer. A few pieces were overripe and would need to be thrown out, so I set them aside. Ah, such a waste, but that was life.

"This is amazing!"

I glanced over my shoulder at the girlish squeal behind me, to find that Maddy had taken her first bite of a real apple. She devoured it in record time, then raced over and went to grab another one.

I caught her hand to stop her, and gave her a playful grin. "Don't eat too many, you'll get sick. Plus, we've got to save some for dessert."

She pouted, but obediently retracted her hand.

What a good kid. Although I was not the most maternal person by nature, I still reached over and gave her a pat on the head.

"Okay, now I need a big bowl, a real big bowl. Is there one here?" I asked her, and her eyes lit up. She nodded rapidly, glossy black tresses flying all around her face, then she scampered off to fetch a big plastic bowl from one of the low cupboards. She came rushing back a moment later and held the bowl up to me triumphantly.

"Perfect." She beamed at my praise as I took the bowl from her little hands and put it on the table. "So what we're going to do, is we're going to wash all this fruit, cut it up, and put it in the bowl all mixed together. That's a fruit salad."

"Ooohh." She sounded genuinely amazed, and my heart melted a bit. I'd honestly forgotten how adorable little kids could be.

"Yeah, it's very yummy. " I picked up a few pieces of fruit and offered them to her. "I'll do the cutting, but my foot hurts so I should sit down as much as possible. Can you wash the fruit for me?"

Madeline nodded enthusiastically, and snatched the fruit from my hands. She scampered over to the sink and started washing them with a determined thoroughness. While she was busy, I rose to find a knife in one of the drawers and a chopping board in a cupboard, then returned to the table. I wasn't kidding about my foot hurting. All the walking I'd been doing recently was starting to make it ache something terrible.

Still, it felt good to be doing something useful for others; I felt helpful, productive and a little bit domesticated.

I'd even go so far as to say it made me feel like a good person.

I hadn't felt like that in a long, long time.

V. L. Dreyer

Chapter Fifteen

Maddy and I had finished our project and returned to her bedroom to play with her dolls when the ruckus started.

My head shot up. I was on my feet a moment later, immediately alert for danger. My hand instinctively went to the pockets of my cargos, but I swore when I realised my taser was not close at hand. Maddy gasped and giggled at my naughty language, but she didn't seem concerned at all.

"Granddaddy's back, Granddaddy's back!"

She leapt to her feet, chanting gleefully, and skipped out of the room before I could stop her. Concerned she might be mistaken, I hurried after her as fast as I could, but she was small and nimble and was gone before I even made it to the door.

Oh great. I'd lost my charge on my first day of babysitting duty. For all I knew there was a hoard of mutated infected coming this way right now.

Thankfully, I was wrong.

"Out the way, Maddy-monkey!"

The voice was deep and commandingly male. It took me a second to realise that it was Michael's voice, and that he just sounded a little different when he was out of breath. He rounded the corner a moment later, burdened by a huge box of god-knows-what but looking flushed and excited regardless. Madeline was bouncing around him trying to see what was in the box, full to the brim with energy in that way only a small child can be.

I grabbed the little girl as she passed by and gently restrained her to keep her out of the way as the loot-procession moved past us. It took them a couple of trips to bring in all of the goodies they found, with the men carrying the heavier items and insisting that Skylar only carry lighter objects. As much as their chivalry seemed to piss Skylar off, it gave me a bit of a warm feeling to see men being gentlemanly in this day and age.

She stopped beside me after one trip to catch her breath and greet Madeline, and while we were talking she mentioned that they found a lot of useful things in the store alongside the general home wares. They found camping equipment, tools, gardening utensils and even seeds that they suspected would probably still be viable. Although there was no space to grow them here, they brought them all anyway since they might prove vital in the future.

I agreed, of course. You never knew what you'd need one day. Even if we never used the seeds, a rake could be a handy weapon in a pickle. Besides, every one of us was aware in our own way that we couldn't keep living off the skeleton of a dead society forever. Eventually, we would need to fend for ourselves and become self-sufficient.

They wouldn't let me do much to help with the unpacking due to my injury, so I settled for keeping Madeline distracted and out from underfoot. For whatever reason, she was extremely excited and possessed more energy than all of us adults combined. As I followed her around, I found myself wondering how my mother had managed to do this for all those years. No wonder she always looked so tired.

In the end, I distracted the little girl by getting her to help me make dinner. There wasn't much that we could do that was terribly creative, but we did our best with the resources at hand. By combining canned meat with tinned Italian-style tomatoes, we managed to craft a fair approximation of spaghetti bolognese. The packets of dried pasta that we found in the storage room were a little bit floppy, but when they were cooked they tasted just fine.

When the exhausted survivors finally finished their task and filed into the kitchen, Maddy sat them down around the table and handed out plates and utensils like a pint-sized maître d'. She took the job so seriously that everyone was smiling by the time the food was ready. When I served up the food, it was met with exclamations of surprise and delight. As I found out later, no one really bothered to try and make something that resembled real food anymore.

I never did either, so I understood. I just felt like

impressing my newfound family in some small way. To them, I probably looked like a puppy desperately wanting a pat on the head, but nobody said anything.

After dessert, which was a treat for everyone, they thanked me one by one and trundled off to bed. The doctor and Maddy went one way, Skylar and Ryan another, but Michael stayed behind to help me clean up.

"Thank you for doing that," he said as he stacked the dirty dishes in the sink, while I was busy clearing the leftover food off the table. I glanced at him and found him smiling at me. "I haven't eaten like that in a long time. You're a good cook."

A hot flush crept into my cheeks at his praise and I looked away, feeling embarrassed. "My mother would disagree with you. She kept trying to teach me to cook, and then getting frustrated with me and chasing me out of the kitchen." The warmth faded away as my thoughts drifted back to my family, and I found myself staring down at the table thoughtfully. "I miss her."

That was the first time I had admitted that fact to another human being since my grandmother died. It was kind of cathartic, to tell someone the truth about how I felt. I didn't quite know why I felt like I could talk to Michael so freely, but something told me that he would understand.

"I know." His voice was soft and thoughtful, barely audible over the sound of the sink filling with water. "I miss my mother, too. All of my family. Especially Sophie."

Even though I was still out of practice at reading expressions and tones of voice, it sounded like the first time he had admitted that to anyone, as well.

Perhaps it was. He'd taken it upon himself to act as the de facto leader of this group, which meant he had to be the strong one, the one who always stayed positive for the sake of everyone else. Admitting that he could be hurt was difficult for him. Even with my rusty social skills, I sensed a great need in him that had gone ignored for far too long.

"Do you want to talk about it?" I offered tentatively, uncertain how my offer would be taken.

He shook his head, and stared intently at the filling sink as though it were the most important thing in the world. "Not really." After a long moment, his shoulders slumped and he looked back at me. "But I guess I should talk to someone."

There was so much pain in those kind eyes that I wanted to run over and comfort him right then and there. But I didn't. I couldn't. I was frozen with indecision. While I hesitated, he opened up and told me the story of his pain.

***

All of his life, Michael had known that he wanted to be an officer of the law.

As a child, he was that kid who always showed up to fancy dress parties in a police uniform — with the exception of a brief stint when he was six, when he decided that he wanted to be an astronaut instead. The infatuation with outer space lasted all of a couple of weeks before he lost interest and went back to his original dream.

He grew up in an affluent suburb of east Auckland with his parents and his older brother. His mother was born and raised in Beijing, while his father was of mixed race, a union of European and Asian bloodlines who had been born and raised in New Zealand.

They met while his father was in Beijing on business, fell in love and married. Michael was three and his brother was six when the family returned to New Zealand in search of a brighter future for their children.

The children were raised bilingual and multicultural from an early age. Michael's mother was intensely ambitious when it came to her children's futures, the way Chinese mothers sometimes are. She insisted that they learn multiple languages and instruments, and always demanded that they do well in school.

His father was much more relaxed and was perfectly content to let Michael do whatever he wanted, but it was his mother who was the dominant parent in their union and it was her will that ruled the nest. Michael's childhood was one of school and endless tutoring, with very little time for friends or fun.

For years, his mother tried to convince him to become an architect or an accountant or a doctor, but Michael stayed resolute. He watched his brother grow up and go off to university, following his mother's dream of a good career, but Michael didn't care about money or prestige. All he wanted to do with his life was to protect and serve.

By the time he finished high school, Michael was fluent in four more languages in addition to the English and Mandarin that they spoke at home. He was an excellent student with top grades, head prefect and a prominent member of the athletics team. He could play the flute and the cello with reasonable competence, and showed a genuine talent for the violin. Although he had few friends, all of his teachers agreed that he was a diligent, intelligent and affable young man with a bright future ahead of him.

In spite of all of that, Michael never doubted for a second which career he would choose.

He could have been anything, but the only thing he wanted was to be a police officer. Every ounce of effort he put into his studies was just another means to push himself a little bit closer to that goal. The same day that he graduated from high school, he applied to the Royal New Zealand Police College and was accepted. Six months later, he graduated with honours, and was offered a position in Hamilton.

Eager to be about the career he'd longed for all his life, he took the position and moved south. In spite of the move and the clashes with his wilful mother, he was a good son and loved his family. He returned to Auckland often to visit them, and made sure to always be there for important family events. He was there for his brother's graduation from university and his wedding, and there for every Christmas. He was there when his only niece, Sophie, was born, and he was there for her first birthday.

When the plague first started to spread, the constables were kept well informed. He told me about the dread he felt in the pit of his stomach when he heard the news that the infection had reached New Zealand's shores. He'd spent what felt like forever trying to phone his mother, his father, and his brother and sister-in-law, trying desperately to reach anyone in his family.

There was no answer; the phone lines were always engaged. No one answered his emails or his text messages. It was like they were simply gone.

Then the riots started and he was too busy to think about his family anymore. Day and night, he was out trying to calm the panicked populace of his adopted home, only to see them fall ill one by one. The only person he could rely on was his partner, an older police officer that he'd been paired with to help him learn the ropes.

But then his partner got sick.

By the time Michael fought through the crowds to get him to the hospital, he'd lost the ability to speak and his eyes were glazed over. The nurses swept him away without a word, leaving Michael to do his job alone.

By that stage, the riots were starting to fade. People were just too sick to put up a fight anymore. Michael did his best to make them as comfortable as possible, but there was nothing he could do to help them. Exhausted and helpless, the young police officer spent every day and every night out in the city helping anyone that he could, while waiting for instructions from his superiors on what to do.

The orders never came.

At last, he returned to the police station only to find it completely abandoned. Everyone was gone, from the administration staff to the senior sergeant. For the longest time, he sat alone in the break room, the very room we were in now, as he tried to figure out what to do.

Like all of us, he'd heard through the media that there were some people with a natural immunity to the disease, but he never considered that he would be one of them. He never imagined that he would be left all alone with no one to guide him. He was just 22 years old, from a sheltered background and a career where he was still used to having someone to boss him around and tell him what to do.

Now there was no one.

He looked me in the eye when he admitted that he'd been terrified. I knew he was ashamed to admit it, but I just nodded. I understood. I had been, too.

"I abandoned my post," he told me flatly without breaking eye contact. "I took my squad car and went north, along the motorway towards Auckland. The only thing I could think about was finding out what happened to my family."

He explained that halfway there he came across overturned trucks blocking the entire span of the motorway, forcing him to abandon his car and travel the rest of the way home on foot. It was more than twenty kilometres, but he walked and walked until finally, he reached the house where he grew up.

The house was empty, the door thrown wide and partially broken off its hinges. He saw signs of looting, but no blood and no clue that told him where his parents were. There were no messages, no notes and the computer was gone so he couldn't see if there were any half-written emails that they just never had the chance to finish. He told me how he used the last of the battery power in his cell phone to try and ring theirs, but again there was no answer.

Frozen with indecision, he waited for hours to see if perhaps his parents would return. He sat in his favourite armchair, the one he'd spent many hours in doing homework while he was growing up, and stared at the door. Hoping, praying.

His parents never came. No one did. Finally, he forced himself to make a decision on his own. He needed to find out what happened to his brother.

It was close to sunset when he reached his brother's house. Again, the door was unlocked so he let himself in, and called out his brother and sister-in-law's names at the top of his voice. There was no answer. On the wall near the door, the telephone hung off the hook; the endless dial tone was a low, sad sound. He picked it up and set it back in the cradle, not sure what else he could do.

Then, he heard the baby crying from upstairs.

He raced up as fast as he could go, taking the stairs two or three at a time, to find his tiny niece sitting in her crib. She was exhausted, filthy and starving from being trapped there for so long without food or water; her bed had become a cage.

When she saw him, the two-year-old cried his name and reached for him frantically with tiny, grasping hands.

He scooped her up without a moment of hesitation and carried her back down the stairs to her high chair. Although he had no children of his own, paternal instincts kicked in and soon the toddler was fed and changed.

She was terrified though, he told me. Terrified of being abandoned again. Any time he put her down, she started crying. Any time he left her line of sight, she screamed. He was desperate to leave before he went crazy, but he couldn't leave the baby behind. It just wasn't an option.

While he was gathering the little girl's things in preparation for their departure, something out in the back yard caught his eye. He told me how he went outside with the baby huddled in his arms, and found his brother and sister-in-law standing there in the semi-darkness on the lawn.

They were completely unresponsive, and stared off into space with cold, glazed eyes. They didn't even blink when he and Sophie called out to them, nor did their eyes focus when he moved into their line of sight and waved to them.

They were already gone.

Sophie was too young to understand. She cried and cried when he took her away; she didn't understand why they were leaving Mummy and Daddy behind. She didn't know what he knew, that once the infection took their speech away, there was no turning back. That wasn't his brother anymore, it wasn't little Sophie's mummy and daddy.

But how could he possibly explain that to a two-year-old?

Fuelled by terror and a desperate need to protect the one family member he had left, he took the tiny child and carried her south. He walked non-stop through the night, pausing only to eat, drink and feed Sophie, and then he picked her up again and walked some more. Eventually, Sophie fell into an exhausted sleep in his arms, but still he walked on. He'd never walked so far in his life, and by the time he reached safety it felt like his legs were about to drop off.

With no other option and no one to give him a better idea, Michael took his precious cargo back to the only safe place he could think of – his home away from home in the crew quarters beneath the Hamilton police station.

There, he raised her like his own daughter, and taught her all the hard lessons he had to learn to survive in the world after humanity was gone. He watched her grow, taught her to read and write, played with her she was little, and told her stories about her daddy from his own childhood.

He was always honest with her and never babied her. He took her with him when he was scavenging because experience was the only way that she would learn. Sophie had been a sweet and intelligent child who learned quickly, and soon became as useful as any of the adults who later joined the group.

***

"If only I hadn't been so lenient." He finally turned to look at me, his eyes filled with so much sadness that my heart dropped into my stomach. "If only I'd insisted that she stay home where it's safe. I only turned my back for a second.

"I didn't notice that she'd run off. We were out poking around, and I guess she saw something that caught her eye. I have no idea what it was, and I guess now I'll never know. I only heard her scream, but by the time I got to her it was too late. The infected had already torn her throat out and it was— hitting her. She was still alive, but only just. I managed to get it off her, but she was bleeding out and I knew she was dying. I tried to get her home, but she didn't make it."

Michael drew a deep, rough breath and put a hand over his face, like he didn't want me to see his emotion. But I knew and I understood. It was a fresh wound, still raw. It had only been a few days since he watched the little girl he loved like a daughter die a horrible, painful death. Even after so long alone, I still felt all the human emotions, like sympathy, remorse and grief.

In that moment when he needed me most, I put

aside my fear of other survivors completely. I wrapped my arms around him and just held him, not saying a word while he grieved for the poor child snatched away long before her time.

With each of us distracted in a different way, it wasn't until much later that any of us realised that we'd forgotten one important thing: night had fallen, and the kid named Dog still hadn't come home.

That was an oversight that we would come to regret.

Chapter Sixteen

I slept poorly that night, tossing and turning in my bed as my mind went over and over Michael's story. For the longest time, there had only been one story in my head, and that was my own. I had never even considered the terrible things that other survivors had gone through, and now my psyche was in distress.

In my nightmares, it was me making that long, long trek between the cities, frightened and alone except for a little girl begging and begging and begging to see her mummy again.

Please, please, she pleaded in my dream, twisting her little hands in the fabric of my uniform. Her little face was a blur, since my subconscious didn't have a face to give her.

I want my mummy...

Just before dawn, I awoke in a cold sweat, unsure whether it was the nightmare that had interrupted my sleep, or some sound I heard. Years of living on my own had left me a very light sleeper. I felt like I might have heard something, but I couldn't be certain. I lay awake in the dark, straining my ears for anything out of the ordinary, but I heard only silence. I brushed it off as a figment of my imagination, then rolled over and closed my eyes once more.

Then I heard it, clear as a bell: A whispery voice begging for help, but struggling to form the words. I came awake instantly and was out of bed a second later, dressed in nothing but a grey nightshirt. There was a wet cough beyond the door and a faint scraping sound.

I froze, listening intently.

The noises were so soft that I could barely hear them. I was the closest, so it seemed unlikely that anyone else would hear them at all. It was up to me to investigate.

I fumbled for my taser in the dark before I switched on the light. My room was as I'd left it. The noise was definitely coming from outside. I thought I could hear someone crying, and then there was another sodden cough. Whatever was out there, it couldn't possibly be a threat. It sounded pathetic, injured. Harmless.

I didn't feel reassured. My back was up, so to speak, and I was ready for a fight.

Then my sleep-addled thoughts darted to something that someone said the day before. I think it was Michael. He mentioned another survivor, a deaf boy that was staying with them. I thought back to the previous night, and realised I hadn't seen anyone matching that description come back to the bunker. I was paranoid, but I wasn't stupid; I swiftly put two and two together.

Taser in hand, in case whoever or whatever had injured the boy was still nearby, I threw open the door and stepped out into the murky hall.

A moment later, the weapon slipped from my fingers and clattered to the ground. My hands flew up to my mouth in horror.

There was so much blood. So much blood.

"Dr Cross!" I turned and raced down the corridor with no thought of my foot at all, panic and adrenaline dulling the pain. When I reached the doctor's door, I beat on it with my fists and screamed his name as loud as I could until finally it opened.

"What? What is it?" The doctor looked sleepy and confused. I couldn't get the words to come out the way I wanted, so I just grabbed him by the wrist and dragged him back to where the wounded survivor lay in a puddle of blood.

I'd seen enough death in my lifetime to know how much blood is in the human body. I could hardly believe that poor boy was still breathing.

The kid lifted his head and looked at us pitifully with his one remaining eye; the other had been torn from his head along with half his scalp. Flesh hung in tattered strips off the bone around the empty socket.

"Help..." Blood dribbled from his lips as he struggled to speak, but then he coughed again. It was a terrible spasm that racked his entire body with pain, and blood sprayed from his mouth across the cold concrete floor.

"Oh, sweet mother Mary." Dr Cross dropped to his knees beside the young man, ignoring the blood that soaked his trousers. I heard a cry behind me, and turned to see that Skylar and Ryan had joined us. The doctor looked at us and started issuing orders.

"Skylar, fetch my medical kit, now." He words were a command and Skye jumped to obey them. "Ryan, go check all the outside doors are closed. And you—" He pointed at me. "—go fetch Michael!"

I nodded and raced off, limping as fast as my body would let me. The leader of the group slept in a different area of the building, so he was unlikely to have heard the racket we were making – or so I assumed.

As it turned out, I underestimated exactly how loud I'd been screaming. As I rounded the corner into the corridor that led to Michael's room, I found myself face to face with a broad, bare chest. I crashed into it before I could slow down, and almost bowled him off his feet.

He managed to brace himself just in time and caught me before I could fall.

"I heard something..."

I was out of breath from the run and the panic, and struggled to form coherent words. I only managed to get out one: "Dog."

It was enough. Michael looked in the direction that I pointed, immediately understanding what I meant. He set me back on my feet and raced off, with me in hot pursuit. Every second was precious, while a human life was bleeding out on the floor.

I was the last to return to the group besides Ryan,

who was still off checking on our security. During the short time I'd been gone, Dr Cross had acquired a bundle of towels and was trying frantically to stem the blood flowing from the young man's terrible, terrible wounds.

The face wasn't the worst of it, I realised with horror. Poor Dog's torso was a mess of deep cuts, with chunks of flesh missing completely in a number of places. His left hand was gone, severed at the wrist and pumping blood from the ragged stump. The doctor had managed to staunch it with a tourniquet, but I feared it was already too late.

"Help me get him into his bed." The doctor looked at Michael, who hurried over to obey. He knelt to carefully lift the youth in his arms, trying hard not to jostle him but the injuries were so extensive that it seemed like an impossible task. The boy looked so small and fragile compared to Michael's lean bulk that in my imagination he weighed next to nothing. With half of his face missing, I couldn't even guess at his age.

Silently, I hoped I would have the chance to ask him one day.

Dog cried piteously, his one remaining hand grasping at Michael's shoulder as he was lifted. He was in excruciating pain and fighting for his life, I realised. Terrified. Alone. Trapped in a dark, silent world. His one remaining eye darted about but blood hindered his vision, and I could see the muscles inside the empty socket twitching convulsively to match. The sight was almost enough to make me throw up.

The poor boy. I'd never really wished death on another human being in my life, but right now I found myself praying he would die soon just so that he wouldn't have to suffer any more. It seemed impossible for us to save him. I couldn't bear to watch his torment, but I couldn't just run away and hide. Nobody should ever have to die alone.

Suddenly, the boy's good eye cleared and found Michael's face; recognition flashed across what was left of his.

"Muh... Muh..."

He stumbled over his words, obviously trying to say his friend's name, but he couldn't get it out. Tears gathered in his eye and he began signing frantically with his one remaining hand, trying to express with his own language what he couldn't do with the spoken word.

"Calm down, buddy. You're home, we've got you." Michael tried to reassure him as he carried him to his bed and gently lay him down on the sheets. I wondered if the boy could even see him clearly enough to read his lips. The moment he was safely down, the doctor shoved Michael away and went to work trying to save the poor kid's life before he bled to death.

Skylar and I huddled by the door, watching with mute despair as the doctor began his makeshift surgery. When Michael joined us, Skye handed him a towel from the bundle she clutched. He was covered in blood from moving poor Dog to his room, and he accepted it without a word to wipe himself down.

Once he was as clean as he could be, Michael

tossed the towel out into the hall and looked around to check on the rest of his group. He took one look at me then put an arm around me and pulled me up against his side. My expression must have been transparent as glass – I was pretty upset. Okay, really, really upset. I felt no desire to protest, strike him or shove him off. I just hugged him back in silence, shaking like a leaf from the adrenaline and horror of it all.

I'd seen wounds before, terrible wounds, even wounds that I'd inflicted – but I'd never felt so helpless.

Ryan returned, out of breath from his run.

"The doors are all locked, I don't think anything followed him in," he announced breathlessly and joined us in our huddle. He took Skylar's hand to comfort her, and looked around at the rest of us. "There's blood everywhere. Is he...?"

"He's alive, but I don't know how much longer he'll last." Skylar's voice was grim.

I half-expected the doctor to yell at us and tell us not to give up hope, but he was too busy to even notice us. This was not some TV drama where the patient always makes a miraculous recovery by the end of the episode. Our reality was so much more brutal.

A life hung by the slenderest of threads.

With a flash of guilt, I realised that it came down to me, one choice made in a heartbeat. If I'd slept a little bit deeper, then we would have awoken come morning to find nothing but a corpse in a puddle of blood. It might have even been Madeline that found him. Somehow, that thought was even more horrifying than anything else.

I'd almost missed the sound of the poor boy's struggles. I'd almost decided to just roll over and go back to sleep. Tears welled up in my eyes and I brushed them away hurriedly, trying to reassure myself that there was nothing more I could have done. But try as I might, I couldn't quite shake the unreasonable feeling that somehow, this was my fault.

The four of us stood dumbly for ten minutes before Skye excused herself to go check on Madeline, and Ryan left to go start the job of cleaning up the blood before it congealed. Michael offered to help him, but Ryan declined. Someone needed to stay with the Doc in case he needed anything.

He was right, of course, so we stayed. One by one, the doctor stitched torn flesh back together where possible, or bound it as best as he could where it was not, until the youth was a mass of bandages with just one eye and a patch of soft brown skin visible. The eye was closed in blessed, drug-induced sleep.

Thankfully, Dr Cross stockpiled anaesthetics. Just looking at those injuries made me feel nauseated – I could only imagine how poor Dog felt. It seemed like it was only sheer willpower that had kept him alive for so long.

At last, exhausted, Dr Cross sat back and looked at us. His face was a mask of regret. "That's the best I can do, but he's lost a lot of blood. He needs a blood transfusion, but even with one I'm not sure he'll live."

"But there's a chance he'll survive?" Michael asked,

his voice sharp and hard.

Dr Cross hesitated, then shrugged. "There's always a chance."

Michael nodded curtly and slipped his arm out from around me. He moved past me, further into the room, and dragged a worn old chair close to the bed so that he could sit down. He offered his arm to the doctor without a word, who stared back at him in confusion.

"What are you—"

"I'm O-negative, the universal donor. *Do it.*" Michael's voice was a hiss; looking startled, the doctor nodded and started setting up his equipment for a transfusion.

Great, more needles. I already felt queasy, but at the same time I didn't want to leave Michael to suffer alone. That seemed so wrong. Although my moral code might have been a little askew after all these years, I still had one. Michael was my friend, and he was doing something very brave. He deserved my support. Lacking any other option that was remotely useful, I sat down on the floor beside his chair and rested my head against his leg.

He looked surprised by the gesture, and stared down at me thoughtfully. I felt a gentle hand stroke my hair as we both tried to ignore the needle being inserted into his arm. Even though no words passed between us, there was a silent understanding: I was offering comfort, and he was accepting it. I took his hand in mine and put my cheek against it, giving him what support I could from simple closeness and human warmth.

It was true that I was socially retarded, but I wasn't without instincts. There were risks associated with what he was doing, but I understood why he *had* to do it. It was his friend's life at stake. If there was even the slimmest chance that he could help, then any risk was worth it. If he didn't, how would he live with himself afterwards?

I closed my eyes and tried to ignore the metallic scent of blood, just waiting for it to be over.

***

When the transfusion was done, I helped Michael back to his room. He was pale and shaky from blood loss and did not complain when I tucked him back into bed with doctor's orders to stay put. Feeling unexpectedly protective, I brought him some fruit and water a few minutes later, and waited with him while he ate.

When he finally closed his eyes to rest, I left him to it. I closed the door softly and padded back out into the hallway with barefoot stealth, to check on the doctor and Dog.

The doctor looked exhausted, and was intensely focused on his patient. I suspected that he would get so wrapped up in his patient he'd forget about himself, so I brought him some food and water as well.

It took a fair amount of bullying to get him to take food with his patient struggling for life. Eventually, I managed to convince him that Dog stood no chance at all if his doctor fainted from hunger when he needed him most. When I was sure I could trust him to take care of his own needs as well, I departed and went off to check on the others.

Maddy was still sleeping, innocent as the child she was, so I left her in peace. I found Ryan and Skylar hard at work mopping up blood, so I joined them instead. Three sets of hands would make the work go faster, and there was an awful lot of blood. We worked in silence for some time, until Skye finally got up to go take the soiled towels off to be washed, leaving me alone with Ryan.

His head came up and he watched her until she was out of earshot. When she was gone, he turned to me with a worried look on his face.

"Skye told me what you said to her yesterday, about the immunity."

My heart sank, but I nodded. "I only know what I've read. I don't know if there's more to it, or maybe they were wrong."

"We don't want to risk it." His voice was soft. "We're going to leave, go south, try and find a little farm somewhere. We want our baby to be born as far away from danger as possible."

This time my heart went the exact opposite direction and leapt up into my throat. "You're leaving? Have you— have you told Michael yet?"

"Not yet. We only decided last night." Ryan looked down at the puddle he was mopping, a myriad of emotions playing across his face. "We're not really a hundred per cent sure what we're going to do. From what you've said, there's a whole bunch of other dangers out there. And now these– things, these mutants, killing us one by one."

"You're just thinking about your baby's safety. I understand." I felt sick at the thought of losing my sister after I'd only just found her, but equally sick about leaving sweet Michael and little Maddy behind. And the doctor, too. I was still a little uncertain about how I felt, but I understood why he'd said those awful things about me and I was in the process of forgiving him. "Maybe we should all go. It would be safer in numbers."

Ryan looked at me with a mixture of hope and despair. "Do you think they would?"

"I don't know. But like you said, it's not safe here anymore." I tossed a bloody towel out of the way, then I looked at his earnest young face and offered him a faint smile. "We'll talk about it with Michael when he recovers. I know a place we could go, for a while at least."

"Really?" His expression brightened.

"Yeah, there's this town south of here that I spent some time in." It felt strange to willingly share my haven with others, but it also felt like the right thing to do. "It's as safe as any other place I've seen down there. It could probably be even safer if we put a little effort in to fortifying it."

He nodded, and hope brought a smile to his freckled face. I offered a silent prayer that I wasn't leading the lad to his death, or worse.

Only time would tell.

***

In spite of everyone's best efforts, the kid named Dog died two days later, surrounded by the group of survivors he'd come to call his family. Just before he passed, he managed to tell Michael what happened to him with awkward, one-handed sign language.

"He was with his dog when they attacked him." Michael was translating for us, signing back to the boy to confirm he understood what he was being told. The boy nodded stiffly, his one good eye almost glazed over. "Several infected knocked him down, and they were eating him when his dog attacked them. His dog fought for him while he ran away, and then he came home as fast as he could."

Eating him? I felt sick at the thought and leaned against Skylar for support. Judging by how pale she was, she was caught up on the same word as well.

Dog's hand was trembling as he signed, making it hard for Michael to understand him.

"What?" Michael looked confused and upset, signing to the young boy and speaking out loud for our sake. "Of course you'll go to Heaven one day, son, but not yet."

Dog smiled weakly up at him and shook his head, then signed one last sentence before he rested his head back on his pillow and closed his eye. With one last deep, rattling breath, he left our mortal world of suffering to explore whatever lay beyond.

We all knew instinctively that he was gone, even before the doctor leaned over to check his pulse. Skye burst into tears and hugged me, while I stood dumbstruck, not sure how to feel. I hadn't known him at all, and now he was one more person that I would never have the opportunity to meet; I felt a sense of grief and loss for the friendship we would never be able to share.

I would never have the opportunity to ask him how old he was. Never have the chance to ask how he got his name. We would never get to share those moments of laughter and camaraderie or any of the other things I longed for over the years.

I looked at Michael, and found him staring at that young face, that seemed so very small against the pillows.

"What did he say?" I asked, even though I was afraid to hear the answer.

Michael looked at me, his expression unreadable. At first, he didn't quite seem to understand the question. It took a second before comprehension sunk in, and then he closed his eyes and smiled weakly.

"He said he was going to go see Sophie again. He promised to tell her how much we all loved her." His voice shook and cracked, but somehow he stayed strong.

I didn't. That was enough for me. I melted down in tears, and cried for what felt like a very long time.

***

We buried them side by side, in Soldiers Memorial Park. It seemed like an appropriate place to entomb survivors who had spent their whole lives fighting an impossible enemy against insurmountable odds, and it was a beautiful green place where the huge, old willow trees overhung the river.

A nice place to spend the rest of eternity.

Wildflowers had already begun to grow atop Sophie's grave. As the men lay Dog into a hole beside her, I marvelled at how swiftly nature reclaims us when we are gone.

I knelt and picked a particularly beautiful flower that grew at my feet, and wonder briefly what species it was. I didn't know, but it was lovely. I stepped close to the grave and I dropped it atop the corpse before they began to shovel the dirt onto him. Perhaps the flower's seeds would sprout and cover the grave with its children.

The sun felt far too bright to be putting someone so young into the earth. I had found out his age after all, from Michael and the others. He was only twenty-three.

I blinked back tears as I retreated to where Skylar stood holding Madeline, who watched blankly as the men laboured to shift the dirt back into the hole. She looked up at me as I neared her, then suddenly a bright smile lit up her young face.

"Don't worry, Miss Sandy." She reached out and took my hand. "Mummy and Sophie will take good care of him."

I smiled weakly back at her, uncertain what I believed. Once I had been like her, innocent and full of absolute trust. Now, I wasn't so sure.

In the golden sunshine that filtered through the leaves, we watched the men working, the sweat glistening on their backs. It was the heat of summer and even under the shade of the trees, it was swelteringly hot. Although I hadn't been outside in days, I already longed to retreat back to the cool, dark bunker that had become home so quickly.

But I couldn't. There were important things that needed to be discussed and time was of the essence. I waited until they patted down the last shovelful of earth, and everyone got their chance to say goodbye. On the way back to the car, I drew Michael aside with a gentle touch on the arm.

When the others were out of earshot, I told him about my conversation with Ryan two days before and about the fear the young couple held for their baby. That combined with the threat from these new mutated infected made me feel a sense of urgency to get out of the area, but I desperately wanted to convince him to join us. I couldn't fathom the thought of leaving him behind.

"If two of us are going, then we should all go. She's my sister so I have to, but she's going to need the doctor when she gives birth, and we all rely on you for leadership." I paused for breath as the words tumbled out, worried by his peculiar expression. "We need to get out of here, get away from those things before they kill us all. You know what I mean, right?"

He nodded slowly as he mulled over what I said, his expression distant. When he finally spoke, his answer was not the one I was hoping for. "You're right. You should go somewhere safer. I'll remain here, and kill as many of those new things as I can."

"What? No!" I must have exclaimed louder than I meant to – I saw a couple of faces turn towards us, watching curiously. Ignoring them, I reached out and grabbed his hand. "You have to come with us as well."

"Why? You don't need me. I haven't done a very good job at protecting any of you so far." Somehow, he seemed to look like a lost little boy despite his stiff posture. Gazing up at him, I realised that he felt responsible for the deaths of those closest to him. My heart did a somersault in my chest.

"Don't be silly. " I squeezed his hand firmly. "We do need you, and you have done a very good job of protecting us. Bad things happen sometimes – it's not your fault. We need you, Michael, now more than ever." Caught in a sudden, confusing surge of emotion, I brought his hand to my chest and wrapped my fingers around it. "*I* need you."

He stared at me, bewildered, until finally the pieces seemed to click together in his head. Then he looked away, towards the car full of people whose lives depended on him.

Finally, he took a deep breath and nodded once.

Just like that, the decision was made. We would all leave the only home he'd known for more than a decade and together, we would travel to another place. They were putting their faith in my knowledge as they set out into the unknown.

I just hoped that I had enough knowledge to keep us all alive.

Chapter Seventeen

Having a plan of action helped to keep everyone from falling apart in the wake of Dog's death. When we returned to the bunker, Michael called a meeting to discuss the options for our departure. It was agreed by universal consensus that Ohaupo was the place to go, since it was the only place any of us had been to recently that was still secure and reasonably well supplied, with ready access to farmland.

What to do with the supplies in the bunker was an issue. The only functional vehicle we had was my utility, and if we crammed everyone into it then there would be no room left for anything else. We needed to find more vehicles.

As the only member of the group with any mechanical knowledge, however rudimentary it was, that task fell to me. The others began organising what needed to be taken with us, and packing it into anything they could find that would make it easier to move.

There was also a new rule in the group: Nobody was to go anywhere alone, or without a weapon. Since the only weapons we had were my pistol and taser and Michael's shotgun, the new rule meant only two of us could leave the bunker at any one time. After what happened to Dog and Sophie, it seemed like a reasonable precaution.

I spent the first morning after Dog's death in the bunker's underground garage, examining the vehicles the others deemed unsalvageable. Since they had no idea what they were looking at, I had decided to take a look at the wrecks myself before I wrote them off.

I discovered that the majority of the vehicles were either completely useless or only good for parts, but there were a couple I thought I could fix up with a bit of effort. One in particular caught my eye – a large prisoner transport, with barred windows and double-locks on the back.

I was lying on the ground beneath the transport van when Michael came looking for me around midday. I saw his boots walk past, and then he stopped and looked about before cautiously calling my name.

"Sandy?"

"Down here." The sound of my voice from an unexpected direction made him jump. He looked around, confused, before finally noticing my feet sticking out from beneath the transport. With a soft grunt, he eased himself down to ground level to peer at me.

"What are you doing down here?" he asked curiously.

"Salvaging." I gave him a playful smile.

He raised a brow. "And?"

"Well, I have good news. A few of the spark plugs needed to be replaced and some of the cables were perished, but I've managed to salvage replacement parts from one of the other trucks. I think once the battery is charged, this one will be good to go."

I finished up what I was doing and eased myself out from under the van. Michael offered me a hand up and I took it, glad for the assistance. Once I was back on my feet, I grabbed a rag I left nearby and used it to wipe the grease off my hands.

"That is good news," he agreed, examining the solid-looking van with an approving eye. Like me, he knew at a glance that we could fit a lot of good supplies in the back of a vehicle that size. Those kind, dark eyes shifted back to me, and he gave me a quirky smile. "You missed a spot."

"Ehh?"

"Right here." He reached over, and wiped a spot of grease off the tip of my nose. I felt my cheeks burn at the contact, but he pretended not to notice.

"Oh, thanks. Didn't see it. Remind me to enjoy another hot shower before we leave." I sighed. The thought of losing the hot water was too tragic to imagine.

"No hot water where we're going?" He looked equally disappointed.

"Not unless we can find a heating coil before we go." I shook my head. "I turned that township upside down looking for one before I hurt myself, but they were all blown."

"Hmmm." He stared thoughtfully off into space. "Actually, I think I know a place. A plumbing supply store. I found it a few years ago, but I didn't need anything at the time so I left it untouched."

"Add that to the list of things we need to do before we go." I heaved another long-suffering sigh, and then shot a sideways glance at him. "What about weapons? Any hunting stores here? I'm not familiar with the area."

"Nothing in the way of guns, if that's what you're asking." Michael grimaced and shook his head. "There used to be, but they were looted or burned out in the riots, and someone cleared out the gun lockers down here before I had a chance to look." He paused for a moment, then flicked an uncomfortable glance at me. "I got my shotgun off a corpse, in the early days right after the riots. We've found a few others since then but they were all too rusted to be any good to us."

"Damn. Well, at least you've got spare ammunition." I decided that it was politic to change the conversation at that point – Michael looked a little uncomfortable talking about weapons, and I couldn't blame him. It was a cultural thing. We Kiwis always were peaceful little birds. "So, what are you doing here, anyway?"

"I came to call you to lunch, madam." He put on his best charming smile and sketched a mocking half-bow. "We need to make sure you put on some more weight before we go."

The playful wit and the quick, appraising glance he gave my physique made me flush all over again. Suddenly I felt awkward and uncomfortable. I wasn't sure how to deal with such obvious flirtation.

I settled for my usual defence mechanism: sarcasm.

"What, are you saying I'm too thin?" I put on an offended face. "I'll have you know that the emaciated look is totally en vogue at the moment."

Thankfully, he took my comment the way it was intended and laughed. Without being invited, he slipped an arm around my waist, and I let him. Despite my nerves around other people, there was just something about him that put me completely at ease.

"Ah, mademoiselle." Michael faked a French accent teasingly. "I am afraid that your fash-ions are somewhat, how you say, out of date?"

I smiled, my embarrassment alleviated by the levity. In the week I'd spent in the bunker enjoying good food and minimal exercise, I'd gained a decent amount of healthy weight – a fact which he clearly hadn't missed, either. As we walked, I caught him glancing down at me on occasion, studying me with interest.

"What?" I asked at last, curious and slightly unsettled by his glances.

"Just thinking that you're filling out rather nicely," he answered softly. The humour was gone now and replaced by that gentle kindness that I'd come to appreciate. And something else.

I would say that got me blushing, but my cheeks were already on fire. Aside from sunburn, it was the biggest disadvantage of being as fair as I was – the slightest blush was painfully obvious.

"Are you calling me fat?" I retorted, I didn't know how else to react, so I fell back into humour.

He, however, did not.

"No." His voice was a whisper, and his arm tightened around my waist. I tensed, but his strength was tempered with gentleness. Suddenly, he stopped walking and caught my chin, to turn my face up towards his. "Never."

There was more to the word than just the obvious, I could sense it. He didn't even have to say it; I saw it in those dark, fathomless eyes as I gazed up at him, frozen with indecision and confusion.

He would never hurt me.

He would never let anyone else hurt me.

He would never leave me all alone, unless I told him to.

His face was so close to mine that I could smell his scent, feel his breath on my skin. Even so, the kiss caught me by surprise. The wild part of me panicked, terrified and desperate to get away, but for once it was held in check by the rational, intelligent part of me.

That was the part of me that longed to be close to someone, to be cared about again. That was the part that was so fascinated by my growing attraction to the man who had almost killed me and then saved my life within the span of a few minutes. That was the part of me that wanted this kiss so badly.

My eyes closed as his lips tasted mine, softly, as

though expecting at any moment that I would panic and flee. He was right, of course. He understood me so well already. If it had been anyone else, then I would never have let that kiss happen. I would have fought him for all I was worth.

Not with this man, though. I'd come to understand him in the short time we'd known each other. I understood that he had nothing but the best of intentions for me, and that when he kissed me it was because he meant it.

I drew a sharp breath when our lips parted, my heart racing, my mind surging with a mix of fear and longing. When my eyes finally opened, I found him looking down at me with a bemused smile on his face. I felt a stab of concern. "What now?"

"I just had a silly thought." He looked a touch embarrassed as he trailed gentle fingers along the length of my jaw. "Like, maybe I should thank you for not hitting me."

I stared at him.

"You hit like a truck!" He exclaimed, sounding defensive.

"Um— you're welcome." My brain was in a million places all at once, and I couldn't quite process his humour. Sensing my need for time, Michael let the conversation lapse into silence and led me the rest of the way to the kitchen. Just before we arrived his arm slid away and I found myself experiencing a sense of loss that I hadn't expected, a feeling that left me even more confused.

"Why is my sister the colour of a tomato?"

Skylar's voice cut through my confusion like a knife, and I shot her an embarrassed glance. She eyeballed me and Michael both, like she sensed something was going on, but Michael only shrugged and let me keep my privacy.

I felt a flood of relief at his discretion. Of course, Skye would be the first person I talked to if I decided I wanted to talk, but I needed the time to figure out how I felt before I said anything to anyone.

I eased myself into a chair to take the weight off my injured foot, mumbling something non-committal about not feeling well. With a knowing smirk, my sister set a bowl in front of me, and put a fork in my hand.

The group dynamic had changed since my arrival. They had gone from each making and eating their own food to sharing group meals at every opportunity, cooked by whoever felt like being adventurous that day.

Frankly, most of us were terrible cooks, me included. But eating together, sharing stories and camaraderie, it brought all of us a little bit closer together. Not to mention, all of us agreed eating off crockery tasted better than eating out of a can.

It also helped us to learn more about one another, and it gave Skylar and me the chance to get closer. She had been just a sweet little child when I last saw her, and now she was a spunky teenager with a bun in the oven.

I had discovered that I liked her a lot, as a person. Despite being eight months pregnant and looking like she was about to pop, she was a bundle of energy and rarely complained about anything.

It felt like her belly was almost as big as she was, and yet she was up and about from the crack of dawn, doing laundry or organising supplies or poking around in the kitchen. If something needed doing, you could count on Skylar to think of it before you did and be halfway through doing it by the time you got there.

This morning, I'd woken to the sound of joyful squeals, and emerged bleary-eyed from my room to find her chasing a delighted Madeline up and down the corridors with gleeful abandon. When she paused to catch her breath, she explained that she'd caught the child moping, and a good game of chase seemed like the easiest way to keep her spirits high.

Though I hadn't quite accepted the thought of being someone's aunt, I really hoped her baby would be okay. From the way she was with Maddy, I knew she'd be a fantastic mum, just like ours was for us.

Although she readily admitted that Ryan saved her and kept her alive all these years, it was quite obvious that she was the one who wore the pants in their relationship. He doted on her like an adoring puppy and was perfectly happy to follow her instructions in any circumstance. More than once, I'd seen her handing out orders and him trundling off about her bidding with a dopey smile on his face, perfectly content with his lot in life.

Given how young they both were, it was kind of adorable.

The doctor was a different story. I learned that he was kind of a loner by nature and preferred to spend his free time reading quietly in his room. Although his face was set in a permanent scowl, I'd come to realise it wasn't because of some deep-seated anger at the world — it was because he was short-sighted. He had glasses, but the prescription was ten years out of date and the lenses were scratched all to hell.

That knowledge came as something of a relief, since he had slightly intimidated me when I first met him. It was nice to know that most of the time, if he was glaring at me it was not because he was mad at me, it was because he couldn't see me properly. We'd come to a grudging understanding over the last week, and while I wouldn't call our relationship anything warmer than cordial, we had found a mutual respect for one another.

Now, Madeline was truly an enigma. I'd come to the realisation after spending some time with her that, although she was just a child, she was intelligent to the point of being brilliant. As much as we all instinctively wanted to protect her from the world, she always seemed to know what was going on around her. She flip-flopped between periods of childish play and moments of intense, adult clarity that never ceased to surprise me.

Sometimes I wondered if she could actually read minds.

Although she got bored swiftly with adult conversations, I often found her watching me doing things that should not interest a seven-year-old at all. Earlier that morning, she had spent nearly an hour watching me work on an engine, asking me questions about everything. Some of those questions were too technical for me to answer.

Right now, she looked like any other child as she shovelled her food down so fast that her grandfather needed to scold her and warn her that she'd choke. Ryan was off in his own world that completely revolved around Skylar, and Skylar was talking to me.

"So, how's it going?" She prompted while she spooned her culinary creation into a bowl for Michael. He took it gratefully, and settled himself into the chair beside me as though it were the most natural thing in the world.

I tried to ignore him and focused on my sister.

"It's good. I found a couple of salvageable engines, though only one vehicle large enough for what we need. I've got the battery on charge overnight, so with any luck it'll be good to go tomorrow morning."

"When did you learn to fix a car anyway?" Skye peered at me askance as she served up her own lunch, and then sat down opposite me. I just shrugged sheepishly.

"Well, in Year Twelve I decided to do a practical class, and automotive engineering was the only one I could get into without a ton of prerequisite classes." I didn't want to explain that Dad got me interested in cars in the first place, so I chose an answer that didn't dredge up old pain. "Who would have thought it would end up being the only useful thing I learned in school?"

"Handy. I wish I'd gotten the chance to go to high school." Her eyes drifted out of focus, and one hand absently rubbed her swollen middle I knew what she was thinking without her having to say a word – that she wished her child would have that chance, as well.

"You weren't missing much." I tried to distract her with humour. It worked, sort of.

"Oh, really now?" She laughed. "What about Robert? And Bryce? And Harry? Oooo..." One by one, she named all my high school boyfriends, then playfully made kissy fish lips at me. Michael shot a look at me with raised eyebrows, and I felt the heat rush back into my cheeks. Suddenly, I wished I could just crawl under the table and die.

"How the hell do you even remember their names?" I demanded, fighting the urge to run away and hide. Or maybe kick my sister to the moon. Yes, that seemed like an appropriate response. "I barely remember them at all."

"Well." This time, it was her turn to look embarrassed.

My anger faded, replaced by curiosity. "Well?"

She blew out a sharp breath, and then finally admitted. "I named my Ken dolls after them, all right?"

"You did what?" I was flabbergasted. Why on earth would she name her dolls after my high school boyfriends?

"Well, I named my Barbie after you." She hung her head like she was admitting something humiliating. "It seemed like a good idea at the time, okay?"

I stared at her while I processed that information. She named her doll after *me*? She loved that doll. It went everywhere with her, to day care when she was tiny and later on to primary school as well. I remembered Mum having to pry it out of her hands when it was bedtime. If Mum failed to tuck the doll into its bed at night, she would kick up such a fuss. One time she got so loud that the neighbours complained, thinking someone was being murdered in our house.

"Aww." My brow furrowed and I fought an unreasonable urge to cry. "That's so sweet, Skye. I never knew."

"Well, don't go telling everyone now," she shot back dryly, tilting her chin up in a petulant manner that reminded me of our mother when she was teasing Dad. "They'll start thinking I have a heart or something."

I immediately forgave her for embarrassing me in front of Michael. How could I possibly be mad over something like that?

Overcome by a flash of almost unbearable affection towards the young woman that had once been my baby sister, I reached over and squeezed her hand. She didn't say anything, but she gave my hand a squeeze back.

She understood.

Chapter Eighteen

Shortly after lunch, Michael and I took Skylar to examine the prisoner transport I had managed to salvage.

"This is good," Skye murmured thoughtfully to herself as she circled the van, examining it from all angles. "Very good, but I think we need another one."

I looked at Michael, who nodded thoughtfully. "She's right. From what you've said, the supplies down south are limited. We should take as much with us as we can."

"Particularly medical supplies." I nodded my agreement. "There's almost nothing down there. That's why I had to come north to begin with."

"There are a lot of things we need to take." Skye sighed, bracing a hand against the small of her back to stretch her spine. "We need more vans."

"How many of us know how to drive?" I glanced back and forth between them, uncertain.

"You, me and the doctor," Michael answered without hesitation, ignoring the irritated sound Skylar made. "Skye and Ryan say that they know how, but I'd prefer not to trust them behind the wheel of a heavy vehicle."

"We may not have a choice. I can't really drive with this." I gestured at my foot. "And we need as many supplies as we can carry."

Michael grunted and Skylar beamed. I raised a brow, but neither of them explained what was going on between them, so I just had to guess it was some kind of inside joke.

"Okay, so we need to find one more. A van or a light truck, something along those lines then." I looked around the garage at the other vehicles and shook my head. "We'll need to look outside. Everything we have here is either too small to be any use, or too far gone to fix."

Michael stared at me, his exasperation fading into a deep frown. Concern etched itself across his handsome face. "Are you sure you can handle a trip outside? You're still wounded."

I felt a surge of warmth at his concern. It was nice to know that someone cared.

"You can't keep me locked up in here forever." Feeling a little bold all of a sudden, I gave him a fearless grin and limped off towards my room. "Besides, you'll be with me if anything goes wrong. Go get your kit on, officer. Time's a'wasting."

Behind me, Skylar snickered.

***

I found it kind of funny how in one short week, I'd adapted to a life where I no longer had to carry everything I own on my back like a tortoise. It wasn't all that long ago I was so paranoid I took my taser with me even for something as simple as a dash to the ladies' room. I'd grown comfortable in this bunker though, and I no longer felt the need to have my hand on a weapon at all times. Those things I once considered vital necessities now sat in my room, in a neat row upon the table by the door.

I stood looking at them for a minute, thinking over the changes that had happened in my life in such a short period of time. I was a creature of habit, but it was interesting how quickly those habits had changed. One by one, I checked that my necessities were all in working order and packed them into the pockets of my fatigues, until all that was left was the gun.

I stared at the weapon, wishing that I didn't have to take it with me, but I knew in my heart that I did. If that horrible weapon was the only thing standing between me and death, then Mum and Grandma would forgive me for using it. It wasn't the gun's fault, it was only a tool. It was the disease that had taken them away from me, and now I had Skylar to protect, not to mention my unborn niece or nephew.

"It's not going to bite you, you know."

Michael's voice almost made me jump out of my skin. I spun around to face him, startled half out of my wits by his sudden appearance. He was leaning casually against the doorframe, watching me with his eyebrows raised, but he didn't move from the spot until I calmed down.

I shoved the gun in my pocket and buried the wave of embarrassment I felt at my overreaction. He knows that I'm... quirky, what's one more piece of evidence? Just as I was about to say something snippy, he distracted me with something completely unexpected.

"I made you a present."

"Eh?" I blinked owlishly.

"To help you while your foot heals." He reached out the door and grabbed something that was out of my line of sight, and then thrust the haphazardly-constructed wooden object at me. It took me a moment to realise that it was supposed to be a crutch. So *that* was what I'd caught him working on the other morning.

That was sweet.

"Oh, thank you." I couldn't say anything to him, but I was a little afraid to put my weight on it. It wasn't well made. My Year Seven woodwork teacher would have called it shoddy at best. Still, I tested it and it held up well enough, so I gave him a grateful smile. He looked so pleased that I liked his gift I couldn't quite remember why I had been preparing to get defensive a second ago.

"You'll heal faster if you keep your weight off your foot." He shrugged and beckoned for me to follow him.

We returned to the garage to gather up the basic tools we'd need for the trip, with me trailing behind while I practiced my crutch-walking all the way.

Although the petrol was running low, we agreed that taking the Hilux made more sense than going on foot. We needed to find some more fuel for our trip south anyway, so by taking the truck we could do both at once.

Michael helped me into the passenger seat and climbed into the driver's seat beside me. The engine spluttered when he turned it over, but it started on the second try; the noise worried me, but I pushed my concern aside for now. Carefully, he turned the truck around and drove it up the ramp that lead to the automated parking garage doors. They clanked open after he leaned out the window and swiped a card against the lock, and then off we went.

The sunlight seemed so bright after being indoors that I had to shield my eyes. For a moment, I thought I saw movement out of the corner of my eye, but by the time my vision adjusted there was no sign of anything out of the ordinary. Michael didn't seem to have noticed anything, so I dismissed it as a figment of my imagination.

We drove for a while, slowly dodging around debris of a hundred different kinds. I watched where we went with my GPS in hand, but Michael knew where he was going and didn't need any guidance from me. After ten years in this city, he knew the ruins like the back of his hand. Still, I felt the need to keep busy, to keep my hands and mind distracted.

Being alone with Michael had me twisted all up in knots. Without something to distract me, that kiss was all I could think about. There was just something hypnotic about his boyish charm. I found it hard not to think about how close he was right now. About the taste of his lips on mine, the scent of his skin, the feel of his hands that were so strong and yet so gentle.

I shook my head to try and clear it, and then rubbed a hand over my eye, pretending to be distracted by an errant bug. To my relief, he didn't seem to notice that anything was amiss.

When did my hormones get so out of control? A week ago, I would have – and had – sooner slugged him than kissed him. It had been so long since I'd felt any kind of attraction to another human being, that it made me so uncomfortable that I couldn't think of anything to say. Thankfully, he didn't seem bothered by the silence.

Still, I was relieved when we arrived at our destination. He eased the car off the road into the forecourt of a long-abandoned petrol station, and I was glad for the distraction.

The place was desolate, the forecourt cracked and overgrown with weeds as nature battled to reclaim what was hers. The pumps stood like lonesome soldiers of some forgotten war, their faces shattered by the riots a decade ago. I was out of the car by the time Michael switched off the engine, hobbling my way over the uneven ground towards the glass shell that protected the petrol station's attached convenience store.

The spider-web of cracks in the glass made it difficult to see inside – more remnants of the riots, I assumed. Somehow, no one had managed to get through the door or any of the surrounding windows. That was unusual, since service stations used to stock all kinds of food, alcohol, cash and car maintenance items in addition to fuel. In my experience, they were usually the first places to get ransacked.

And then I saw something that made me realise why the rioters had left this place untouched.

Through the fractal lens of shattered glass, I saw a hunched figure standing behind the counter, still clad in the decaying remains of a forecourt attendant's uniform. He didn't move. He didn't pace. He didn't fidget. He just stood there, a perfect statue of eternal plebeian servitude.

Michael came up behind me, and immediately saw what I was looking at. "What do we do?" His voice was a whisper, but he needn't have bothered; the creature was completely unaware of our presence. I shot him a look, amused that for once I knew how to proceed and he didn't.

"We do this." I smiled confidently, and raised my makeshift crutch. With a sharp thrust, I used the foot of the crutch to smash out the night service window near the cashier's left arm, sending shattered glass flying everywhere. The cashier didn't move, even when shards of glass tinkled across the service counter and the floor around his feet. He was way beyond caring. Content that he was unlikely to attack me, I reached through the hole and released the security lock. It disengaged with a rusty click.

With my free hand on my taser, I tucked my crutch back under my arm and led the way into the building. Although the goods were untouched, there was little that would be any use to us now. Most of the food here had been fresh, sandwiches and baked goods. The stench of decay hung heavily in the air. The only things of use were a few cans stacked on one shelf, but it was the stuff in the auto-care section that caught my eye.

"Take as much of that as you can carry." I pointed Michael towards a display of precious motor oil near the counter. He hurried to obey, while I hobbled around to take care of the unfortunate cashier. Much as I had done for dear old Benny, I dispatched the poor fellow with a quick jolt to the back of the neck. He collapsed with a disturbingly wet thud, as if he was already liquefied on the inside and the only thing that kept him in human shape at all was his skin.

"Off you go to the big service station in the sky, mate." I'm no good at eulogies, but I offered him a quick prayer anyway. "Sleep well."

Michael stared at the corpse for a moment, then looked at me and nodded silently.

Between his strength and my experience, we stripped the building of useful resources and disengaged the lock on the petrol pumps. Luckily for us, there was more than enough gas left in the underground tanks to fill up the Hilux and all the barrels we brought along with us to store fuel in.

After we capped off the last of them, I looked at Michael. "That should keep us going for a while."

"Yes. Most of the people around here were more interested in mobbing the pharmacies and hospitals than the petrol stations." He frowned deeply, and the expression on his face said that he remembered the riots first hand.

His tone made me consider how lucky I'd been, in a manner of speaking. By the time I returned to civilization, the riots were long over – everyone was already infected. For some reason, that thought disturbed me more than usual today.

"Let's go check out that plumbing supply store while we're here." I made the suggestion as much to distract myself as from any real desire to go. I had a funny feeling in my gut, like something bad was about to happen and I didn't know what. As we climbed back into the truck, I found myself watching the bushes intently, like I expected something to come screaming out of them at any second.

Nothing did.

Yet, my brain added perversely. I muttered a low curse under my breath.

"You have a potty mouth." Michael shot an amused sideways glance at me.

"And you have ridiculously acute hearing." I flicked him a glower.

Urge to brood... rising...

Thankfully, he took the hint and left me to my sour mood, instead focusing all his attention on finding the thing that most closely resembled a roadway. In some places, it was hard to tell. Nature was determined to reclaim this city, so the roads were overgrown and wild. A drive that would have taken five minutes before took twenty now, but at least it was an uneventful twenty minutes. Finally, we pulled up outside a shop that looked remarkably intact, aside from needing a bit of a clean and a fresh coat of paint.

"I guess no one wanted to loot a plumbing supply store," I commented dryly. "If only they knew that plumbing supplies would be more valuable than gold one day."

"Hey, look back there." Michael pointed, distracting me. I followed his finger to a garage next door. There, an old seven-seater minivan waited patiently for the service that would never come.

"That's perfect." I eased myself out of the truck and onto the ground. "See if you can find the keys; I'll go get what we need from the store."

Michael hesitated, torn by indecision about whether to follow me or do as I asked. I was already halfway to the store by the time he made up his mind and headed off to look for the keys.

In retrospect, I should have known better than to split up. I mean, in horror movies, someone always got killed when they did that. So, guess who got the kudos for the stupidest idea of the day?

That's right, it was me.

The store had seen better days, but aside from a thick layer of dust things were mostly just the same as they had been left years ago. Tarnished brass display fixtures hung on the wall, above models of sinks and shower units. The place was small and cramped, so I was forced to pick my way carefully towards the stockroom in the back.

The door was locked. Undeterred, I lowered myself to my knees and drew a small set of lock picks from one of my pockets. This lock was one of those old, simple ones, and I would have no problem opening it. After a few minutes, it made a satisfying click and I knew I was in. I levered myself back to my feet and switched the set of lock picks for my taser.

The door swung open to reveal a room hazy with dust, abandoned to its fate long ago. A quick sweeping glance reassured me there was nothing more threatening than rat droppings and the odd cockroach inside. Despite the dust, whoever used to be in charge of this stockroom kept it well-organised and I found what I needed without difficulty. There were a number of spare elements there as well, so I grabbed as many as I could carry.

There were a few other things that I thought might come in handy as well, so I added them to my armload of loot. I had no intention of coming back to this place any time soon.

Still, you never knew.

With that thought in mind, I pulled the door closed behind me as I left, until I heard the lock click back into place.

Then, leaning heavily on my crutch with my free arm full of supplies, I hobbled back to the truck. It took some awkward juggling to get the rear cab's door open but somehow I managed it, and when I did I set my treasure down on the back seat.

As I was shutting the door, I realised something. It shouldn't have taken that long to find the keys or to give up and come looking for me. Where was Michael?

I froze, head tilted, listening for the telltale sound of his footfalls, or the soft hiss of his breath against the silence of our empty world. I heard nothing. Hmm, that was worrying. He should have been back by now.

I managed to take a single footfall towards the garage before the blast of a shotgun discharge shattered the mid-afternoon silence.

"Oh, fuck." Sorry, Mum. I picked up the pace, using my crutch like a pole to vault myself over fallen debris. "Michael? Michael!"

My answer was a blood-curdling, inhuman scream.

I rounded a corner into the alley that ran behind the building, and found my friend pinned to the ground beneath the weight of a female undead, frantically trying to protect his face from her ragged fingernails. He had the shotgun held crosswise, using it to keep her at bay, but while he was protecting himself there was no way for him to go on the offensive.

"Sandy!" He saw me and called my name, his breath coming in ragged gasps as he battled to keep the undead off him; her ragged nails were mere centimetres from those kind eyes that I adored. "Sandy, run. *Run!*"

I ignored him.

In three strides I crossed the gap between us,

screaming at the undead creature until her head jerked up to stare at me. She howled a bloodthirsty wail, mouth wide to reveal bloody jaws.

"No, fuck *you*!" I screamed right back at her as I swung the crutch with all my might, using it like an impromptu cricket bat.

The undead flew backwards and crashed into a low wall a few feet away, but even with her skull caved in and most of her face gone, she was still trying to get up. I was on her before she could right herself, and jabbed the crossbar of my crutch down into her throat to pin her to the ground. The taser was out of my pocket and crackled to life within a heartbeat, ready to deliver its high-voltage payload.

And deliver it did, when I crammed it down into the bloody socket where the creature's face used to be. Electrical current surged through the its body, and made her limbs jerk convulsively as she lost control of her nervous system.

My chest heaved with exertion as I stumbled back, only to be caught by Michael's strong hands. Like me, he was panting, struggling to catch his breath. Adrenaline had our hearts going at a mile a minute, and it took a second for me to notice that he was covered in blood.

"Is that yours?" I gasped, pointing at the stains. He shook his head and pointed wordlessly at the jerking corpse; I nearly fainted with relief. Then the still-living carcass distracted me. I stared at it, not quite believing what I was seeing. It was still trying to get up. "Oh

Christ, those aren't death throes, are they?"

Michael shook his head, rendered speechless by his brush with death. It came down to me, then, while he was still recovering.

"Watch her. If she manages to get up, shoot her." I righted my crutch so I could use it for its intended purpose again. It was slippery with blood and other fluids that I'd rather not have thought about, but there was only one thing on my mind and it wasn't grey matter.

I returned to the abandoned garage, and it didn't take me long to find what I needed: A bottle of methylated spirits, left behind by the former occupants. I imagined they had used it to clean equipment, but I had a much simpler use for it.

An impromptu cremation.

I snatched up the bottle and hobbled back to the rear of the building, where I found Michael guarding the flailing infected with focused intensity. When he saw me coming he lowered his shotgun and hurried to meet me. As he drew closer, he spotted the bottle in my hands and anticipated my idea. He took the spirits and undid the cap, then upended the bottle over the writhing corpse.

Oh god, it was trying to howl, but all that came out of its shattered face was an infuriated gurgling. Its tongue flailed through the bloody mass that had once been a pair of jaws, disembodied and horrifying. My gorge rose.

Thankfully, Michael had his nerve back and took

care of the gruesome task for me. Once it was burning, we left the corpse behind us and hurried back to the front of the building, to put as much distance between us and the stench of death as we possibly could.

Back at the Hilux, Michael rounded on me with anger on his face. "I told you to run – why didn't you run? You could have been killed!"

I'd never seen him angry before, but I was too riled up on adrenaline to care. My back was up and I was still in fight or flight mode. Social graces were completely out the window.

"And I said *fuck you*!"

"No you didn't – you said that to her!" He yelled, and jabbed a finger back in the direction where the creature burned.

"Whatever– I don't even– Shut up!" My patience was gone, and my pulse pounded deafeningly in my ears. There was only one thing on my mind, and I needed to sate it before I went mad.

The crutch clattered to the ground when I lunged at him, taking him completely by surprise. He tripped, and then I had him pinned with his back up against the car before he knew what hit him. The kiss was hot and hungry, passionate, fuelled by our recent brush with death. It was a completely different kind of kiss to the tender taste he'd sampled earlier in the day. It was animalistic. I'd almost lost him before I even had the chance to get to know him, and I was furious about it.

Not at him, though. I was furious at myself.

It was my stupidity that almost cost this sweet, kind

man his life. My moronic need to show him how strong and independent I was. It was so idiotic. I felt like a fool.

Our lips parted after a moment that seemed to last forever. I shoved myself back away from him, now out of breath for a completely different reason. He stared at me, both of us still riled up but our anger was fading into... something else.

Perhaps he understood me a little bit better now, after seeing me fight to protect him. Even if I lacked the means to eloquently express my attraction out loud, he seemed to understand that I couldn't have abandoned him just because he ordered it. Like him, I would do anything to protect someone that I cared about – even if it cost me my life.

All of a sudden, it felt like we had far more in common than we initially realised.

***

It took us a while to coax some life out of the minivan, but we got it going long enough to get it back to base.

It was spluttering and making some very upset noises by the time we finally pulled into the parking garage, with me behind the wheel of the minivan and Michael in the Hilux. Still, we were home and safe, so I'd have time to get it running smoothly before we left again. As the gate rumbled closed behind me, I breathed a sigh of relief at being back in our nice, secure bunker again.

The relief didn't last long. Shortly after we disembarked, we both stopped and stared at each other, uncertain of what we were hearing. There was a sound echoing around the bunker, a terrible sound, and it was coming from inside the building.

It took us a few moments to figure out that it was the sound of a little girl screaming in terror.

We both took off running simultaneously, though with my foot almost crippled, Michael soon drew out in front of me. The further into the belly of the bunker we went, the worse the noises became. Madeline's muffled screams were interspersed with those bloodcurdling yowls that were steadily becoming all too familiar to us, punctuated by the intermittent wet crash of flesh on wood.

There was another screech, followed by the sound of wood splintering, and Maddy screamed again. The sound was followed by an older female voice issuing orders that we couldn't quite make out: Skylar.

Michael rounded the corner ahead of me, his shotgun loaded and aimed from the hip. The discharge roared in the narrow corridors and made my ears ring, but I didn't care about the discomfort or the pain in my foot.

All that mattered right now was Maddy and my little sister.

The door the undead was beating upon was a bloody mass of splinters. The creature was so intent on getting at the victims inside that it had torn pieces out of its own flesh as it was trying to get through.

Michael charged it, unloading the shotgun again and again, until the barrel ran dry and he was forced to stop and reload. The creature was taken completely by surprise by his vicious assault, and now it was on the ground with its head and shoulders churned to a bloody mess by hot shards of metal. His attention was completely focused on it, so I turned mine towards our family.

Through the door, I could hear Maddy crying and the sound of someone in pain.

"We're here – is everyone all right?" I shouted, leaving Michael to vent his temper on the creature he had cornered.

"Sandy? Oh, thank god." It was Skylar's voice, and I felt a surge of relief. There was the sound of moving furniture, then the door flew open and Skye was suddenly in my arms, hugging me tight around the neck. I hugged her back and did a quick headcount, finding everyone alive and accounted for.

Alive, but not necessarily well.

Ryan was groaning on the bed, bleeding badly from several nasty cuts across his chest and left arm. The fact that they were not yet stitched and bandaged told me all I needed to know. Skye and the doctor had barricaded everyone inside the room, and they'd dedicated all of their strength to keeping that terrible undead thing out.

There wasn't much left of it now. I released Skye and turned my attention to Michael. I moved up behind the former police officer and grabbed his forearm before he could unleash another shot into the bloody mound of flesh. His eyes darted towards me, wild and full of bizarre, mindless berserker rage. I somehow instinctively knew that the emotion wasn't directed at me, but rather that something snapped inside his mind. I stared back at him, keeping my gaze level and unflinching, and my voice soft and soothing.

"You're wasting ammunition."

He blinked and stared at me, then looked at the undead thing. It was shredded by a dozen blasts of buckshot, its body reduced to a few twitching limbs, its torso all but liquefied. He nodded dumbly and handed his shotgun to me, then began the gory process of picking up the writhing limbs from the puddle of body parts.

Now there was a sight that I prayed I would never have to see again. I could only be thankful that the face on that corpse didn't belong to someone that I cared about.

I followed him as he moved the corpse outside, and guarded the door with vigilance while he piled the pieces together and poured accelerant over them. When the pile was alight, we returned to the bunker.

The others were taking care of one another, and Michael was clearly in shock. He didn't say a word to anyone, not even me. I was the one that locked the door behind us, and I was the one that took him by the hand and led him to the bathrooms. I was the one who stripped the blood-splattered clothing off us both, and I was the one that guided him into a hot shower.

He just stood there, like a statue, while I soaped his muscular frame, making the kind of soft, soothing sounds that I didn't know I had in me. Still, I understood in some intuitive way that a part of him was shell-shocked beyond comprehension for a while, so I bathed away the blood that soaked us both and then bundled him up in a towel and guided him to his bed.

He didn't seem to notice my presence at all. He obeyed my every touch without showing a response. I sat beside him until he fell asleep, gently stroking his hair the way that a mother might. Finally, exhaustion won out over the shock, and his eyes closed.

My clothes were far too repulsive to put back on, so I was dressed only in a towel wrapped around my midsection when I went off in search of the others. I found Skye and Madeline in the kitchen, huddled together. Maddy was sobbing uncontrollably, but Skye was aware enough to look up when I entered the room.

"Michael?" she asked softly, as though afraid to hear the answer.

"He's asleep. I think, you know... Sophie..." Skye nodded. I didn't have to explain further. "What about Ryan? What happened?"

"It attacked us in the storage room, while we were packing." She suppressed a shiver as she explained the story. "Ryan tried to protect me, and got a bit torn up. I managed to get it off him and shut it in the room while we ran, but it got out.

"We barricaded ourselves in the doctor's room, and then you two arrived." Tears welled up in her eyes but she blinked them back, showing a remarkable degree of personal strength. "I don't know what we'd have done if you hadn't gotten here when you did."

"Don't think about that." I put my hand on her shoulder and gave it a gentle squeeze. "We arrived in time, that's all that matters. Is Ryan going to be okay?"

To my relief, she nodded. "He bled a bit but not nearly as bad as Dog; Doc says he'll be fine, but it'll take some time to heal."

"Then I guess it comes down to the McDermott sisters to save the day again." I leaned down to give both her and Madeline a hug. Her smile was weak but determined. Feeling a flash of affection towards her, I brushed the hair back from her forehead, and planted a light kiss there. "What's most important is that everyone survived the day. But, the first rule from now on is that no one goes outside until we're ready to leave."

"Amen to that," she agreed wholeheartedly.

V. L. Dreyer

Chapter Nineteen

I spent most of that night awake, patrolling the corridors with shotgun in hand while the others slept intermittently. Occasionally I'd see one of them up and about, anxiously roaming the halls unable to sleep, but I was simply too keyed up to sleep. I did try for a bit, but I ended up getting up again, feeling this overwhelming need to protect the people I'd claimed as mine. My friends. My family. Mine, mine, mine.

The infected would take them over my cold, dead body.

It was hard to tell how many hours that passed in the dimly-lit corridors of the bunker, but with unrelenting determination I checked each and every single room in that warren for anything that even remotely resembled a threat. There were a lot of rooms, and I was still dressed in the nightshirt I had intended to sleep in, but by God I would bring hell upon anyone or anything that threatened my family.

A week ago, I wouldn't have even considered walking around half-dressed when there was a chance people might see me, but something had changed since then. They'd all seen my legs before, on the night of Dog's ill-fated return, so modesty seemed like such a waste of energy in the face of impending doom.

As far as I could tell, it was the darkest part of the night; that time right before the dawn when the body should be in its deepest sleep. I padded along the hallways with barefoot stealth, the cold concrete numbing any pain I may have felt in my wounded foot. I was indulging a compulsion, a need. There was no logic in it, not tonight.

One by one, I checked on my family. Ryan, stitched and bandaged, lay asleep on the breast of his would-be wife, who had finally settled into a fitful doze herself. The next room on, the doctor slept upright in bed, propped against the wall with his little granddaughter snuggled against his tummy. Safe. Serene. Oblivious to the world.

Good.

I moved on to the last of them, the furthest one away and the one who gave me the most confusing feelings of all. I silently opened his door and found him awake, sitting on the edge of his bed with his head in his hands. For a moment I thought he might be crying, but then I realised he was just trying to organise his thoughts.

I lowered the shotgun and cleared my throat softly, alerting him to my presence. His head came up, and he stared at me blankly for a minute before recognition dawned.

"I'm sorry..." he murmured, lowering his head back into his hands. "I don't know what came over me."

"I do." I slipped into the room and closed the door behind me. I put the shotgun down and sat beside him on the bed, to rest my hand reassuringly upon his broad back. "It was shock, Michael. It happens to us all."

He looked at me, those dark eyes unreadable, but his expression was solemn. "I'm supposed to be tougher than that. The leader. I-I froze..."

"You're an officer of the law, not a soldier." I pointed out softly. "You're not meant to be a battle-hardened warrior. That's not your role. Your role is the protector, the community leader who exists to keep us safe. What you did was exactly what you were meant to do." I put my arms around him and drew him against me, trying my best to ignore his nakedness. "You protected us."

He slumped against me, and I found myself supporting most of his weight. His voice was just a whisper when he spoke. "I did a piss-poor job of it, yet again."

"No, you didn't." I stroked his cheek, feeling the roughness of his stubble against the curve of my neck as he leaned against me. It sent a shiver down my spine. "If it had just been me all alone, they probably would have died – and I would have joined them."

He sighed, his breath hot against my skin, but no words accompanied it this time.

"It's okay, you know." I stroked my fingers through his hair, trying to reassure him. "There's only so long you can possibly be strong. Something has to give eventually."

"But I have to be strong." His voice was weak, and his face so close I could almost feel the brush of his lips against my skin when he spoke. "For all of us, I have to be strong."

I drew away from him, and cupped my hand beneath his chin until his eyes rose to meet mine. They were so sad right now, so hopeless. I'd always wondered what people meant when they talked about puppy-dog eyes, and now I understood.

"You don't have to be strong when you're with me," I whispered, and then kissed him softly.

At first he didn't respond as though uncertain of what to do, but after a moment his hands slid around my waist and drew me gently up against him. His lips parted and the tip of his tongue flicked out, tasting me tentatively, perhaps afraid I might bite him.

I didn't, of course. That familiar hot prickle crept up the sides of my throat and brought heat into my cheeks as his head tilted to draw me deeper into the kiss. Oh God, I'd forgotten what it felt like, to really kiss a man, a man that I cared about and wanted to get closer to. It felt so good, so right, like I could fall into that kiss and just live in there forever.

I felt a gentle hand upon my thigh, creeping up beneath my night shirt to trace the line of my underwear. Our lips parted, and his head dipped lower, to the side of my neck to press soft kisses against the sensitive skin there. My heart raced and my breath came faster, responding to his touch. Part of me was terrified and wanted to run, but it was only a very small part; the rest of me wanted that touch so badly that it almost hurt.

Those strong hands lay me back on the bed while his lips explored my throat, my collarbone and down to leave a trail of kisses across my skin. The buttons of my nightshirt came open as though by magic, exposing my skin to the cool air. I shivered, but the cold had nothing to do with it.

His kisses drifted lower, into the crevice of my breasts. There he lingered, breathing deeply for the longest moment before he drew back just enough to look at my face. His dark eyes searched mine, seeking my thoughts, my needs, before they drifted down across the curve of my bosom.

The softest sound escaped him, a sound I recognised as one of deep longing and need that had been held in check for far too long. His tongue flicked out and danced across the sensitive apex of my left breast. The feel of it made me gasp out loud, and his breath was so warm on my skin that it left me quivering. He was so handsome, so strong, so... everything that I needed.

His lips touched my navel, and kissed a soft trail down further and further. I wondered briefly where my knickers had gone, then realised that somehow he had managed to slip them off me without my even noticing.

Oh, but his lips were going even lower now, and I found myself not caring anymore. He was so very gentle, careful not to even scrape my skin with the stubble of his chin. Oh, and his tongue... what was it doing down there? My mind was so addled by arousal that I could barely keep track of what was going on anymore.

I couldn't remember ever being so turned on before, not even with Harry, who was my first, so many years ago. It had been so long since then, a long time since I wanted anyone to touch me, and I wanted him now. I wanted him so badly. More than anything I'd ever wanted in my life.

But then, while I was weak and at my most vulnerable, the memories came crashing down on me like a bucket of ice water. The flash of hot pain, of violation, of humiliation. Violence, so much violence. I cried out again, but this time it was a sound of blind, animal terror, and then I forced poor Michael away from me, terrified beyond words of a phantom that only I could see.

The knives cutting my skin, the burns, and the harsh sound of laughter as the men gloated over my beaten frame. In my memory, a fist struck me and I fell, crying, begging, alone and terrified. Oh God, I was so afraid.

An uncontrollable sob wracked my body. I was on my feet without thinking, fleeing from him, fleeing from his bedroom, fleeing to anywhere where the spectre couldn't find me. I left him staring after me, confused, aroused and hurt. I could hear him calling my name but I couldn't respond.

He didn't understand why I rejected him in the

moment when he, too, was at his most vulnerable. He couldn't possibly understand. I didn't understand.

They laughed and laughed, mocking me with their horrible, naked bodies.

Do you want it, little slut? They gurgled drunkenly in my memory, the faces blurred by time into the faceless ghosts of a past that could not be forgotten. All I remembered was the terrible tattoos and the corpulent, repulsive bodies. And the pain, so much pain.

No, no, I begged, *please, anything but that.* But they didn't listen. It hurt, it hurt so much. They made it hurt, because it gave them pleasure to watch me suffer.

I ran, or at least hobbled, as far and as fast as I could, and soon I found myself back in the locker room. Feeling unclean beyond words, I stripped off my nightshirt and flung myself beneath a blast of hot water.

The water hid the tears. The warmth between my thighs mocked me, teased me, and made me question myself and everything about me. Everything about everything. Why didn't I fight harder? Why didn't I kill myself when I had the chance? Why did I now want to do something that had caused me so much pain before?

How could I ever want to be with a man again? How could I even consider making love to one? He would hurt me; they always wanted to hurt me.

It's my fault, my battered psyche told me. *I brought it on myself. I'm a bad person.*

I'm dirty, unclean. No one will ever love me again.
I hate myself.

My shoulders shook convulsively as I slumped against the wall, pressing my face to the rough concrete. The strength faded out of me and I slid down the wall, to curl up into a wet, shivering ball in the corner of the shower stall.

I had no idea how long it was before Michael found me, huddled beneath the water that did nothing to wash away the feeling of terrible sin. I had cried all my tears and there was nothing left to spare, but I was off in a world where everything was terrible, bloody and violent. A world where I was the victim, and yet somehow I thought it was my fault.

Where was a psychologist when you needed one?

"Sandy?" His voice was so soft and gentle that it cut through my nightmare, but I didn't have the strength to reply. I heard the shower curtain twitch, then the water turned off and strong hands bundled me into a big, soft towel. The animal part of my brain screamed and flailed and told me to flee, but I was too exhausted to even move.

Wrapped up and dripping, he carried me to a nearby bench and cuddled me into his lap. His touch was so soft and his voice so soothing that it finally began to calm me down again. I shivered and turned my face against his chest, where I found him dressed in crisp blue fabric. My eyes flickered open and I saw that he was fully clothed, dressed in his police uniform.

I'd never seen him wearing that before.

It was a wise choice of attire. The uniform soothed me in some way I didn't quite understand. I had been raised to trust the police as a child, and that trust persisted into my adult years.

That's why he's wearing it now, I realised numbly. For me. To show me who he really was, and why I didn't need to fear him. The uniform embodied everything about him, and everything that I trusted.

"It's okay," he whispered soft, soothing nonsense in my ear, and stroked my hair in a way that oddly mirrored what I'd done for him not so long ago. In spite of everything, I snuggled closer, finding comfort in his warmth.

He was still aroused, I realised suddenly – I could feel him hard against my hip. But through cloth, it was so much less threatening, less real.

A flash of affection overrode my panic, followed by guilt for making him suffer. I could only imagine the discomfort of going from a state of intense arousal to where we were now. Yet, he was trying so hard.

"I'm sorry." My voice was hoarse from crying. "I'm so sorry. I just... I just... I-I..."

"Sandy." He tilted my chin up to make me look at him. "I know. They trained me to recognise the signs of..." He hesitated for a moment, reluctant to say the word, and his arms tightened protectively around me. "...abuse."

I made a sound that wasn't really a word at all, but more of a whimper. He'd figured out what I couldn't put into words. He did understand.

With gentle fingers, he stroked my cheek and down along my jaw, then kissed me again, just quickly and tenderly. The kiss ended almost as swiftly as it began, and didn't give panic a chance to resurface.

"I want you, Sandy," he whispered, "and I want you to be my lover. I've never had a lover before..." His words trailed off, and he broke eye contact. "...but I've waited a lifetime, I can wait a few more days, a few more weeks. A few more years if I have to. Until you're ready. Until then, just know that I'll always be here for you. I'll never let anyone hurt you again. I swear to you, on my life."

I had no idea what to say, so I just stared at him – but it was okay, because he knew that I understood.

"When you're ready," he added softly, as he gathered me up to carry me back to my own bed, "you just tell me, and I'll be waiting for you."

***

I slept late that morning, later than I'd done in years. When finally I awoke, groggy and confused, I found myself with strong arms wrapped around me and the warmth of a human body pressed against my back.

Then, it all came crashing back to me.

I slumped against the pillow and let the comfort of his arms soothe me. After we'd finished speaking, he had carried me back to my bed and tucked me in, then he got up to leave. Suddenly terrified of being alone, I had panicked. I'd grabbed his hand and begged him to stay.

Please, please don't leave me...

He stayed. He snuggled into bed beside me,

keeping his trousers on to make himself as unthreatening as possible. I appreciated the effort, considering that I was naked as a jaybird and too exhausted to get dressed at the time.

It was okay. True to his word, his touch stayed innocent. He lay behind me with his arms wrapped around my waist and his face snuggled against the back of my neck. I shifted slightly but he didn't move, still fast asleep.

I lay there for a while, just thinking. Wondering what I'd gotten myself into.

He's never been with a woman before, I thought, and found myself mulling over that point in my head. Was it really such a surprise, though? He had been 22 years old when all this happened, and he'd grown up in a carefully monitored environment of study and personal development. He was a good guy – still is a good guy – and had been too wrapped up in his studies and his ambition to waste time on girlfriends and frivolous relationships.

The concept of one day having a wife and children had been a very distant thought on that day ten years ago when our world changed forever.

I wondered if he regretted those lost opportunities now, when the only chance he had at love was with an underweight blonde with severe psychological issues. He didn't really have many other options. The only other females about were Skye, who was enamoured with someone else, and Madeline, who was seven.

Don't think like that, I scolded myself when I

realised what I was doing. There were still plenty of other women left in the world, and he'd chosen me. I smacked my self-doubt across its dirty little face, and shoved it back into the deepest recesses of my brain where it belonged. I refused to let it control me and ruin what I might be able to develop with this kind man in the future.

With one of my demons successfully conquered – for now – my thoughts drifted back to Michael again. I felt a little disappointed at myself for wondering if he was the father of Skye's baby. In retrospect, it seemed so obvious. He was just the kind of man who was protective by nature and respectful to everyone, particularly women. He would have protected her regardless of whose baby it was. My brief bout of jealousy had been completely misplaced.

I shifted a little in his arms, feeling wrung out and exhausted from the night's adventure. My body had responded to him with such intensity that I still felt the dampness of past arousal between my thighs. It had faded now to a dull discomfort, like an itch that went unscratched.

Was the discomfort much worse for him? I had explored my sexuality in high school as most young people did, and I understood in a distant sort of way just how uncomfortable it was for a healthy young man to go unsatisfied. Poor Michael had gone for more than ten years without satisfaction – and then there was me, getting him all riled up like a dirty temptress and leaving him in the lurch.

Okay, now I felt bad. He'd been so sweet to me, and in return I'd put him through such hell that he really didn't deserve. Somehow, it made it even worse that he'd been so nice about it. As much as he tried to be strong for the others, he had let me in to see the vulnerable young man inside him. Now I felt like I'd kicked a puppy.

I lay there, pondering ways to make it up to him, until I finally came to a decision. There were ways that I could thank him for his kindness and let him experience blessed relief without putting myself back into panic mode. It would take a good deal of courage on my part, and some obedience on his, but I felt like I could do it for his sake. The attraction that I felt towards him was so intense and so genuine that I wanted to overcome my demons somehow, and that would only come with effort.

It was being vulnerable that made me freak out, I realised. Being sprawled on my back with a man atop me, no control about what was going to happen to me. If I took back my control then I should be fine. I sensed that Michael would probably let me.

I rolled over within the circle of his arms and turned towards him, gazing down at his handsome face, so peaceful in sleep.

Oh, but I shouldn't wake him, my inner voice crooned, but I smacked it aside as the voice of cowardice. He'd be perfectly happy with being woken up this way.

I drew a deep breath and let it out slowly. We were

so close together that my breath stirred his eyelashes. The stubble on his chin had grown overnight, I noticed with a detached fascination. I'd forgotten how swiftly a man's beard grew.

With one gentle hand, I slid my fingertips down across his belly to trace the contours of his abdomen. It rose and fell slowly in time with his breath, and I found myself marvelling at the warmth that radiated from his skin. Something else that I'd forgotten, I guessed.

My fingers found the waistband of his trousers, and carefully undid the top button. The zipper slid down, and I discovered that in his hurry to catch me the night before, he had neglected to find his shorts. No wonder he had been so insistent about keeping his pants on when he climbed into my bed.

I suppressed a smile at the thought, and slid my hand down the front of his trousers. In spite of myself, I felt my own breath begin to quicken when I felt his body respond to my touch.

So did his, for that matter. His brow furrowed and he stirred against me before his eyelids cracked open. A second later he was fully awake, lying stiff in bed beside me.

"What are you doing?" His voice was a harsh whisper; I silenced him with a finger across his lips.

"Shh..."

With a firm but gentle hand, I pressed him onto his back. He obeyed reluctantly, and his eyes went wide when the blankets fell away to reveal what I'd been doing to him in his sleep.

"But—" He tried to protest, but I shushed him again.

"Just lie still and follow orders, officer." I put on my best playful tone to mask my own nervousness. Making a great show of confidence, I slipped a leg over him to straddle his thighs, my bottom resting upon his knees. "We're going to play a game. I want you to pretend that I'm your sergeant, and you're my good, obedient constable."

"Ah…" There was a flush of colour creeping up the sides of his throat and I felt a surge of pride at his reaction. "…but… my sergeant was an ugly old man."

Way to ruin the mood, Mike.

"Okay, well pretend I'm your sergeant, if your sergeant was a sexy twenty-something girl." I gave him my best approximation of a sultry pout. He laughed and nodded his consent.

"Ah, okay. Y-yes, ma'am."

Then he shot me a salute. With me pinning him to the bed, his pants unzipped and naked above the waist, it struck me as the funniest thing I'd ever seen. It took all of my willpower not to burst out laughing and completely destroy the mood once and for all.

"Much better." I play-acted, letting my confidence grow with time. He was letting me play, even if it made him uncomfortable, and that reassured me. He seemed to understand that I needed this to bolster my own personal confidence, and he was willing to let me try. "Now, you have been such a good and understanding person, that I feel I must reward you for your loyalty.

Sadly, I'm all out of medals, so we'll have to find something else that'll do for a reward."

"Ehhh?"

He just looked totally bewildered now. Okay, I'm not good at this game. I sighed and rolled my eyes.

"Oh, just shut up and enjoy yourself, would you? I'm a little rusty, so try to make encouraging noises or something." For lack of a better response, I fell back into sarcasm to get my point across.

He looked down at his crotch, then looked back at me. It was a confused look, like he couldn't quite figure out what I was about, but he still seemed inclined to let me do as I pleased to him.

That was what I needed.

I eased myself back a bit and leaned down and planted a playful kiss upon his stomach. I felt his deep intake of breath as he realised with shock what I planned to do. I glanced up and met his startled gaze then narrowed my eyes and gave him a flirtatious smile.

As it turned out, I wasn't as rusty as I thought.

***

Later, we lay contentedly in one another's arms, his eyes closed and arms wrapped around me possessively. Though he tried to say something, all that came out were whispered half-words that meant nothing.

It was fine, though. I knew what he meant.

Frankly, I just felt better for no longer being that crazy bitch that runs off screaming and flailing because a cute guy kissed her. Not that he would ever dream if calling me that, but that was how I'd been thinking of myself.

Sometimes the worst critic was the one inside your own head, and I hated that feeling. I hated knowing that I was judging a good man against the template of other people's wrongdoing. Worst of all, I hated knowing that I had hurt him. He'd made it clear that he didn't judge me for that, but his opinion of me was still secondary to my own. I had to follow my instincts, and do what felt right to me, and my conscience.

I let him have a couple of minutes to rest and recover before I cleared my throat and gave him a gentle nudge.

"Time to get up, sleepy-head. Day's a'wasting."

He grunted and opened one eye to give me a glare. It didn't last long, though. It faded as I smiled back at him playfully, then melted into a look of contented relaxation. He started to lay his head back down, but I wasn't having any of it – and neither was he, since I took the blanket with me when I extracted myself from the warmth of his embrace.

I heard grumbling behind me as I dressed in some of the spare clothing I'd acquired since my arrival. My normal clothing would probably be almost dry by now, but getting it would mean prancing through the hallways butt-naked, and I wasn't *that* self-confident.

Jeans and a t-shirt would do. Not my usual attire, but functional and, more importantly, clean. As I pulled the shirt over my head, I felt strong hands sneak around my waist.

"What's this, then?" Michael whispered in my ear, his lips so close enough that I could feel his breath. I shivered.

"What's what?" I turned my head just a little, to look up into his eyes.

He said nothing in return, just smiled knowingly. One of his hands crept up beneath my shirt, across my belly, until his fingertips grazed the curve of my breast. I felt myself flush at the touch and suddenly I understood the question.

"Oh, that, um..."

He grinned at my embarrassment – or was it the fact that I didn't pull away?

"You clearly have no idea how hard it is to find a decent bra in this day and age." I finally gathered the wits to reply. "I only have *one*, and I left it in the bathroom last night."

It was true. Good lingerie was hard enough to find before the end of the world; afterwards, it was nearly impossible. Since it was made of such light fabrics, it doesn't last long to start with, and when you lost one it took forever to find a replacement.

"Oh." He seemed a little disappointed at that answer, and his hands drifted back down to rest on my hips. "Here was me, getting all excited and you were just being practical."

I turned within the circle of his embrace and slipped my arms around his waist in a moment of uncharacteristic boldness. "Well, at least you can comfort yourself with the fact that you're the only one that knows?"

His expression brightened. "That... is true."

Amused, I pressed a quick kiss to his lips, then released him and took his hand instead. "Come on, the others will probably be frantic with worry since we didn't show up to breakfast."

"Hu-uh?" He looked dazed and still a wee bit sleepy. "What time is it?"

"Almost midday, I think."

"Ah, cripes. They've probably sent out search parties by now."

Suddenly wide awake, Michael took the lead. He opened the door and led me out, leaving me to admire just how nice he looked in his uniform. While I was dressing, he had put his shirt back on and straightened himself up. Now, he looked like a real police officer at last.

Call me a sucker for a man in uniform.

"I should go find the doctor," I admitted reluctantly, loathe to let go of his hand. "I need my bandages changed." I'd gotten them soaking wet again the night before, and wet bandages were a breeding ground for bacteria.

"Yeah. I should find Skye and see how she's getting on with the packing all by herself."

We looked at one another and a flash of understanding passed between us. Neither of us particularly wanted to leave the other, and yet we must. The look was long and charged with tension, but finally I released his hand.

"I'll see you soon?" I tried not to sound too hopeful, but failed miserably.

"Count on it." He smiled reassuringly, then turned with a wave and headed away from me.

I hate to see you leave, but love to watch you go, I thought, my demented brain dredging up yet another stupidly clichéd old quote from the deepest recesses of my memory. I shook my head to distract myself, and then limped off in search of the doctor.

***

It didn't take long to find him. He was a creature of habit as well, and I already knew his patterns. After a thorough scolding taking so long to come and see him, he sat me down and pulled my foot into his lap to strip off the soggy bandages.

"Again, you get these wet." He sighed, a sound of long-suffering annoyance. "How many times must I tell you to keep them dry?"

"I know, I know; I'm sorry. I had a momentary lapse of judgement." My explanation was weak, but I didn't feel like telling him the truth. I liked it better when what was developing between Michael and I was our little secret.

"Mm-hm." The doctor stared at me over the rim of his spectacles. "'Feeling ill' again, were we?"

Oh great. He even made the air-quotes with his fingers. I could feel my cheeks turning red all over again.

"That's what I thought." His lips narrowed to a

disapproving little line, then he turned his attention back to my bandages. He dried and cleaned the wound, replaced the gauze, and bound it all back up again in a clean bandage. "Do try to keep this one dry, won't you?"

"I'll try. Sorry, doctor." I looked down, feeling a bit like a scolded child. He grunted, clearly not believing me, and hauled himself back to his feet with an audible creaking of joints. I rose as well and made to leave, but he stopped me with a gesture.

"I've prepared these for you in case you start 'feeling ill' again, I insist that you begin taking these immediately." He shoved a scrappy box into my hand and stared at me sternly over his glasses. "One first thing in the morning, every morning, and do not miss a day."

"What?" I looked down, and then realised with a flash of distress what the box contained. "Oh."

Birth control medication.

"I don't care what you and the boy get up to." His voice was snappish and abrupt. "I know you're both young and full of energy and feel the need to go throwing yourselves around, but the last thing we need right now is for another one of our able bodies to be burdened with a pregnancy. And for the love of God, don't waste them – the ingredients for these are getting very hard to come by."

I wanted to curl up in a corner and die of embarrassment.

"One, every day, at the same time." He repeated

himself and held up a finger, like he didn't expect me to understand what he was saying without it. "And do not miss a day."

"Doc, I don't even... you know, get a 'monthly' anymore." I hesitated, feeling so uncertain that I didn't know what to say. "I don't think I can get pregnant, even if we were... you know. Not that we are."

Technically.

"Not yet, no. You've been too malnourished." He adjusted his glasses and hiked them back up on his nose. "Your body probably wouldn't have the strength to support a foetus to full term just yet, but there's always a chance – and there's also the matter of miscarriages. Just take the pills. Better safe than sorry."

I nodded and fled from him, red as a beetroot.

He was right, of course – that was, if I ever got over my issues long enough to do anything that would put me at risk of getting pregnant. I didn't want a child right now. I was in no position to care for one.

And I was just too fucking crazy for a baby. Nobody wants a psycho for a mum.

I deposited the box in my room and hobbled off towards the garaging area, intent on distracting myself with work. I got about halfway there before something else caught my attention: the sound of raised voices coming from the direction of Michael's room.

"Tell me!" It was Skylar's voice, and she sounded pissed.

"No! It's none of your business." That was

Michael's voice, and he sounded... peculiar. I rounded a corner and found myself confronted with a bizarre scene. Skye had Michael cornered and was poking him threateningly in the chest with her index finger. Michael looked confused and a little bit afraid.

Despite being five inches shorter than me, with a tiny frame that made her belly look like a bowling ball by comparison, my sister was kind of terrifying when she was pissed off.

"You *will* tell me." Skye's voice was low and threatening. "Or else I'll have to—"

"Look, there she is; ask her yourself!" Michael pointed at me, distracting Skylar's attention. The second her attention wavered from him, he was off like a shot, fleeing down a corridor away from us.

"Sandy!" Skye was on me in a heartbeat, and grabbed me by the shoulders, then she was shaking me until I was afraid my head would pop off. "Where have you been? I was worried sick."

"Jesus, Skye." I squeaked and wriggled out of her grasp, then backed away, holding up my hands defensively. "I just slept in."

"But your door was locked so I thought you were out, but I couldn't find you anywhere. I couldn't find Michael until a minute ago, either, and the car was still in the garage, and... and... and..."

This time, I grabbed her and gave her a solid shake.

"Calm. The fuck. Down," I told her in no uncertain terms. She bristled, but I didn't give her a chance to protest. "I was just in bed. I had a late night and I was tired. I locked the door because I don't like people barging in on me unannounced."

Yes, that was the reason. Not because I had a half-naked man in my bed. No, not at all.

"You could have just knocked if you were so worried." I added. "I probably would have been annoyed at being woken up, but at least you would have had an answer."

"Knocked?" Skylar looked confused.

"You know, tapped on the door until I responded?" Was she being serious right now?

"Oh... I always thought that was just something the doctor yelled at me when I opened his door."

I felt the overwhelming urge to facepalm. Oh, right. She was eight when the world ended. Eight-year-olds don't knock. "You haven't been living here much longer than I have, have you?"

"About six months." She shrugged, then suddenly seemed to remember that she was at my throat for a reason. "Wait, but if you were asleep, then where was Michael? I looked all over for him. He wouldn't go outside alone..."

She trailed off as the pieces began to fall into place, staring at me.

I avoided eye-contact, trying very hard to prevent myself from turning red again and giving us away.

"Sandy." Skye's eyes narrowed. "Look at me."

I looked anywhere but at her, fighting the urge to flee that rose in my chest.

"Look at me!"

I cleared my throat and pretended to be fascinated by my feet, while silently plotting my escape route.

"Sandrine McDermott, did you sleep with Michael?"

Oh crap, she was on to us. Time to go.

"Hey, get back here!" She squealed, as I dashed off as fast as I could go.

Go, go, race of the cripples.

Luckily for me, I was quicker in spite of my injury, what with her belly being so swollen that she could barely waddle at a fast pace. When I was out of her line of sight, I ducked into one of the many rooms in the underground maze, and dropped down behind an old desk to hide. I heard her footsteps patter past, and then sighed softly in relief.

"Your sister scares me."

I almost jumped out of my skin; I hadn't noticed that Michael was hunkered down close by until he spoke. He looked back at me with the most embarrassed expression I'd ever seen.

"Hey, you abandoned me." I gave him a sad-puppy look, though in truth I didn't really blame him. "I'm so mad at you."

He shrugged helplessly. "She was accusing me of everything from eating you to stealing your soul. I had no choice. At least she won't kill *you*. Me, I'm not so sure about."

"Yeah, you're probably right. Okay, I forgive you."

Michael helped me up, his hand lingering in mine even after we were back on our feet. He turned my hand over, as though studying it, then brought it to his lips and kissed the tips of my fingers. "Good. I'm not sure I could bear you being angry with me."

I smiled at him and stepped in close, to press a soft kiss against his cheek. "Yeah, me either. Let's go get some work done before Skylar finds us."

Hand in hand, we left our hiding spot and went off about our business.

Chapter Twenty

Michael and I snuck around like thieves for two whole days while our group prepared to leave its home, stealing what moments of privacy that we could. Skylar became something of a menace and demanded the latest gossip at every turn, but eventually she began to grudgingly accept that neither of us were interested in sharing the details of our tryst.

During the process of stripping the bunker of everything that we could carry, I came across a set of walkie-talkies. They were good, solid things, heavyweight with rechargeable batteries. When I showed them to Michael, he told me that they were police issue. He recalled that he had found them in the bunker when he first moved in, and put them into storage in case he needed them some day.

We need them now, I reasoned and put them on their chargers. The next morning, they crackled to life chirpily and a few minutes later I had them working.

As we were preparing for our departure, I assigned one to each person, and explained to each of them how to use it.

"If anything goes wrong, if we get separated, if you get lost or attacked, call the rest of us," I included in my instructions. "Don't hesitate. Even if you see something but you're not a hundred per cent sure what it is, call us. It's better safe than sorry."

Yes, I blamed myself for Ryan's injuries, though I hadn't admitted it to anyone. I kept my shame a secret, bottled up deep inside where the only person that it could hurt was me.

But it was a lesson learned, a lesson that I prayed none of us would ever have to repeat.

As the sun rose on the third day, the six of us gathered one last time in the parking garage. The trucks were all packed and our scant personal possessions were crammed in amongst the supplies. We looked around one last time, making sure everything was switched off and locked, and said goodbye to the place that had been our home. For me, it was only ten days; for Michael, it was a third of his lifetime.

For Maddy, it was the only home she'd ever known. Despite that, she was practically bouncing off the walls with excitement, ready for an adventure. The rest of us were quiet, determined and intense, ready to fight our way free if we had to.

Michael issued orders and assigned each of us to a vehicle. Madeline and Skylar were placed in the minivan in the middle of the convoy so that we could protect them easily. They were the two most vulnerable members of our group, and we wanted to have them somewhere safe. I half-expected an outburst of rebellion from Skylar, but it never came. She was simply delighted by the fact that she was going to be allowed to drive.

Ryan and the doctor would bring up the rear in the bulky prisoner transport, with the doctor behind the wheel. Despite his injuries, Ryan was alert and capable with the hand not swathed in bandages. Although he couldn't drive in his condition, he could keep a lookout and fight if he needed to.

With my blessing, Michael armed him with my handgun and cleared a space in the back of the van for him to sit in, so that he could watch the road behind us for danger. Although he looked disappointed at being separated from Skylar, Ryan acquiesced without protest on the understanding that he was still protecting her.

Michael and I would lead the convoy in the Hilux, as both the most capable fighters in the group and the only ones that knew where we were going. My foot was almost healed but we didn't want to risk it, so Michael took the wheel.

Before he climbed in, he handed me his shotgun. He'd already briefed me on how to use the weapon, how to reload the shells and how to fix it if it misfired, so I felt confident that I could defend us if necessary. Ryan and I flanked the roller door while everyone else went to their places, checking that our weapons were loaded and the safeties were off.

The garage reverberated with the sound of three

engines starting at once. I swelled with pride that not one of them stumbled and died. A job well done. No time to pat myself on the back, though. It was time to go.

I looked at Ryan and he nodded to indicate that he was ready. With the shotgun tucked in the crook of my arm, I reached over and swiped the key card against the lock. The door began to rise, with a rusty clanking that felt loud enough to wake the dead – or at least alert them to our presence.

Side by side, Ryan and I approached the opening door, our weapons aimed at the entrance. Bright morning sunlight crept through the gap as the door rose, sneaking across the floor to attack our feet before it gradually illuminated the rest of our bodies. It was just after dawn and the sun was already intense. A wall of heat washed over us in stark contrast to the cool darkness that we were used to.

It was time.

I led the way, my footing cautious but the limp was almost gone. In a militaristic crouch-walk, I stalked the entrance at an angle, clearing the right side before I rounded to the left. Just as we had practiced, Ryan covered my back as I stared about for any sign that we had been detected. After ten seconds, he moved up to join me, back to back, and added his eyes to my search grid.

Nothing moved. With fluid footsteps despite our injuries, we slid further out into the daylight, far enough to check every bush, every crevice that might hold some horrible dead thing. The only corpses we saw were the kind that didn't move.

The door whined in protest as its tiny automated brain decided that it was time to close. I returned to the entrance to swipe my card again, and to give my signal to the others waiting in the garage below.

Michael led the charge, surging up the ramp with a heavy foot on the accelerator, and kicked up a breeze that stirred my hair as he passed. He cleared the entrance in a few seconds, and came to a halt a short way down the street to wait for the rest of the convoy to assemble.

I gestured to Skylar to come next and she did – eventually. It took her a few tries, and in the process she somehow managed to bunny-hop an automatic engine. It took all of my willpower to fight down the urge to laugh. Instead, I gave her the thumbs-up sign in encouragement and waved her on out the door.

The doctor came last in the prisoner transport, which groaned and struggled to clear the ramp with its heavy burden. For a moment I worried it wouldn't make it, but then it was over the lip and out into the street beyond.

I cast one last glance around the garage as the door rumbled closed again, and silently said goodbye to all the dead cars that I would never have a chance to bring back to life. Then the door shut with a heavy clank, and it was all gone to me. There was no need to lock the door; it was keyed to the card in my hand. Without the card, no one was getting in.

Although we were leaving, we agreed that everything we left behind was still ours. We left it all stored safely, on the off chance we might have to come back for something.

All of us hoped that we would never have to.

I returned to Ryan, who was watching for trouble while the rest of us moved out, and gestured to him that it was time to move. He nodded and fell in beside me as I escorted him to the rear of the prisoner transport, and there I helped him up into the nook we'd left clear for him.

"Don't forget to lock the door from the inside," I reminded him as he settled in. He gave me a lopsided smile in return.

"I remember, sis."

Sis? When did that happen?

"Pft, you don't get to call me that until you marry my sister." I snorted and gave him a playful smile.

"Working on it." He grinned brightly, then slammed the door and locked it securely.

I was the last one left exposed, and I did not like that feeling. With great effort, I fought down a spurt of panic and hurried to the passenger door of the Hilux. A second later, I was inside and pulled the door closed behind me. The locks clunked as Michael engaged them, and only then did I feel secure.

I pulled on my seatbelt, then grabbed my walkie-talkie off my belt. "Everyone lock up tight. Don't open for anyone you don't know."

What I got in return was a series of silly answers

and fake military jargon. Even Michael picked up his radio and added a "Roger-roger, Cap'n!" in a nasally falsetto, garnering laughter from the others.

I rolled my eyes and clicked the microphone off as we pulled away from the bunker, and left our home behind us.

***

The sun rose higher in the sky, and brought with it the stinging heat of midsummer. The trip was torturously slow considering the short distance we needed to travel. The roads were in even worse condition than I remembered, and the heavier vehicles struggled in many places. Our Hilux had no issues with the terrain, and its big tyres carried us easily over the roughest ground – but the others were not so lucky.

It took us almost an hour to reach the southern edge of the city. I breathed a sigh of relief when we finally cleared the outskirts and found the shattered concrete ribbon of the highway that wound its way out through the flat, green pasturelands towards our destination.

I was just beginning to relax when the radio crackled to life, and nearly gave me a heart attack.

"I see something, I see something!" Maddy was screaming and sounded terrified. "I see something *moving*!"

There was a weird, muffled sound, and then Skylar's voice came on. "Please disregard that emergency broadcast. Madeline has just seen her first cow."

"What's a 'cow'?" We heard the little girl's voice in the background. Skylar heaved a long-suffering sigh, and then the line crackled off.

Michael and I glanced at one another, and then burst out laughing.

It felt so good to have someone to share a laugh with.

***

A slender tree had fallen across the road since the last time I'd come this way, effectively blocking the path. It wasn't a big one, but there was no way the vans would get past it unless we found some way to move it.

The Hilux rolled to a stop, and Michael grabbed his radio. "We've got a blockage. Everyone stay where you are."

The radio crackled to life.

"What kind of blockage?" I couldn't quite tell which one of the others it was.

"Just a tree down, nothing dangerous." He unfastened his seatbelt, then clipped the radio onto his belt and climbed out. I followed him, shotgun at the ready as I scanned the horizon.

"Calm down, Sandy. It's only a tree." Michael gave me one of his quirky smiles, but I was not convinced.

"Not necessarily." I shook my head. "I've seen raiders use something very similar as a trap for travellers. You'll forgive me, but there is a reason I'm this paranoid."

He had nothing to say to that, and just silently acknowledged that he was out of his element. With my weapon held at the ready, I soft-stepped towards the tree, and angled around the fallen trunk until I could see the base. The sure way to know if it was a trap or natural deadfall was to figure out whether the trunk had been cut.

The stump was shattered, rotten, eaten through by insects. I immediately relaxed and called over my shoulder to Michael. "It's okay, it's just deadfall. It's probably not a trap, but keep your guard up anyway."

"*Probably* not a trap?"

"You never know." I shrugged. "People can be opportunistic."

"This is a very depressing conversation." Michael sighed as he drew up behind me, to help me examine the tree for the best way to get rid of it.

"Welcome to the world outside your nice, safe bunker, sweetheart. It's depressing out here." I answered dryly, then prodded at the deadfall with my boot. "It's rotten through and all soggy. We should be able to cut it easily enough and move it in sections."

"What about towing it out of the way with the four-wheel drive?" He looked at me for guidance, but I shook my head.

"Maybe in chunks, but if we try to do that with the whole trunk it'll just crack. Look." I shoved at the trunk with my foot, and showed him how the bark was spongy and moved beneath my foot. Squish, squish, squish.

"All right. I'll go find an axe." He deferred to my judgement without a word of complaint, and headed off towards the rear of the convoy.

I pulled my own radio off my belt and clicked it on. "Guys, Michael's coming to get the axe. Does anyone know where we put it?"

Crackle.

"I've got it," Ryan said.

"You hear that?" I called after Michael, and he waved to acknowledge that he had.

A few minutes later, he was back with the doctor and Ryan beside him. Between the three of them, they made short work of the rotten tree while I patrolled the perimeter of our little caravan on the lookout for trouble. I stopped to chat briefly with my sister and Madeline while they waited, but I didn't linger for long.

As I was returning to the front of the queue to check on the guys, something in the distance caught my attention. I stretched up as tall as I could and I shielded my eyes against the sun. Something was moving, and moving with far more vigour than a cow or a sheep.

"Guys." The low, urgent tone of my voice got their attention immediately. "Did any of you bring binoculars?"

Without a word, Michael drew a pair out of his vest and handed them to me. They were small with a low magnification, but they were enough. I focused on the movement in the distance, and then swore softly.

"We have a pig incoming," I told them softly, keeping my voice low and calm to disguise my concern.

Then, something else caught my eye, another flash of movement. Smaller and quicker – and running for its life. My whole body tensed. "It's chasing a person!"

"A living person?" Michael strained to see what I was seeing, which was a solitary survivor fleeing from 350 kilograms of rampaging, infected pork.

"Definitely alive – for the moment."

The others looked at me for guidance, but I wasn't sure what to tell them. If I were on my own, I wouldn't have stood a chance so I would have had to leave that survivor to his fate.

But between the four of us, though...

I looked amongst them, and saw faces that ranged from determination to fear. It was Michael that made the decision for us, though, in that soft, deep, commanding voice he used when he'd made up his mind about something.

"We can't just leave him to die."

We all nodded, and I battled a mixture of relief and terror. We were going to fight a pig. A massive, undead, rampaging wild boar. This was madness.

Still, someone needed to organise us now that the decision was made, and they were all looking at me.

"Doctor Cross, I would appreciate if you stayed with the girls." I glanced at him, and saw his relief. "You're our last line of defence in case the worst happens." He nodded his agreement and moved off, leaving me with Michael and Ryan.

I turned to them and pointed at the gun Ryan held. "That little peashooter won't do anything more than piss it off. If it gets close to you, use the axe."

He nodded. I turned and handed the shotgun to Michael.

"What about you?" Michael looked concerned as he took the weapon, but I just smiled and pulled out my taser.

"I'm bait," I answered with a giddy kind of confidence that was based more on bravado than real courage. "Remember, these things charge. They're much stronger and faster than they look, but they can't turn quickly. Stay light on your feet." Suddenly, I was feeling almost buoyant, charged full of adrenaline – ready to do the impossible.

The survivor saw us and turned, pelting towards us as fast as his legs would carry him. The paddocks were uneven and full of hidden obstacles; I silently prayed he wouldn't lose his footing. If he fell, the creature would be on him in a heartbeat.

The taser cracked to life in my hand. I strode forward, and felt the two men fall into place on either side of me with their weapons at the ready.

"Be prepared to scatter," I told them softly, calmly. "We should be able to confuse it. It won't have much of a brain left."

The stranger was shouting and waving at us, so I waved back and gestured for him to keep coming. He was close enough now that I could see the sweat glistening on skin the colour of milky coffee. I wondered how long he'd been running for, because he looked close to collapse.

The pig was hot on his heels, its head down and snorting furiously. Then it saw us, and it squealed a terrible sound. The running figure was forgotten as it turned its attention onto us.

"Wait for it." I kept my voice low and soft, to keep them calm.

The creature stopped and stared at us, making the kind of noises that would echo in my nightmares forever. Low, deep squeals, sounds that no pig should ever make. It stomped its hoof, slowly swinging its head from side to side.

The horrid thing was already half decomposed, with innards hanging out in places and patches of muscle lay bare beneath tattered skin. Its spinal column stuck out, white and naked against rotted flesh. I focused on that, and flexed my fingers on the taser.

Then, suddenly, it charged.

The three of us scattered in a neat three-pronged formation, just as we planned. The men with the guns put distance between themselves and the pig, while I cut it so fine that I could smell the pig's terrible stink as it barrelled past me. I struck without hesitation, and jabbed my taser at the exposed bone of its spine. Electricity surged along the biological conduits intended for an entirely different kind of current, and the creature screamed.

It was slow to turn towards me, hindered by my attack. As I retreated, Ryan darted in and struck at it with the axe, swinging the weapon overhead with all the strength in his one good hand. He struck in the same place that I had, aiming for the exposed bone, but he missed and the axe bounced off.

The shotgun roared a moment after Ryan retreated, peppering the beast's side with hot shrapnel. It screamed again, a terrible, blood-curdling sound. It was turning on the spot, almost spinning in place, struggling to decide which of us to charge first.

It chose Michael.

The pig took him by surprise and bowled him over, knocking the breath out of him. It was on him in a second, and he barely had the chance to get the gun up in time to defend himself. It bit down on the shaft of the gun, which did little damage to the weapon itself but it prevented him from firing and forced him to twist himself awkwardly to keep out from beneath trampling hooves.

Ryan and I leapt forward and went on the offensive. I struck it behind the ear with my taser, while Ryan hacked away at its spine. Finally, one of his blows slid between the vertebrae and severed its spinal cord.

The pig's hind-quarters collapsed, distracting it for the few seconds that Michael needed to yank his gun around into position to fire.

The shell exploded in the pig's mouth, and penetrated the soft membrane at the back of its throat. Shrapnel exploded within it, and sent hot shards scattering about, dicing what was left of its brain.

The pig died unceremoniously, and this time its death was permanent.

It took all our combined strength to drag Michael

out from beneath the corpse before it collapsed, but we got him free just in time. I was relieved to find he was uninjured aside from some bruises and the ringing in his ears from the shotgun blast so close. He shook his head to clear it as we hauled him to his feet, then we looked down at the pig with a mixture of amusement and confusion.

Then Michael looked up and grinned at us both.

"Bacon, anyone?"

***

It felt amazing to laugh together, all of us feeling the rush of victory. We made our way back to our convoy together, slapping each other on the back and administering high fives all around.

When we arrived, we found the stranger leaning against one of our vans, talking to Skylar and Dr Cross. He looked exhausted and was out of breath, but as we drew closer we could hear his words.

"—sickness. They sent a couple of us out looking for a treatment. Then the fucking pig—"

"What are the symptoms?" Dr Cross interrupted him, adjusting his glasses absently. His face was already set in the scowl he wore when he was thinking about something intensely.

"Diarrhoea mostly, you know, real nasty diarrhoea. Vomiting. Some of them have a fever." The kid glanced back over his shoulder and his expression brightened when he saw us closing in. "Hey! Oh man, I owe you fullas my life. I don't know what I woulda done if you hadn't been here."

"Glad to help, mate." Michael took the lead and approached the stranger with an extended hand. The youth grabbed it and shook it enthusiastically, reaching out with the other to clap him on the shoulder.

"I can't believe that fucking pig, man. I heard about them on the news but never seen one before. It bowled me right off my bike. Hell, you folks are heroes!"

"Hell's the word for it; that was one scary bundle of demon-pork," Michael agreed, then he glanced back at me and gave me one of those smiles that made my heart race. "Luckily for all of us, we have an expert along."

I felt my cheeks burn, but I hung back and sidestepped behind Ryan. My inner paranoia warned me away from the stranger-danger, but the others seemed relaxed and the stranger looked friendly, so I wasn't in too much of a panic.

"An expert? Damn. You're real lucky." The stranger shook his head and ran a hand back through his tight black curls. "Bro, I'm still freaked out."

"You and me both," Ryan commented dryly, then shot a curious look at me when he realised that I was hiding behind him. "Let's not do that again anytime soon."

"Agreed." The stranger nodded, then extended his hand to Ryan as well. "Hey, I'm Hemi."

"Ryan." The redheaded youth awkwardly shook the offered hand with his one good one, and then he proceeded to introduce the rest of us.

"So what are you doing out here?" Michael asked curiously, and shot a glance at the doctor. "You were saying something about a sickness?"

"He was telling me that his *whanau* live near here, and that a lot of them have been getting sick recently," the doctor piped up with the information he knew, and then Hemi nodded exuberantly.

"Yeah, man. Real nasty sick in the stomach. Puking and crapping all over the place."

Now there was a pleasant thought.

"Did you get sick, young man?" The doctor fixed Hemi with an intense, wary look.

"Nah, I'm good. That's why I volunteered to go looking for medicine."

"I'm rather relieved to hear that." I peered at the youth with natural suspicion, but he didn't seem to mind. He just laughed and nodded.

"Me too, man. Me too."

"So, you guys have a community?" Skylar suddenly joined the conversation, her curiosity getting the better of her at last.

"Yeah, there's about a dozen of us. We built us a *pa* southwest of here." He used the Maori word for a fortified town, but it was a word that most of us were familiar with from the time before the plague. Then he looked around at us and gave us a lopsided smile. "We can trade, if you have medicine. We've got cows and sheep, so we can trade beef, milk or lamb. Or wool, if any of you guys are knitters. Maybe other things, depends what you want."

"Weapons?" Yes, that was me. Surprise, surprise. I felt exposed, like we needed more to protect ourselves.

"Guns?" He shook his head. "Nah, sorry. We only have one old rifle and we use it for hunting. A few knives, but nothing good for fighting with."

Damn. Couldn't blame a girl for trying.

"It's okay." Michael shrugged. "If we can help you, we will. You can return the favour later. It's more important to get your people feeling better."

Hemi's eyebrows shot up, and he gave Michael a long, sideways look. So did I for that matter. We had the opportunity for trade, and he was willing to just give away our advantage?

As though reading my mind, Michael looked back at me and gave me one of his sweet smiles. I melted a little bit, and smiled back; his smiles were so addictive.

"That's generous man, real generous." Hemi bobbed his head thoughtfully as he mulled it over, then he flashed another one of his lopsided grins. "Not a lot of trust left in this world, but I ain't gonna say no when the *whanau* need help, you know. Appreciate it, guy. We owe you one."

Michael nodded, and gestured for the doctor to do his thing.

While Dr Cross spoke to the young man in great detail about all kinds of colours and consistencies I didn't want to think about, Michael drew me aside. Together, we walked to the front of the convoy, and put the Hilux between ourselves and the others.

Once we were alone, he took my hand in his and drew me in close to him. The kiss was quick and feather-light, for fear of sneaking Skylars hunting us down.

"You were amazing out there." His voice was a breathless murmur as he wrapped his arm around my waist to draw me up against his lean frame.

"Me?" I was bewildered by the compliment. "You were the one that killed it."

"No, *we* killed it, with teamwork. " He slipped his other arm around my shoulders, and his fingers softly caressed the back of my neck. "But you... you were magnificent. So confident and graceful. I didn't know you had it in you."

"Oh."

His lips were on the side of my neck now, planting tender kisses across my skin. A little nuzzle, and then I felt the softest nibble on my earlobe – it sent a lightning bolt right through me. My back came to rest against the truck's door, pinned by his strong hands.

"Ah, M-michael..." I tried to protest, but my heart wasn't in it. His breath was hot and heavy across my skin, and I could feel the swell of his rising arousal despite the body armour he wore. "W-what about—"

"Shh..." he murmured and silenced me with a kiss. "They can't see us back here. What they don't know—"

"What we don't know, huh?"

Uh-oh.

Skylar stood a few meters away, her arms folded across her chest and a look of smug satisfaction on her face.

"I knew it!" She jabbed an accusatory finger at us, then turned on a heel and skipped off.

Michael groaned, and reluctantly released me. "Can't we get a moment's privacy around here? God."

"Of course not." I sighed and straightened my clothing. "This is what happens when six people live in close proximity for too long. No one has any privacy."

"Well, I sure hope we can find our own space in this new town. What I wouldn't give to have you all to myself for a while." He paused and gave me a long, thoughtful look that made me tingle all over.

"Oh, really?" I lifted my brows, half-teasing and half-curious. "And what would you do with me if you had me?"

"Well." His voice dropped to a low, throaty purr. "I would have to spend some time exploring you. Catalogue your most sensitive spots." He reached a hand up and stroked a curl of hair from my cheek. "Or at least, the ones you'll let me touch."

"Hmm," I murmured and turned my head to nuzzle at his palm. "We should *definitely* try and find our own space, then."

He shot me a wicked grin, and then took my hand to lead me back towards the others.

***

It took some time for the doctor to work out the medication required, and the prescriptions for the number of sick people Hemi described. As he worked, we learned more about the group that Hemi came from.

He told us that his *whanau* consisted of about a dozen Maori survivors from across the region, who had banded together gradually over the course of the last ten years with a communal need to survive and keep their old traditions alive. They had built their village on the edge of one of the local lakes a few years ago, and had lived there in relative seclusion ever since.

After speaking with Hemi for a while, the doctor reached the conclusion that human occupation had inevitably tainted their water source.

"Make sure you boil any water that you're going to drink or are going to use to cook or clean something that you're going to eat." Dr Cross handed out information and medication with his usual efficiency. "Be sure to get the sick people to drink as much clean water as you can; they'll be quite dehydrated by now."

Hemi nodded happily, and examined the little box full of prescription bottles. "And everyone who's sick gets one of these, three times per day with a big glass of water. Got it. Thanks, doc." On a sudden impulse, the youth snatched up the doctor's hand and shook it vigorously.

"You're quite welcome, young man." The doctor looked flustered but pleased by Hemi's gratitude. As grumpy as he appeared to be, he did always seem to get a thrill from helping a patient. Medicine really was his calling in life.

"Hey, where are you folks heading to?" Hemi

looked back and forth between us, his dark eyes sparkling with youthful exuberance. "The *ariki* will want to come visit you. *Homai o homai*, eh? A gift for a gift."

Michael hesitated for a moment, and then made the decision for the rest of us.

"Ohaupo. We're planning to settle there." He sounded a little unsure of himself, but Hemi didn't seem to mind.

"Oh, eh? Sweet as, I'll let her know." He grinned, and there was nothing but genuine friendliness on his young face. "We'll come visit you, bro; bring you some presents."

Something about the youth put me at ease. In spite of my learned paranoia, I found myself liking him. He was no older than my sister, and there was a real openness to his character that made him instantly likeable.

A thought came to me suddenly as I watched him, and then I reached out to touch Michael's arm. He turned and looked at me, surprised, since I'd mostly stayed quiet throughout the conversation.

"Tell him about the mutants."

Michael immediately understood what I meant. Even if this tribe did turn out to be hostile in the end, it would be cruel not to warn them about a potential threat that might spread into the local area.

Michael summed up our encounters with the mutated infected in as few words as possible, glossing over the painful details of the deaths of his friends. Despite his brevity, he got the point across quite efficiently. By the time he finished warning the youth of the impending danger in Hamilton, the kid's smile was gone.

"No wonder you folks were after weapons." He looked back and forth between us, wide-eyed. "Had me worried for a second, but now I get it. Man, that's scary. I better get home fast, tell the boss. She'll decide what we do."

"Be careful." Michael nodded his agreement and stepped back. "We haven't seen anything this far south aside from the pig, but there's no way to be sure."

"Yeah. Stay safe, bro." The kid nodded respectfully to Michael, and then to the rest of us in turn. He looked up at the sun to get his bearings, and then with a wave he was off at a long, loping jog towards the south-west. We watched him go, then turned and looked at one another.

"We should probably get moving before it gets too hot." I ran my hand over my brow deliberately. The others nodded their agreement.

Suddenly, Michael chuckled. I looked at him quizzically, not quite sure what the joke was at first. He knitted his brows and rolled his eyes heavenwards.

"We never did finish moving that tree."

***

It didn't take us long to finish removing the deadfall, though. In no time at all, we were back on the road, picking our way slowly towards the township of Ohaupo. It was just after midday and the sun was high overhead, burning down on us with an exhausting intensity.

"Ugh." I groaned and plucked my singlet away from my sweaty tummy. Even with the windows rolled down, the humidity was getting unbearable. "I never thought I'd be fantasising about a *cold* shower."

"Mmngh," Michael agreed unintelligibly, half way through taking a long drink from his water bottle. He swallowed and sighed heavily, then offered the rest of the bottle to me.

I took it without thinking and drank deeply, even though it was warm and tasted a little brackish. After the last few drops rolled down my throat, I sighed as well and plunked my elbow on the edge of the window.

Suddenly, a thought struck me, and it was so silly that it made me giggle.

Michael glanced at me, bemused. "What are you chortling at?"

"Just a thought." I pulled a face and shook the empty drink bottle at him. "Is sharing your water with another survivor the post-apocalyptic equivalent of sharing your juice box with the cute girl you like in kindergarten?"

"What?" He chuckled and shook his head. "Where did *that* thought come from?"

"I honestly don't know. Maybe it's heatstroke?" I shrugged and shot a sideways look at him. "Are you going to push me over so you can sneak a look up my skirt now?"

"Why, of course not." Michael feigned offense at

the very suggestion, then his eyes narrowed, and a wickedly flirtatious grin danced across his lips. "If I wanted to get a look up your skirt, I'd just ask politely... and maybe kiss you on that spot on your neck that makes you go all gooey."

He had a point. When he kissed me *there*, I was putty in his hands.

I was about to say something cheeky back when he interrupted, his tone gone from one of playful flirtation to one of pure excitement. "Hey, hey look!"

Ahead of us, the details of a tiny township were beginning to emerge from the heat mirage. I sat up straight and scanned through the haze until I spotted familiar landmarks.

"Yes, this is it." It was hard to contain my excitement as I confirmed his suspicions, and then I fished my radio off my belt to inform the others about the good news. "Attention all passengers, please be advised we will be reaching our destination in a few minutes. Please ensure your seatbelt is fastened, and your tray table is in a secure, upright position."

A chorus of cheers echoed from the others. No one was any happier about travelling in the heat than I was.

I dropped the radio in my lap, and flopped back in my seat with a sigh of relief. "Thank goodness that's over."

Chapter Twenty-One

We toured slowly through the town of Ohaupo. Michael followed my directions as I pointed the way through the township, until at last we eased to a halt in front of my familiar old video store.

"I've claimed that flat up above the store." I pointed it out to Michael proudly. He looked, and then gave me an odd sideways glance. I laughed at his expression. "It's nicer than it looks, I swear."

"Hrm. I don't know, Sandy." He looked worried, and I knew that feeling well – it was the feeling of being exposed and vulnerable. "Everything seems so... open. It doesn't feel very secure."

"We can't live in a bunker forever, honey. We'll turn into mushrooms." I gave him an impish grin, and leaned over to reassuringly rub his thigh. "Don't worry, there are ways to make this place secure, too. I've explored pretty much the entire town and only found one infected, plus I know exactly where we can stay."

"Only one infected?" His brow furrowed. "Surely there must have been more people living here than that."

"Yeah, about that – don't go into that function building we passed."

"Oh." He paused for a long moment to think that over, and then looked at me again. "Group suicide?"

I nodded, and he grimaced.

"As loathe as I am to destroy perfectly good shelter, we may want to consider burning the whole building down." I glanced back over my shoulder and struggled to suppress the chill that rolled down my spine. "There are a lot of bodies in there. A lot."

He just nodded and looked grim as he put the Hilux into park and killed the engine. We climbed out and went back to check on the others. One by one, they disembarked and stood around, smelling the air. A cool breeze blew, and it smelt fresh and clean after the cloying stink of decay that hung over Hamilton.

"Where do we go?" Skylar asked, absently plucking her sticky t-shirt away from her neck. Even in the shade, it was humid.

"Well, I was staying above the video store, but it backs onto a small motel." I looked back and forth between them. "There's a half-dozen rooms upstairs that are clean, dry, and zombie-free. You have to go through a staircase in the lobby to get to them, so you've got a natural choke point to defend."

"Sounds good." Michael nodded for me to take point. "Let's go take a look."

We gave everyone a moment to lock up their respective vehicles, and then I led the way. Madeline, fresh from a nap in the car, skipped ahead of us singing happily to herself, despite our best efforts to keep her from running off. The rest of us moved as a group, weapons relaxed but ready in case they were needed.

We picked our way across the cracked pavement past my store, and took the side road to the left. The entrance to the motel was an old glass door that was webbed with cracks, yet still solid. The hinges protested as I shoved it open and led the way into the dusty darkness.

The lobby was nothing to write home about, just an open space no bigger than the average living room. It was decorated with a faded reception desk and a couple of overstuffed couches off to one side. On one side of the desk, an archway led out to an overgrown courtyard. On the other side, stairs led up into brilliant sunshine. Magazines ten years out of date decomposed on the coffee table.

"We should be able to bolt this from the inside, but it'll take a little lubricant on the hinges." I gestured to the front door, then led the way further inside.

A bunch of keys sat on the front desk, exactly where I'd left them two weeks before. I picked them up and headed upstairs. The staircase let out onto an open-air landing; the motel was like an old Roman villa, built in a square with a courtyard in the centre. Half a dozen doors flanked the upper landing, each with a number on it that had once meant something to someone.

I'd gone through them all in my initial exploration and at the time I mentally catalogued their contents.

Now, I used that knowledge to point out the ones that were immediately liveable to the others, separating them from the rooms that would need work to become habitable.

Each room was a self-contained unit, with a bathroom and basic kitchen functionality, while there was a larger kitchen on the bottom level that had once served as a small restaurant. Much like the rest of the building, the downstairs kitchen was filthy and it would take all our combined efforts to get it in functioning order again.

Still, after they had looked around for a while, the others agreed that this old motel would work well as our new home.

***

The next few days were spent hard at work, turning our little motel into a fortress. We scavenged enough boards from the other buildings nearby to cover up all the downstairs windows and the fire exit at the rear, to leave the front door as the only way in or out of the complex. As I predicted, with a little maintenance the front door closed and locked easily, and we slept soundly at night.

Each of the others chose their own rooms. Ryan and Skylar claimed the honeymoon suite, amidst exclamations of delight at the sheer size of the bed, and the bright morning sunshine that the room got. The doctor took a two-bedroom suite on the opposite side of the building, so that Madeline could have her own room. He was thrilled by the idea of being able to close off her mess when he didn't want to look at it anymore, and I couldn't say I blamed him.

Michael, on the other hand, chose a small room right on the corner of the building that was once the owner's personal office. The sole reason for his choice was that the room had a window less than two meters from the upper floor of the video store where I preferred to stay. His window lined up almost exactly with the one on the tiny landing of my loft, close enough that we could almost touch if we leaned out.

Between the two of us, we constructed a walkway between the two buildings. It was really just a couple of planks for a floor and ropes for handrails, but it was strong enough to support our weight when we wanted to duck back and forth to visit one another. Which we did, often.

Michael swiftly came to appreciate my affection for the little loft, particularly the soft double bed. After the narrow, rock-hard cots that we had been sleeping on in the bunker, the beds here felt like sleeping on a cloud.

On the third morning after our arrival, I awoke to the sound of birds chirping and Michael snoring contentedly beside me. I rolled over and looked at him, and found him sprawled on his back with his arms and legs flung in all directions. He looked so peaceful that I couldn't bear to wake him.

I rose and slid out of bed, careful not to disturb the blankets draped over him. Stretching languidly, I moved out to the living area to open the curtains, and let the bright morning sun wash over my naked body. It felt so good to be able to walk around freely without the fear of running into a curious seven-year-old. I liked kids, but sometimes it was nice to be able to be an adult without little eyes peeping in.

Feeling relaxed and refreshed, I wandered contentedly around my living space, opening the windows one by one to let in the morning breeze. True to his word, Michael had been using his time alone with me very well. Although I still couldn't quite conquer my fears completely, we'd learned so much about our own limits through experimentation and play. Every day, he was helping me to hate myself a bit less.

I sighed and looked down at myself, considering the curve of my breasts, my stomach and legs. It had been years since I'd had proper female curves. With a healthy, regular diet and exercise, my body was gradually leaving starvation mode. I was starting to feel healthy and fit again, and it felt good. I had breasts again. That fact made me happy, and made Michael even happier. I didn't even realise how much I'd missed having a proper bust line until there was someone in my life that I wanted to share it with.

My foot had been healing cleanly, and last night the doctor had finally announced that I no longer needed to keep the bandages on. It still ached, and it was pink and tender, but the stitches were out and I was more or less functional again. I stretched the foot out in front me like a silly, naked ballerina, to examine the scar. It wasn't pretty, but my foot was working again and that was all that mattered to me.

Full of energy after a good night's sleep, I danced back through the bedroom to the en suite, and flicked on the shower. It had taken some doing, but with time, determination and lots of bad language, I'd managed to get the hot water cylinder working again. Skye insisted I do hers as well, so once I knew the trick to it I ended up fixing everyone's.

I didn't mind at all. The work kept my mind active and my days busy, and Michael kept my nights... interesting, and exciting. My lips quirked into a smile as I slipped beneath the hot water and let it cascade over my face and down my body like a hot caress. I closed my eyes and ran my hands back through my hair, enjoying the feel of hot water cleansing me.

All of a sudden, there were sneaking fingers blocking the falling water as hands crept around from behind to cup my breasts. I opened my eyes and looked back over my shoulder, to find my lover grinning impishly back at me.

My lover, I thought possessively, and spun beneath the water to face him. Driven by the heat of the water and my own surging emotions, I wrapped my arms around his neck and drew him down into a kiss.

Mine, mine, mine.

Though I supposed if you wanted to be technical, we weren't lovers yet. Over the last few days, we'd done everything but the final act of consummation. Little by little, he was coaxing out my inner harlot, that saucy young thing I had been in my youth before harsh reality tore it away.

And yet, no matter how much I wanted to, I couldn't quite bring myself to take that final step.

God, how much I wanted to, though. I longed for it, I thought about it constantly and even dreamed about it, but every time I tried to gather the courage, the spectres lunged out of their hiding place and chased me back. Michael had been so patient with me, and he never tried to put any pressure on me to do anything I was uncomfortable with. Over the time we'd spent together, my trust in him was growing, to the point where I could feel it turning into something deeper.

It scared me a little bit, but at the same time it was exciting and new. If there was one thing in this world that I knew for sure, it was that I wanted to be with him one day, when the time was right and we were both ready. In the meantime, he was helping me to repair the damage that bad men had done to me over the years.

His hand caught the small of my back, and drew my belly up hard against his as he kissed me deeply. The heat of the water had always been something that made my desires stir – and now I had the fantasy man to go along with the steamy shower. I wanted to have him so badly, to be pinned to the wall and ravished in that hot, hot shower, and yet... I couldn't. Not yet.

Soon? A part of me begged, writhing in unsatisfied torment.

Soon! The rational part of me demanded, hating so much being the victim.

But the part of me that was the victim wasn't so sure just yet. It didn't know what it wanted, and it was so afraid.

***

Half an hour later, the hot water finally ran out. Exhausted, flushed and not nearly as clean as we probably should have been, we finally managed to pry our hands off one another long enough to get dressed.

Everyone else had already figured out what was going on between us by now. There were no secrets in a community this small. Still, there was an unspoken agreement between Michael and me, that we would keep our business as private as possible. It was driving Skylar crazy.

After ten years of only having one person with her, someone whose business she already knew intimately, she was gossip-starved and desperate to talk about something new. Still, sisters or not, I liked having something that was mine and mine alone. Michael seemed to be a private person by nature, and I respected that. Neither of us were willing to indulge Skye's need for gossip just yet.

When Michael and I finally made our way into the communal kitchen to join the others for breakfast, hand in hand, Skylar gave us a knowing look but didn't say a word. As we settled down at the breakfast table, she sauntered over to give us both the hairy eyeball.

"I'm making omelettes. You two okay with that?"

"Oh, you found the chickens?" I grinned at the

thought of savoury, nutritious food, and she smiled back at me.

"Yup. I found a vegetable garden, too, so I've got tomatoes and parsley as well." She looked so proud of herself. "I hope no one's allergic?"

We all shook our heads and she grinned brightly, then waddled back to her stove to get cooking.

"Shame we don't have some toast and Marmite to go with it," I reminisced dreamily.

"And don't forget the bacon." Michael's comment was laced with dry humour; we all laughed.

"So, we were talking earlier," Ryan piped up as the levity faded. "We've got this jungle happening in the central courtyard right now, but if we cleared out all the weeds and bushes, then we could plant our own vegetable garden in there."

Skye added her input to the conversation, as she cracked eggs into a huge bowl. "That way even if something happens and we have to lock this place down, we'll still have a secure source of fresh food."

"That's a good idea." Michael nodded slowly, then looked at me for my thoughts.

"Yeah." I glancing thoughtfully around at the ring of faces. "We could transfer some of the adult plants from the gardens outside. I think I saw some hydroponics equipment out at one of the farms, too."

"We could clear out one of the downstairs rooms." Ryan was sounding excited now. "If we bring back that equipment, we can grow all kinds of things."

I looked around at the faces that had become so

familiar to me in such a short period of time, and felt an unexpected surge of affection towards them all. Then I noticed a strange little smile on Dr Cross' face, and shot him a curious look. "What are you grinning at, Doc?"

"Oh, nothing." He chuckled softly. "I was just thinking that you young folks sound as excited as my late wife when she first saw the big gardens behind our first house. She loved to garden." The doctor sighed softly, and absently raised a hand to stroke Madeline's hair. Maddy, of course, was off in her own little world, playing with her dolls, and didn't even seem to notice.

"Oh, good." I grinned right back at him. "Hopefully you can tell us how to not kill things, then. I'm pretty sure no one in this room has ever planted a vegetable garden before."

Embarrassed chuckles from the others around the room answered that question – apparently, my guess was bang on the money.

"Ah, I see." The doctor shoved his glasses up his nose, but for once the smile lingered on his face. It was nice to see him happy for a change. "I've been volunteered as the king of the vegetable patch. I shall try my best to teach you youngsters what you need to know."

"After breakfast." Ryan grinned, and everyone else agreed. Skylar's savoury concoction was just about done, and to our deprived noses it smelled like the most delicious thing ever made in the entire history of the world.

We waited impatiently while she finished cooking,

our grumbling bellies whining in protest about how long it took to cook. Once it was served, the food was devoured with delighted gusto; more than one of us suffered a burnt tongue in our haste, but it was well worth it. I couldn't remember a breakfast I'd enjoyed more.

"You're getting good at this, Skye," I told her after I finished my last bite, while settling back in my chair to digest. "I think you've inherited Mum's culinary skills."

"Thanks." She beamed, glowing from the praise. "I'm really enjoying it, actually. Cooking, I mean. I found some cook books while I was exploring the other day, and looking through the pictures has got me feeling so inspired."

I smiled at her enthusiasm and nodded. "Well, if we can find the ingredients, I'm sure no one will mind if you experimented a bit and tried out some of the recipes."

A chorus of grunts came from the menfolk that we both took to be agreement.

"I'd love to, but there are so many words in there that I don't know." Skylar sighed heavily. "I'll have to get someone to help me read the recipes."

I stared at her, but it took a second for what she'd just said to actually sink in. When it did, my eyes widened in surprise. "You can't read?"

"I can, sort of." She looked taken aback by the accusation, and a little offended. "But not very well. I was eight, Sandy. Eight! I only got to go to school for a few years, so I didn't get to learn much. I haven't had very much practice since then so I'm just not a good reader."

Her tone stung; it was so full of bitterness, something I hadn't heard from her before.

"I didn't mean it like that, sis." Suddenly on the defensive, I held my hands up in front of me as though to ward off a physical attack. "I just mean, you know. I hadn't thought about it. Don't worry about it though, we'll teach you."

"Yes, we absolutely will." Dr Cross' voice cut in, surprising us since he usually spent our mealtimes in silence. "You shall join Madeline's lessons immediately. So much of human history is now only available in the written form; it is critical that each of us understand it so that we can keep our language and our history alive. The written word is the only reliable way that we can preserve our history for our children, and our children's children."

Skye was speechless for once in her life and sat staring into space for a while, with her hand rubbing protectively over her swollen belly. I could see that the doctor's words reached her – particularly the very last of them. Finally, she nodded.

"Okay. If nothing else, then I'll learn for the baby's sake."

"And don't forget the cookbooks." Ryan chipped in helpfully. Someone kicked his ankle under the table, and he yelped. I wasn't sure if it was Skylar or one of the men, but either way everyone laughed.

***

The day grew hotter and hotter as the sun climbed higher in the sky. I paused in my work to wipe the sweat from my brow with the back of my hand, and then peered upwards.

It must be February, I thought absently as I considered the heat mirage that radiated off the ground and the roof of our building. February was the hottest month of the year, and with all the time I spent outside I had a good sense of the rise and fall of the seasons even if I didn't know the exact dates. This was by far the hottest day that I'd felt all year.

With a group effort, we had managed to clear the biggest weeds from the garden before the sun climbed high enough to reach our courtyard. The men had strained and strained to pull them out; some of those weeds had grown into small trees over the years. Eventually, we won the battle, and then we combined our forces to lug the unwanted greenery away.

Digging out the smaller weeds was going to take time, though. I was on my hands and knees in the dirt with a trowel, digging them out one by one. I twisted out one rampantly overgrown dandelion and flung it over my shoulder without looking, in the general direction of the pile on the concrete behind me.

"Hey!" A voice yelped. I glanced back and saw Michael brushing dirt off his trousers from where the plant hit him. He kicked the weed into the pile, and then joined me in the dirt. "Geez, attacking me with weeds now? What did I do?"

His voice was only teasing, so I smiled and tilted the

wide brim of my hat back to look at him. "You were clearly trying to sneak up on me, so it was self-defence."

With a grin, he grabbed one of the little gardening forks we'd scavenged from around town, and set about helping me to gouge out the verdant weeds. My gaze lingered on him a moment longer, admiring the way his broad shoulders glistened with sweat in the sunshine. He'd ditched his shirt at some stage and was clad only in dirty jeans. It was a pleasant sight – until I realised that his fair skin was starting to turn red.

"You're getting sunburnt," I warned him. The combination of his ethnicity and the length of time he'd spent living underground made him even more vulnerable to the sun than I was, but at least I was smart enough to wear a hat.

"I know." He sighed and absently rubbed a hand down his arm, then shrugged and gave me a sideways look. I noticed the bridge of his nose was red as well, as was his forehead and upper cheeks.

"Get inside, you. You're getting roasted," I scolded him and shook a dirty finger at him. "We've got enough things trying to kill us without adding melanoma to the list."

He mumbled something inarticulate and yanked out a weed. I leaned over and snatched it from his hand, then tossed it aside. "Oh no, you don't. Inside, right now."

He gave me a sulk that made my innards quiver, but I wasn't going to let him injure himself for the sake of pride. In the time I'd known him, I'd learned that the biggest danger to Michael Chan's health was not zombies or food poisoning, but his own stubbornness. I knew that he considered our safety and health far above his own, and tended to ignore his own condition until it was almost too late.

I hauled myself to my feet and dusted my knees off with my hands, then stripped off my dirty gardening gloves. I dumped them at my feet, put one hand on my hip and offered the other to him.

Loathe to admit his own weakness, he stared at my hand for a second, and then pointedly looked away.

"Ahem?" I wiggled my fingers deliberately, until finally his shoulders slumped in surrender. With a long sigh, he took my hand and let me help him to his feet, then he trailed along behind me as I led him into the shade.

"I'm fine, really." He was still protesting when we found the doctor in the midst of organising one of the storage rooms. The doctor took one look at him, and then started scolding him like a naughty child.

Michael promptly put on his whipped puppy expression, but neither of us were having any of it. Between the two of us, we bundled him off to one of the bathrooms and bullied him into a cold shower.

"But I'm fine!" He spluttered beneath the chilly flow, sending cold droplets flying in all directions.

"You feel like it now, but you won't in an hour." I gave him a stern look that told him I would brook no arguments from him. "Trust me."

"I'm afraid your lady friend is quite right, young

man," the doctor agreed. "It may not look or feel so bad right now, but the damage is already done. You're inside for the rest of the day, doctor's orders."

Michael visually deflated and slumped in against the shower's wall. "But what am I supposed to do inside all day?"

"Clear out one of the rooms for the hydroponics." I sighed and pulled off my hat. "I'm going to go this afternoon when it cools down a bit, and see what I can scrounge up. Right now, I don't think any of us should be out there. It has to be 32 degrees in the sun."

"Mmn." The doctor made an inarticulate noise of agreement. "Go fetch them in, Ms McDermott. I'll keep an eye on our good constable here."

"But I'm fine!" Michael was still protesting weakly, but he'd given up the fight.

"Sure you are, lobster-man." I chuckled, and reached over to trail a fingertip over his wet shoulder. The water felt so cool and nice I almost wanted to join him. "You seem to forget you've been living in a basement for the last ten years. Your skin has forgotten what the sun is."

Michael mumbled something inarticulate in return. The doctor caught my eye and rolled his, as if to comment on Michael's foolishness. I smiled at him and then left them to it, content to know that my sweetheart was in good hands.

Luckily, the others were not half as stubborn as Michael was; they were already filtering in out of the sun on their own. When I caught up to Skye and Ryan, they were heading for the kitchen. Ryan plodded along contentedly behind my sister, his arms burdened by an old plastic washing basket filled to bursting full of freshly-picked lettuces, tomatoes, cucumbers and green beans.

Skylar waddled ahead of him with her arms wrapped around an enormous watermelon, her gait awkward but determined. The melon was almost as big as her belly, so I hurried over to help her with it – or at least I tried to, but she refused to relinquish her prize.

"No, I've got this." She shooed me away, and vanished into the kitchen.

Ryan gave me an amused look and lifted a shoulder in a shrug. "Yeah, I tried that too. There's no helping her when she's got it in her head to do something."

I chuckled and nodded – I understood that stubbornness very well. It was a family trait. "What about you? You sure you should be lifting that with your arm?"

The youth looked down at his arm, which was still swathed in bandages, and then shrugged.

"Probably not, but I'm not letting *her* do it." He grinned and tilted his chin in the direction Skylar had gone. "It's all good, though. We're almost there." Then he adjusted his burden and followed Skylar into the kitchen, with me trailing along in their wake.

"Salad for lunch?" I queried curiously, and reached over to snatch a juicy tomato from the basket when Ryan set it down on the table. I held it to my nose and inhaled deeply, enjoying the garden-fresh scent. There was nothing quite the smell of a freshly-picked tomato.

"A'yup, and watermelon." Skylar beamed with pride as she rolled the massive melon along the bench and up onto the chopping board.

"That thing is huge, Skye. Think I should get the axe?" I was only half kidding. The thing really was ridiculously enormous. She actually paused to consider that option too, before shaking her head firmly.

"Nah, I don't want anything that touched that gross pig anywhere near my watermelon. Ry, come hold this while I get the knife."

"Oh god, I'm going to get killed, aren't I?" Ryan laughed cheerfully as he trundled over to do her bidding.

I couldn't help but join in the laughter. "Well, I'll leave you two to it, then. Have either of you seen Maddy?"

"Not recently." Skylar shrugged, unconcerned. In the three days that we'd been in the area, we had yet to see a single thing that even remotely resembled a threat. "She followed us towards the garden, but scampered off while we were picking veggies. I figured she must have gotten bored and come home."

"Sweet as, I'll go find her. Doc says it's time to come in out of the sun." I waved to them both and headed out. My first port of call was to head upstairs and check her room, but when I got there the room was empty.

"Made-line?" I called as I wandered through our little fortress, sticking my head into each room to check for her. After a few minutes, I came to the conclusion that she wasn't inside. Although I felt a brief stab of concern, I fought it back down and convinced myself that wherever she was, she was probably just fine.

She'll just be off playing somewhere, I decided as I headed back downstairs to fetch my hat. The sun was so intense that I didn't really want to go back out into it, but I had my orders.

As I crossed the threshold from the lobby to the street outside, the heat hit me like a wall. I lifted a hand to shade my eyes as I peered up and down the street, and called the girl's name again. No answer.

If I were a kid, where would I go?

I thought about it for a minute, and ran over the options the town had to offer that would interest a seven-year-old. There weren't many places to play here, except–

With a flash of cognition, I snapped my fingers and jogged off in the direction of the old primary school not too far from our base of operations. If I remembered correctly, the place had an extensive but overgrown playground in the yard. If I were a bored child, that was definitely where I'd go.

I ducked down a weed-choked walkway that ran between two houses, a pathway that had once been used by children as a shortcut to their school. The homes had big, old trees in the yard, with branches that hung so low that I had to duck beneath them as they tried to snatch away my hat, but the shade was a welcome respite from the intensity of the midsummer sun. At the far end of the corridor, I emerged from beneath the trees and stood squinting in the bright daylight.

Sure enough, there was a little figure playing on the swings. As I drew closer, I could hear her chattering away to someone or something I couldn't see. Since there was no reply, I assumed she was just talking to her dolls.

"Hey, Maddy," I called to her as I crossed the overgrown field, following her path of crushed grass towards the swings. Surprised, she turned around to look at me. After a second she waved happily, and beckoned me over.

"Miss Sandy, look, look what I found. Look!" She squealed gleefully and pointed to a climbing frame nearby. I followed her finger with my eye and looked up.

Lo and behold, who was sitting up there but my little friend Tigger. She'd grown a lot in the two weeks I'd been gone and now lay basking contentedly in the sunshine.

"Well, look at that." I grinned, pleased to see the little housecat was fine. I may or may not have been a little bit worried about her while I was away, so it was a relief to see she had stayed happy and healthy in my absence.

"It's so cute!" Maddy twisted on her swing, looking bright-eyed and excited. Suddenly she spun the swing around to face me, and stared up at me with enormous eyes. "What is it?"

"It's called a kitten." I tried hard not to laugh; it wasn't her fault that she'd grown up in a world without pets. I reminded myself just how limited her experiences were, and expanded on my answer for her benefit. "A kitten is a baby domestic cat."

"Oh, like Puss In Boots?" Her eyes were so wide I was almost afraid they'd pop right out of her head.

"Sort of, except real cats walk on four legs, not two." It was starting to get really hard not to laugh, her expression was just too cute. "I named this one Tigger when I was living here before. Like from Winnie the Pooh?"

"Ohh. Tigger like a tiger, because he's got stripes?" She looked delighted by my childlike logic, and hopped off her swing. "Tiggers-Tiggers-Tiggers are wonderful things, their heads are made of rubber and their tails are made of springs!" She chant the old rhyme gleefully and bounced around the yard.

"Yes, yes they are. And Maddy-monkeys need to come inside for lunch." I grinned at her and offered her my hand. She bounced over to take it, and together we walked – and bounced – back towards our little fortress.

Behind us, Tigger stretched and rolled onto her back to watch us go. Just as we were about to leave her line of sight, she hopped up and scampered after us, to follow us back home.

***

Lunch was a noisy affair that day, full of boisterous joy and happy mess. Madeline had never eaten watermelon before, and she was quick to announce it was her new 'favouritest food ever', to the amusement of the adults.

Since I lacked Madeline's sweet tooth, the salad was the bigger treat for me. Skylar had even added some hard boiled eggs for protein, just the way Mum used to when we were little. I ate several helpings before I was satisfied, and then sat back in my chair to watch the others stuff themselves.

There's going to be a few sick tummies tonight, I thought to myself with amusement.

The only one not joining in on the feast was Michael, who sat beside me in silence, picking quietly at his food without much interest. I watched him for a minute before I finally decided to check on him.

"Are you okay?" I asked softly, and reached over to stroke his knee in case my question was lost in the din.

The others didn't notice, but he did and shrugged absently. I looked at him closely and noticed that the sunburn was getting darker as the burn settled deeper into his skin. I resisted the automatic 'I-told-you-so'; just as we had predicted, he hadn't realised how bad the burn was until hours after the damage was already done. Now, he was in pain.

I knew that pain well, and so I rose to fetch another bottle of cool water for him from the fridge. Without a word, he took it and drank deeply, then gave me a weak smile. "Thank you."

"Of course." I rubbed his knee softly, sympathy twisting my gut. Sunburn could be a terrible thing.

Finally, the doctor noticed the conversation and joined in. "I made him some aloe vera gel, if you want to help him put on another dose." He fished a jar out of his pocket, and offered it to me across the table. I accepted it with a nod and then looked at Michael, who rose from his chair without a word.

He followed me out of the kitchen and plodded up the stairs behind me to his room. There, I sat him down in an old wooden chair beneath the window. He slumped into it with his chin resting on the back rung, staring miserably out the window.

"Ah, you poor thing," I murmured as I knelt on the floor behind him to study his burns. He was in too much pain to have put on a shirt.

"Doc says it'll take days to get better." He flinched as he folded his arms under his chin to give me better access to his burned back. He heaved a long sigh and murmured plaintively. "Make it better?"

"You know that I would if I could." I opened the jar of cream to examine the contents. The gel smelt strange and pungent, but I scooped out a generous helping anyway and lathered it across his broad back. His sigh of relief just about broke my heart, and he immediately relaxed beneath my touch.

With gentle fingers, I spread the gel over his shoulders and upper biceps, then up the back of his neck. Even the tips of his ears were burned, so I added a dollop on each and gently rubbed it in.

"You should lie down for a nap," I suggested as I tended to him, to which he grunted inarticulately and didn't answer. "I mean it. You'll feel better, and it'll keep you out of the sun."

He looked back at me with those sad puppy eyes. He'd already learned I was vulnerable to those kind of silent, appealing looks, but I was building up a resistance to it. Unrelenting, I helped him to his feet and guided him to his bed. I lay him down on his tummy and leaned over him to fluff his pillow. A hand tried to sneak up beneath my top while I was bent over him, but for once I pulled away.

"Sleep," I told him firmly as I disentangled myself, and he sighed sadly.

"I should have listened to you." His voice was muffled by the pillows.

"Everyone has to learn their own lessons." I ruffled his short hair reassuringly. "Sleep, honey. I'll bring you some dinner later on and you'll feel better tomorrow."

"Thank you," he mumbled and closed his eyes. I stood to leave him, in case I distracted him with my presence. I left the jar of gel beside his bed and I slipped out of the room, closing the door behind me.

When I turned to walk away, I almost ran straight into the doctor, who was waiting outside. I backpedalled to avoid running him down, then stopped and stared. There was a very strange look on his face.

"Ms McDermott, might we speak?" His voice was low, almost a whisper. He shot a glance back over his shoulder to make sure we weren't being observed.

"Of course." I was a little bewildered, but followed as he turned and lead the way back towards his room.

When we arrived, he closed the door behind us, and then he stuck his head into Maddy's room to check if she was there. Evidently she wasn't, because he returned a moment later with a deep frown on his face.

"Ms McDermott – Sandy – I need to ask you for a favour." He sounded strangely nervous. "It's regarding your sister."

Suddenly, I felt a cold chill run through me. "Skylar? Is she all right? Is the baby—"

"She's fine at the moment, but I am concerned for her," he said, cutting me off. "She is at a very delicate stage of her pregnancy, when she should be resting and taking it easy, but as you know she resists all attempts to convince her to rest. I have tried to speak to her about it, but she brushes it off and ignores me."

"You want me to talk to her?" I cringed at the very thought. "I can try, but I don't know what good it'll do. We've only known one another as adults for two weeks."

"But you are sisters, and blood runs thicker than water. She loves you. I hope that she will listen to you, or else..."

"...She could lose the baby?" I whispered, horrified by the thought.

The doctor shrugged. "That is one possibility; more likely she will injure herself. But, we are in a dangerous and unsanitary environment, and she neglects to acknowledge that she is particularly vulnerable right now. If she were to cut herself and get an infection, like you did, it could complicate the pregnancy. Given our limited access to medical technology, complications of any kind drastically increase the chance that she could lose the baby – or her own life."

I grimaced, feeling a surge of mixed emotions. Part of me was worried, while part of me filled with cold anger. What was it with the people in my life deliberately putting themselves at risk?

"I'll talk to her right now."

The doctor nodded, but his concern did not seem to lessen. I felt like time was of the essence, so I let myself out of his room and hurried off, looking for any sign of my sister.

I spotted her downstairs doing exactly what she probably shouldn't be: lugging a heavy box from one room to another. Ryan was trailing along behind her, protesting, but she was too stubborn to let him take it. The anger welled up to overwhelm my caution, so I raced down to intercept them.

I took the stairs two at a time, and then sprang around the corner to take them both by surprise. Without giving her a moment's notice, I snatched the heavy box from Skylar's grip and shoved it into Ryan's arms instead.

"Hey!" Skylar exclaimed in alarm, but I wasn't having any of it. I grabbed her by the arm and dragged her off towards the nearest room, and didn't give her time to protest or pull away.

She sure tried, though, but I wouldn't let her. I dragged her into one of the storage rooms and slammed the door behind us, then grabbed her by the shoulders and gave her a hard shake.

"What the hell is wrong with you?" she protested at the rough treatment and tried to shove me off. Despite all her determination, I proved to be physically stronger than her and managed to keep her restrained.

"You need to stop it." My voice hard and threatening. It was the kind of tone that I'd never used on my baby sister in my entire life. I could see her getting angry but I refused to let her go. "You are almost nine months pregnant, Skylar McDermott. You need to slow the fuck down and start taking care of yourself. "

"Oh, so the doctor's been whining at you too, has he?" she snapped with bitter sarcasm, and again tried to shove me away, but she just couldn't shake me.

"Stop being so fucking stupid, Skye. You are going to *kill that baby.*" I was practically snarling now, so angry that it took all of my willpower to fight down the urge to slap her. My choice of words did a better job of it than my fist ever could have, though, and her eyes widened in shock. When I suddenly released my grip on her shoulders, she was so stunned that she stayed exactly where I put her.

I jabbed a finger at her pointedly. "I know that you think you're invulnerable, but you're not. You're human, and you're subject to human weaknesses. So is that baby," I redirected my finger at her midsection, "and she has more than enough to worry about without her own mother trying to *murder her* with stubbornness. Frankly, I would very much like the chance to meet my niece or nephew one day, so knock it off right now or I will lock you in your room until you go into labour. Got it?"

She stared at me with huge eyes, shocked beyond words by my harshness. I wasn't generally the most threatening person. Frankly, I was a skinny little doll-faced slip of nothing – but I was Skye's big sister and she'd never seen me angry before. Judging by the look on her face, it scared the hell out of her.

Finally, she gathered her wits enough to nod quickly. I narrowed my eyes at her, and she seemed to understand instinctively that meant I would not brook any more of her headstrong behaviour if it put her baby at risk. She couldn't hold my gaze; her eyes dropped, and a hand rose protectively to her tummy. I suddenly realised there were tears gathering in her eyes, and I felt a mixture of victory for making her see sense, and guilt for making my little sister cry.

"I don't want my baby to die," she whispered.

"I know, Skye. I know." I softened my tone to comfort her. "That's why you have to slow down, for your baby's sake. Your body is more fragile than you know."

My anger had done its job, and now that it was no longer required it began to drain away. I reached for her and drew her into a hug made awkward by the very baby we were trying to protect, sandwiched in between us. She hugged me back, and I felt tears soaking into my shoulder.

"I'm just so scared." Her voice was watery and

muffled against my shoulder. "I don't want my baby to get the infection. I feel like I can't do enough to keep her safe."

"I know." I hugged her close and stroked her hair, as if she were a little girl all over again. As much as I knew that she needed the shock to protect her growing baby, I hated to cause her distress. I was comforting myself with the gesture just as much as her, and trying to reassure myself that it was in the name of the greater good.

After all, what were sisters for, if not giving you a kick in the pants when you were being an idiot, and borrowing your favourite sweater with no intention of ever returning it?

Chapter Twenty-Two

The fire crackled, roaring up into the night sky, while we stood around with hoses at the ready in case the flames decided to spread.

I watched with mixed feelings as the blaze consumed the ambiguously named 'Function' building, along with the dozens of bodies housed within. We decided that this was best way to keep the area safe for Skye's incoming baby, and to keep the risk of infection to a minimum. The makeshift graveyard would become a crematorium.

There were four of us there: Michael, Ryan, the doctor and me – Skylar had decided to stay at home with Madeline. Since our talk almost a week ago, Skye had finally accepted her condition and started to spend most of her time indoors cooking or focusing on her studies, or in the courtyard tending to our little garden.

Tonight, she had actually volunteered to stay home, complaining of a persistent headache. I was relieved by her decision; the nearer she got to full term, the more I worried about her.

Goodbye, Benny, I thought to myself as I watched the flames rage. I really hoped that there was a Heaven, and that his sweet Margie was waiting for him there.

That thought made me sad. I hoped there was something more, anything more, than just this world of suffering that we knew. Somehow, Michael heard my sigh over the crackle of flames and he reached out to put his arm around me. I'd told him everything over the course of the last week or so, even about old Benny and his wife.

Well, no. Not quite everything. There were still some things that I held back, even from him. Things that had happened to me over the years that I didn't want to think about, let alone talk about. I couldn't even bear to say the word out loud. It was such a terrible, terrible word.

The worst four letters of the English language.

I leaned against his side, as the fire we had set so carefully consumed the function hall, and the café and bar next door. The buildings were separated from the other ones nearby by some distance, but we still practiced great caution in our act of arson. We had waited until the heat-wave had passed and rain had come this morning. The ground was dry again by the time we started the blaze, but the morning's rain reduced the brittleness of the plants and the buildings nearby and lessened the chance that our fire would spread.

Regardless, we'd hosed down the nearest buildings before we planted accelerant in the bar and café. Then, we waited until we saw more clouds on the horizon, promising another shower on the way. They came just before sundown, when the air was still and humid. We judged the time just right for our bonfire to begin.

The fire had caught quickly and burned with a furious intensity that worried us at first. None of us were professional arsonists, but we all remembered the warning signs about the summer fire danger from our younger days.

The flames had raged unabated for hours, and now there was hardly anything left – just the most basic framework and the roof. Then suddenly the roof caved in with a terrible noise and an explosion of sparks, reducing the buildings to flaming rubble. A few smouldering ashes drifted towards nearby buildings, but we were tense and alert, and doused them quickly before they could land.

Something cold and wet struck me on the top of the head as we retreated back to a safe distance again. I looked up, and another raindrop splattered me right between the eyes. The next thing I knew, it was coming down in a torrent and we were caught in the deluge. After the intense heat of the past week, none of us really seemed to mind.

The flames burned so hot that it took another hour before they died down completely. When they did, they left behind only ashes and a few shards of human bone where there had once been a building. A building where so many people had taken their own lives.

I let sadness wash over me in the darkness as the

flames retreated. The rain turned everything to a hot, muddy soup, which would probably bake to a crust in the sun when the storm passed. We would return another day and bury the ashes and bits of bone deep within the earth, but for now it was time for my bedraggled group of survivors to go home.

We gathered up our things, and trudged off to wash away the stench of smoke, and retire to our beds.

***

It was still raining the next morning when the sun slipped up over the horizon. I came awake slowly to the sound of rain on the roof, my face buried in the back of Michael's neck. My breath ruffled his short hair as I heaved a sigh, and I felt him stir.

"G'morning," I greeted him, and he murmured a sleepy reply. Lost in a pleasant doze, we snuggled together listening to the sound of the rain on the roof for a good, long while, before a different, alien sound finally brought us both awake. It was the sound of a small engine moving down the road outside our building.

I opened my eyes reluctantly and rose, to pull on a t-shirt and underwear. Content with being halfway-decent, I wandered out into the living room to investigate the unfamiliar noise. Hemi waved up at me when he spotted me peeking through the curtains, and I waved back. He was soaked to the bone from the rain, but his smile was broad as he sat back on the farm bike to greet me.

"*Kia ora!*" He called when I opened the window and leaned out. "We've come to visit, brought you some *kai*. Where are your friends?"

"Probably still sleeping," I called back, amused. "It's the crack of dawn, and we didn't realise you were coming. Give us a minute and we'll be downstairs."

"Sweet as." He gave me his funny, lopsided grin, and settled down on his bike to wait.

I pulled back from the window and returned to our bedroom, where Michael was stretching languidly in bed. It took all of my willpower not to get distracted admiring the tan he'd acquired over the last week.

"Your friend Hemi is here to visit. Put some pants on, you nudist."

He grinned at my teasing and rolled out of bed to do just that. A few minutes later, when both of us were properly dressed, we trundled downstairs to greet our visitors.

Although I was always concerned about our security, we left most of our weapons behind. I kept my taser in my pocket just in case, but no guns. I had to admit that I felt a little naked confronting another survivor relatively unarmed, but Michael was unconcerned.

By the time we walked out the front door, Hemi was off his bike and waiting for us. A woman had joined him, and the two stood comfortably in the rain exchanging light banter in their native tongue. When we emerged, Hemi grinned brightly and approached us both with a hand extended.

"G'day, mate – sorry to wake you."

"*Kia ora*, mate. *Haere mai*." Michael greeted the young man like they'd been friends all their lives, with a warm handshake and a broad smile. I hung back and watched them, amused and secretly impressed by Michael's social graces. Not only did he speak sign language, but he spoke decent Maori as well. I knew the basics from back in school, but I could never quite tell the contexts apart. He didn't seem to have any problem with it at all.

Suddenly, I realised the woman was watching me, and I tensed up instinctively as I was assessed. My attention turned to her as well. I felt oddly uncomfortable, uncertain whether I was being considered as a potential friend, enemy or rival.

The strange woman was unabashedly beautiful, with creamy brown skin and long dark hair that fell in wild waves down her back. Her lips were full and sensual, the lower one stained by a *moko*, a Maori tribal tattoo that curled down across her chin. Although she looked older than I am, her skin was smooth and unflawed by age, and there was no trace of grey in her hair.

But it was her eyes that struck me most. Although dark and framed by long lashes, they spoke a whole other language to the rest of her body. There was a confidence in them, a quiet strength and a hypnotic personal magnetism; she held my gaze unflinchingly, and I was caught by her charisma.

I wasn't afraid to admit that I felt a little bit

intimidated. Those beautiful eyes held such deep intelligence that I felt small by comparison. I found myself trapped by her charm, hypnotised, afraid to make eye-contact but equally afraid to look away.

In the end, it was she that broke the staring contest, not I. Hemi spoke her name to introduce her to Michael and so she looked away, leaving me feeling shy and uncertain as I lurked in the background.

"This is my mum, the boss-lady." Hemi had his usual impish grin on, and the strange woman smiled In return. The expression softened her beauty, and I felt my tension ease a little.

"*Kia ora*." She accepted Michael's outstretched hand with grace. "My name is Anahera. I lead what little is left of the Waikato *iwi*." Then she looked straight at me, and gave me a smile that made my heart race. "And what is your name, my dear? You are being very quiet."

I felt a surge of panic as all eyes turned towards me.

"Sandy. Sandy McDermott." I managed to get out my name before anxiety overwhelmed me, and I looked to Michael for rescue. He understood immediately that my self-confidence was low and stepped in on my behalf.

"She's a bit cautious around strangers." He glanced at me to make sure it was okay to tell them; I nodded, to give him my permission. "She's had a few bad experiences with other survivors."

Anahera nodded her understanding, and then she approached me with a grace that was almost feline.

When she was close enough, she went to take my hand and I allowed her to gently draw me in, to press the tip of her nose to mine. Having a stranger so close to me made me tense up, but I knew it was only a *hongi* – a greeting – and that she meant me no harm.

"It is good to meet you, Sandy McDermott," she said softly as we parted. "Hemi says I have you to thank for the fact that I still have a son."

My cheeks started to burn, but I managed an unsteady smile. "It was a group effort. Michael made the killing blow."

"She's also modest," he commented dryly as he wandered over to put a protective arm around me. "We're just glad we could help."

"And you did, more than you know. Between your doctor's medicine and his expertise, you may have saved my entire *whanau* as well. I feel that we owe you a debt that can never be repaid." Anahera bowed her head in respect, and said a few words in her native tongue that I didn't understand.

Michael seemed to, though. He smiled and bowed his head in return. "You honour us with your presence, *ariki*."

"Bah." She flapped a hand. "That title does not fit me. I am no chieftain, just the only one of us left with any ability to organise these slackers into some kind of community. Before this happened, I was just a teacher."

A teacher, huh? I thought to myself. *With cleavage like that, it's a wonder that her students got anything done...*

Oh crap. Was I jealous?

I suddenly felt ashamed of myself, and lowered my gaze thoughtfully while Michael led our guests to the entrance of our motel and invited them inside out of the rain.

"My brothers will be here shortly with your gifts," Anahera mentioned while we were leading her inside. Just inside the entrance, she stopped to admire the building. "Ah. I see you have built a *pa* of your own here. Well done."

She nodded her approval, and stepped out into the rain to examine our little vegetable garden. The moisture didn't seem to bother her, and I found myself distracted, admiring her curvaceous figure with some confusion. She was so beautiful, I found watching her fascinating.

Then came a flash of panic when I realised that Michael would be just as attracted to her natural magnetism as I was. I looked up at him, and found him... looking right back at me. He smiled and touched my chin, lifting it up just a little for the softest of kisses, while Hemi was distracted following his mother.

I couldn't believe it. Someone so beautiful right in front of him, and he only had eyes for me? Even *I* wanted to stare at her all day, and I wasn't even inclined that way. Either I was the luckiest woman alive, or my new lover was crazy.

You know what? I think I'm okay with that, I decided after a moment of careful consideration.

"Are these strawberry seedlings I see here?" Anahera called to us, attracting our attention to where she was pointing. When we nodded, she made a sound of delight and wandered back over towards us. "You have many plants we don't have. Would you be willing to trade seeds some time?"

"Share and share alike, my friend." Michael smiled, all boyish charm and diplomacy. "We know of a patch run wild not far from here, and we're happy for you to help yourselves so long as you leave some for us."

"You are rare, generous souls." Anahera's smile was so radiant that it made my stomach do a flip-flop. "I am pleased to have you as our neighbours. Too many have become wrapped up in themselves in these self-absorbed days, and forget that community is what will keep the human spirit alive."

I felt an odd mix of emotions: A swell of pride at her praise, coupled with a sense of guilt that I would have handled things so much differently if I were the leader of our group. She was right, and I was one of those selfish ones. Without Michael's sweet soul to temper me, I was just another greedy survivor clutching her precious scraps of a shattered civilization. I didn't like that feeling.

"I agree completely." Oblivious to my internal conflict, Michael beckoned for the visitors to follow us. "Come and meet the rest of our community."

Although Michael led the way, he kept his arm looped around my waist in a manner that was both protective and a little bit possessive. I couldn't help but wonder if he had seen me looking at Anahera, and was feeling just as jealous as I had been a few minutes ago. There was no chance to ask him or reassure him now, though. A moment later, we entered the kitchen where the others were sitting around the table discussing breakfast.

Introductions were made, with Anahera showing delight over the littlest members of our company. She greeted Maddy like an adult, and spoke softly to her until the child beamed and nodded happily. Then her attention turned to Skylar, who blushed and smiled shyly when the older woman crooned over her belly; she looked both confused and pleased by the attention at the same time.

"When are you due, dear one? It must be soon, surely?"

Skylar nodded and rubbed a hand over her belly as though to soothe her unborn child. "In about a month, a little less. Very soon."

"Ah, it must be terribly uncomfortable in this heat." Anahera sighed softly. She reached over and hovered a hand above Skye's belly, then shot the young woman a quizzical look. Skylar nodded her permission, so Anahera gently rested her hand upon her tummy. "I remember being pregnant with my youngest son at this time of year. It was terrible. I spent half my time soaking in a cold bath just to keep the swelling in my ankles at bay."

Skye smiled at the understanding, and rubbed the side of her belly. "I do that sometimes, too. Well a cold shower, anyway. She kicks more when it's too hot, so the cool water calms her down."

"Ah, feel her kicking now." Anahera laughed, and it was the sweetest sound I'd ever heard. "I think she knows we're talking about her."

Skylar's smile faded, though, replaced by an intense concern.

"I'm sorry to ask, ma'am, but... have any women in your community had babies since the outbreak?"

Anahera drew back and stared intently at my sister, clearly sensing there was a reason behind the question.

"No. I am the only woman in my community, and I will not take another man since the plague took my husband." Her head shifted a little, tilting to one side. "Why do you ask, dear?"

"Oh, well." Skye looked at me, uncertain what to say.

Despite my instinctive reticence, I stepped in to the rescue. "There was some research that I read; it said that immunity is not necessarily passed from mother to child. We're worried that her baby might get infected."

Anahera's expression changed to one of concern. "I am afraid I have no information to give you, but I pray that does not happen."

The conversation was interrupted at that point by the sound of quad bikes outside. Of course, I felt anxious that we were about to be attacked, but no one else looked worried. Anahera quickly informed us that it was just her tribe-mates arriving with their gifts for us.

Anahera and Michael led the way back outside, with the rest of us trailing along in a rag-tag group strung out behind them. I brought up the rear, and was the last one to step back out into the moody weather. By the time I left the building, the leaders of our two groups had descended on the quad bikes and were chatting about something I couldn't quite hear.

I lingered near the doorway, feeling mildly uncomfortable. More strangers to worry about, more potential dangers. My inner recluse was not happy. While the others splintered off to investigate the newcomers, I stood quietly in the doorway, watching Michael. Even at a distance, I found his presence reassuring. A humid breeze caught my hair and tugged a few loose tendrils across my face. I reached up to pluck them out of my eyes, and tuck them back behind my ear—

—and then I froze as a cold sensation shot right through me from the back of my throat to the tip of my toes.

There were three quad bike riders standing in a gaggle off to one side, obviously members of Anahera's tribe from the Polynesian cast of their features. They stood in a group watching the leaders chat, shoulders slouched and hands in pockets. They were oblivious to me.

I wished I could say the same. Two of the three faces were unfamiliar to me.

The third one was not.

The shaking began as a faint trembling in my hands

when recognition hit me. Then came the panic in icy, surging waves that rippled through my body from head to toe, and made my body shake harder and harder until I thought that I could hear the sound of my bones rattling in their joints.

Skylar said something to me but I couldn't hear what she was saying over the rush of noise in my own eardrums. I took a step back, and then another, but my back hit the wall beside the door, and I couldn't quite assemble my thoughts enough to turn around.

I knew that horrible face, with its flat, oft-broken nose.

I knew the tattoos that wound across his brow like a wicked serpent.

I knew that corpulent body, the one that hid thick muscle deep beneath its fat.

Oh god.

Skylar was looking at me and I knew that she was concerned, but I couldn't understand what she was saying. I couldn't breathe.

Oh god. Oh god.

It was the spectre from my nightmares, my tormentor, the one that writhes and hits. I heard the sound of flesh striking flesh, and I felt the pain all over again.

He was here, in the flesh. The demon was here, in my home.

I had prayed so hard that I would never see him again.

I felt hands on me and then I felt myself being

dragged inside until I could no longer see the demon that haunted me. Once he was gone from my sight, I collapsed both literally and figuratively. The hands caught me as I fell, and supported me.

"Sandy? What's wrong?"

I heard my sister's voice, but it sounded like it was coming from a million miles away. Stars danced around the edge of my vision, and I felt like I was falling, falling, falling...

The next thing I knew, I was lying down with a semi-circle of concerned faces hovering around me: Skylar, Ryan and Madeline. They were familiar faces, friendly faces, and yet I couldn't put aside the uncontrollable, animal panic. I couldn't speak, couldn't control my limbs.

I suddenly realised that I was crying, but I was too afraid to make a sound.

"Maddy, go get your granddad." I heard Skylar speaking, but the little girl shook her head.

"No... we should get Mister Michael."

"What? She needs a doctor, not her boyfriend." Skylar leapt to her feet to go fetch the doctor herself, but Maddy sprang up as well and grabbed her by the hand to hold her back.

"You don't understand; the bad man is here." The little girl stared at her intently, then repeated the words with an intensity that made my shivering all the worse. "*The bad man is here.*"

Skylar stared at her, not quite comprehending what she was saying for what felt like forever. Finally, something seemed to come together in her mind. Her eyes widened in shock.

"The—" She hesitated for a moment then made a snap decision. "I'll go get Michael."

All this time I felt like I was paralysed, watching some terrible play unfold before my very eyes. It was less than a minute before Skylar returned, but it felt like an eternity. Michael was with her, my kind, sweet Michael, and his concerned face joined the circle that floated above me.

"Jesus... Sandy? Sandy, what's wrong?" His gentle fingers caressed my cheek, and came away wet with my tears. It took all of my willpower to raise my hand just a little bit, but it was trembling so badly I couldn't coordinate it enough to touch his hand.

"The bad man is here." Maddy came to my rescue again, and repeated the words softly for Michael's benefit. Like Skylar, he stared at her in uncertainty. Then, driven by some sixth sense, he reached for me and gathered my shivering body up against his broad chest, to cradle me close against him.

His warmth was like a pillar of light to my ice-cold mind, the tonic that I needed to coax my frozen muscles back to life. A convulsion shook my entire body as I wrapped my arms around his waist, and buried my face in his chest.

"Sandy, sweetheart." His voice was a gruff whisper, and he stroked my hair softly as I clung to him. "Talk to me. Tell me, which one of them did it? Which one of them hurt you?"

The sobs wracking my body left me mute and inarticulate, but Maddy knew. How does she always know?

"The one with the bad drawings on his face." She stared at Michael like he would know what that meant, with an intensity that just didn't belong on the face of a little girl.

"Bad drawings? Do you mean the tattoos?" he questioned her softly, but she was only a little girl and didn't know what that meant.

"What's happening?" A new voice entered the fray, one that I recognised as Anahera. There was a gasp, and then another body joined the circle around me. "Is she all right?"

Michael's voice was like ice, so cold it practically froze the hot summer air.

"Are you aware that one of your brothers is a rapist?"

There it was. The R-word. The worst four letters of the English language, and spoken from the lips of the man I cared about. I muffled a sob against his chest.

"What?" Anahera's voice was soft but it carried so much dangerous intensity that for a moment I felt a wave of irrational alarm. They were going to hurt me, going to hurt my sister, hurt my unborn niece, hurt my Michael.

No, no!

But I couldn't see her face. I didn't see the anger, the unbridled fury that bubbled up from deep within her. I did not know that it wasn't targeted at me. Oh, but I could hear her voice, the hiss of her breath through clenched teeth. "Which one of them did it?"

"T-the one with the tattoos..." I managed to summon the will enough to name my abuser, unable to bear the thought of little Madeline having to say the words again.

There was a sound like a growl from the beautiful woman, an animal thing of wild and primal fury, and then she was up on her feet and gone. Suddenly I was afraid for her, afraid for my family, and my instinct was to fight.

I struggled against the palsy that held me, unintentionally fighting against Michael's grip as well – but he understood. His strong hands helped me to my feet and kept me upright until I could stand on my own. I shook off the dizziness and headed to the door, with my family hot on my heels.

As I made it to the doorway with the others in a gaggle behind me, I could hear the sound of raised voices arguing back and forth in the Maori tongue.

Then I heard the distinctive sound of a fist striking flesh, and I was afraid, afraid that Anahera was being attacked.

As it turned out, I needn't have worried for her. It was her fist that I heard, and the target of her ire was the very one that was causing my distress. He was screaming at her, spitting curses around a mouth full of bloody teeth, but he was held back by the three other men of his tribe. His leader struck him, again and again with astounding strength, until her knuckles ran with his blood.

He didn't look so terrifying now, not when he slumped semi-conscious in the arms of his captors, and his own leader kicked him so hard that I saw teeth fly.

Then, panting heavily with exertion, she gestured to her companions and they dropped their captive in the dirt. She saw me, trembling amongst my family, and she turned to face me.

"He would not deny it," she spat the words like they tasted bad, as enraged as a wild cat. "All these years he's lied to us, told us that his only crimes were petty thefts." She jerked a finger at the slumped man, and her brothers hauled him back to his knees. "This is the one, dear heart? You are sure? He is the one that hurt you?"

I could only nod; there was no way I would ever forget that horrible face.

"Wait."

There was a voice behind me, and then Michael stepped by me with the strangest look on his face. "I didn't realise it before, but I think I know this man as well."

"From where?" Anahera spoke softly as she stared at him, her eyes narrowed dangerously in the grips of an irrational berserker rage.

Michael circled the prisoner, and stared at him from all angles, his brow knitted deeply in thought. "I used to work for the police force. I know his face. I just... need a moment to remember."

Silence descended over both groups as Michael

stared at that terrible face from every angle. I stood back drawing deep breaths, trying to keep the shaking in my limbs under control. I worried for my sweetheart, but I was afraid to move closer. I wasn't sure whether I would faint again if I did, or whether I would attack like a pack animal and tear that terrible man apart.

Suddenly, Michael drew a sharp breath and straightened up.

"I remember now." He looked at me for a long moment, and then his dark eyes returned to Anahera. "He was a wanted man, but the riots hit before we could catch him. I'm sorry to say that Sandy wasn't his first victim."

"What did he do?" Anahera's voice was like ice. I could see her twitching, barely in control of her anger. Michael stared at her, almost as though afraid of telling her the truth – or perhaps he was afraid of what he would do to the man himself if he spoke the words out loud.

"He abducted a pair of little girls." Michael closed his eyes and swallowed hard. "Twins; it was all over the news when they went missing. They were... five or six." I felt my stomach drop to my knees. I remembered seeing those sweet-faced children on television. It was one of the last things we saw before the plague became everyone's news. Michael's voice was heavy with sadness as he continued. "He... violated them, strangled them, and then threw them into the Waikato River.

"My colleagues found them." Michael grimaced

and shook his head. "One of the girls was already dead, but the other one was still alive. She lived long enough to name her killer, but then she died in hospital. He was her uncle. They distributed pictures of him to everyone in the precinct, and it was all hands on deck looking for him. I don't think I could ever forget those tattoos."

In the silence that followed, tears sprang unbidden into my eyes again. I remembered those little girls. It had been weeks between when they went missing and when they were found. Someone had kidnapped them and tortured them for a long, long time.

Just like me.

It was the softest little noise that broke the silence, but it wasn't a sob or a cry – it was a growl. I looked up and saw Anahera shaking with pent-up fury, her dark-eyed gaze focused on the half-conscious man held up by her brethren. They dropped him unceremoniously in the dirt and stepped back, as though sensing something terrible was to come.

"You–" Her voice was a husky whisper as she rounded on the man, her feet planted wide apart, her hands clenched to fists. "–are not *my brother!*"

The last part wasn't spoken, it was screamed. She punctuated the sentence with a kick so brutal that it sent the tattooed man rolling through the dirt.

Screaming in wordless fury, she chased after the crumpled form and stomped on him again; I heard the tell-tale sound of ribs snapping at the force of the blow. Her voice was so loud, so charged with pure rage that it startled birds out of the trees nearby and sent them fluttering away in distress.

At last, exhausted, she stepped back and took a deep breath to calm herself, then turned and looked straight at me.

"Is he really your brother?" I stared back at her, horrified by the idea.

"No, not by birth. I consider all the men of my group to be my brothers, in the sense that common interests bind us into a form of adopted kinship. But, this one betrayed me, and everything that we stand for. He is a murderer. There are no judges anymore. No juries. In *my* tribe, the only just punishment that I see is death." Her voice was dangerously soft, her eyes unreadable. "But, you are the last living person that he sinned against, dear one. His punishment is yours to decide."

"Mine?" The statement didn't quite sink in straight away. She wanted me to decide the fate, the ultimate punishment for the man who had held me captive for days; brutalised me again and again until I was so traumatised that even years later I felt crippling fear every time I met a stranger.

This was the man who had left me so emotionally damaged that I struggled to trust even good people, people who were kind to me and showed me generosity far beyond what I deserve.

This was the man that had broken my psyche so badly that I was afraid to make love to the man I adored.

This was the man who destroyed those beautiful

little girls, and god knows how many others since then.

It was his fault.

His fate was mine to decide.

But, did I want the blood of another human being on my hands? It was true that I'd killed before to save myself, but only in the heat of the moment and never in cold blood. That was how I'd escaped from him, three years ago. He'd gone somewhere, and left his lazy, drunk accomplice to use me as he pleased. He'd been careless; now he was dead.

Did I want the ringleader dead as well?

Yes, I did – but also no. Not like that.

"I don't want him to die." My voice was so low and breathless that it forced Anahera to draw closer to hear my words. "He doesn't deserve a quick death. I–" I could hardly believe I was saying this. "I don't know. I think he deserves to suffer, like he made me suffer all of these years. Like he made those little girls suffer. I just want him to understand what he's done to us."

"What do you want me to do to him, dear heart?" The woman spoke softly to me, her anger diluted by the pain she saw reflected in my eyes.

I shook my head and fought as tears gathered in my eyes. "I don't know. I don't want to know. Just... make him understand. Make it so he'll never want to hurt another girl ever again. Please?"

Anahera watched me quietly for the longest minute, and then nodded slowly. "I understand, child. You do not wish to cause another person pain, but you must so others like you never have to feel it. I will do for you what your kind soul cannot."

I nodded, speechless, my face frozen in an attitude of distress. This woman, this teacher-turned-leader — she knew my innermost thoughts.

There was a soft sound of steel on leather, and then a long, curved knife appeared in her hand. "Go inside and rest, dear. This man will never hurt you or any other person ever again."

Michael stepped in and gathered me to him, then hurried me away, but not before I saw the other group pick up the fallen man from where he lay in the dirt and drag him off. They took him far away from our home before they began his punishment, but it wasn't far enough.

Even as Michael was tucking me into his bed where I felt safe and protected, I could hear the prisoner screaming.

Chapter Twenty-Three

The sound of the man's torment haunted my dreams, but in spite of that I slept deeper and longer than I had in years. The spectre no longer haunted me, mocking me, hurting me; the spectre was gone. It was no longer an immortal, inhuman thing, but a physical being that I could fight off and destroy if I needed to.

I wasn't afraid anymore.

It was dark when I awoke, and the room was faintly lit by moonlight through the open window beside the bed. I could hear the sound of breathing in the dark, soft and even, but didn't feel the warmth of a familiar body beside me. I rolled over and saw the faint outline of the man I had come to care about so much, sitting in his chair by the window. The faintest glint of steel told me that his shotgun rested in his lap.

He was protecting me.

"Michael?" I whispered his name in the shadows. He snapped awake at the sound of my voice; I heard his sharp intake of breath, and saw his outline moving.

"Sandy? You're awake?"

"Yeah." I yawned softly and snuggled down in the soft blankets. "Why are you all the way over there?"

"You need some space right now." His voice was soft, but he still rose from his chair to sit on the edge of the bed instead. Close enough for me to reach out and touch him, which I did.

"I'm... okay, I think." I sought out his hand in the dark, and when I found it I twined my fingers through his and felt comfortable and content. "Are they gone?"

"Yes, hours ago." He shifted a little bit and drew my fingers up to his lips to press a soft kiss against them. "They left their gifts and went, and they took him with them. The woman, Anahera, said that they were going to take him as far away from here as they could before they let him go."

"What did they do to him?" I wasn't really sure that I wanted to know the answer, but morbid curiosity drove me to ask.

"I'm not sure." His voice was soft, but I felt him tense up and knew that he was lying. I may be socially inept, but I wasn't stupid.

I decided to let it pass. Would knowing really help me to heal? No, it wouldn't. My imagination could fill in the blanks. I sighed and sat up, to lean against my sweetheart's broad back. "I wish I knew how to feel right now. Part of me wishes I'd just let her kill him."

"I know," he murmured, and then heaved a sigh himself. "To tell you the truth, I almost did it myself. If Anahera hadn't been there, then I might have... might have..." He trailed off, and I felt his body tense up again.

"I know," I whispered, and slid my arms around his waist. There was no need for him to finish the sentence. I knew what he was thinking. Still, there were so many questions left unanswered, about everything. "Michael?"

"Hm?" He glanced over his shoulder at me.

"Why do you think he did it? Not just to me, but to the others. God knows how many women he's murdered over the years."

Again there was silence, but this time it was while he thought it over. Finally, he spoke again, hesitant and uncertain.

"I think that he just didn't care. I've seen men like him before, men that think women just exist to please them. They have no respect for the sanctity of human lives." I heard a deep intake of breath, let out as a sharp exhalation a moment later. "People like that don't deserve to live."

I pondered that response and weighed my conflicting emotions against one another. He was right, of course. Some people were just born evil, and no amount of nurturing or punishment would break them of the habits that nature had bred into their psyches. As much as I'd have liked to put some logic to my former tormentor's decisions, there simply wasn't any. I was just unlucky. He'd seen me all alone, and that was enough. If not for a moment of luck weeks later, that would have signed my death warrant. I couldn't help but wonder how many other lives he'd already snuffed out.

I lay my head against my policeman's back and closed my eyes as I sifted through my muddled feelings. On the one hand, I felt terrible being the source of someone else's misery. On the other, he deserved it. Those little girls didn't deserve their fate, but they certainly deserved justice. I was sure there were others out there like me, whether they were alive or dead.

But now I'd had my justice. That feeling brought with it a sense of peace. What was there to be afraid of, if that man was no longer a threat? I smiled to myself and snuggled closer to him, enjoying the warmth of Michael's skin beneath my cheek. In my lowest moment, he'd not only stayed true to me, but he'd helped me to get that justice.

While Anahera had been the judge, jury and executioner, Michael was my officer of the law. My protector. My hero.

"Michael?" I whispered his name again, a flush of warmth rising in my cheeks. It'd been such a long time coming, but at last I truly felt safe.

There was a faint sound of movement as he turned towards me, and then his big hands drew me up against his chest. I snuggled in against him happily, feeling content and relaxed.

"I think I'm ready," I whispered the words softly in the darkness, and trailed my fingers along his stomach. I could feel the heat of his skin beneath the light t-shirt he wore, and I longed to strip it away and have him all to myself.

One of his hands cupped my chin and tilted it

upwards and his lips met mine in the darkness. He kissed me slowly and tenderly for what felt like forever, before finally drawing back to give me a quirky smile that I could only half see.

"No, you're not."

That was not the answer I expected.

"What? Yes, I am!"

"No, you're not, and neither am I." Although it was dark, I could see and feel the edge of tension about him, and it was not a kind of tension I recognised. I didn't like the way it felt. Still, his hands were gentle as he ran his fingers through my long hair. "Sandy, if we were to do this now, it wouldn't be about you and me. It would be about him, and revenge."

I froze, not sure what to say to that.

He did, though. His voice dropped low as he cupped my face in his hands. "I don't want that. I want to wait until it's perfect and we're both ready for it. I want it to be about us, just us, no one else. This isn't just about sex to me, you know that. This is about the fact that I love you, Sandy McDermott – and I want you to love me back."

"Y-you... what?" Did he just say what I thought he said? It took me totally by surprise in a moment when I was already off balance.

But Michael, he just smiled enigmatically and silenced me with a kiss.

⚜ ⚜ ⚜

The thought that someone loved me galvanised me

for days. Although we didn't speak about it again, I found myself in a rare good mood that nothing seemed to be able to shake. My foot had finally healed enough that I could walk around without pain, my family was safe and gradually settling into a comfortable routine, and I had a sweet, kind man that loved me.

Loved me. Loved *me*. In spite all of my flaws, he loved me.

I wasn't angry at him for rejecting my proposal that night, because in reality he was right. If we had made love, it wouldn't have been as special when the wound was still so raw. Amongst other reasons, it would be his first time ever and he deserved more than a wild fuck fuelled by hatred and revenge, and I wanted our first time together to be special, too.

I often thought of the man whose name I had never learned over the days that followed. Eventually, my feelings of guilt faded, replaced by a strong sense of relief. Although he was still alive out there somewhere, he had lost his demonic countenance within my mind and my nightmares. It seemed apt that Anahera was the weapon of his punishment – another woman, the avenging angel for his victims.

I hoped his other victims could feel the sense of relief that I felt now, if they were still alive. If not, then I hoped they rested easier for knowing they had been avenged.

I wondered if perhaps I would have to face him alone someday, if he might come after me. For the first time, I was no longer afraid of that thought. He was no longer a faceless, mocking beast that writhed and hurt me in my memory. That memory had been overwritten by one where he was just another human being, just as weak and pathetic as the rest of us. The difference was that he had chosen to act out and try to make himself look strong by taking advantage of those that were weaker than him, something that I would never do. That was what made him less than what any normal person could ever be.

If it ever came to a point where I had to kill that man, I had decided that I'd think of Anahera and try to be strong like her. My initial admiration of her had grown into something more like hero-worship, although I knew as well as anyone that it was ridiculous to worship someone who was just as human as I am. She was just as flawed on the inside, and yet she showed so many traits that I coveted – her emotional fortitude was just one of them. I truly hoped that one day, I would grow to be like her.

Beauty tempered by intelligence. Ruthlessness tempered by compassion. Strength tempered by gentleness. She was everything I wanted to be. She reminded me of my grandmother, my namesake and the woman who had inspired so much of my early life before I lost her to the plague. I thought having a new, living role-model would be good for me in the long term. I could only hope that having her to look up to would help me grow as a person. Was there anything else that anyone could ever really ask for?

In the days that followed, my group was well-fed

but not entirely content. We spent most of our time tending to our little garden as a safeguard against winter's inevitable arrival, but there was a thread of disharmony that ran through every conversation. Not everyone was happy about the punishment that Anahera had meted out on our behalf. Even I, the most socially inept of us, sensed the discontent amongst the group and it made me feel uncomfortable.

On the third day, Michael found me sitting alone in the kitchen in the middle of the afternoon, brooding over a cup of black coffee.

"Why the long face?"

I almost jumped out of my skin when his voice broke the silence, and promptly spilled hot coffee all over myself and the table.

"Ah, shit." Sorry, Mum. "Ow. Michael! Don't sneak up on me like that," I complained, as I leapt up to go run my hand under a cold tap. I heard him chuckling behind me, and then one strong arm slid around my waist from behind.

"Sorry," he murmured softly in my ear, then planted a kiss upon my cheek. "So, why the long face? Are you sulking again?

I paused for a long moment and thought over my answer, then I let out a deep sigh and shrugged. "I've been thinking about him."

Michael nodded. I didn't have to explain which 'him' I meant. "He's long gone, honey. You don't have to worry about him anymore."

"It's not that." I switched the tap off and turned

around to face him, though I couldn't quite meet his eye. "It's... I don't know if we've done the right thing, Michael. How do we know what's right and wrong? It used to be that we had people specially trained to do this for us, but now what do we do? If the law falls into the hands of the people that it's supposed to be protecting... I'm not sure I like where I can imagine that taking us."

Michael went silent as he thought over what I was saying, and then he nodded again. "We do need some form of justice, but not just lynch-mob justice."

"Exactly." I put my arms around his waist and leaned against him, but for once his strength couldn't banish the troubled thoughts from my mind. Eventually, I sighed again, and looked up at him. "What do we do?"

Michael stared off into space for a few seconds, looking lost in thought. "I have an idea, but I think it should be a group decision. Let's get everyone together."

"Okay." I nodded my agreement, and hurried off.

Twenty minutes later, we had our entire group – all six of us, including Madeline – gathered together in the kitchen around the table. As our leader, Michael stood at the head of the table while everyone settled into their places.

"Thank you for coming," he spoke in that soft, deep voice of his, the one that always carried a note of strength and command. "As you all know, we recently had to deal with an issue that has left many of us feeling troubled. I think that we need to address the matter, and set up rules for the future. As Sandy once pointed out to me, the world outside our nice little bunker is not a safe place. We already have our own code of conduct, but we need to establish some method for dealing with things when they get out of hand."

"You mean, what do we do if someone *else* tries to rape our women and murder our children?" Skylar asked, her face pale and tense. Out of all of us, she had been the one most vocal in her discontent, which didn't surprise me. "We should have killed him. The just thing to do would have been to kill him!"

"You don't know that," the doctor interrupted, and waggled a finger at Skye like a disapproving school teacher. "Who are we to decide if a man lives or dies? If we start murdering people wantonly, then we become no better than they are. Who are we to play God with the lives of others?"

"But now he knows where we live," she argued back vehemently. "What if he decides that he wants to come after us for revenge? What happens then? What about Sandy – or me and Maddy? We're just his type!"

"Enough." Michael held up his hands for silence, and then looked each and every one of us in the eye. When he got to me, he gave me a soft, reassuring smile. He could see that I was tense and nervous, but his smile made me feel better. "What's done is done. We can't change that. We're going to be alert and careful in case something does happen, but what I've gathered you here for is to work out a way to prevent this kind of disharmony from happening in future."

"You said you had an idea?" I spoke up softly to prevent further argument from breaking out, and he nodded to me.

"I do." The young man looked up and around at us all, then smiled. "I suggest that in future, we use a system not unlike the one that we had before the end, to ensure that justice is had for all. If a crime is committed, then we appoint one person to act as an adjudicator and consider the evidence. If the person is found guilty, then all of us vote on the punishment. The adjudicator would be the person who has the least emotional investment in the crime that occurred. That way, everyone has a chance to have their say, but we're not driven purely by emotion."

"Who suggests the punishments?" I asked, genuine curiosity replacing my discomfort. It was an interesting idea, but I shouldn't have been surprised. Michael was our paragon of justice.

"The victim, if they want to," he answered, "or if they're not comfortable then the adjudicator can. It's unlikely that any of us could be completely impartial towards someone that hurt one of our friends, but I think that's as close as we're going to get."

"That... does seem fair." Skylar had calmed down enough to look interested in the discussion, and beside her Ryan nodded thoughtfully.

Michael and I looked towards the Doc, and he nodded as well. "I also agree with your proposal. I feel it is important that we do everything we can to avoid descending back into barbarism."

"I think it's a good idea." The little voice that spoke up was the last one that we expected: Madeline. We all turned and looked at the girl, who stared back at us with huge, solemn eyes. "There are bad men out there. Lots and lots of bad men. Some bad ladies, too. We should be careful. We don't want to become bad like them. Do we?"

None of us quite knew what to say to that, but it settled the issue once and for all. By universal consensus of all our members, we created our own internal judicial system. I think that we all felt better for having that, even if we hoped that we'd never have to use it.

Chapter Twenty-Four

A few days later, I found myself wandering through our motel looking for my sister, feeling relaxed and content with my lot in life for the first time in what felt like forever.

I drifted past the hydroponics room, but instead of Skylar I found the doctor focused intently on the tiny seedlings while he instructed his granddaughter in their care. They were oblivious to me, but I stood and watched for a moment anyway. A surge of affection rose in me. Although we share no blood ties, they were becoming like family to me.

Mutual survival bonded you in a way I'd never understood before. Now that I did, I felt strangely complete.

I left them without alerting them to my passing and moved on.

A few minutes later, I peeked into the communal lounge, where I found Ryan and Michael lost in conversation over some point of maleness that was completely irrelevant to me. Again, I retreated without being seen, and left them to their bonding as I moved on in search of Skylar.

When at last I found my little sister, she was where I least expected her to be: In her own room, curled up in bed despite it being the middle of the day, looking pale and unhappy. She wasn't asleep though, and when I stepped into the room she looked up at me with sad eyes.

"Hey, you." Suddenly concerned, I forgot all about the reason I was looking for her, and crossed the room to seat myself on the edge of her bed.

"Hey." She gave me a pathetic look, and nuzzled miserably at her pillow.

"What's wrong?" I reached out to her instinctively, and brushed a strand of hair off her cheek.

"I feel like crap." Her answer was blunt and without embellishment. "My head's been hurting for days and I feel like throwing up all the time."

Concern twisted like a knife in my gut.

"Have you told Doctor Cross?" I whispered the question, fighting down the urge to panic.

She shook her head. "I don't want to worry anyone..."

"I'm sure you'll be fine." I tried my best to sound reassuring, then leaned down to plant a kiss on her forehead, just like Mum used to do when we were little. The memory made her smile, but it was a weak smile. I straightened up again and looked down at her worriedly. "Let me get Doctor Cross anyway, just in case."

She nodded softly, and that was permission enough for me. I patted her head one last time, then rose and went off in search of the doctor. He was exactly where I last saw him, so it didn't take much effort. When I told him what she'd said to me, he nodded thoughtfully.

"Pregnancy comes with many aches and pains and mysterious illnesses all the way through, particularly towards the end," he said in that self-assured way of his, the doctor's voice that says everything will be just fine. "I'll go check on her anyway."

"Thank you, doctor." I gave him a smile to mask my own worry, and watched him leave to check on her. Maddy skipped along after him, singing quietly to herself, and left me alone.

'I don't want to worry anyone.'

Something about the way she'd said that bothered me immensely. Skye was never one to mince words when she was feeling slighted or unhappy about something. Why would she suddenly change her mind completely?

Unless she knew in her gut that it was something serious.

I shook my head to dismiss the thought. If it had been something serious, then the doctor would have picked up on it before. He'd been watching Skye like a hawk through the last few weeks of her pregnancy. It seemed unlikely that something serious would miss his attention so completely. She was probably just feeling hot and bothered in the humidity, like the rest of us.

I decided that a present was in order, to cheer up

both the parties involved, so off I went to get my things. Once I had my taser and my radio safely in my pockets, I set off on a scavenger hunt to find the perfect gift for my little sister.

In my head, I ran through the list of appropriate things that I'd seen over the last few weeks. Something for the baby would be best, but the question was what?

There was a home not far away that had once housed a young family. I remembered that there were toys and children's books scattered all over the living room. That seemed like a logical place to start. I broke into a jog and headed off towards the building in question, feeling a surge of simple joy over the fact that I could run again.

It was a quaint little home, surrounded by small gardens and what was left of a white picket fence. Once, it had been someone's dream home. Now, the paint was cracked and peeling, baked by ten years' sun with no maintenance, and the garden was a jungle just like all the others. The gate shrieked in protest when I opened it and then I picked my way along the remains of the garden path towards the front door.

I had left it unlocked when I last visited, and everything was exactly the same as it had been weeks before. To my left, a tiny kitchen and dining room stood beneath a thick layer of dust. To my right, an archway led to a small living room, with cheap, overstuffed couches in front of the television. Toys still scattered the floor.

I bent to examine the toys, searching for something

suitable, but none of them seemed quite right to cheer up Skye today. Perhaps when the baby was old enough to play then I could come back for them, but for now they stayed where they were.

A narrow staircase led to the second floor. I scampered up it, feeling light-footed and agile. Doorways flanked the hall leading to a couple of bedrooms. The first one I opened had obviously once belonged to a young girl. Dolls lay discarded where they fell, stuffed animals lined the bed, everything was pink and pretty, all ballerinas and fairies and princesses. It looked just like Skye's room before the outbreak. For once in my life, that thought made me want to laugh instead of cry.

The second room I cracked open was more promising; it was the baby's room. It was hard not to think about the fact that both of those innocent children were dead now, but I tried to ignore that as I crossed the room to peer into the crib.

A little pink blanket lay folded across the foot of the bassinet. I reached out and touched it, marvelling at its softness. Upon it sat a little matching teddy bear, waiting to receive the newest addition to the family, the one that would never come.

It will now, I thought, and that cheered me up. These were just perfect. I gathered up the teddy and the blanket, and gave both of them a gentle shake to rid them of the dust, then I hurried out of the little house and headed back towards my home.

A few minutes later I bounded up the stairs towards

Skylar's room with my prizes clutched to my chest – only to find myself confronted by a small group of people standing outside the door. Everyone was there, except for the doctor and Skye. Concern returned like a sledgehammer, and this time it socked me full in the jaw. I hurried over to join them, my gifts forgotten.

"What's happening?" I whispered and tried to push through them to get a better view. No one had an answer for me.

Panic swelled up in full force, so I squeezed my relatively small frame between the men and burst into my sister's room. I found the doctor bent over her, so intently focused that he didn't notice my arrival until I was right beside him. Skylar lay unconscious on the blankets, her skin so pale and waxy that there was no way that this could be normal.

"She appears to have contracted an infection." Dr Cross' soft voice broke the silence as he checked a small thermometer resting in my sister's mouth. Even I could see that the fever burned painfully high.

"But how? We've been so careful to keep her safe." Tears leapt unbidden into my eyes, blurring my vision.

"Pregnant women are just more susceptible to infection than any other normal, healthy adult." The doctor's frown was more intense than usual. The last time I'd seen his scowl etched that deeply was when he was tending to poor Dog. That expression did nothing to reassure me. "It may have been something she ate. Sadly, we do not have the facilities to run blood tests to figure out exactly what it is. I am giving her the strongest broad-spectrum antibiotic we can safely give her in her condition, and we'll just have to hope that it's enough."

I felt an arm creep around me and realised Michael had joined me. His support was very, very welcome. As soon as I felt him there, my strength drained away. I sagged against him and let him lead me away from the bed so that we weren't in the way. There was only one chair in the room, so he sat and drew me into his lap, then held me close while we waited.

Darkness fell, and Skylar still didn't wake up.

***

Late that night, a scream tore me from my doze; a terrible, bloody scream of unbearable pain.

I was up a second later with Michael right behind me, and we hurried to the bedside where I found the doctor struggling to hold my sister down. She was writhing in agony, and I realised with horror that there was a terrible red stain spreading below the waist of her nightshirt and inching across the blankets beneath her tormented young body.

"Help me," the doctor begged us for aid, and we both leapt in to try and hold my frantic sister. She was oblivious to us all, and her body seemed to hold an unnatural amount of strength. A third set of hands joined us; I glanced up, and saw Ryan's ghost-pale face join us while we struggled to control her convulsions.

Suddenly the doctor was holding a syringe, and while we controlled her he injected it into Skylar's pale, sweating arm. It took a minute before she relaxed as the painkillers took effect, but even once the convulsions stopped she was whimpering and her eyes rolled in her head. It was a terrifying sight.

The blood was spreading.

"She's going to lose the baby." I clung to Michael for support through the shock and horror of that realisation. The doctor blew out a short breath, and a look of regret pinched his brow.

"Yes." His shoulders slumped, and he looked at me with the kind of expression that made me want to run and hide rather than hear what he was going to say. "And I'm not sure I'm going to be able to save her, either."

I felt like I'd been punched in the face, or the gut, or maybe both. I had found my baby sister, alive after all these years, and I was going to lose her again after just a few short weeks? It seemed impossibly cruel and so terribly unfair.

"No... no, no, no, please – you have to save her!" The words tumbled out of me without control, pleading, as if through sheer force of will I could save my sister.

"I have no intention of giving up, Ms McDermott, but you need to understand that there is a strong possibility that she may not make it." The doctor shook his head regretfully, then seemed to steel himself. "Please leave the room; I will call you if I need you."

Although the doctor's voice was soft it felt like he'd yelled at me. Michael had to drag me bodily from the room. I fought to stay even though I knew there was nothing that I could do, driven by primitive instincts that have no real name. Eventually I gave up and sank into Michael's arms, my emotions surging with such strength that I couldn't figure out which one of them to respond to first.

It was all a matter of time, and hope. I had no choice but to put all my faith in Dr Cross' skills, pray that they would be enough.

***

It was breakfast time but no one felt like eating. My sister's screams were raw and primal. Every time one of us relaxed, another scream would come and put us all back on edge.

I managed to doze for a few minutes with my head lolling against Michael's shoulder, but it wasn't enough to actually rest. I felt wrung out and exhausted, emotionally drained and tense to the point of snapping.

At one point, Ryan rushed out from the sick room and summoned Michael for his skills as a blood donor, leaving me alone with little Madeline.

She had no wisdom for me today.

A short time later, Michael returned looking pale and woozy, but he refused to go to his bed. He sat beside me once more and wrapped his arms around me, letting me bury my face against his chest.

Even his warmth couldn't hide the terrible sound of my baby sister in agony. My sweet little baby sister. I loved her so much that it was unbearable.

Eventually, the screams trailed off to a distant, pathetic sobbing, then they stopped altogether. A few minutes later, an exhausted Dr Cross emerged from the sick room and found us huddled together. We looked at him expectantly, but he just shook his head.

"I have done all I can." His voice was hoarse and regretful, and he wouldn't make eye-contact with me. "Only time will tell now."

The memory of an identical statement made just before Dog's death flashed through my mind. I was up before Michael could stop me and dashed past the doctor, back into my sister's room.

Ryan sat on the edge of their bed, cradling something wrapped in the soft pink baby blanket I had intended as a gift for my sister. As I drew closer, I realised that it was the baby.

It was dead.

The baby's skin was a terrible shade of blue-purple, and its tiny face was contorted and stiff. Tears ran down Ryan's cheeks as he looked down at the tiny child in his arms, the terrible litany of loss written clearly across his freckled face.

"We were going to name her Kylie, after her grandmother," he spoke softly when he saw me, and cuddled his firstborn daughter, dead before he had the chance to know her. "Kylie Sandrine Knowles-McDermott. That was going to be her name. She was going to have beautiful blue eyes like her mama, and my freckles, and we were going to teach her to sing and read and play games with us. We were–" His voice broke, and he trailed off into sobs of terrible grief, the tiny body clutched against his chest.

I didn't know what to say. There was nothing I could say that would make this better. The baby was dead, and with her all their hopes and dreams for a family together.

Behind him, my sister lay unconscious, her breathing shallow and uneven. Her skin was waxy, and so very pale I felt like what little hope I had left would never be enough to save her.

The tears gathered in my eyes and I let them fall unhindered as I knelt beside her bed. In my mind's eye, she was still that sweet-faced little girl I adored. She would always be my baby sister.

My one living relative.

My best friend.

I took her cold, clammy hand and pressed it to my cheek, praying that somehow, someway, she might hear my words and fight a little harder.

"Please, Skye, please. Don't leave me."

***

To be continued, in The Survivors Book II: Autumn.

Kiwiana Language Guide

Aotearoa — The Maori name for New Zealand, literally "The Land Of The Long White Cloud".

Bush — Specifically, "native bush". This term refers to an area of native forest, which is characterised by a particularly thick shrub layer dominated by indigenous ferns and bushes – hence the colloquialism. Native bush is often very thick and dark, and can be very difficult to travel through as a result.

Cark It — To die. *Example: "We were half-way to Tauranga when the car carked it."*

G'day — Colloquial version of "Good day".

Hangi — Maori culture, an underground oven used to cook food.

Hongi — Maori culture, the pressing together of the nose and forehead in a greeting. Used in a similar fashion to the handshake in Western culture. Symbolises the mixing of the breath of life integral to Maori folklore.

Kai   Maori, "Food".

Kia Ora   Maori, "Hello".

Kumara   A sweet potato.

Maori   Relating to the original peoples of New Zealand. May be used to refer to their cultural traits (*e.g. "she tried to live by the traditional Maori ways."*), language (*e.g. "he spoke Maori."*) or ethnicity (*e.g. "my grandmother was Maori"*). The Maori culture evolved from Polynesian migrants that arrived in New Zealand around 1,000 years ago.

Mate   A contextually sensitive word that is usually used in place of the word "friend". Can be used sarcastically or in threat just as readily as being used in a friendly fashion, *e.g. "You're going to regret that, mate."*

Pā   Maori, can refer to a village or settlement, but usually describes a hill fort.

Rēwena   Maori, literally "ferment/rise". In terms of bread, it refers to a traditional Maori potato bread.

Credits

Concept & Story:	Victoria L. Dreyer
Editing:	Holly Simmons
Cover Art:	Alais Legrand
Graphic Design:	Alyssa Talboys

***

Financial Support

Prior to the release of this novel, the author ran an online fundraising campaign to help with the costs. Without the generosity of these lovely people, *The Survivors* may not have been possible.

Adrienne Smith
Clare Stones
Dennis Swanson
Rebekah Andrews
Sarah Hayward
Sonia Rudolph

And of course, the anonymous donators who requested not to be named. Thank you.

V. L. Dreyer

About The Author

Born in Auckland, New Zealand, Victoria Dreyer began her career in the most peculiar of ways - as the writer and illustrator of graphic novels. Although her ultimate dream was always to become a novelist, she spent many years exploring other mediums before finally returning to the one she felt most comfortable with - the written word.

Ms Dreyer is a voracious reader, and in addition to the post-apocalyptic genre she also enjoys reading and writing science fiction, modern fantasy, and the paranormal romance genres.

She currently resides in West Auckland with several flatmates, a large collection of books and two very spoiled cats.

http://www.vldreyer.com

Printed in Great Britain
by Amazon.co.uk, Ltd.,
Marston Gate.